ABSORBING LIVES

LT ANDERSON

Published in the United States by Rogue Street Entertainment, LLC.

Absorbing Lives / Les and Taylor Anderson (LT Anderson)

Summary: When the elite Changers harnessed immortality and the ability to change their appearance at will, they erased State lines and walled off sections of the country as human breeding farms. The Punks rebelled when they discovered the Changers absorb the lives of innocent people to retain their eternal life. To regain control of their breeding farms, The Changers are preparing high-tech AI Mutants to eliminate the Punks.

Edited by Eliza Dee from Clio Editing - clioediting.com
Book Formatting and Beta Read by Lisa Gilliam - lisagilliam.com
Cover Design by Dane from Ebook Launch - ebooklaunch.com

ISBN-10: 1-7321795-1-4 Paperback
ISBN-13: 978-1-7321795-1-6 Paperback

Visit us on the Web! www.ltanderson.com

*ABSORBING LIVES is dedicated to society's rejects.
To the commonplace, average and ugly. To the blemished,
imperfect, unattractive and flawed, old and young, freckle-faced
and scarred, the fatsos and the beanpoles, the slow, the geeks, the
loners, the outcasts, the freaks and weirdos.
You are perfect.
Never change.*

CHAPTER 1

Krystal

THE SWAMP COOLER IN THE small two-bedroom, one-bath house offered little relief from the waning autumn humidity, even at 10:00 p.m. Krystal Peterson's greasy hair stuck to her forehead, resembling smears of brown ink, and her white tank top hugged her braless torso like a wet straitjacket. She glared at the skinny, grotesque loser in the mirror. She was positive her looks had caused the crack—the one that ran diagonally from the middle of the left-hand side across to the top right. *Twenty-nine point five percent of my body, assholes,* she thought. The doctors said the burns covered thirty percent. She knew they were wrong, because she had meticulously measured every millimeter of gnarled, withered skin on her body.

Krystal laughed, because now it didn't matter. After all, being a Changer had its perks. Krystal liked the idea of living forever, but she *loved* that she had the capacity to change her appearance at will. In the dim light, she closed her eyes and raised her arms above her head. Face to the floor, she crossed her legs. The vibration began at her feet, crawled up her body and shot out the tips of her fingers. It lasted exactly one point six five seconds.

She stepped back to survey her new look in the mirror. Pretty, with an edge. Tight. Tough. Jet-black hair.

A quick wardrobe change completed the transformation. Black on black on black: a black Underground Punk Band T-shirt strategically cut to expose a gray tank top over a black bra, black jeans with a black leather belt holding just the right number of studs, and black boots. *I'd give me a ten…maybe eleven.*

She closed her eyes again. A membrane lining the inside of her eyelids displayed critical information regarding her status as a Changer.

CITIZEN NUMBER: 1.999.780.001
SECTOR: 001 WEST USA
ACTUAL AGE: 26 YRS 2 MOS 15 DAYS 21 HR 14 MIN 33 SEC
CHANGE DISPLAY CONDITION: 21 YRS 6 MOS 15 DAYS FEMALE
EXPIRATION: 2 MOS 16 DAYS 2 HR 45 MIN 27 SEC
ABSORPTION STATUS: CRITICAL

Cool, she thought. *I still have over two months before I time out.* Krystal ratted her hair and tossed the comb onto the dinky second-hand dresser. She grabbed her cell and keys, picked up her wallet, stuffed it into her back pocket and hooked the wallet chain to a belt loop. *I'm outta here.* Her keys jingled as she passed through the narrow wood-paneled hallway.

"Where are you going?" her mother called out from the small dinette next to the kitchen.

"I already told you, out."

"When are you coming home?"

Krystal ignored the second question and closed the front door. She let the spring-loaded screen door slam shut behind her, hopped down the front steps and crossed the yard to her mini pickup, parked on the street. She turned the key in the ignition and hand-cranked the driver's window down, releasing the musty, gasoline-flavored scent of the truck's interior. Her cell vibrated under her thigh. She held it up for a quick look as she pulled away from the curb.

Curtis

Krystal put the cell on speaker and tossed it onto the dash in front of the steering wheel. "Hey."

"*Hey, babe. Where are you?*"

"My street. I'm on my way."

"*Oh. I thought you said ten thirty.*"

"Right." She slowed the mini pickup. "Hey, I got traffic ahead."

"*Okay. See you in a few. I love you, babe.*"

"Of course you do." She tucked the cell back under her thigh, made a California stop, turned right and crossed the railroad tracks.

A large electronic sign atop the old ten-story building on her right negated the need for a streetlight on this corner:

JOIN THE ELITE.
BE THE PERSON OF YOUR DREAMS TODAY.
EXPERIENCE IMMORTALITY TOMORROW.
RECEIVE THE CHANGE!

Long ago, the Changers had harnessed immortality and the ability to change one's appearance at will. This combination of powers had become a monetary boon for the Changers. In the beginning, there were humorous ads—amaze your friends and family, change your appearance. Then the ads appealed to the more rational person—live an easier, longer life. The final hook—everyone's doing it, so join the party, be one of the elite, live forever. Krystal had seen the sign so many times it was nearly invisible to her.

She rolled up to a stop sign and stared at an old three-story brick building. She'd heard stories about how it used to be a Bank of America. Now it was a clothing store. She imagined how it must have been when it had been a thriving bank. That was before the Perimeter, before the Wall. *Quiet tonight*, she thought.

The staccato slapping of a hand on her passenger-side window jarred Krystal from her temporary vegetative state. She glanced to her right.

Scotty Van Buren.

"What the shit, Scotty?" Krystal unconsciously stiffened her right leg, pushing down on the already-depressed brake pedal. She felt the seat springs on her back, bulging out of the thin vinyl.

"Open up!" Scotty was smiling, full-toothed. Even when he wasn't smiling, he always appeared to be smiling—the result of the way the corners of his mouth turned slightly upward. He thought it was cute. Krystal saw it as a permanent smirk that befit his personality. The smug look suited his overall appearance: GQ look with a perfectly trimmed haircut, khaki dress pants, formfitting sweater with the dress-shirt collar sticking out and brown loafers.

The look fit Scotty perfectly as a spy for the Changers. His role kept him inside the Perimeter most of the time. Spying on the Bystanders gave him what every Changer needed—unlimited access to innocent lives for absorption. He used his position as Liaison to the mayor to his advantage, becoming friends with Bystanders and select Punks.

Krystal reached across the seat and flipped the manual lock upward. She flinched as the little pickup bounced hard to the right when Scotty hit the seat.

"Head out of town—Outpost 100." He slammed the door. Scotty's expensive cologne blended well with his flawless smile, but mixed with the petrol-inspired scent of the truck's interior, the smell was gag-worthy.

"Why? I have plans."

"Just do it." Scotty looked out the back window of the little truck. "You don't want to miss this."

"Doubtful."

"Fine, then—it's mandatory. Just do it."

Ooh, the serious smirk. One of these days I'm gonna wipe that serious smirky-smirk off your face. A series of flashing orange strobe lights on the water tower caught Krystal's attention as a high-pitched alarm screeched to life. "Shit."

"Mutant alarm." Scotty shrugged. "Good thing we're not staying."

Krystal jammed the gearbox into first and lurched it twice

through the intersection before heading out of town. The couple drove in silence for several minutes until the pickup approached a traffic signal.

Krystal hurried the vehicle through a yellow light at the rural highway crossing. "This is bullshit, Scotty." The suspension on the little pickup hit bottom after its flight over a small rise on the other side of the intersection.

Scotty squeezed the grab handle above his head. "It's not bullshit. You've skipped out on two meetings. Levi wants an update on your progress. He wants to know what the Punks are up to, and he wants to know now. This is a mandatory meeting and I've been ordered to escort you personally."

Krystal downshifted the mini pickup at the next intersection. A group of Punks stood beside a heavily armored guard house blocking the highway.

Scotty looked at Krystal. "What's up with this? These checkpoints aren't usually manned."

The Punks had set up small checkpoints in the Wall after the rebellion. They had designed guard shack-style structures to monitor ingress and egress of citizens within the Perimeter. When the Punks signed the Treaty that gave them control of the interior, fear of Changers breaching the enclosed cities waned, the Punks relaxed and they deactivated the minor checkpoints.

"I don't know," Krystal said. "They haven't used them in years—last time the Punks felt friction with the Changers. Let's just hope I have friends here and we breeze through."

One Punk was stationed inside the guard house. *C'mon, open up*, Krystal thought. *You know my truck.*

Krystal slowed to a stop and rolled her window down. "What's up, guys? You know me."

The little truck tilted slightly when the Punk leaned inside. "It's late. You're too close to the Perimeter."

"You know me, Slade. Just open up."

Slade wiped his sweat, forehead to neck. He looked across the cab. "Who's this turd?"

Krystal shivered imperceptibly at the scent of Slade's breath.

His bottom lip bulged from an overworked wad of tobacco. A crusty brown trace of dried snuff lined his lips and the corners of his mouth. "That's Scotty. He's a friend of mine."

"Still hanging out with Bystanders, eh?" Slade backed up as he opened the driver's door. "All right, everybody out."

The Punk on the other side opened the door, and the pair stepped out of the truck. "What the hell, Slade?" Krystal winced as Slade's sweaty hand pinched the skin on her shoulder.

"Up against the truck, Peterson."

"What, you're patting me down?"

Slade grabbed the back of Krystal's collar and slammed her against the vehicle. "Best be cool, girl."

Krystal tasted the blood from her bottom lip at the same time she saw the red smear on the roof of the mini pickup. She felt the pressure of the big Punk against her back. *This is taking forever.* Her vision blurred. She stiffened when the hand squeezed her crotch. "Damn you, Slade."

"Gotta do what we gotta do." He backed up and looked over the roof of the truck. "She's clean. How's Sparky over there?"

"Nothing here. He just smells funny."

"Off you go, Peterson."

Krystal lunged at the big Punk, punching him squarely in the chest. "Totally unnecessary, Slade." She dropped backwards onto the truck seat and slammed the door before grinding the transmission into first gear.

Slade chuckled as he shoved his hands into the pockets of his leather vest.

Krystal chirped the tires as the gate arm swung skyward.

Scotty smiled across the seat at Krystal. "Friends?"

CHAPTER 2

Curtis

CURTIS DYER HUNG UP HIS cell as he pulled his armored Chevrolet van into the driveway of his parents' two-story country-style home on the outskirts of Tremayne. His recent promotion within the Punks Organization hadn't sat well with his parents, particularly his mom. His new status came with perks, the best of which was private living quarters at Checkpoint One at the Perimeter.

Curtis bounded up the wooden steps to a large well-lighted porch. His lanky six-foot frame made two steps at a time a breeze. Knowing the doorbell was broken, he pounded his fist on the heavy wooden door. The broken doorbell was one of many small repair projects his dad never seemed to find the time for.

Curtis's mom sat at a small desk in the dining room, staring intently at a laptop. She jumped at the knock. "What? Come in!"

"The door's locked." He surveyed the familiar wooden deck area: two wooden patio chairs with faded floral cushions, a love seat–sized porch swing with matching cushions, a round glass-and-steel table with no chairs around it, a stack of paving stones from an unfinished project, and numerous small terra cotta pots with begonias in need of a trim. His thoughts drifted to Krystal, stirring butterflies in his gut.

Mrs. Dyer slapped the laptop shut and pushed her rolling office chair away from the desk. "Coming." She waddled to the entryway and opened the door, just a crack. "Oh, hi." She fidgeted with the useless chain lock on the doorjamb.

Curtis peeked in with one eye. "Hi, Mom. Just checking to see if you need anything before I head home."

"This is your home, hon—you know I've told you that."

Curtis moved his head from side to side, viewing his mom through the slit with first one eye, then the other. "I know. I don't see Dad's car. Do you need anything?"

Mrs. Dyer finally removed the little brass-colored chain from its hook and opened the door. "I made a pie today. It's apple, your favorite. Would you like to come in and have a bite?"

Curtis smiled. Apple pie wasn't his favorite. His mom only assumed it was since apple pie was always his choice at family gatherings when the only alternative was fruitcake. "I can't tonight. I have to get back. I've got Perimeter duty."

"You know your father and I don't approve. Those are rough characters. Too rough. You're not like them."

Moths flicked the porch light. Curtis spun his key ring around one finger. "Well, if you don't need anything, I better get going."

As he turned to leave, a high-pitched ear-piercing alarm sounded in the distance. Reflexively, Curtis reached around his back to his waistband for his 9mm Beretta handgun.

"Oh, dear," Mrs. Dyer said.

"Mutants again, Mom. Drop the window shields and close the safety door behind me," Curtis ordered.

Mrs. Dyer frowned. "But you're not going out now, are you?"

Curtis smoothed a hand over his seven-inch blond Mohawk before slipping on a pair of fingerless leather gloves. "I have to, Mom." He leaned over and kissed his mother's forehead. "I'm leaving. Now get in the house."

Mrs. Dyer patted her son's arm. "Just be careful."

"I always am." Curtis hurried to the van.

"I love you, honey," Mrs. Dyer called out from the porch.

Curtis closed the door and fired up the van. He stuck his arm out the window as he backed down the driveway. "Love you, too, Mom."

CHAPTER 3

The Assignment

A FEW MILES OUTSIDE THE PERIMETER Wall, Krystal swung her vehicle into an expansive driveway on the right. She braked to a stop and waved her cell in front of a small keypad on a post just left of the driveway. A large wrought-iron gate split in the middle and swung inward. Krystal crawled the little pickup through the gate and paused until it closed behind her.

"Why do you need an eight-foot wall around this place?" Krystal asked. "You can't see in or out with these stupid trees anyway. And why do we call these *outposts*? It's a *mansion*."

"It's what we call them. Just a place to keep an eye on our interests. Oh, watch it driving over the creek. Maintenance is supposed to fix that left rail tomorrow. Just hang a little to the right."

"I can't believe the Punks ever agreed to these outposts," Krystal said.

"All part of the Treaty. It's a give and take—they monitor inside the Wall with their little checkpoints and we monitor outside with our outposts."

Krystal shook her head. "Those little shacks are minor checkpoints. Checkpoint One is a huge complex."

"Exactly," Scotty said. "Punks built the main checkpoints in the Wall like regular fortresses. So we built our outposts as big as we wanted."

"Right. According to the Treaty, Changer Outposts are supposed to be limited to one-bedroom bungalows, no larger."

Scotty smiled. "Get real. You know we do what we want." He shrugged. "Guess you just answered your own question about eight-foot walls and monster trees."

"Yeah, okay. Well, hang on a sec while I call Curtis. I was on my way to meet him when you hijacked me."

"He's a loser, Peterson," Scotty said. "I can't wait till you take him out."

"Hey, babe. Yeah. I got sidetracked by Scotty. Yes. I'll be there. I'm just not sure when. Okay. Yeah. Bye."

Krystal hung up. "Who says I'm taking him out?"

"It's your assignment, Peterson. You have to absorb a high-ranking Punk. That's the message Levi wants delivered—that we can get to the Punks anywhere, anytime." Scotty tried his best to appear bewildered. "You know all this."

"It's my choice. Curtis Dyer isn't the only high-ranking Punk I'm close to."

"Prove it, then. I haven't seen that you're close to any other Punk, let alone high-ranking."

Krystal shut off the engine and turned to face Scotty. *Okay, listen up, smirky-smirk.* "I'm not sure he's the right choice."

"I heard your conversation with Dyer just now." Scotty raised an eyebrow. "If I didn't know better, I'd suspect you're confusing your emotions with your assignment, and your loyalties. Wouldn't be good if you fell in love with your mark." He opened the passenger door and stepped out of the little truck.

Krystal got out, closed the door and addressed Scotty across the roof of the vehicle. "Why are you on my back about it? This is my assignment, and who I take out is my decision." Krystal's keys jingled as she pointed at her chest with her thumb. "*My* decision."

CRICKETS CHIRPED AS KRYSTAL AND Scotty walked toward the mansion. The two entered through huge front doors. Krystal followed Scotty into the large round marble-floored foyer. She looked up at the ceiling, open through to the second floor and marveled at the ostentatiousness of the structure.

"This way," Scotty said, making an immediate left into the library.

Krystal loved the scent in the library: wood, leather and sweet pipe tobacco. She bristled when she saw the young olive-complected woman sitting at one end of a brown leather couch. *Silver Long, I hate you*, she thought as the woman tapped away at a virtual keyboard on the glass coffee table in front of her. She deliberately stepped on Silver's shiny black boots, which lay off to the side of the couch.

"Hi, Van Buren," Silver said without looking up from the keyboard. "Peterson."

Krystal flopped down on the leather sofa opposite Silver.

Scotty leaned on the edge of a large mahogany desk positioned face-out on one wall. He crossed his arms. "Do you have all the information, Long?"

"Got it." A holographic monitor appeared, revealing a detailed profile. Krystal's picture popped up next to a series of charts, spreadsheets, narratives and statistical data. "You have a high-ranking mark named Curtis Dyer?"

"Maybe."

"She does," Scotty said.

"Maybe so." Krystal's eyes narrowed as she turned to Silver. "But I haven't finalized him as my choice to absorb."

"We have been monitoring your activities, Peterson." Silver flipped to a second screen on the display. "You're moving at a snail's pace. The order directs your immediate action. This comes from the highest levels within our organization." She smiled at Krystal. "That's why we're here. You have less than three months until your Change times out. Each absorption gives you twenty-four months, at best. Consequently, the choice has been made for you. You *will* absorb Curtis Dyer."

"What's that database, anyway?" Krystal asked. "How do you know so much about my activities?"

"It's the chip in your head, Peterson. You know, the one implanted at the Underground when you became one of us."

For decades, the Changers had experimented with cell mutation, chromosome regeneration, protein absorption and chip implantation as a means to extend life. The ability to effect physical change upon oneself merely by thought was an unexpected bonus. Now, every Changer can live forever and change their appearance at will. And because every Changer receives an implanted chip, the Organization tracks every Changer.

Silver stopped smiling. "Your deadline for action has passed. Complete the assignment, period."

Scotty shook his head. "Your contract with us goes beyond normal circumstances, Krys. When I introduced you to Levi, that alone put you in the spotlight. You're special, not a Lottery pick. You are bought and paid for by the Changers Organization. If you recall, you said you'd do *anything* to repay us for the gift of Change you received."

Krystal shifted on the couch. "A figure of speech."

Scotty stood from the desk and walked over to the couch. He sat next to Krystal. "No one heard it that way. You are specifically beholden to Levi."

"Need I remind you how you got here, Peterson?" Silver tapped the keyboard as she eyed the monitor. "Let's see, you had no place to go. No family, no contacts of any kind. Then along came Scotty. Two years before you received *our* gift of the Change, a girl in Tremayne disappeared. You saw an opportunity in this tragedy. One day, you showed up in town and coincidentally looked exactly like the missing girl. There was a lot of hoopla and a big celebration in Tremayne because the *missing girl* had *returned*. So you played the amnesia game and this poor unsuspecting woman you call 'mommy' accepted you into her home. You, Miss Peterson, received the home life you never had as a child." She looked at Krystal. "I do believe you owe us. It's time to pay up."

Krystal's scalp bristled. "Okay, so, let's say I complete this assignment. That's the payback, right?"

"Sorry, hon," Silver said. "You're in it for the long haul. No matter what you do, you are not released from Levi's grip until he says so."

"And if I fail this assignment?"

Silver's eyes widened, ever so slightly. "Let's put it this way, Peterson. Don't think crossing Levi grants you death. That would be the easy way out. Levi will not allow you to time out and die. You'd only get death if our leader is feeling generous."

Krystal sat on the couch, silently rubbing the hourglass-shaped brass fob attached to her key ring.

Silver glanced at the time on her cell. "I think we've made our point. I've got less than four hours to be back at the City."

A man wearing a black jumpsuit appeared at the doorway to the library. "Excuse me, ma'am, the Hyperloop is available."

"Thanks, Aames. I'll be right there."

The man turned and exited toward the rear of the mansion.

Silver scooped up her laptop from the coffee table. "I better get my butt in gear."

Krystal stood. "I take it we're done?"

"Yeah, that's it," Scotty said.

"Then I'm outta here, too."

"I'm staying here. It's almost midnight. Trains will be running soon, and the checkpoints are closing in a few minutes."

"Big deal. Trains don't scare me, and I can drive a few miles out of my way to hit the main portal."

Scotty shrugged. "Suit yourself. Just don't get out of your truck. I heard some rumor about mutants running wild out there after dark."

"I'll take my chances."

THE AUTUMN AIR FLASHED INTERMITTENT cool drafts as Krystal accelerated down the curvy back road toward the Perimeter checkpoint.

Tired of her clumsy words and the voice of her thoughts, Krystal squeezed her eyes shut and shook her head. Her mini pickup screeched around every corner. She opened her eyes, removed her bandanna and shoved it into the glove compartment.

When she hit the rural highway, she downshifted without stopping at the intersection and pressed hard on the accelerator pedal. The little truck shot to eighty miles per hour.

Krystal winced at the stiffness in her shoulders. The swirling wind in the cab swept the hair from her face, rushed through her brain and disintegrated the cobwebs from her mind. She thought about Curtis. She thought about Scotty and Silver, the heavy-handed frisking at the Perimeter. The thoughts clung like litter to the filter of her brain.

"*He's a loser, Peterson.*"

"*You need to make up your mind.*"

"*I love you, babe.*"

No! Krystal shook her head. *I love you, Curtis! How can I end your life? Damn you, Changers. Yeah, I owe you. But I hate you and everything you stand for.*

"*Be who and what you want to be.*"

"*Live forever.*"

Krystal slowed at the only large curve in the road, but she didn't slow enough. The rear end of the little truck broke free and swung around to meet the front. Sliding sideways down the highway, she hit the brake and turned the wheel sharply to the right. Too late. The front of the truck hit the shoulder and dove into the ditch on the side of the road. Her head slammed against the roof and the glove compartment popped open. The little truck plowed through the first row of orange trees in the adjacent grove, rolled over once and landed upright. The engine died.

"Ow, shit." She shouldered the driver's door open and fell out onto the ground.

crickets

Krystal stood slowly and grabbed her lower back. She stepped up to the dirt shoulder. She put her palms to her face, rubbed her eyes and fell to her knees. There was no let-up from the voices in her now-throbbing head. "*I can't think of a better choice for your big assignment.*"

What am I gonna do? Tears formed in Krystal's eyes. She smoothed her hands over the top of her head. She felt the tangles in her hair and knew her fingers would never make it through. "Dammit." Tears dropped between her legs, forming tiny craters in the dust.

She remembered the day she had become a Changer. From the beginning, Krystal was a pawn. She possessed every negative trait and experience the Changers loved. She was the perfect balance of needy and defiant—she'd never stood a chance. She had been passed from bad home to foster home to foster home, and finally to the street before Scotty found her.

The *accident* only served to magnify the pain. It wasn't the physical pain from the burns. It was the added rejection for being ugly. To Krystal, school had been a nightmare from which she'd found it impossible to awaken. Social classes tended to gravitate toward each other. The upper class hung out with the rich, the middle class with the middle class, the poor with the poor, and the losers with the losers. Krystal had never found her crew. Until Scotty. Until the Changers. She would have agreed to *anything*, and she *had*.

The highway checkpoints are gonna be closed by the time it takes me to walk, Krystal thought. She checked the battery on her cell: 16%. *Shit.* She turned the brightness down to almost zero and shoved it into her back pocket. A train horn sounded in the distance—two long tones. *Hmm, just leaving town. I'll head that direction and sneak in on the tracks.*

Krystal stepped off the road on the other side of the highway and headed toward the sound of the train. She wiped the sweat from her forehead and shivered. *So cold. What the heck? These boots were not made for walking, I'll tell you that much.*

Ignoring the pain in her back, she trudged forward through the short sagebrush, intermingled with tall grass. *Agh!* She tripped on a root, exposed from the last heavy rain. *Gotta keep moving.* Her once-jet-black jeans and boots quickly faded to grayish-brown from the foliage.

Krystal never saw the log. She felt her knee twist and squeezed her eyes shut when her face plowed through the heavy bush in front of her. "Ow!" The outcry wasn't from her knee, or her face—

now streaked red from the branches. Krystal pulled a pencil-sized branch out of the meaty side of her thumb. "Aaagh!"

Cradling her injured hand with the other, she pulled out her cell and rolled onto her back. She checked the battery again: 12%. The words Krystal texted blurred as tears again filled her eyes:

I need you. Don't know where I am.

CHAPTER 4

Traveler

A CLOUD OF DUST ENGULFED THE fifty-year-old nondescript minivan as it skidded to a stop at the edge of a sand dune in the Southern California desert. The driver got out to stretch, leaving the creaky door open. He looked down. A drop of sweat trickled off his forehead and fell from his nose, forming a sun-shaped splat on the toe of his leather boot.

He leaned into the cab and shouted through the cage that divided the front seats from the rest of the van. "How you girls doing back there?"

The man was distinctly aware of the grit that chafed his neck, his armpits, the back of his knees and his groin. His legs prickled with sweat beneath his coat. He removed a canteen from the center console of the van. Tilting the titanium container to his dry lips, he finished off the water, feeling a sandy remnant against his teeth in the last few drops.

"We need water," a female voice said.

A second young woman pounded the metal floor inside the van. "It smells like a locker room in here. Let us out."

The man tossed the empty canteen onto the passenger-side floor of the van. "What's the matter, number three? You giving me the silent treatment?"

"Suck it, scumbag," a third girl replied.

"Okay, three, I'm calling you Miss Feisty from now on. You get to be first in the Arena, just because Levi likes a good show." The man closed his eyes and faced the stars, just beginning to show. "Yeah, I think I'll recommend you be the main event tonight," he muttered. He drew his duster upward, gathered it in front of him and tied the long trench coat's straps around his waist. He was grateful to be wearing shorts; his legs shivered involuntarily in relief as the cool evening breeze dried the matted hair on his calves and thighs.

Looking east toward the river, the man squinted. No signs of life. He removed his battered Stetson and strained his eyes to the west at the silhouette of a small group of dark hills, scarcely discernible against the muted sky.

"Hey, Miss Feisty." He pounded an open palm on the side of the van. "Let's you and me go for a little walk."

"No way, asshole. I'm staying with my friends."

The man stepped to the back of the van and opened the door. His keys jingled against the interior cage when he twisted the lock open. "It was your choice to jump the train, Missy. Shoulda caught a ride someplace else. Finders keepers, you know. Now you're mine."

"I don't belong to you."

The man grabbed a fistful of the girl's hair. "Get *out* here." When she hit the desert floor, he slapped a ready-made leather strap around her neck and wrapped the slack around his wrist. He clamped the lock back onto the cage and slammed the van's door.

"The rest of you pretty ladies wait here. I'll send you some dates to escort you to my little oasis." He heaved a guttural laugh that lasted until he slammed the driver's door shut.

"You look stupid with that coat tied around your waist like that."

"Okay, Miss Feisty, out in front."

THE MAN GAZED INTO THE dark distance at the main entrance to the Underground. The Changers had established the Underground as their Elite Headquarters after the Punks' rebellion became a force to be reckoned with.

Resistance to the high-tech world and the Changers' rule had begun slowly at first. A small contingent of Bystanders had rebelled. The moral compass of the rebellion had resisted the absorption of the innocent to feed the elite.

The rebels had deleted their social media accounts, dropped their satellite entertainment, and gone off the grid to deny revenue to the Changers. Word of mouth had spread their message quickly—stand against the high-tech takeover of one's existence. They'd insisted on being individuals, not part of the mass sellout.

They were called Punks because they had a beef with the profit--driven world. They were about not buying into society and the quest for money, just for the sake of having more than the next guy. For them, it wasn't a fad. They were a serious culture. They were specifically against doing things to be part of the average person's idea of the new, high-tech society. Their attitude came from inside each individual person.

Resistance to the Changers grew among the military and the common person—the factory workers, the mechanics, the farmers, the doctors, nurses, students and teachers—and they joined the rebellion. But the resistance was not without technology. Rebels in the high-tech community declared their independence and allied themselves with the Punks.

So, the Changers struck back. They confiscated weapons and destroyed factories and manufacturing plants. They deprived the Punks of their science and technology. And they developed the Underground.

The main entrance was thirty feet high and a quarter of a mile wide. Multiple layers of reinforced high-strength steel framed triple-thick bulletproof panels of glass. From this distance, the entrance was merely a sliver of blue light against the foothills. Tonight, the man would not access the Underground through the main entrance.

His feet twisted and turned on the sharp multisized rocks beneath him. The man guided the girl toward the nearest dark hill, scrambling between increasingly larger rocks. Small tufts of sagebrush scratched his legs. His sweaty feet slipped and writhed within his boots. The grit between his toes and under his feet chafed his skin.

"Be glad you got those tennis shoes on." The man stopped at a narrow opening in the rocks, removed his hat again and wiped his forehead. "Down you go." He shoved Miss Feisty headfirst into the opening and let go of the strap. The man followed and disappeared down into the portal.

Moments later, the man stepped into a familiar stone foyer, girl in tow. He felt a cool breeze from the Underground and paused. "Love that fragrance, don't you? Kind of like"—he sniffed the air—"cinnamon and peaches."

The girl crammed her fingers between the leather strap and her neck. "You smell like piss. That's all I smell."

He shrugged and continued downward through the smoothly polished passageway. He stopped at a tinted glass wall blocking the corridor and spoke into a microphone on the wall. "It's me."

Voice recognition technology prompted a soothing reply from the female attendant. "*Welcome, Traveler.*"

"Yes, I've got a Rogue here, and another load up on the surface. Send a security detail to retrieve the others. Take this one off my hands and have them all stripped, shaved and delivered to the Arena."

The female voice replied, "*Confirming, the Arena. And how many in the party?*"

"Three." The man smiled. "And it's not a party yet, but I'm sure we'll make it one."

"*Yes, sir. Security detail has been dispatched.*"

CHAPTER 5

The Punks

THE LATE-EVENING AUTUMN AIR FELT perfect for driving with the windows down. *Convertible would be nice*, Curtis thought. He turned the volume up on his radio to compensate for the added wind noise.

At 10:30 p.m., Curtis pulled into a parking lot in front of the Punks' main checkpoint at the Perimeter. He cruised the Chevy van past the largest of several groups of Punks. A few noticed Curtis's vehicle. A couple of the guys tilted their chins up in acknowledgment.

From the center of the crowd, a pretty red-haired girl stood on her tiptoes, smiling and waving to Curtis. *Ah, Melody*. He returned the wave and thought about the time he'd had a crush on her. That was sixth grade.

To the uninformed, they all looked alike: dressed in a myriad of denim, leather, plaid, army camouflage and leopard print. Guys and girls wore flight jackets and vests, warmers, T-shirts with band names, safety pins of every imaginable size, metal studs and spikes. Some wore obviously custom, one-of-a-kind T-shirts with both random and patterned cuts in the fabric. Many in the crowd wore studded and spiked wristbands, with belts over multi-zippered jeans and skirts.

Their footwear ranged from sneakers, creepers and army boots to Mary Janes and pumps. Most had no discernible brand name.

Hair among the crowd was you-name-it individual. No style was specifically in, but nothing was necessarily out: Mohawks, bihawks, trihawks, bitch handles, long, short, spiked, straight, teased, layered, bleached, colored, accessorized and plain.

They were smokers and nonsmokers, shy and outgoing, tattooed and pierced—or not. They sat, stood, crouched and knelt on chairs, benches, tables and walls. Each individual was his or her own person. The group was a family of individuals.

Curtis's new rank afforded him an assigned parking spot. He checked his look in the rearview mirror. *Hmm, Mohawk's a little weak*, he thought. He got out of the van and closed the driver's door, wincing when the window hardware rattled inside.

Melody greeted Curtis as he sauntered up to the crowd of Punks. "Hey, buddy!" She mussed his hair with both hands. "Your hawk's droopy tonight."

"Yeah, I drove with the top down," he joked. "What's happening around here?"

"Not much. The Changers are unusually quiet tonight. We're just shootin' the shit."

"Cool."

"So where's Krystal? I haven't seen her lately."

Curtis shrugged. "She was gonna meet me, but something came up."

"Too bad, I wanted to say hi. Maybe I'll give her a call later." Melody flashed a look over her shoulder into the crowd. "You notice things are strange around here lately?"

"Oh, you haven't heard?" Curtis liked how Melody's eyes kept their sparkle, even when she worried. "There's a lot of friction between our groups right now."

Melody frowned. "Changers and Punks?"

"Yeah. Word on the street is the Changers are planning an offensive of some sort."

"Wow. What about the Treaty?" Melody smiled nervously.

"You know, the arrangement where we provide their dinner and they leave us alone."

"Yeah. But the prisons are almost empty, right?" Curtis ran a hand through his Mohawk. "We're doing what we can." He sighed. "But no one's naive enough to think we could really stand up to them like last time. Their technology just keeps advancing."

Melody shook her head. "No way, Curtis. We're damn strong. We could kick their asses."

"Yeah, we're strong. But the days just keep going down, you know? And the days turn into years and nothing changes. Seriously, how long can this cycle we're in last?"

"But we have a good life as Punks."

"It's life," Curtis said. "But is it really *living?*"

"You have a point. But I'm putting my money on us." Melody grabbed Curtis's wrist and turned back to the group. "C'mon. I want you to meet someone." She dragged Curtis to the approximate center of the crowd, dropped his wrist and stepped over to snuggle up to a guy twice Curtis's size. She wrapped her arms around the guy's waist and laid her head on his bicep.

"Johnny, this is my friend, Curtis. Curtis, I'd like you to meet Johnny."

Curtis extended a hand. "Nice to meet you, Johnny."

Johnny tipped his chin slightly upward. Curtis dropped his hand. He shoved his hands into his back pockets, thumbs out.

Johnny stared at Curtis. "So is this your old boyfriend or something?"

Melody slapped Johnny's arm. "Johnny! I said Curtis is my friend."

Curtis ignored the comment and looked at Melody. "Whatever. I gotta talk to Dion anyway." He turned to the side and slipped between Melody and a faceless leather vest connected to some jeans and army boots. "See you later, Mel."

"See ya. If I'm gone, say hi to Krystal for me if she shows up." Melody's attempt to touch Curtis's arm failed, and he disappeared into the crowd.

CURTIS FOUND DION AND JIMBO near the edge of the crowd by one of the fire barrels. Dion had assumed the role as leader of the Punks after a skirmish with the Changers had taken the life of his uncle, Angelo. Angelo's death had thrown the Punks' organization into disarray. Although power struggles naturally occurred, Dion had risen to the top due to his cool head and his ability to make a decision under pressure. Raised by his dad, Dion was a man's man. His mother had disappeared when Dion was five years old, and he barely remembered her.

During Dion's early years as the Punks' leader, Jimbo had come to Dion's side as the top enforcer. Dion had grown to depend on the ever-loyal Jimbo to squelch attempted uprisings by rogue factions within the organization.

"Curtis, m'man," Dion greeted him. "So, what's up?"

Curtis bumped fists with his two friends. "You tell me. Anything new about the Changers moving on us?"

"Nothing new there," Dion said. "Seems to be more mutants out and about, though."

Jimbo's eyes widened. "Man, you shoulda been here earlier. We killed a fuckin' monster tonight!"

"Great," Curtis said.

"So there's that," Dion said. "Plus, we heard a rumor about some sleaze bag going around kidnapping people outside the Perimeter."

"What the heck for?" Curtis asked.

"Don't know. Sounds like some random masochistic sonuvabitch. Been happening after dark."

"Yeah," Jimbo said. "With that, and all those mutants out there, who would chance going beyond the Perimeter after dark?"

Curtis turned up the collar on his leather jacket and shoved his hands into the pockets. "You guys think all this strange stuff is related?"

"Who knows?" Dion lit a cigarette. "All I know is, something's up with those bastards. I can feel it. Which brings us to you, buddy."

"Me?" Curtis asked. "Why?"

"You have Perimeter duty tonight. You packing?"

"Always. You know that."

"Better grab one of the ARs," Jimbo said. "It's hairy out there."

"I don't need an AR-15. My Beretta will do."

"You can zip off thirty rounds way faster with an AR."

Dion blew a smoke ring. "Take an AR."

"All right, man. If you guys insist."

"We insist," Dion said.

During the rebellion, the Punks had lost weapons facilities but salvaged the castings and molds and the ability to manufacture AR-15s. Consequently, the AR-15 was a staple for the Punks. They stole technology from the Changers, defended what their meager resources could defend and abandoned the rest.

"Cool. But, hey, before I head out, did you guys meet Mel's new friend? I haven't seen him around here before."

"Boyfriend," Jimbo clarified. "He's her boyfriend."

"I met him." Curtis glanced in Johnny's direction. "He's kinda hard to miss. Even without the Trojan, his head sticks out above the rest of us."

"Here comes Ryker, guys," Jimbo said. "Let's ask him."

Ryker walked over to the friends and brushed his wavy brown hair off his forehead.

"Hey," Dion said. "Wanna do the meet-and-greet with Mel's new boyfriend? Curtis met him."

As Dion's best friend, Ryker had naturally floated to the top of the Punks' organization. His home life, or the lack of it, influenced both Ryker's graciousness and his penchant for fighting. Raised by a drug-addicted single father, he had been the unwilling recipient of regular beatings, just for being a kid. The last most severe thrashing had driven him to hang out at Dion's almost full-time at the age of ten.

Dion's dad, Pops, had raised Ryker like he was one of his own. Ryker liked that Pops gave so much and expected nothing from "his boys," other than to pull their own weight around the shop.

In Ryker's mind, it was a good exchange. *I don't have to be around my scumbag dad, and I don't have to sleep with one eye open.*

As kids, Dion and Ryker had fought a lot—regular fist-flying, blood-drawing brawls, mostly started by Ryker. Cool-headed Dion shrugged it off because he knew Ryker had it in for his piece-of-shit dad. The fights almost always started after Ryker had been with his father. They usually ended in a draw, because Pops would only let it go on for just so long before breaking it up. *"You guys are brothers, now get cleaned up,"* was the usual epilogue from Pops. And they had no choice. Deep in their hearts, Dion and Ryker knew they were brothers.

Ryker looked at Curtis. "You met him. What'd you think?"

"He's a poser."

"Good enough for me." Ryker clapped his hands once. "Let's go, guys."

About a dozen people—including Curtis, Dion and Jimbo, followed Ryker.

When they reached Melody and Johnny, Melody acknowledged the group. "Hey, guys!"

Johnny turned to face them. He remained expressionless and silent.

"Hey, Mel," Dion said. "Kinda thought maybe you might want your boyfriend to meet some of the crew."

"Sure!" Melody wrapped her arms around Dion's neck. He one-handed the return hug, leaned into Melody and placed his right arm around her waist.

Johnny muscled his way between the two friends. "Hey, hands off my girl!"

Dion smiled and raised both hands in a "no foul" gesture. A number of the Punks around the trio broke into a mildly subdued laughter.

"You gotta be kidding me," Ryker said. He stepped forward and put one arm around Melody's waist. He cradled her neck with the other hand, dipped her backwards and planted a full, closed-mouth kiss on Melody's lips. "Hi, Mel!" He smiled.

"All right." Johnny puffed up. "That does it, asswipe."

"Johnny," Melody said. "These are my friends. Ryker and I have been friends for years. We grew up together."

Johnny moved toward Ryker. He grabbed Melody's studded belt from the rear and forced her behind him. "What's up, dude? You need a girl to stand up for you? Can't you defend yourself?"

Ryker raised his eyes slightly to meet Johnny's. "Hard to defend yourself against crassness and naïveté."

Johnny's mouth opened, exuding the faint scent of Budweiser mixed with clove cigarettes.

Ryker smirked. "What, were the words too big for you?"

Johnny nudged his chest against Ryker's. "Don't push me, asshole."

"C'mon, Johnny." From behind him, Melody grabbed Johnny's shoulders. She sprawled butt-first to the ground as he shrugged her off.

Curtis stepped forward from behind Dion. "Hey."

"Don't you start with me." Johnny raised his arm to backhand Curtis.

Ryker struck a blow to Johnny's arm, deflecting its intended target—Curtis's head. Curtis ducked under Johnny and rushed to help Melody to her feet.

Johnny's eyes were locked on Ryker. "Let's go, tough guy."

Dion slipped Ryker a set of brass knuckles. Ryker removed his glove and gripped the weapon in his right hand. "We don't need to do this, Johnny."

"I'm gonna whip your ass worse than you ever felt it from your daddy!" Johnny made his move, lunging at Ryker.

"*No!*" Melody screamed.

Ryker's gut flinched at the reference to his father as the memories flooded his head. He attempted to shake off the comment. *No, you don't.* His left hand caught a wad of Johnny's vest and shirt. *Try this on for size, Dad.* His right fist connected. Johnny's cheek glowed pink.

Ryker's follow-up right hand never reached its mark. Johnny caught Ryker's wrist midflight.

"Johnny, stop!" Melody pleaded.

"Dion, let's give him a hand," urged Jimbo.

Dion waved him off. "Give it a minute."

Ryker felt extreme pressure from Johnny's grip. Using his left fist again, Ryker rabbit-punched Johnny's face. The other cheek reddened. Johnny squeezed Ryker's right arm, forcing him to his knees.

"Johnny, please!" Melody cried.

Jimbo and Dion stepped up to Johnny. Each grabbed a bicep.

"Okay, big guy," Dion said. "You proved yourself."

Johnny sneered. "Let go of my arm, wimp!"

Ryker's right hand felt hot.

Curtis watched beads of sweat break into streams and trickle down Ryker's temples.

Ryker strained. *Damn, this guy is strong.* Ryker heard his ulna snap. Mind-numbing pain shot through his arm and launched into his chest like a lightning bolt. "Aaahhh!" His knees weakened and his legs went limp.

Johnny grinned and shoved Ryker's shoulder with the bottom of his boot, then shrugged off the other two Punks. "Nice try, pussy!" he whispered.

Ryker grabbed his shoulder with his left hand. The brass knuckles fell from his right hand and clinked onto the dirt. The skin on his fingers, stripped back from his grip on the brass knuckles, oozed blood. Sweat dripped from his forehead and stung his eyes. His fingers involuntarily pointed at the ground, his wrist swollen and limp from the broken bone inside.

Johnny kicked the brass knuckles at Curtis. "Don't even think about messing with me." He turned and walked toward his car, pausing long enough to grab Melody under one arm. "Let's get outta here."

"No, you don't," Dion said, his 9mm handgun pointed at Johnny.

Johnny turned to see Dion, Jimbo, Curtis and three others, guns drawn, facing him. Melody squirmed to get away as he pulled her closer. "You're hurting me," she said.

"Get over here. You're going with me." Melody stumbled and tripped as Johnny dragged her to his Cadillac, keeping her between him and the row of armed Punks. He shoved her into the car on the driver's side and followed her in.

"Only reason he's in with us is because of Mel," Jimbo said. "Too bad I never had a clean shot."

CHAPTER 6

Levi and Silver

L EVI YAWNED AS HE STEPPED into the elevator through the door inside his suite in the Underground. He selected 101— *Secure Mode*—and tapped the light switch twice. The ceiling lights in the cylindrical tube dimmed, and a soft purple glow illuminated the borders around the top and bottom. When the door opened, he walked into a spacious room.

On the far wall of the room were twenty-one arched doorways, each with a slick red titanium door. The huge room was equipped with highly polished furniture appointed with plush cushions of cotton and suede. Seven couches complemented twelve huge chairs. Glass-topped end and coffee tables reflected ambient lighting from the ceiling and floor. Silver, blue and white titanium chaise lounges dotted the room. Scale models of various cities and Perimeter Wall designs rested on glass shelves within arched niches in the walls.

Levi loosened his tie as he crossed the room and paused in front of the third door from the left. Pressure sensors in the floor caused the door to swish open. It closed quietly behind him as he stepped in.

The water in the shallow pool in the floor of the small semicircular aluminum-walled room was tinted blue-green. The Underground's filtration system continuously replenished the bathing pools with clean, heated water, so each pool was always fresh and clear.

Levi adjusted the room's music volume to a whisper before disrobing. He slipped quietly into the bathing pool and sighed. He slid below the surface of the water and savored the slick, polished floor of the pool as it caressed his slight frame. Through the crystalline liquid, he ran his hands over his body, examining the many familiar scars for the umpteenth time. His mind drifted as he closed his eyes. Cupping his hands, he brought the water to his head and stroked his cheeks. He felt the ripples, the pits, the disfigurement.

He thought about his childhood—the bullying, the taunts, the regular beatings. He saw himself lying in the gutter when he was ten years old and remembered that he had vowed to even the score. He had looked up at the boys, the girls who'd stood around and laughed, the jerks, the bullies. *I'm going to be somebody one day. On that day, you'll regret how you treated me.* Slowly, his downturned lips curled into a smile as he dozed into a half-sleep.

Levi stirred at a faint tinkling sound in the main room. Sufficiently relaxed, he stepped out of the pool and dried himself. He stood tall, breathed deeply and pounded his bony chest three times with both fists. He walked to a corner of the tiny room and stood with his back to the entrance. Hands at his sides, he dropped his chin slowly and deliberately to his chest. He felt a familiar vibration on the soles of his bare feet. The vibration migrated upward, increasing in intensity and thickness as it rose, completely engulfing his body.

stillness

The vibration ended with a loud *crack* as Levi's body convulsed once, then twice. He slowly turned his face to the ceiling and raised his fists above his head.

"I am Levi!" he screamed.

He turned to face a full-length mirror adjacent to the pool and viewed his body. Gone were the scars, the blemishes, the imperfections. He was rejuvenated, toned, muscular and strikingly handsome. He brought his voice to a whisper as he looked himself in the eye.

"Yes! Today is the day. The retribution begins." He donned a pair of slippers, put on a floor-length silk robe from the closet and tied the sash at his waist.

LEVI STEPPED OUT OF THE round chamber and into the main room.

"It's about time. I was ready to send in the paramedics." Silver reclined on one of the atomic-style chaise lounges, sipping a glass of wine, a tablet in her lap. "We've got some business to discuss." She swished her silky black hair from her face. "Wine?"

"That would be nice," Levi said.

Silver set her glass on the end table adjacent to the chaise and walked across the room to one of three wet bars.

Levi watched her as she pulled the already-open bottle from a glass ice bucket and removed the cork. "You know I enjoy seeing you *fix* my wine more than I like the wine itself."

Silver smiled without turning around. "Yes, Leader." Her figure-hugging black romper just covered the lower curve of her buttocks. Black pumps extended her olive-toned legs by three inches. "I know what you like." She waited, watching the mirror behind the bar until Levi was standing at her back.

"Ooh, Levi. Of all your personalities, it's times like this that make me like this one the best."

He slipped his arms around her waist and kissed her neck.

Goose bumps swept up Silver's arms and washed down her back. She threw her head back and spun around to face Levi. Still holding his glass of wine, she embraced his neck with both arms and kissed him. He pulled her close and pressed his body against hers.

"Feels like you're in no condition to discuss business right now," she whispered. "You've really put me in the mood for an absorption, dear."

He smiled. "But I've made arrangements for a special event in the Arena tonight."

"You know I love the events in the Arena. I'm just in the absorbing mood." She cocked an eyebrow. "Would certainly give me added energy for after the show."

Levi leaned back, clasping her waist. "All right. I must confess, I've brought you a surprise."

She smiled. "Oh, you know I love surprises."

Levi let go of her waist, slipped his hand into hers, and motioned behind him. "Room One, your favorite."

"Nice. How—"

"I placed a personal classified for you. He thinks he's in a hotel in Tremayne, and he believes you like him."

Silver turned toward Room One. "Are you going to watch?"

Levi smiled. "As always. But make haste. The Arena awaits." He eyed the silky smoothness of the young woman strolling across the room. *She is beautiful.*

Silver entered Room One and closed the door behind her. Levi turned and pressed a small button on the bar top. The mirror behind the bar split in the center, revealing a large flat-screen video monitor. He sat on one of the barstools and adjusted the volume as the monitor flashed to life. The screen displayed the scene inside Room One: a king-sized bed with a nightstand on either side, a fireplace, a small writing table and two occasional chairs.

A man who appeared to be in his midtwenties stood to greet Silver. "*Thanks for waiting, babe.*" Silver smiled at the man. They embraced and kissed.

"*You're so worth the wait,*" the man whispered.

Levi operated a remote control to manipulate multiple cameras in the room. He switched between five different angles until he was satisfied with the view.

"*Love is always worth waiting for,*" Silver hissed. She unbuttoned the man's shirt and moved her face close to his again, wrapping her mouth around his bottom lip and sucking it in. The man encircled Silver's waist and drew her toward him. In a flurry of activity, the couple tore at each other's clothes, dropping them, casting them aside like nothing in the world mattered. The couple fell onto the bed, entwined and engulfed in a passion reserved for lovers.

Levi guided a camera downward to the bed.

The heavy, naked petting escalated. Millions of nanobots,

generated by an implant in the Changer's brain, mixed with her saliva and flowed into the man's throat. The atomic infiltrators found their way into his bloodstream with lightning speed. The bots sliced into the cells before drilling down to the man's DNA, extracting the telomerase and sending the youth-inducing enzyme back to its master.

Liquid in the man's organs turned to steam—a result of friction from the activity of the microscopic intruders.

Levi observed goose bumps on the man's arms. In the dim light of the room, he saw his skin flush to a deep reddish hue. The man's activity became more frenzied as Silver's seemed to slow. She wrapped her arms in an iron grip around his neck. Her legs locked around his hips. She rolled the man over and assumed a top position. The man whipped his head back and forth to avoid the face of his lover. His hands moved around to Silver's shoulders. She grabbed his hair and held his head steady to inhale the bots from his mouth back into her system.

Levi watched the man try to push Silver off, but the Changer's grip tightened around the man. His moans turned to shrieks of agony. His movements grew more frantic. Levi noticed the man's skin. He appeared older, wrinkled and leathery. The man grew more desperate. He fought harder, tearing his own skin against Silver's hard, smooth body. His skin slipped and slid on the bone. His muscles withered beneath his skin. The man's shrieks became forced, guttural heaves and his skin flashed white. The video monitor overexposed momentarily, and the room on the screen went dark except for the flickering fireplace.

Silver sat up on the bed, her blood-streaked bare back to the camera.

A remnant of the man's body lay wrinkled and withered, entangled in the sheets.

Levi smiled and poured another glass of wine.

CHAPTER 7

The Arena

CEILING LIGHTS REFLECTED OFF THE highly polished black rock floor of the indoor arena. Heavy gold drapes separated arched niches in the wall of the round room. Plush theater seats with matching gold upholstery sloped elegantly around the room toward the caged-in stage at the center.

Fred Garrison sat with Levi and Silver in a luxury box reserved for top echelon Changers.

Fred had been Levi's top adviser for decades. He had been one of the lead scientists on the team that had developed the Change technology and had been the first to receive the Change after Levi. Interestingly, Fred had opted to receive the Change exclusively for immortality—he had always been satisfied with his outward appearance. Early on, he'd experimented with changing his looks for the experience only, always reverting back to his normal appearance. But, like Einstein's regret over his letter to FDR encouraging research into development of nuclear weapons, Fred Garrison regretted his participation in, and contribution to, the Change project. The absorption of an innocent life to extend one's own had weighed heavily on Fred's conscience from day one. He'd resolved to reverse the process one day.

Levi nudged Fred's elbow. "I sense a splendid show tonight."

Fred smiled. "Best seats in the house."

"WHAT'S SO SPECIAL ABOUT THIS ONE, Leader?" Silver asked.

Levi patted Silver's hand. "The main event. I hear she is referred to as Miss Feisty for good reason."

"Oh? Think maybe we caught a Rogue that actually stands a chance of surviving?"

"Has a Rogue ever survived a mutant in this setting?" Fred asked.

Levi laughed. "There is always a first time, my friends."

Silver leaned away from Levi and eyed him with mock suspicion. "You're so smug. Where are you finding these participants?"

"I have my sources, dear." He smiled.

"Obviously," Silver said. "You're like a cat. You always seem to know everything, but never tell."

Levi stopped smiling. "It's my business to know everything."

The lights dimmed. The crowd in the packed theater fell silent— the unwitting human orchestra of an invisible conductor.

"Ladies and gentlemen!" a male voice boomed over the sound system as the rhythmic beat of a corporate anthem rose in the background. Multicolored lights flashed in sync, their stop-and-stutter timed perfectly to the music. "Welcome to the show!"

The audience burst into a frenzied applause of awe and approval. The swirling music pounded throughout the Arena, flawlessly matched to the hypnotic light show. The crowd arose from their seats and clapped in time.

A male announcer walked briskly through a caged corridor from one side of the room into the cage and stopped center stage. A spotlight followed him obediently, smoothly and precisely. The colored lights ceased as the music slowed to a murmur.

"Ladies and gentlemen, tonight, by executive command, we bring you the main event first!"

The announcer motioned with authority to a door in the Arena wall at the far side of the caged corridor. "Let me introduce to you… Miss Feisty!"

The door in the wall opened. Two guards escorted a young woman, naked and bald, through the corridor to center stage. The announcer exited, followed by the guards.

The Arena erupted in applause.

The woman at center stage turned in circles, surveying the crowd. She stopped when she spotted Levi. Their eyes locked.

Levi smiled as the woman raised both hands to flip him off.

A red light over the door in the wall flashed. The woman turned toward the door and backed up to the wall of the circular cage.

The music stopped. All house lights dimmed except the lights illuminating the cage. As the door opened, the woman climbed the wall of the cage and pressed the back of her shoulders against the steel mesh roof.

The mutant rushed through the corridor to the center. The cage door automatically slammed shut.

"That's hideous," Silver commented.

"The latest mutation. Man and pig," Levi said. "You like?"

"You've outdone yourself, Leader," Fred said.

"I can't believe you're using humans for your experiments, sir," Silver said.

Levi chuckled. "You *are* jesting, correct? Humans are the *main* ingredient. It's the beast that is the variable."

The momentum of the mutant carried it up the side of the cage toward the woman. The mutant snapped at the woman's leg, tearing off a small chunk of skin.

Perfectly timed, the woman let go of the cage ceiling and followed the mutant down, feetfirst. She landed one foot on the creature's neck and one on its rib cage before rolling onto the floor. She rose to a crouching position.

The mutant lay momentarily stunned.

The Arena crowd cheered.

The woman rushed to the man-pig and gripped its neck with both hands. The mutant animal twisted quickly and regained its footing. The woman lost her grip and ran to the cage wall. The beast raced behind her and grabbed her ankle in its mouth.

The woman screamed as she attempted to climb the wall, the mutant still attached to her ankle.

The crowd cheered again.

The woman dropped from the wall and managed to turn around. She began kicking the mutant with her free foot—rib cage, gut, head. The beast growled and shook its head, attempting to separate the woman's foot from her leg. The woman gave up the kicking and fell forward onto the beast, arms wrapped around the mutant's hindquarter.

The two rolled across the cage, each attempting to gain traction on the slick, now blood-covered floor. The woman grabbed the beast's testicles and tugged hard. The mutant animal growled as it yanked her ankle and left the woman's foot on the floor.

The contestants separated, facing each other. The mutant growled and charged the woman. She braced herself as best she could on one leg and a stump. The beast leapt into the air and latched onto the thigh of the woman's good leg. The woman swung a fist into the air, missing the mutant. She went down with a thud.

Blood from the woman's femoral artery spurted onto the floor of the cage. The mutant was relentless. The woman swatted the air with her fists. The beast drug the woman backwards, yanking and tugging at her thigh.

The woman stopped moving. The jaws of the beast remained clamped to the woman's leg as blood pooled onto the floor.

"She was competitive," Levi said. "I knew she would be."

Fred turned his head to the side. "Yes, that was bad."

The red light over the door blinked. Two guards walked down the corridor to the cage door. The mutant remained in place, locked onto the woman.

One guard slid a rifle through the cage door and shot the mutant with a tranquilizer. The lights around the cage dimmed as orderlies arrived through the side door to clean up the stage.

The Arena crowd stood and applauded politely.

Silver sipped her bottled water. "Hmm. The mutant proved to be feistier than Miss Feisty."

CHAPTER 8

Platforms

Curtis stopped the modified four-wheel-drive Chevy van in the middle of the dirt road and shut off the engine. He got out and walked over to the thirty-foot-high Perimeter Wall. He leaned against the wall and lit a cigarette.

Where are you, Krys? Curtis pulled out his cell and tapped the maps app. He zoomed in on Krystal's icon on the app. *Whoa. What the heck are you doing way over there?* He texted Krystal:

On my way. Keep your phone on.

Curtis heard the frantic rustling in the bushes right before the rushing animal hit him in the shoulder. He dropped his cigarette and reached around to the back of his waistband. *Shit, gun's in the van!* He scrambled to the passenger door and yanked on the handle. The heavy armor plating welded to the door put him at a split-second disadvantage he couldn't afford.

The animal hit him in the other shoulder. The door slammed shut. Curtis ran around the front of the van and reached through the driver's window. He snatched his Beretta off the dash. When he turned around, he saw the shadow of the beast coming at him from the rear of the van. He aimed the 9mm and squeezed the trigger. The mutant animal hit the ground and skidded to a stop at Curtis's feet.

Holy shit, that thing's ugly. Curtis jumped into the van and fired up the engine. He flipped on the lights all around—headlights, front light bar, rear light bar, side spots. *Outta here.*

The armored van bounced up and down as Curtis navigated the dirt road toward the railroad tracks. The array of lights illuminated the terrain for thirty yards in every direction. *Hit the tracks and head north on the train frontage road*, Curtis thought. *I'm coming, Krys.*

KRYSTAL CONTINUED WALKING TOWARD THE lights of the train. *At least Punks control the trains*, she thought. *Just gotta stay on the tracks.*

"Hey."

Krystal slowed and squinted.

Four figures rose from prone positions on either side of the tracks. Krystal shielded her eyes from their high-powered hand-held spotlights.

"Stop where you are," the gruff voice shouted.

"Who are you?" Krystal asked.

"Never mind that. Who are you? And what're you doing out here?"

"She looks like one of us, Stringer," the smallest of the four said.

"We got no clue who she is," Stringer said. He approached Krystal. "So, like I said, who are you?"

"My name's Krystal. Now, who are you guys?"

"Doesn't much matter," Stringer said. "What are you doing out here at this time? Curfew started hours ago."

"I don't know you guys. I don't have to tell you anything. And why are you wearing sunglasses at night?"

"None of your business. With that attitude, one thing's for sure—you're coming with us."

"Hell I am."

Two Punks grabbed Krystal by the shoulders.

"Yep, you are." Stringer whistled and motioned to his right.

A Humvee parked about twenty yards off the road fired up, lights blazing, and roared to the edge of the tracks. Stringer walked over to the driver's side of the vehicle. "Get her up to the platform. Tell Wade I want her acid-tested."

"You got it, man," the driver replied.

"No," Krystal objected.

Stringer shrugged at Krystal. He motioned to the two Punks holding Krystal. "Put her in the Humvee."

The Punks lifted Krystal off her feet, muscled her into the vehicle and shut the door. One Punk pounded a hand on the roof before the Humvee headed toward the front of the train.

CURTIS PEERED THROUGH THE WINDSHIELD of the van, narrowed by the sheet metal around the glass. *What have we here?*

Two Punks with spotlights approached the driver's side of the van. Curtis clicked the power locks on the doors and pulled to a stop, engine idling. He glanced in the right-side mirror and noticed two Punks standing in the dark on the other side of the van.

"What's up, guys?" Curtis asked the biggest Punk.

"Hey, Curtis. Perimeter patrol?" Stringer asked.

"That's right. Anything happening out here tonight?"

"Not much. It's pretty quiet. Found a couple of strays wandering around. Sent 'em up front."

"Oh?" Curtis slipped his Beretta off the dash and placed it on the van's console between the seats.

Stringer smiled. "Yeah. One was a little combatant. Didn't want to tell us anything. She was a real pistol."

"Hmm. Well, my partner and I got separated back there a ways. We were attacked by one of those mutants."

"You okay?"

"Yeah, we killed it. But like I said, we got separated. I'm gonna make a quick run up front and take a look."

"Go for it, man. Sucks you got separated like that."

Curtis bumped fists with Stringer. "Thanks, man. Don't work too hard."

"Never do."

Curtis pulled slowly forward.

Stringer stepped back from the van. "Oh, hey, about your partner."

Curtis stopped. "Yeah?"

"Hope you find him."

"Thanks."

IT'S LIKE HIGH NOON AROUND *here*, Krystal thought as the Humvee pulled to a stop at the front of the train. Floodlights at the prisoner hand-off station illuminated the area for seventy yards in every direction.

Krystal tried the door on the Humvee. Locked, and no button. She looked at the driver's eyes in his rearview mirror. "So what's your name, anyway?"

"Just sit tight. That's not gonna matter in the long run. No use us getting all close and everything."

Krystal sat back and watched the activity at Platform One. Changers on the receiving side. Punks on the train side. One at a time, prisoners were led off the train and into a caged neutral area.

"What's going on here?" Krystal asked.

"Acid testing. Why do you ask? You sure acted like you knew what it was back there on the tracks."

"I, uh, I didn't know. Acid testing just didn't sound like something I'd like to participate in."

"All right. So, you see the guy on the receiving side of the platform? That's one of *them*, a Changer. He's like the head Changer for this shift. He gives the okay to receive each person coming off the train. Guess they've had some of their people leaving their group. Don't want to be Changers anymore."

"Why would that be?"

"How do I know why? That's just how it is. So, anyway, they drop some acid onto the forearm of every person we deliver now. If they burn, they're Bystander people—good for the Changers to eat, or *absorb*, or whatever they call it. If the acid turns the skin green and hard, that's a Changer."

"So if it's a Changer, they just let 'em go because they aren't good for absorption—I mean, to eat?"

The driver laughed.

Krystal looked at the exchange station atop the platform. The barrel of a rifle, from inside the train behind an armored sheet, stuck out through a slot into the neutral cage.

"What's so funny?" Krystal asked.

"That guy in the cage is a Changer. Watch."

Krystal saw a flash from the barrel of the gun next to the cage. The Changer's head jerked sideways and he dropped to the floor of the cage. Blood from the fatal wound flowed through a grate in the center of the cage floor.

"What the hell?"

The driver laughed again. "We can't let Changers run around loose. It's the same as we'd do if we found 'em in town. Treaty says no Changers inside the Perimeter."

Krystal wiped her sweaty hands on her jeans. "So that's what happens to any Changer caught by the patrol?"

The driver looked at Krystal in the rearview mirror. "Changers on the platforms get their choice. That guy, the head Changer, decides. Some of the ones we find are flagged to go through."

"Why?"

"We don't know for sure. We've heard the Changer's leader likes to do special things with some of 'em. They call 'em Rogues. We don't know any more than that and we don't care. We just follow the rules."

CURTIS CHECKED THE GPS ON his cell. *Well, she's around here somewhere. At least her* phone *is.* He approached the hand-off station slowly and found a pull-through parking spot next to the platform. *Where are you, Krys?*

Curtis exited the van and shoved his Beretta into the back of his jeans. He lifted the AR-15 from its mount and slung the strap over his shoulder before locking the door.

Two well-built Punks, a male and a female, approached Curtis from the front of the platform. "Hey, stranger," the girl said.

"Hey, Winter, Raymond." Curtis bumped fists with the two Punks.

Winter's dark skin stood in stark contrast to her bleached white cornrows. Her gym-chiseled physique was accentuated by her sleeveless leather vest and tight-fitting jeans.

She glanced at Curtis's van. "Perimeter patrol tonight, eh? What brings you out this far?"

"My partner and I got jumped by a mutant. We got separated."

Raymond's black hair, buzzcut on the sides and slicked back across the top, reflected the bright platform lights. "Yeah, those things are beginning to be a real pain in the ass. You guys need help?"

"Kind of. I'm looking for my partner."

Winter rested her hand on the butt of her holstered pistol. "Who is he? I may know him."

"She," Curtis said. "It's Krystal Peterson. I think you've met her, Win. She's a fourth-level lieutenant."

Raymond spoke into a microphone on his shoulder. "Wade, do you copy? We got one of the Perimeter patrol here looking for a lost partner. You know anything about that?"

Curtis looked up at the platform. A Punk, obviously in charge, waved down toward Curtis.

"Is that for me?" Curtis asked.

"Nah," Raymond said. "He hasn't replied to me yet."

Curtis turned around to see what Wade was waving at. He saw two Punks escorting a disheveled female toward the platform.

"Wait, that's Krystal."

The two Punks with Curtis turned toward Krystal and her escorts as Curtis hurried past them to meet the trio.

"Whoa, what're you doing?" Raymond shouted. He and Winter ran past Curtis to meet Krystal and the other two Punks. They turned around to face Curtis.

Krystal's eyes widened. "Curtis!"

The driver eyed Curtis suspiciously. "What's up, Win?"

Winter glanced at Curtis, then Krystal. "Perimeter patrol. Curtis is looking for his lost partner. Looks like he found her."

"Yep. That's her. Let's go, Krys."

"Wait a sec," the driver said. "I got orders from Stringer to hand her over to Wade. She's getting acid-tested. Stringer's my boss, and Wade okay'd the test. I can't hand her over to you. I got orders."

Winter nodded to Raymond. "Tell Wade it's Curtis down here. He's vouching for her."

Raymond exchanged a few quick words with Wade before addressing Curtis. "Wade sends his greetings, and his apologies." He looked at Krystal. "You guys be careful out there."

The Punks detaining Krystal opened their hands, fully releasing her.

Curtis dropped the AR-15 from his shoulder and handed it to Krystal. "Let's get back to work."

The four Punks stood silently and watched Curtis and Krystal head to the van.

"For some reason, I don't trust her," Winter said.

Raymond shook his head. "Well, you got the instinct, girl."

CURTIS FLIPPED ON THE VAN's light bar. "Got Moses working overtime tonight."

Krystal fastened her seat belt. "Why do you call that thing Moses, anyway?"

"Holy Moses. You know, *parts the darkness*." Curtis smiled. "Like the parting of the Red Sea."

"You're an idiot."

"Just one of the reasons you love me, babe."

Krystal fingered the AR-15 in her lap and stared out the window. She felt the tears rising and rolled the window down, hoping against all odds the cold night air would dry the flow before it began. But it began. And the tears flowed. She didn't wipe them away. She looked down. And she cried.

Curtis skidded to a stop. He threw the transmission into park and turned to face Krystal. "Babe, what's up? What the hell is going on with you?"

Krystal hung her head and stared at her hands. Tears fell onto the back of her hands, trickled down her wrists and soaked into her jeans.

Curtis reached out and gently touched her chin, pulling it toward him. "Babe."

She looked at him through long, wet eyelashes. Her waterproof mascara was no match for the flood. "I love you, Curtis. I love you, but I can't!"

"Krys, you're gonna make me cry, too. What are you talking about?"

"There's so much you don't know about me," Krystal sobbed.

"But I love you. There's nothing you could tell me about yourself that would make me not love you."

"Why? Why, Curtis? Why do you love me?"

"I don't know what it is. We come from the same mold. We both had some pretty serious shit go down with us when we were kids. We joined the Punks about the same time. And—"

Krystal looked up. "And what? What, Curtis?"

Curtis was bewildered. "And you're the most beautiful thing my eyes have ever seen."

Krystal locked eyes with Curtis. "You're the only one who sees me that way. There's so much I want—so much I *need* to tell you."

Curtis turned off the engine and unfastened his seat belt. "I'm right here, babe. It's just me and you."

"I don't know. I don't fit in…anywhere."

"What are you talking about? Krys, I'm dying here," Curtis pleaded. "Give me something."

Krystal pulled away and turned to face the open window. "I can't."

"Can't what, Krys? Look, I'm an open book to you. You know everything about me. I'm holding nothing back."

"Oh, Curtis, you would die if you knew the real me."

"Then I'll die loving you. Tell me. Please."

Krystal slumped in the seat and faced the dash. "All right. I'm…"

Curtis held his breath.

"I'm…I'm a…"

Krystal's head slammed against the door sill. The pale metallic claw tangled in her hair yanked again.

Curtis swiped his Beretta from the dash and pointed the barrel at the open window. "Duck!"

Krystal grabbed her hair and dove to the floorboard of the van.

A muscular white torso flashed past the open window. Curtis squeezed the trigger. *Dammit.*

The creature moved to the front of the van. Curtis cranked the engine to life and threw the transmission into drive. His foot smashed down on the accelerator. Every wheel on the four-wheel-drive van spun wildly, throwing rooster tails of mud behind and to the sides. The van fishtailed and spun in a circle. Curtis whipped the steering wheel left, then right, then left again. He flipped a switch on the dash and Moses sprung to life. When the huge push bar on the front of the van crashed into the creature, it grabbed the side rails and hung on, its huge black eyes locked on Curtis.

"Get the fuck off," Curtis shouted. He slammed on the brakes and the creature lurched backward, its metallic claws still gripping the rails. Curtis jammed the transmission into park and jumped out of the van. The mutant moved swiftly around the van and lunged at Curtis. He clicked off four rounds before the beast fell forward, smacking its head on Curtis's Beretta before hitting the mud.

"Krys, are you okay?" he called out.

Krystal stepped out from in front of the van. She was holding the AR-15. "Never had to fire a shot, babe."

CHAPTER 9

Battle Plans

LEVI STEPPED INTO THE WIDE hallway outside his quarters and greeted the guard with a nod.

"Good evening, Leader. I trust the facilities are as you expected?"

"They're awesome, as usual. Now move out of my way."

"Sir?"

"I said, move. I'm fashionably late for an important meeting."

Lately, Levi had become more obsessed with destroying the Punks. Since the Treaty, the Punks had been shipping death row inmates and criminals sentenced to life to the Changers.

Levi was tired of the arrangement. He knew the Punks' strategy was to control the Changers' life source. He knew this would eventually lead to the extermination of the Changers, or at best, the end of their ability to live forever. *I think I've been patient long enough. We must prepare our forces to strike, to remake the world the way it is destined to be. We will cultivate and assume control of our own human breeding farms.* To accomplish this, Levi knew he had to do away with the middleman that stood in the way. *We must eliminate the Punks.*

THE SLICK STAINLESS-STEEL DOOR SWISHED closed behind Levi as he entered the main conference room. His twenty top commanders and department heads filled the large black conference table.

The ceiling intercom emitted a familiar female voice as Levi seated himself at one end. *"Holding all correspondence, Leader."*

"Long, how is our new Mayberry marketing strategy progressing in Bystander territory?"

The oblivious, go-along-get-along majority within the Perimeter had become known as the Bystanders. They weren't Punks and they weren't Changers. The Bystanders filled their days with the old ways, all the while waiting for the next big free thing the Changers had to offer. The Changers recognized this as an opportunity.

Intensive marketing encouraged Bystanders to remain inside the Perimeter, to retain their Mayberry lifestyles. The Changers subsidized food, housing, education and transportation for the Bystanders as a way to retain favor and keep the Bystanders ignorant of their lot in life. Happy Bystanders were exactly what the Changers needed to ensure their immortality.

Silver occupied the seat directly to the left of Levi. "The Mayberry Campaign is coming along nicely, sir. I am impressed with the analytics, if I do say so myself."

"Splendid! Keep them happy. Once we're rid of the Punks, the Perimeter Walls that *we* financed will form the perfect holding tank for our sustenance." He looked at Fred. "Garrison, what is the report on Rogue numbers with regard to our conversion project?"

Fred, seated to Levi's right, tapped a virtual keyboard. "The major issues are manpower, scheduling and supply."

"All right, one at a time. Manpower."

Fred pulled up a hologram in the center of the table. "As you can see by the spreadsheet, we've got one hundred technicians working eighteen-hour days in shifts. We—"

"Double the technicians, work twenty-four-hour shifts."

"Yes, Leader. That—"

"That solves manpower and scheduling," Levi interrupted again. "What's the supply issue?"

Fred pulled up the next spreadsheet. "Here's a graphic showing the ratio of Rogues being brought to the City versus the quantity sent to the Arena holding cells. There are not enough Rogues allocated for Chybrid conversion."

Levi raised an eyebrow. "Oh, really?"

"Yes, sir. You might want to ease off on the entertainment aspect a little. Or at least confine it to Bystanders or Punks going up against the mutant errors, instead of using perfectly good Rogue Changers."

Levi looked around the conference table. "I trust you, Garrison. You are ballsy enough, if I may use that term, to be forthcoming and truthful instead of blowing smoke up my ass."

"The only other issue," Fred continued, "is that too many Rogues are being terminated at the prisoner hand-off stations."

"But we have Changer spies inside the Punks."

"We do, sir. At this time, I'm not sure why that's happening."

"Macey," Levi barked. "Look into that and report back to me in one week."

Marvellus Macey scribbled some notes onto an electronic tablet. "Sir."

"Good work, Garrison."

"Thank you, Leader," Fred said as he turned off the holographic display.

"Dennis." Levi looked to the far end of the table. "Supply issues aside, what is the status on our Chybrid conversions?"

"On target, on time." Thomas Dennis turned on a large monitor on the wall behind him. "You're viewing the assembly building now. The smaller picture-in-picture shows our technicians performing some preliminary tests."

"Good. I would like to view the facility directly after this meeting."

"You're on my schedule," Thomas said.

"Van Buren, Logan."

"Sir," Scotty said.

Levi's eyes narrowed. "You two have complete control over the Demoralization Campaign."

"It's under control, boss," Johnny said.

Scotty did his best to hide his irritation over Johnny's lowbrow demeanor. "Sir, we've got it covered. The operation will take place at the upcoming Lottery. Silver is in the loop and will be tracking the statistics."

Levi looked at Silver. "Well?"

Silver smiled. "We've heard the Punks are aware of some unfounded rumors about an offensive coming from us. As you know, that will occur when we roll out the Chybrid project. They aren't aware of the Demoralization Campaign. It's vital this Campaign is carried out prior to release of the Chybrids. I believe Van Buren is ready and capable."

"I like it," Levi said. "What is your plan, Van Buren? Dispense with the details."

Scotty couldn't help smiling. "Massive absorptions inside the city limits of Tremayne. We're literally rubbing the Punks' noses in the mud of our presence."

CHAPTER 10

Tremayne

E ARLY EVENING OF THE DAY before the Lottery, Curtis drove to Krystal's house. He moved slowly down the quiet, shady street. Roots from mature trees intermittently distorted the sidewalk sections. Shadows from the trees stretched across the road—exaggerated silhouettes of the old giants—slowly becoming one with the approaching night. A cool autumn breeze whipped the leaves into miniature whirlwinds over the street, only to be broken up by the curb on the other side.

Curtis parked his van parallel to the curb in front of Krystal's house. He ran a hand over his Mohawk and checked his look in the rearview mirror before stepping out of the car.

Krystal hopped off the porch and ran across the dirt-grass yard to greet Curtis with a peck on the cheek. "Downtown, I guess," she said as she stepped into the passenger side of the vehicle.

Downtown normally saw crowds on Thursday nights, but this night was busier than usual. Residents readied themselves for the next night's sign unveiling to kick off the Lottery celebration. This year, the crowd was more subdued than usual. The tension and uncertainty of dealing with mutant creatures running wild had taken a toll. It didn't help that the Punks had grown anxious and irritable.

"Hey, check it out," Krystal said. "Scotty's over by the new sign with Drew and Sydney."

"Looks like Syd's headed this way," Curtis observed. "I'm gonna catch up with the guys."

"And leave me here to shoot the breeze with Sydney?"

"You'll be fine. I won't be long."

Krystal surveyed the street. She watched Curtis greet the others.

"Hey, Krystal," Sydney said as she approached.

Krystal tipped her chin up. "What's up?"

"Not much. Just thinking about the Lottery. It's more like a memorial service to us. I wish the Punks would put a stop to it."

"Can't. It's part of the Treaty."

"Well, it's stupid. At least the weather's supposed to be cooler," Sydney said. "Plus the locals supposedly got a team together to help keep the mutants out."

Krystal laughed. "You mean the rednecks? Oh, I feel *much* safer knowing they're here to protect us."

"Why don't you worry about mutants, or anything for that matter, Krystal?" Sydney asked. "You act like you're in a protected group."

"Eat me, Syd. You're in the top social class. We know you look down on us Punks."

"Not all of you. You're where you are by choice. So am I."

CURTIS, SCOTTY AND DREW WANDERED down the street.

"Hey," Curtis said. "I heard Mayor Kutch is going to be a special guest at the Lottery."

Drew nodded. "Heard that, too. And why not? He's more of a figurehead, not much else. Our mayor's about useless."

"Sorry I can't agree with you guys," Scotty said. "I'm still Liaison to the mayor, you know."

A cold gust of wind swept across the street in front of the trio.

Drew pulled the collar up on his jacket. "I'm kinda feeling sorry for all those people hoping to see their names on the Winners Sign. I mean, thousands put their names in the Lottery every year and only four are chosen. Kinda blows."

"They all stand the same chance to win," Curtis said.

"I agree with you there," Drew said. "But I mean, how do the losers feel when they don't see their names? Do they just go back home and feel like losers for another year?"

"Do you know any of them?" Curtis asked. "Send 'em to one of the Punks' Checkpoints. We'll put 'em to work."

"Yeah, I don't think it's work they're looking for. They're looking to be accepted."

Curtis stopped walking. "You know what, Drew? We don't judge."

Scotty stopped to inspect some fruit at one of the temporary booths. "Come on, guys. It's obvious by the Lottery the Changers will take anyone, too."

Curtis exaggerated a laugh. "Sure, for the right amount of money."

Drew had hated the Change technology from the beginning. When it had first been introduced to the public, rich people had lined up in droves to receive the Change. Celebrities, politicians, white-collar criminals, investment bankers and Wall Street executives had come first. Then, ordinary people had mortgaged homes, cashed in retirement accounts and taken out personal loans to get it. But it wasn't the steep initial cost that Drew despised.

"The price for keeping it is too high," he said. "Immortality and changing your looks isn't worth killing innocent people."

As with everything else the Changers offered, there was a catch—the Change required maintenance. To maintain the Changed status, one must absorb the lives of other living humans.

Curtis sighed. "Sure, but the Lottery people get the Change so they can alter their looks. They'd get it for that, even if immortality wasn't included."

"I guess they think it's worth it because they don't like who they are," Drew said.

"It's not who you are," Scotty said, sniffing an orange. "It's what you end up being."

CURTIS STOPPED AT THE CORNER. He tilted his head forward and squinted. From the shadow of the Tremayne Park gazebo, three boys were running toward downtown. "Hey." He motioned to Scotty and Drew. The two trotted over and stood next to Curtis.

The faces of the three boys were flushed pink and streaked with sweat. The dark-haired boy, slightly in front of the others, jumped up and pulled a red alarm handle on a green post at the corner of the sidewalk about thirty yards from Curtis.

The mutant alarm sounded from atop the town's water tower.

A woman screamed. The crowd of people scrambled in ten different directions. Car doors slammed. Steel barriers auto-closed on stores and restaurant windows.

"Oh shit!" Drew whipped his head around in time to see Krystal across the street herding people into the old bank building. When he looked back at the boys, he saw the mutant.

Drew had seen pictures of these pesky mutants before. The last image from an article on the Tremayne Daily News website looked like a cross between a dog and a pig. He had heard no two mutants were alike. This one had the body of a large monkey and moved on all fours. The head and face were grotesquely humanlike.

"Curtis," Scotty shouted. "Your gun."

"Got it." Over Scotty's shoulder, he saw the last shop door close. A heavy metal safety door covered the entrance from the inside.

The expansive downtown intersection was instantly void of humanity, save for Curtis and his friends and the three boys. All traffic lights blinked red.

"Get over here," Scotty shouted at the three boys. "Get in the light."

The mutant lunged at the slowest boy. Its claw caught the blond boy's heel and the boy skidded to the pavement at Scotty's feet.

Curtis took aim, but the mutant pivoted and raced after the second boy. The boy ran toward his friend in the street. "You okay?" He turned around to see the mutant grab the dark-haired boy by the top of his head.

The mutant bounded back to the ground with a handful of hair, pivoted and headed toward the blond.

That monkey's part human, Curtis thought. "I can't get a shot," he yelled.

Drew lunged at the creature with his hands in the air. "Rah! Over here!"

Curtis aimed again. "Drew, get back."

The mutant swatted Drew's leg, knocking him off his feet.

The ear-piercing alarm continued.

The second boy ran his fingers quickly through his thick mop of light brown hair. He helped his friend to his feet. The three boys stood in a tight circle, back-to-back-to-back.

The mutant circled the boys, ignoring Curtis and his friends. Curtis watched the beast leap vertically into the air and swat two of the boys on top of their heads with its front claws. It used its rear claws to push off the dark-haired boy's chest.

Curtis circled the boys as the mutant danced a sickening, humiliating dance, up, over and around the three boys. "I can't take a shot. It's too close to the kids."

"Hang on," Scotty shouted. He circled the morbid dance act, moving ever closer to the beast.

"Scotty, watch out," Drew yelled as the disgusting creature sprang straight at his friend.

Scotty ducked and thrust his hand in the air, catching the mutant under its jaw. He fell backwards, gripping the mutant's throat with one hand. He flipped the mutant over his head as the creature clawed at the air. The mutant hit the pavement with a thud. Without letting go, Scotty stood and turned around to face the creature. He squeezed the throat of the beast as it wriggled frantically on its back in the street.

The three boys turned to watch, wide-eyed as the mutant's activity slowed to intermittent twitching.

Curtis stood, mouth open, Beretta in hand.

Scotty locked eyes with the mutant dog-monkey. He squeezed tighter. The mutant's twitching ceased. "Dead," Scotty said.

Curtis tucked his Beretta safely away as a pickup truck full of rednecks skidded around the corner and screeched to a stop.

The driver threw the truck into park and jumped out of the

cab. Two other guys piled out the passenger door. "Hey," the driver screamed at Curtis. "Get off the street. Get to shelter."

Four guys with shotguns hopped out of the truck bed and into the street. "Where is it? Why are you guys out here? Can't you hear that alarm?"

Scotty picked up the limp mutant by the scruff of the neck and walked over to the pickup. "You looking for this?" He tossed the carcass into the truck bed.

"Bob," the driver shouted at one of the shotgun guys. "Shut that alarm down."

CHAPTER 11

Bad All Over

Ryker tossed his empty beer bottle into the huge recycle bin.

"Lucky shot, Ryk," Jimbo said.

"You make your own luck, partner. Like I always say, the harder you work, the luckier you are."

Jimbo dropped a dry stump of wood into the burn barrel. "Whaddaya think the Changers are up to?"

Ryker retied his trademark black bandanna and pulled it tight. "I dunno, man. But I keep trying to fit all the pieces of the puzzle together."

"There ain't that many pieces," Jimbo said. "You got mutants, and you got rumors of an attack."

"Yeah, there's more than that, though." Ryker slipped the blade of a long bottle opener into the cast on his forearm. "Sucker itches."

"What else is there?" Jimbo asked.

"Take Mel's boyfriend. What's up with him?"

Jimbo laughed. "I'd like to kick his ass, too, man. But Mel's okay with him, you know? Besides, you full-mouth kissed his girlfriend right in front of everyone. What'd you expect the guy to do?"

"Stand up to me. I was baiting him, you know me."

"Yeah, so what's the big deal? How's that a piece of the puzzle?"

"We're all family, man, that's all. This guy acted like an outsider. I mean, sure, I wanted to fight him to see what he was made of."

"So you accomplished your goal."

"Yeah, maybe." Ryker rubbed the outside of his cast. "But family would know where to stop. The guy literally broke my arm. That wasn't cool."

"I agree. But I still don't see how that fits. What're you getting at?"

"He's new to the Punks, Jim. How'd he know about my dad, my home life growing up?"

Jimbo lit a cigarette. "Grapevine, maybe?"

"Hey, outside of you, Dion and Winter, no one's supposed to know. I've just been thinking about it."

"That's tough, man. You know we'd never spill that."

"Well, did you hear about Krys getting hassled by Slade at Checkpoint Seven the other night?"

"Yeah, I heard. Everyone knows Krys and Slade don't get along."

"It wasn't Krys," Ryker said. "She had that Bystander with her, Van Buren, the mayor's Liaison. Roman patted him down. He said the guy was really talking shit."

Jimbo swallowed hard on his last swig of beer. His eyes narrowed. "Whoa, Liaison to Mayor Kutch? What'd he say?"

"Like, 'Be cool, little man. You don't know who you're messing with.' Something like that."

"So Roman got in his face, right?"

"No. Strangely enough, he let it go."

"What?"

"Yeah, it's not like him. Roman is one of the most badass mothers I know."

Jimbo flicked his cigarette butt into the burn barrel. "Makes no sense. We gotta have a word with that guy."

"See? That's what I'm talking about. I guess he mentioned it to Slade, and Slade told Dion about it."

"And?"

"And Dion asked Roman about it. He told Dion Van Buren gave him the willies. I guess Roman started roughing him up a little, you know, the Roman way. That's when he started mouthing off. Roman said he knew all about his criminal background. Said he ruin his family, including his granddad's business."

"What the heck?"

"Yeah, what the heck is right. Like Johnny knowing about my P-O-S dad. That's what I'm talking about—another puzzle piece."

"Right," Jimbo said. "But the pieces don't fit. Johnny's one of us. Scotty Van Buren's a Bystander."

Ryker noticed the revolving orange warning light above the Perimeter gate the moment the alarm chirped to life.

"Mutant in town," Jimbo said.

"Where's Dion?"

"The Depot."

"I'm heading over," Ryker said. "Secure the gate and put everyone on alert."

Ryker kick-started a dirt bike parked about ten feet away from the burn barrel. He flipped up the kickstand and roared off. He checked his waistband for his 9mm. *Yep*.

Dion stared intently at a monitor situated on a huge stainless-steel console. The monitor displayed a series of blinking dots on a map of Tremayne.

"How many we got in Tremayne?" Ryker asked.

"GPS is showing 325. Not everyone's checked in, though," Dion said.

"I didn't know so many of us were there tonight. Have you heard from Curtis?"

"Yeah, there's pre-show stuff tonight for that stupid Lottery tomorrow. I got Curtis's car here, but he hasn't checked in."

"How many others?"

"None. Everyone else has reported in okay."

Ryker frowned. "I'm gonna give him a call."

Dion stood up and walked across the highly polished concrete floor to the other side of the room. He opened a sliding door on a cooler in the wall. "Soda?"

"Nah, I'm good." Ryker pulled out his cell and flopped onto an expansive sofa next to a desk by the door.

"Give him a few minutes. Hopefully, he's not involved with the alarm."

Ryker set his cell on the desk. "So what are the other Sectors feeling these days? I mean, are the Changers restless everywhere, or do you think it's localized?"

Dion checked the time zone clocks positioned across the wall above the monitors. "Everyone's feeling it. Mountain zone, Central, Eastern. It's everywhere."

"Damn." Ryker glanced at the monitor across the room. "Hey, looks like Curtis is checking in."

Dion walked over to the monitor. "Yep, that's him. Everyone's accounted for."

"So what's everyone else doing about the unrest?"

"Beefing up security, extra shifts in their big cities, the usual."

Ryker stepped over to a large high-tech electronic console. He tapped several buttons and manipulated a touch pad. A huge monitor mounted above the console lit up. "Judging from the info here, I don't see any sign that whatever they're doing is helping. Yellow and orange regions all over the map. Very few green."

"Yep," Dion said. "I see that as a problem."

CHAPTER 12

The Lottery

O N FRIDAY, THE SUN DESCENDED on the western horizon in slow motion. It sat at the edge of the earth as if trying to hold back the evening. Now, the last remnant of the day, distorted by humidity and distance, reluctantly relinquished its presence to the night. Clouds moved in to hide the stars.

Downtown buzzed with activity. Fresh food vendors and other merchants displayed the best of their crops. Multiple booths lined the business district with unique crafts and artwork. Local meat markets fired up their barbecues. Cooks and chefs from the Armenian, Chinese, Mexican, Portuguese and Thai communities prepared their best. Beverages were plentiful, including fresh-squeezed lemonade, sodas, wine and beer.

Residents from far away within the Perimeter arrived early, hoping for the best parking. The streets were crowded when Scotty and Johnny arrived at City Park in the Tesla roadster. A band was setting up sound equipment under the gazebo.

Heavy clouds drifted in.

The guys sat in the car and watched the band members tune their instruments. Scotty took a drag on his cigarette. "Well, I'm ready for the night. Have you talked to Melody?"

Johnny smiled. "Oh yeah, she'll be here."

"You're hardly dressed the part." Scotty eyed his friend. "Honestly, John, a pashmina suit? A little overboard, don't you think?"

"Meh." Johnny shrugged. "I gotta make a couple of changes before the night's over. I figured I'd just be soft and comfy as long as I can." He ran his hand over the sleeve of his sport coat. "Feel it, man. It's super soft."

Scotty wasn't impressed. "Sure, it's nice." He flicked the ash from his cigarette and sighed. "Well, at least you'll get a little pleasure with the pain you're going to inflict tonight."

Johnny eyed Scotty sideways. "You know what, pal? I earn my keep. I deserve a little pleasure."

"Never said you didn't. This is a big event tonight. Just keep your head in the game."

"Don't worry about me. I got everything I need to pull off my end of the operation."

Scotty tossed his cigarette butt into the gutter. "It's my job to worry about you—and everyone else."

"Someday I'm going to have your job, Scott. Must be nice keeping your hands clean all the time. Shit, man, you're pretty much untouchable."

"Keep up that attitude and you'll get that promotion yet. As far as being untouchable—perks of my position, buddy."

"Yeah, I get it. So, hey, big operation tonight. Pleasure first, then the work."

"Whatever order you want. In the end, it won't matter anyway. By the time tonight's over, these Punks won't know what hit 'em."

THIS IS ABOUT AS CLOSE as we're gonna get, I think." Drew parked parallel to the curb about two blocks from the grandstand on Main Street. He jogged around to the passenger side of his pickup to open the door for Sydney.

"Thank you, babe. You're such a gentleman."

People crowded the sidewalks throughout the downtown area. Excited families piled out of their vehicles. Babies rode in strollers, and tots balanced on daddies' shoulders. Countless teenagers formed in groups and social clusters.

The festive noise of the crowd and music drowned out casual conversation.

Two women shouted over the din. "Mayor Kutch says people are coming from all edges of the Perimeter."

"Wow, Drew," Sydney said. "Considering everything, sounds like this is going to be a pretty big event."

"Yeah, that's cool. Hey, when are Curtis and Krystal supposed to get here?"

"They said in time for the opening. It's almost nine o'clock now."

Drew and Sydney hurried up Main Street, weaving their way through the ever-increasing throng of people. The crowd moved as an uncoordinated mass, sensing the time of the Lottery drawing near.

SCOTTY AND JOHNNY MADE THEIR way down the street toward the grandstand. They consciously stayed to the rear of the ever-growing crowd. Facing the enormous drape that covered the Winners Sign, the boys hopped up onto a city bench across the street. Standing on the seat, they leaned against the wall of the old twenty-story bank building.

"Perfect spot, John." Scotty lit another cigarette.

Across the street, a man ascended the steps to the stage in front of the drape-covered wall and stepped up to the podium. *"Testing..." Click, click, click.*

COMING FROM THE EAST, CURTIS screeched his armored van to a halt at the nearest open parking spot, four blocks from Main Street. Krystal swung the passenger-side door open. She slid off the bucket seat and onto the sidewalk. When she slammed the heavy door, a loud bang sounded from underneath the vehicle.

"Great," Curtis said. "Perfect time for a flat." The right front tire hissed. "I know Drew and Syd are waiting for us, but I better fix this now, babe."

"We can hold a space for you," Krystal offered.

"Yeah, just go. If I fix this now, we can make a quick getaway when it's over."

"'Kay. Look for me. Call or text if you have to."

"Yeah," Curtis said.

The tire expelled its last breath of stale air. The streetlight next to the van flickered.

Under the now-dim, fluttering yellowish light, Curtis stood and watched Krystal hurry away. His hands dropped from his hips to his sides in frustration.

KRYSTAL HURRIED TOWARD DOWNTOWN AND stopped at the edge of the nearly impenetrable crowd.

A raindrop landed with a splat on the podium's microphone.

She turned away from the crowd and hurried back down Main Street. She paused next to the VIP stage and stood on her tiptoes. *Can't see a damn thing.* She turned and ducked under the ropes that cordoned off the stage and podium area. Volunteer security personnel were oblivious to her intrusion into the restricted area.

Krystal ran up the stairs and onto the stage. Now above the crowd, her eyes locked on Scotty and Johnny standing on the park bench across the street.

Scotty gazed at Krystal.

Another raindrop fell.

CURTIS LOCKED HIS JACK ONTO the bumper of the vehicle as the flickering streetlight was extinguished.

The adjacent streetlight began to flicker.

"Whoa," Curtis said, startled by the instant darkness. He lost his grip and the handle slipped off the jack, swung down sharply, bounced off Curtis's shin and slid under the van.

SYDNEY TUGGED ON DREW'S SLEEVE. "Look, there's Krystal up on the stage."

From the center of the crowd, Drew raised his arms, attempting to attract his friend's attention. "Krystal!" He jumped up and down, waving his arms.

A couple of overweight security guards lumbered up the stairs.

Krystal caught the two in her peripheral vision. *Great.* She hurried down the steps on the opposite side of the platform to avoid the plodding pair.

"Hey, I think she saw us," Drew said.

"No, she wasn't looking at us," Sydney replied. "I'd say either she spotted someone else or she was avoiding arrest. Look at that." She pointed to the security personnel, now bounding down the stage.

Scotty pointed at the podium. "Hey, John. I just saw Peterson up on the stage."

"Speaking of girls, Mel just texted me." Johnny smiled. "Tonight's the night. Gotta go, pal." He hopped down off the bench and was immediately swallowed by the throng.

Scotty stepped off the bench and headed toward Krystal.

Sprinkling. Great, Curtis thought. *There's no rain in the forecast.* His shin throbbed as he lay on his stomach, groping under the van for his jack handle. *Got it.* His knuckles scraped the oily asphalt as he positioned himself to back out from beneath the vehicle. As he army-crawled backward from under the van, he noticed a vague movement and heard the scuffling of feet. Lying still, he squinted in the dark and tried to focus. It was two people, male and female. He watched as they moved across the street and sat down in the grass under the water tower.

Krystal rounded the corner from the alley behind the mural, then back onto Main Street. At the edge of the crowd, Scotty greeted her. "Hey, Peterson."

"Hey," Krystal greeted him. *C'mon, Curtis. Where are you?*

"Come on and watch with me. I found the perfect viewing spot."

"Yeah, well, Curtis and I are meeting up with Drew and Syd—"

"Drew and Sydney?" Scotty frowned. "Thought you'd be taking advantage of tonight to complete your assignment."

Oh god, get off my back about it, smirk face. Krystal gazed into the crowd. "Whatever. They'll be looking for me."

Scotty grabbed Krystal's wrist. "Oh, come on. They're probably buried in this mess somewhere."

THE MOB IN THE STREET began clapping their hands in rhythm, growing impatient for the unveiling of the Winners Sign and anxious to get on with the celebration.

click

"Ladies and gentlemen… ladies and gentlemen…"

The clapping spread, and the chanting began.

"Ladies and gentlemen, please."

"Just start, Henry," a female voice from behind the speaker urged. "They'll calm down if you just start."

"Ladies and gentlemen. Welcome to the annual unveiling of the Changers' Lottery Winners."

Mixed with the chanting and rhythmic clapping, the crowd cheered.

"Tonight, Mayor Kutch and other elected officials of Tremayne are here as special guests of the unveiling."

The cheering increased. The speaker introduced the city council, the planning commission officials, Mayor Kutch, and the sign's designer.

"DON'T THINK I'LL EVER WANT to be a Changer, Syd," Drew said.

"Me either. These poor people put so much stock in their appearance."

"I know what you mean." Drew shook his head slowly. "It's their overall life experience, too. In their minds, they're rejects. No one accepts them the way they are."

Sydney squeezed Drew's hand. "When you think about it, the Changers accept anyone. Why else would they receive four misfits like these people into their organization every year?"

"You're kidding, right?"

"Well, they do accept everyone," Sydney said.

"Uh-huh," Drew said. "Then they want you to change to be

like them. Whether you pay to get in, or you win the Lottery, you change once you're in."

"You're making my point, babe. People get into the Changers' organization because they want to change—"

"Because they don't like who they are. Because they don't accept themselves."

"We're lucky," Sydney said. "Because we're above-average-looking and relatively intelligent. But I have pity for these people. I mean, look at them. Who would hang out with them...really?"

"Punks would. Punks accept anyone."

"Even these people?"

Drew let go of Sydney's hand. "You know what Curtis told me about the Punks? He said, 'Anyone is welcome to be a Punk. But being a Punk isn't for everyone.'"

"That makes sense when you think about it." Sydney grabbed Drew's hand again. "The Punks are definitely not all good-looking—"

"And they can't all dance, and they don't have perfect teeth. Heck, babe, they come in all shapes and sizes, genders, transgender, nationalities, you name it. Anyone is welcome."

"So you're saying these people should join the Punks instead of the Changers?"

"I'm saying the Punks would accept them as they are."

A HUGE MENAGERIE OF HUMANITY hovered restlessly inside a cordoned off area in front of the main stage. Several of them held umbrellas. Others huddled in small groups holding tarps above their heads. This was not due to any forecast of rain, because there hadn't been one. They used the umbrellas and tarps as protection against the consistent onslaught of tomatoes, soft drinks, beer and spit that rained down upon them from outside the Lottery entrants' circle. Full of hopes and dreams, they had arrived as they appeared in their natural state: commonplace, average and ugly. They were blemished, imperfect, unattractive and flawed. They were old and young, freckle-faced and scarred, the fatties and the beanpoles, the slow, the geeks, the loners, the outcasts, the freaks and weirdos. They hoped to leave as Changers. These were society's rejects. These were the Lottery hopefuls.

THE OFFICIAL VIP SPEAKERS RECITED rehearsed speeches, their voices echoing over the PA system throughout downtown.

Scotty led Krystal to the city bench. The two turned their attention to the stage.

"...*so the inspiration came naturally*," the sign's designer concluded.

"*Thank you, Ms. Greaves. And now, ladies and gentlemen, the moment you've been waiting for.*"

A drumroll began from the band's drummer.

The cheering increased.

The designer moved quickly toward the rope that held the drape over the Winners Sign.

Sydney squeezed Drew's hand.

Scotty slowly blew out a long puff of smoke.

The VIPs on stage rose and turned to face the draped sign.

Krystal stood on the bench with her hands in her back pockets. Her vision blurred and her mind drifted to Curtis.

The artist gripped the rope tightly.

IN THE DARKNESS, CURTIS STOOD up and squinted across the street at the couple, now lying down. *Dammit. Who is that?*

THE GRASS FELT COOL AND soft on Melody's back as she lay under the water tower. "Johnny, we have to talk." She felt every millimeter of Johnny's body where it touched hers. The throbbing of his heart pounded against her chest.

Raindrops sparkled across Johnny's brow. Light brown locks of hair shone black against his forehead. He kissed her.

Melody felt his strong arms, his tender lips. "Johnny..." Goose bumps swept over her body.

Johnny cradled her neck in the crook of his arm and brushed the hair from her face. Stroking her temple ever so gently, he gazed deep into her eyes and rested his cheek on hers. He kissed her, and the scent of their breath fused invisibly together.

Melody's skin tingled and she felt flush. Allover warmth radiated outward from her body. She slipped her hands under his jacket and wrapped her arms around him. Her skin became as hot as his. She closed her eyes. Her veins bulged as her muscles began to pulse uncontrollably.

In a sickening show of sensuality, Johnny held her closer, partly out of morbid self-gratification, mostly to prevent her escape.

THE ARTIST YANKED THE ROPE.

MELODY'S SKIN SHRIVELED, STRETCHING AGAINST Johnny's grip. Her eyes shot open wide and she screamed into his throat. In a long, low huff, Johnny inhaled hot, moist air from his victim. A smile split the smooth skin on his boyish face.

There was a momentary flash of light under the water tower.

The deflated, shriveled carcass of Melody's formerly youthful body lay flat against the wet grass.

The streetlights on Main Street flickered, then were extinguished.

Wide-eyed, Curtis shrieked, jerked and fell backward onto the street.

THE DRAPE FELL FROM THE sign.

The cheering escalated into hysterics.

The beautiful sign displayed the four names of the lucky new Changers.

The hysterics calmed to a buzz and the microphone clicked. *"Ladies and…"*

A scream to the distant north, accompanied by a flash of light, interrupted the announcer. Another scream followed from the east, then two more from the south, then three screams from the west with simultaneous flashes of light.

The buzz of the crowd turned to a murmur. A second wave of

randomly interspersed screams, flashes, pops and sparks wove its way through Tremayne like a snake.

The city froze.

IN THE UNDERGROUND, THE AUTOMATIC door leading to the main control room swished open. Silver Long strode swiftly through the doorway, tablet in hand. "Get me the latest count from the Central California operation."

One of twenty technicians, seated at the rearmost of three consoles that faced the front of the room, typed skillfully into the keyboard in front of him. "One moment, Commander."

The electronic display covering the front wall of the control room showed a map of the western United States, centered on California. The Perimeter, outlined in fuchsia, blinked busily with lighted dots of differing colors.

The technician swiveled in his chair to face Silver. "Commander, two thousand and thirty-two authorized lifespan renewals; twenty-nine Changers in the same location have simultaneously reached suspension. A collection team has been dispatched."

"Beautiful, over two thousand extensions! About those twenty-nine suspensions—what's the collection team's ETA?"

"About ninety minutes by air, Commander."

"Excellent. Have them delivered straight to the lab. Notify me when the team has gathered the bodies and they're en route back to the Underground. Send me a list of the names of the renewals. They're up for promotion. They have infiltrated and executed perfectly. And let me know immediately if there are any more suspensions." Silver swiped and tapped her tablet, then slipped it into a holster on her hip.

"Yes, Commander." The technician swiveled back to the console.

Silver turned to exit the control room. The door swished open, then closed behind her as she turned down the corridor toward the main conference room.

CHAPTER 13

Pandemonium

On Main Street and throughout the downtown area, the lights flickered on in succession from west to east.

On E Street, moths clicked and rustled their silky-soft rag-colored bodies against the spotlights that shone around the Lottery Winners sign. Except for the humming of the PA system, the downtown area was silent, dead to the night.

An inaudible vibration filled the misty night air. Not one standing body moved. Mothers hugged children. Other kids sat still on their fathers' shoulders. Couples held hands. It was as if everyone was waiting for someone, anyone, to make a move.

A third wave of flashes and explosions snaked its way through the downtown area.

The crowd quickly wound back up. Scrambling security personnel surrounded the stage to protect the VIPs. The surge of residents and guests twisted and snarled its way in a hundred different directions. The mob morphed into divisions of disorder and mayhem and quickly became an uncontrollable mess.

Someone pulled an alarm handle.

A strong breeze blew in, and the sprinkling turned to a drizzle.

FROM THE MIDDLE OF THE throng, Drew and Sydney felt the suffocation of the solid whirlpool of bodies.

"Drew," Sydney shouted as she lost her grip on Drew's hand.

The unruly mob carried Sydney toward the outside as Drew was drawn involuntarily to the center.

Drew fell, driven unmercifully to the ground by the humongous, mindless, heartless monster that was the crowd. "Ow." Someone stepped on his hand. "Oof." His temple took a knee. On all fours, he stared at the asphalt, only two feet from his face. Saliva dripped from his mouth. The smell of dirt, slightly tainted with a scent of dead animal, permeated his nostrils. He tried to focus. *That little white spot, what is that?* He focused on a pale yellowish piece of popcorn, smashed flat from hundreds of shoe soles, carelessly abandoned as a casualty of the celebration. Drew noticed the popcorn piece was damp, having found its resting place in a small puddle of melted snow cone. Dizziness washed over him. The grimy popcorn piece, the snow cone mush, the asphalt grit and that awful smell faded to black as he lost consciousness.

AT THE OTHER END OF Main Street, Curtis scrambled to his feet. He dropped the handle of his bumper jack. Pulling his cell from his pocket, he quickly checked in with the Punks at the Perimeter. *Gotta find Krys*, he thought. He started toward the downtown area on foot.

The drizzle became rain.

Curtis speed-dialed Krystal as he ran toward the downtown area. "Hey, where are you?"

"*I'm in the alley behind the bank,*" Krystal shouted into the cell. "*What the hell is going on?*"

"I don't know, babe. Gotta be the Changers."

"*What? How do you know?*"

"I don't. But I'd bet money on it." Curtis ran when he could, tripping sideways, forcing himself in between and through the wave of confusion.

KRYSTAL PUSHED A FINGER AGAINST her free ear. "*I can't hear you!*" A rolling crush of bodies forced Krystal into a tight doorway.

CURTIS SURVEYED THE DOWNTOWN AREA. *Gotta get to the other side*, he thought.

A gust of wind ripped a banner from atop the hotel and deposited it temporarily onto the roof of the bank. A putrid-green taxi forced its way through the throng a foot at a time.

Curtis used the shoulders of two unwary passersby to boost himself atop a city waste bin. He jumped from there to the hood of the taxi and slid to the ground. He half jumped, half body-surfed to the sidewalk on the other side of the street. He put the cell to his ear. "Krys, are you there?"

"*I'm here! These people are crazy! We have to get out of here!*"

"Almost there, babe."

"*I see you! I'm in this little alcove on your side of the alley.*"

As Curtis moved closer, Krystal reached her hand along the wall. She grabbed the sleeve of his leather jacket and squeezed.

Curtis felt the warmth of Krystal's hand and interlocked his fingers with hers. "Krys!"

Krystal pulled with all her might.

Curtis fell into the tiny space on the building. He grabbed Krystal around the waist with both arms and lifted her off her feet as he embraced her.

Krystal smiled. "I knew you'd find me."

Curtis loosened his grip and let Krystal slide down to regain her footing. He held her face in his hands and their eyes locked. "Thank God you're safe." Curtis strained to hold back the flood he knew was waiting to flow from his eyes.

Krystal smoothed his hair from his forehead. "Aw, babe. I'm fine—"

Bodies from the throng bumped Curtis's back as he pulled Krystal's face to his. He kissed her. "I love you, Krys."

"But, Curtis—"

"But what? I love you!"

"How can you think about love at a time like this?"

"DION." JIMBO BURST INTO THE Hangar, followed by two other Punks. "Something big's going down in Tremayne. We got over five hundred checking in, the mutant alarm is going berserk, and the police scanner is nonstop."

Dion and Ryker rose from squatting positions atop a tank-sized armored vehicle.

Geezer turned from a corner of the spacious metal building and removed his round spectacles.

Pops stopped welding and swiveled his face shield up onto his forehead.

"What's up, Jim?" Ryker hopped down to the lower section of the vehicle and used a short stepladder from there to the floor.

"You gotta come to the Depot and check out the board. It's mayhem in Tremayne right now."

Dion lit a cigarette and clinked his Zippo shut. "See what's happening, Ryk, and let me know if I need to come in there."

Ryker removed his bandanna and stuck it into a back pocket. He ran his fingers through his long brown hair. "Show me what's up, man." He and Jimbo led the two other Punks out the door of the Hangar.

Geezer grabbed a rag off a stainless-steel countertop to clean his glasses. He strolled over to the massive vehicle and looked up at Dion. "Whaddaya suppose is happening?"

Pops turned the valve off on a nearby oxygen tank. "Wanna know what I think?"

"Let's hear it." Geezer put his glasses back on.

"Changers. They're makin' their move."

Geezer put his hands on his hips. "What move's that?"

Pops ran his thumbs under the straps on his suspenders. "The move I've been tellin' you about." He twisted one handlebar on his thick mustache. "Told you I been feelin' this for the last two years. I felt it last year when I did that repair over at Platform 60."

"Yeah, I 'member you sayin' you felt something. Nothin' you could put a finger on, though."

Dion hopped down off the vehicle. "He's right."

Geezer pulled at his thin goatee. "You're just agreein' 'cause he's your daddy. We don't even know what's happening. Maybe Jimbo's just havin' a panic attack," he said.

"We'll know shortly, Geeze," Dion said. "You gotta trust the information Ryker brings us."

"Oh, I trust Ryk. He's—"

"I've felt it, too," Dion said. "So has Ryk."

Pops tossed a heavy wrench onto the floor. "See there, you old fart? Dion *and* Ryk's been feelin' it. Why do you think we've been working all this overtime on this project?"

"Yeah, I gotcha," Geezer said. "But if it's them Changers, what's their beef?"

A voice came over the ceiling intercom. "*Dion. You need to see this.*"

Dion dropped his cigarette into a butt can. "Be right back, guys."

Geezer looked at Pops. "That kid of yours is just like you, man."

"He's better, in every way. Smarter, stronger, more cool-headed." Pops spat a tobacco wad into a glass jar. "Best part is, he's a leader. Something I never had."

Geezer stroked his goatee. "Yeah, you were always a loner, I know that. You were always a loner."

Pops smiled. "Yeah, but I always got you, Geeze."

Johnny unlocked the huge aluminum bay door and rolled it to the top. He walked over to the yellow school bus lined up in the first position. He glanced in through the open door. Keys in the ignition. *Good work, guys*, he thought. *Now, where's Zack and Rod?* He walked between the rows of vehicles to the second and third busses in line. *Keys. Good.* He checked the time on his cell.

"Johnny." Zack entered the bus barn, followed by Rod.

"You guys are just in time. This is your first assignment. Wouldn't have looked good if you were late."

"Have you seen that mob downtown?" Rod asked. "It's wall-to-wall people."

"Never mind that. Both of you look like socialites. We're security tonight. Get changed."

"Now?" Zack asked.

"Now," Johnny said.

Zack and Rod stood erect, chin-to-chest. Their bodies blurred as the transformation progressed from the bottom up. Their hair turned black, slicked back—the look of authority. Quickly, the two donned athletic shoes, jeans and yellow polo shirts with the word SECURITY in black across the back.

"Awesome," Johnny said.

"What about you?" Rod asked.

"Don't worry about me. I'll be ready when you get to your vehicle."

Johnny's change was complete by the time he sat down in the driver's seat of the first bus. He unhooked the microphone from the dash-mounted two-way radio. "You two follow me. Don't bother closing the door."

The three busses moved slowly around the outside of the downtown crowd and pulled to a stop in front of a small warehouse just outside the business district. As the air brakes hissed, a security detail of one hundred men and women trickled out the double doors on the front of the building. Their bright yellow polo shirts stood in stark contrast to the dim area lighting. The busses sat idling as their wipers frantically squeegeed the windshields. Simultaneously, the bus doors opened.

Johnny stepped off his bus and motioned to the detail. "This way. You all have your assignments. Round 'em up. Two hundred, no less."

Sixty-five members of the security detail moved into the crowd. The others remained near the busses and formed three human pathways, each leading to a bus.

"Ma'am, move this way. We have seats available for transportation out of the downtown area."

"But my husband—I can't find him."

"If he's nearby, he's probably already on the bus. Just follow the line of security personnel right over there."

"Oh, thank goodness!"

The security detail worked the crowd like a finely tuned machine.

"This way, people. If you need immediate transportation, we have busses waiting. They're filling up fast, please hurry."

A man and his fourteen-year-old son walked up to one of the security people. "Have you seen my daughter? She's sixteen, blond, about this tall."

"Yes, sir. She's headed to the busses. Right this way."

A woman, holding her husband's hand, followed the man and his son. "This way, honey."

"Follow the line, people. We have warm, dry rides waiting for you."

"Oh, you people are lifesavers," another man exclaimed.

Johnny radioed the security detail. *All security personnel, this is Johnny. We're full up.*

Like a synchronized marching band, the security personnel closed ranks and followed the remaining residents back to the waiting busses.

Johnny closed the bus door as the last of the security detail seated himself beside the bus steps at the front. "Everyone, make yourselves comfortable. We'll be making one stop, then you'll all be home in no time."

The three busses followed a two-lane rural road out of town. The residents were excited, relieved, and thankful to be dry and out of the activity back in the City.

"Where do we have to stop first?" a man asked Johnny. "My house is the opposite direction."

"Yes, mine is too," a woman agreed.

Johnny remained silent as the busses sped toward the Perimeter. The residents grew anxious.

"Why isn't he talking to us?"

"Hey, where are you taking us?"

"We'll be home soon, honey. Just be patient."

When the busses finally slowed down, Johnny turned left onto a dirt frontage road paralleling the Perimeter Wall.

"This is making me sick," a woman said as the huge vehicle jostled its passengers over the rough terrain.

The busses rolled slowly to a stop at an abandoned Perimeter checkpoint. Johnny pulled out his cell and tapped out a series of numbers. The dilapidated gate in front of the bus slowly opened. Johnny crept his bus through the opening and into the darkness outside the Perimeter. The other busses followed.

A man screamed from the back of the bus. "No!"

In the darkness, through rain-covered windows, the three busloads of people gasped at the silhouette of a line of boxcars attached to the locomotive engine of a train, quietly idling.

THE CARAVAN OF TWENTY VEHICLES filed in through the main gate at Perimeter Checkpoint One. The gate closed behind them. Four Lenco BearCats on the outside rolled in to block the entrance.

Shortly after the rebellion, high ranking Punks within Lenco Industries declared all vehicles made by Lenco would be available exclusively to the Punks' organization. Military-bred Punks preferred the huge Lenco BEAR on the front lines in battle. The smaller BearCat comprised most of the Punks' fleet for routine patrol and security situations.

The caravan inside parked in a semicircle in front of the Depot.

Jasper stepped out of a heavily armored Humvee and stretched. "Griff, bring the walkie, just in case."

"Got it." Griffin grabbed the two-way radio off the dash mount and closed the passenger-side door.

The Punks piled out of their modified vans, trucks, BearCats and Humvees and met Jasper at the entrance to the Depot. Camouflage netting draped over the building dripped from the rain. Every window on the expansive warehouse-sized building was illuminated from the inside.

Jasper held up a hand. "All right, everybody, listen up. Jimbo's got the gate secured. Griff, Zane, set up two defense details, one around the Hangar and one around the Depot. Everyone else, inside with me."

DION TOOK A SWIG FROM his water bottle and looked up from the control console. "Let 'em in, Jim."

Jimbo unlocked the door and stepped back. "Jasper. Good to see you, man." The two bumped fists.

"Hey," Jasper said. "We relieved your guys on defense detail. Set up two buffers, ten men each. One buffer for here and one at the Hangar."

"The checkpoint's closed," Ryker said. "You set up on the outside, too?"

"Yep," Jasper said. "Fourteen BearCats, six Punks in each, heavily armed."

"Awesome. Take a look at the map here."

Dion expertly tapped the keyboard in front of him. "Check it out. We had six hundred and twenty of us in Tremayne. Five hundred and two reported in. Nothing from the rest."

Jasper frowned. "Whaddaya mean, *had*? What are the trackers showing?"

"That's the problem. Not all of them have GPS devices on their vehicles. Some of them carry trackers, some are cell apps. Nothing on the rest."

"Okay, I'm with you," Jasper said. "That leaves about a-hundred-and-twenty unaccounted for?"

"One-eighteen," Ryker said.

Dion lit a cigarette. "But that's not just *unaccounted for*. Strangely, their trackers disappeared from the map. The lights just went out."

"Wow." Jasper shook his head. "Did you guys send anyone in?"

"Twenty vehicles, six in each. They're standing by for orders."

Jasper turned and looked around the room full of Punks. "So who do we have there? Who's in charge?"

"Curtis," Ryker said. "He's our top rank in the City right now."

CURTIS'S CELL BUZZED. *LACE.*

Lace was a third level commander. She'd received her nickname because of her skin condition, vitiligo. She'd been picked on and ridiculed because of the white areas on her dark skin, but the Punks never tried to convince her the condition was unnoticeable. They saw the beauty in her soul and in her eyes. They saw the beauty in her skin and called her Lace.

Curtis tapped the screen and put the device to his ear. "Lace," he shouted. "What's happening?"

"*Curtis, we're on the west side, just outside the garment district. We have twenty vehicles here, full with reinforcements. I brought your van—we changed your tire. You need to get here ASAP.*"

Curtis stuck a finger in his free ear. "I've been waiting for your call, girl. I got the info from Dion."

"*Give me the word, man. What do you want us to do?*"

"Spread out and form a barrier with the vehicles facing Checkpoint One. Leave two in each vehicle. Everyone else team up in fours and get a handle on traffic at the main intersections."

"*Did Dion tell you it's not just the Bystanders? We have people missing, too.*"

"Yes. That's where we come in. You, me and Krys are gonna find out what happened to them. Just wait by my van."

"*You got it. What's your ETA?*"

"Gimme five."

CHAPTER 14

The Aftermath

DREW WINCED AND RUBBED HIS head. "Where are they taking us?" Sydney stared out at the darkness between the slats of the boxcar. "I don't know, but it can't be good."

"I didn't know Tremayne allowed security personnel to carry weapons. I never would have agreed to get on that bus if I knew they were going to treat us like this."

"Drew, we wouldn't have gotten on this train if they hadn't held guns to our heads."

"Dammit!" A small pool of water fell from the ceiling of the boxcar and landed on Drew's head.

A rather large woman in an overcoat stared at Drew. "Can you keep it calm, sir? There are children in here."

Drew's eyes narrowed. "Can you back off, lady? I've had to put up with your boobs in my face for the last three miles."

"There's no place for me to go. It's crowded in here."

Sydney touched Drew's arm. "Don't worry about her. We have to figure something out before this train stops. Whoever these people are, they're going to be in complete control once we get wherever it is we're going."

The muffled voice of a man came from the other side of the boxcar. "They're Changers."

Sydney's scalp bristled. "Of course. It makes sense. No wonder they all looked perfect. Every hair in place."

"Right," Drew agreed. "That answers the question of why they had guns." He looked up. The rain had stopped, but several large splashes of water sprinkled rhythmically from the ceiling directly above Sydney.

"Someone's up there," Sydney said.

"They're pounding on the roof," Drew observed. "Wait, there's a little hatch up here."

A gust of cold wind swept through the boxcar as the hatch opened outward. A boy with long brown hair swung his head down through the opening. "Shit, Joey. They're in here. All of 'em!"

"Quiet, Will," Joey whispered from atop the car. "Let's get 'em out. We have to hurry!"

"Who are you guys?" Drew asked.

"Tell you later," Will said. "You guys are gonna have to boost people up here so we can help you."

The crowd of people in the car pressed toward Drew and Sydney.

A man held his twelve-year-old son above his head. "Take my son."

"You people are crazy," the fat woman in the overcoat said. "I'm not going up through that hole."

"Okay," Sydney said. "Who wants to try it?"

Hands went up and the crowd of people chattered to life.

Sydney raised both hands in the air. "Shh, people. We have to be quiet."

"Syd," Drew said. "Give me a boost. If I go up first, I can help the others from up top."

"Good idea." Sydney clasped her hands to form a stirrup.

Drew used the front wall of the boxcar and Sydney's shoulder for balance as he stepped into her hands. He reached up and grabbed Will's outstretched arm. Will pulled upward. Drew placed his other foot on the fat lady's shoulder, leaving a muddy boot print on her overcoat as he hoisted himself out the portal.

Drew zipped up his windbreaker to stop what he could of the

cold breeze that hit him as he stood atop the boxcar. He looked at Will. "Thanks, man. Who are your friends here?"

Will pointed at the dark-haired boy. "That's Joey," he said. "The blond guy is Adam. He's watching the back for us."

"Nice to meet you guys." He knelt back down to the opening in the roof. "Now let's get to work."

Joey glanced at the lights in front of the train, now about a half mile away. "We gotta hurry, Will."

The kids came out first, six in all. Then thirty-three others, a mixture of adult men and women. Joey guided them slowly to the back of the car, where Adam waited.

"Climb down this ladder," Adam said. "When you get to the bottom, jump off. It's not that far, and we're not going fast enough to hurt you. Just watch out for big rocks."

Sydney was the last of the people willing to make the move. When she reached the roof, she turned around and stuck her head back through the opening. "Okay, last chance, people. Anyone else coming?"

The remaining Bystanders in the boxcar stared at her in silence. Sydney stood up and walked in front of Drew to the ladder at the other end. Will closed the opening and followed Drew to the ladder.

Drew hit the ground and turned around to see Will, still on the ladder at the back of the boxcar. "Hey, Will!" Drew whispered as loud as he dared.

"Let him go," Joey said. He turned to the small group of escapees. "Okay, listen up, everybody. Look around. Grab a stick or a big rock—but not so big you can't handle it."

"What for?" an old man asked.

"Mutants. You have a long walk back to the Perimeter, and then further into Tremayne. I can just about guarantee you're gonna need a weapon."

"Oh, one more thing," Adam said. "Get away from these tracks, as far away as you can. We abandoned these a long time ago. Only the Changers are using them."

"He's right," Joey said. He pointed to the east. "That way is

Tremayne. Once you get over this little hill, you'll see the lights in the distance. Stay on track. Big guys stay in front, in the back and on the sides of the group to protect the ladies and kids."

"Aren't you the big shot?" the old man said.

Adam handed Drew a baseball bat-sized club. "You'd best be their leader. They're gonna need you."

"Thanks for your help, guys," Sydney said.

Joey and Adam turned and ran toward the train.

Drew watched them in the darkness. He saw Will help them aboard. He saw them give each other high fives, and he shook his head. Club in hand, he turned to the group. "Let's get going."

THOMAS DENNIS PRESSED NUMBER FOURTEEN on the elevator control panel. He and Levi descended to the Underground Production Lab.

"I've instructed Duncan and Macey to meet us below," Thomas said. "They will provide additional information regarding the progress of the projects."

Levi used one of the highly polished walls of the elevator's interior to check his look. He straightened his necktie and brushed the lapels on his bright blue suit. "I expect nothing but the best, Dennis."

Ivan Duncan greeted the two as they stepped out of the elevator into a shiny white corridor. The rhythmic drone of mass-production machinery accompanied the clicking of Levi's shoes on the highly polished floor. Double sliding doors opened with a smooth *swish* as they neared the end of the hallway.

The polished white floors of the huge high-tech lab matched the walls. Framing and ladder-work on the two-story-high ceiling secured various tubes and wiring. Monitors on two walls flashed busily with ever-changing statistics tracking the progress of automated work stations.

Marvellus Macey studied a series of graphs and blinking lights on a control panel. He turned to greet the trio as the doors swished closed behind them. He buttoned his white lab coat and wiped his palms.

"Right this way, Leader," Thomas said. "Marvellus, let's begin with the Chybrid conversions."

"Follow me to the holding area." Marvellus grabbed an electronic clipboard and stepped between two rows of fifty auto-mechanical arms, busily soldering circuit boards.

The trio followed Marvellus to the end of the room through a second set of sliding doors. The mechanical cadence of the machines in the first room faded as the doors closed. The lights in this room were off. A low hum emanated from the Chybrid Holding Area. Occasional clicking sounds accompanied flashing lights on individual information consoles. The consoles hung in three-tiered rows from pipes on the ceiling next to large, illuminated glass-topped pods, also secured to the ceiling. Each pod contained a Chybrid.

"This is Chybrid Holding Area Number One, Leader," Marvellus said. "There are one hundred Chybrids in this room."

"And how many Chybrid holding rooms do we have at this time?" Levi asked.

"Ten rooms, sir. Five of the rooms are currently full."

Levi turned to Thomas. "Well done, Dennis. I'd like to see the procedure. How are we transforming the Rogues?"

"Right this way, sir," Thomas said.

DREW'S FEET BURNED. CONSTANT POUNDING over the uneven surface of the terrain didn't help. He was thankful for the ankle support afforded by his boots. He stopped walking and turned to face the weary group behind him. "How's everybody doing?"

"Any idea how much longer?" It was the old man.

"That depends on our pace. Distance-wise, I'd say we're about a mile out."

"Can't we just get on that dirt road?" A woman asked.

Sydney was stationed near the back of the group. "No. We can't chance it."

"I can't take much more of this," the man with the twelve-year-old boy said. "And my son's dying here. He's more tired and beat than the rest of you."

"I'm fine, Dad," the boy said.

"That's enough out of you!"

"Okay," Drew said. "Take it easy. We don't have much longer. And Sydney's right, we're not walking on the road. It's too dangerous."

"Who says we have to listen to you, anyway?" the old man asked.

"I'm all for walking on the road," the woman said. "I don't see the danger. Those boys told us to watch out for mutants."

"Yeah," the old man said. "Mutants aren't going to travel on the road *only*. They're more likely to be out here in the sagebrush, where they can hide."

"That makes sense to me," the dad said. "Let's go, son. We're taking the road."

"I'm with you," the woman said.

"Let's go," the old man agreed.

"Dad, no."

"Come with me, son. I'm in charge now."

Drew and Sydney stood and watched the four trudge through the brush toward the dirt road, about one hundred yards away. The remaining people in the group looked at each other.

A middle-aged man spoke to Drew. "Look, I've been using my club for a cane for the last half mile. The road would sure be easier. And you can kind of see in the dark up there that it takes a more diagonal route to the lights. That's shorter."

"Lean on me," Sydney volunteered. "We'll do it together."

"Okay, everyone," Drew said. "I can't make you follow me. But I'll get you home. That's all I can say."

Sydney hurried over to the middle-aged man and grabbed his free hand. She threw his arm over her shoulder. "C'mon. Let's go."

Drew trudged onward, followed by the exhausted group. "Watch out for this tree branch," he called back. He kept his eyes on the lights, ignoring his burning soles.

Sydney's back ached from the additional weight of the middle-aged man. "How you doing?" she asked.

"I'll make it. I got family at home. I just keep my mind on them. It's all I can do."

"That's the spirit."

Drew paused and called back to Sydney. "Why don't you two come up here? I'll be able to gauge our pace better that way."

Sydney and the gimpy man caught up with Drew. "This works out better, babe," Sydney said. "I've been wanting to talk to you, anyway."

Drew kissed Sydney's forehead. "What's up, babe?"

"I don't know. I'm feeling a little out of touch. I mean, what's going on in the world, anyway?"

Drew looked toward the lights of Tremayne and resumed the trek. "You seem really upset."

"I am. I'm upset about those wretched mutants. I'm upset about the Changers. I mean, what the heck—kidnapping us and forcing us onto a train? I thought we had a treaty with them."

Drew waved his hand. "Wait a sec, babe. It's not our treaty. The Changers have a treaty with the Punks. We're different. There's no treaty with us."

Sydney stopped. "Why? What's so special about the Punks? Why can't *we* have a treaty with the Changers?"

"That's an easy one. We don't have any power. The Punks have whatever technology wasn't confiscated by the Changers. They have the weapons, the organization. The Bystander people have nothing to offer, and nothing to counter the Changers with. I mean, we run the manufacturing plants, the farming and all that. But that's mostly for us and the Punks, who provide our protection. Bystander people are selfish—everyone living for the next dollar, the next feel-good whatever. They live for themselves and their immediate families."

"We don't all feel that way, Drew. You and I don't."

"Of course not. But some people say it's because we're in a good position. As regular people, we're not poor, we're relatively decent-looking, not sickly, fat, physically or mentally challenged."

Sydney tripped on a rock. "Ow! You're kind of making my point."

"Which is?"

"Which is, if not all the regular people are self-centered or greedy, why are we just sitting around letting the Changers use us for food? Why aren't we working with the Punks?"

"To do what?" Drew asked. "To help protect us?"

Sydney stopped walking. "Can you take him for a while? My back is killing me."

"Sure, babe." Drew slung the gimpy man's arm around his neck and handed Sydney his flashlight. "Here, take this. Keep it pointed low in front of us."

"I don't know, Drew. I hate being in the dark, never really knowing what's going on. The Punks seem to know what's happening."

"C'mon, Syd. The Changers control the media. They control every electronic news site, every television and radio station. All the Bystanders see or hear is what the Changers allow."

"So why are the Punks so hip, so knowledgeable?"

"They're rebels, what can I say? They didn't just curl up and die. They're fighters. They developed their own sources, networks, broadcasts. You just have to know how to find them."

Sydney pointed the flashlight in front of her and resumed the trek. "I guess I knew the Punks had technology. I just didn't know to what extent."

"Yeah," Drew agreed. "A lot of high-tech people joined the Punks when the rebellion started. They were way behind the Changers, but they built on their technology through the years."

"I wish more Bystanders knew what's happening."

"True. So, what do you suggest we do?"

"Team up with the Punks."

"Never happen," Drew said. "They're too tight. Besides, who would we even talk to about that? Only ones we're close to are Curtis and Krystal."

Sydney smiled in the darkness. "That's a start."

Drew stopped abruptly and held up a hand. "Shh, everyone down," he hissed.

About fifty yards away, Drew spotted headlights, bouncing up and down on the road ahead. *We gotta cross that road*, he thought.

Drew lay down in the brush and motioned to the others to do the same. In the headlights of the vehicle on the road ahead, he saw four figures. They stopped walking when the vehicle pulled up in front of them. He saw a man exit the vehicle and walk around to the front. His head prickled. *Those are the people from our group.*

Drew noticed the stranger wore a long robe, or maybe it was a trench coat. He watched the old man greet the stranger while the man, the boy and the woman remained behind him. Drew gasped when the stranger took a step back and hoisted a rifle from under his garment. In the distance, he heard the woman scream as she fell to her knees. The old man held his hands up.

The group of people behind Drew whispered to each other. "Shh," he cautioned.

The man and his son broke from the road and ran toward the darkness, toward Drew. The stranger kept his gun trained on the old man with one hand. With the other hand, he whipped out a long strap and slung it at the two escapees. The strap caught the man's leg while his son kept running toward Drew and the group. The strap wrapped around the man's ankle and stopped his momentum. He fell forward and slammed his face into the dirt. The old man dropped to his knees and clasped his hands in front of himself, as if praying to the stranger would help.

Drew watched the stranger drag the other man back to the dirt road. He winced when he saw the stranger's boot connect with the man's head.

The running boy didn't see Drew and the other bodies on the ground when he reached the group. When he was within her grasp, Sydney jumped up and tackled him. She lay on top of him and quickly slapped her hand over his mouth.

The stranger on the road guided the other three by gunpoint to the rear of the vehicle and opened a door. The trio climbed into the back. Drew heard the door slam.

The stranger grabbed a spotlight from the front of the van and panned it toward Drew. The people hugged the ground. The stranger returned to the van and hoisted himself into the front seat. He heaved a guttural laugh that lasted until he slammed the driver's door shut.

CHAPTER 15

Spies

THE CLACKING OF THE FREIGHT train slowed as it approached the platform. When the air brakes hissed, the three boys hopped off the ladder on the last boxcar and hurried away from the tracks. They lay quietly in the grass until the train came to a complete stop at the platform.

"See?" Will whispered. "Just like I said, only Changers here. Not a Punk in sight."

"Yeah," Joey said. "They may be using abandoned tracks, but that platform is high-tech. Look at those doors. Titanium, maybe?"

"Or steel," Adam suggested. "That would be stronger."

"Stronger, but heavier," Will said. "Those doors move too easily. They're too lightweight. Could be they're made with some kind of silica nanofibers. Maybe even be an advanced form of graphene, who knows?" He adjusted his thermal imaging biocular. "I bet the platform is made of the same stuff. It shows the same heat signature, or lack of it."

"Stronger than steel?" Joey asked.

"Stronger and lighter," Will said. "If it's made of the right synthetic material, they could set up and break down these stations quicker and easier."

"We gotta get closer," Adam said.

Will held up a hand. "Hold up a sec."

"They're pissed," Joey observed.

"Yeah. They're hauling people out of the car we freed all those others from."

Adam panned his scope. "Looks like the head guy is yelling at those guys wearing SECURITY shirts."

"Yeah," Will agreed. "They're in deep shit for losing half a boxcar full of people."

"Uh-oh," Joey said. "They're going for the vehicles."

Will lowered his biocular and brushed his hair back. "And they're headed this way."

"Stay cool," Joey whispered. "They're gonna miss us."

The boys pressed their bodies into the ground while watching the four-wheel-drive vehicles.

"It's gonna be close," Adam said.

The trio placed gloved hands over their heads and faced away as one of the vehicles approached, lights blazing. The vehicle slowed for a series of tightly spaced shallow troughs.

A Changer riding shotgun panned a spotlight in the boys' direction. "Hold up," the Changer yelled to the driver. The vehicle slowed to a crawl while the rider scanned the spotlight over the boys' position. Several other vehicles slowed their pace to match.

"What is it?" the driver asked.

"Nothing, I guess," the rider said. "I must be seeing things. Let's go."

The three boys maintained their positions until the vehicles were a safe distance away. Will looked around and motioned to the others. "All right." He shook his head and brushed the grass from his hair. "Now let's move in."

"You need a beanie," Joey said.

Will ran his fingers through his hair. "You know, you guys look cool with beanies. It's not my style."

"I know," Joey said. "Just looking out for you."

"Yeah, I know you can't help it. Let's have a closer look."

The boys stayed clear of the tracks and out of the lights as they hurried through a small dry ditch. They moved to within thirty yards of the platform. "Down here," Will said.

Adam landed between Will and Joey and spun his biocular around from the back of his neck. "I'm recording."

"Good," Will said. "Just stay low."

THE OLD SOUTHERN PACIFIC LOCOMOTIVE and rickety boxcars appeared out of place against the backdrop of the polished, high-tech platform. The sliding doors of the first three cars lined up to adjacent holding areas on the lower portion of the platform. A sliding gate joined each holding area to the other. The front holding area had three exits to the top of the platform. Each exit led the passengers through a caged tunnel to a solid door at the top of the platform.

"Looks like they're sorting the passengers," Joey said.

"Exactly what I was thinking," Will said. "Question is, why? Adam, zoom in on the top of the platform, where that guy is assigning doors to the passengers."

"Got it."

"Can you pick up the audio?"

"I brought a shotgun mic," Adam said. "It's syncing with the video now."

"Give me an earphone," Will said. He inserted the earpiece and observed the activity on the platform through his biocular.

A Changer wearing a black bow tie at the top of the platform barked orders to the people crowded into the cages. "*Changers, move to door number one. Everyone who's not a Changer, stand by until the Changers have cleared the platform.*"

A voice from the crowd shouted to the Changer with the black bow tie. "*Hey, so Changers are safe, right?*"

The bow tie Changer laughed. "*Yeah, you're safe. Just move on up to the platform.*"

When door number one closed behind the last Changer, the bow tie Changer began sorting the remaining people. He motioned to the guards who were manning the platform. "*Number two, number two, number three, number three, number three...*" The guards opened the doors according to the number assigned by the bow tie Changer.

"I'm not following the sorting here," Adam said.

"Me either," Will said. "Give it a few minutes."

"I think I see a pattern," Joey said. "The little kids and most of the women are going into door number three."

"You're right," Will said. "Not as many people are going to door two. But the ones going in there are all guys, except for a couple of pretty buff women."

"Two older men went to door three," Adam said. "Along with the other women and the kids."

"Uh-oh," Joey said. "There's a Punk. Wonder where he's headed?"

"Door number two," Will said.

The Punk on the platform used both hands to flip off the bow tie Changer before entering door number two.

"Good call," Adam said.

"Pattern's obvious," Will said. "Weak versus strong. I've seen enough. Let's get out of here."

CHAPTER 16

Making A Chybrid

Thomas Dennis and Levi entered the Chybrid Transformation Viewing Room. The entry-activated lighting system that illuminated the floor at the baseboard around the room faded as the door gently closed behind them. The Chybrid Transformation was underway.

Thomas reached into a built-in refrigerator and grabbed two fresh bottles of mineral water. Handing one to Levi, he gazed intently at the two-way mirror that divided the Viewing Room from the Chybrid Transformation Room. "This one's given us a little more trouble than usual." Thomas twisted the lid off his bottle and took several deep swigs. He put the bottle to his forehead and moved it back and forth across his oily skin. "Tried to convince us she's not a Rogue."

"She looks pretty tame to me."

"True. But we've already administered the paralyzing solution." Thomas swished a mouthful of mineral water around to rinse his teeth before swallowing hard. "Look at the bruises on her arms and legs. Plus, the redness and swelling in the cheeks is from self-inflicted blows. This one's a head-butter."

"More like face-butter," Levi said. "Why's she so calm now?"

Two Changers dressed in blue scrubs stood on either side of

the gurney where the unfortunate Rogue lay. "Well, no doubt by now the sedative is beginning to take effect," Thomas said. "We're finding good results with a custom combination of fentanyl mixed with diazepam. Renders the subject's extremities practically useless. She can't hurt herself, and we pretty much have our way with her."

The technician to the Rogue's right fiddled with the controls on the vital signs monitoring device. The other Changer busied herself checking chart data on an electronic tablet. They appeared to be involved in casual conversation.

Fred Garrison slipped into the Viewing Room as a third Changer opened the door to the Chybrid Transformation Room. "Hey," Fred greeted Thomas and Levi.

"Good timing," Thomas said. "The doctor has arrived."

"Yeah," Fred replied. "He and I walked over together." He opened the refrigerator. "Anything good to drink in here?"

"Yep. Everything you like."

The light from the fridge caused a glint on the two-way mirror from the transformation room. The Rogue on the gurney noticed. Her eyes widened. "Help! I know somebody's behind that mirror. Help me, *please!*"

The technician on the left side of the gurney stroked the girl's hair, attempting to calm her patient.

"Are we ready?" The doctor motioned to the Changer on the left, who pressed a button on a remote control built into the tablet. "Burning Love" sounded on the room's speakers.

The patient screamed. "Elvis Presley? What's wrong with you, you—*people?*"

The doctor calmly removed an electronic device from a hanger on the wall behind the patient and nodded to the Changer on the left. The assistant Changer administered an anesthetic through the IV that was plugged into the girl's arm. The patient drifted into shallow unconsciousness.

"What's happening now?" Levi asked.

"Garrison," Thomas said. "You helped develop this."

Fred smiled. "You can tell him. It's your lab."

"Well, it's like this, sir," Thomas said. "That electronic device is used to erase memory. We don't want to harm the brain, but we want to make sure they don't remember anything except being a Changer."

"Makes sense," Levi said. "So how does it work?"

"It's highly advanced electroconvulsive therapy. That device puts out bursts of power, modulated to whatever the doctor deems correct for the patient. The power bursts change the electrical properties of the brain cells that build and contain the memory. That serves to unbind specific thoughts that the electrical properties of the brain cells have imprinted into the long-term memory of the brain."

"Does it hurt?"

"Nah. Look at her, she's basically asleep. That's what's so funny about her getting all bent out of shape." Thomas chuckled. "When the medical team is done with her, the brain will be primed for chip implantation. Once the chip is in the brain, the body will undergo an aggressive muscle-enhancement therapy."

"Superhuman Changers?" Levi asked.

"Correct. We experimented extensively with injections of a gene-manipulated virus on animals. We had a few minor setbacks when we crossed certain animals with others. And maybe a few issues with crossing certain animals with our human subjects, as you know."

Levi smiled. "Makes for nice Arena entertainment."

"Precisely, sir. But at this point, we believe we have it right."

"And the chip implantation?"

"That's the best part, sir. We program the chip, we control the beast."

"Yes," Levi said. "The Hybrid Changer."

CHAPTER 17

Duped

ONE HUNDRED AND TWENTY ARMORED vehicles stood sentry, two rows deep, around the Punks' headquarters at Checkpoint One. Ingress and egress were prohibited. Outside the Perimeter, two additional rows of thirty-six each sat silent, manned and heavily armed. Defensive positions atop the wall extended two hundred yards in each direction.

Wall-to-wall Punks lined the interior of the conference room inside the Depot. Dion sat at the head of the twenty-four-seat conference table.

In the Depot's office, Jimbo monitored the electronic map on the wall. "Final stats are transferred, Ryk," he said.

"Great," Ryker said. "Keep your monitor to the conference room on, both ways. This will be the most important meeting we've ever had."

"Got it, man."

Ryker strode across the office to a nondescript door behind the main control panel. He entered the conference room and took the seat to the right of Dion at the table. "Everything's finalized and uploaded."

"Good," Dion said. He looked around the table. "Everyone listen up. You all know about the massive loss of life at the

Lottery. We have no doubt this is a direct assault by the Changers. Their encroachment violated the Treaty. Because of this, we are in full-on defensive mode. Phase one started with the complete shutdown of Tremayne. Your commanders are stationed at every street, road and waterway, into and out of the City."

Stringer raised his hand. "Dion, how were they able to breach the Perimeter, let alone Tremayne?"

"Good question. Ryker, this one's yours."

"It was simple," Ryker said. "They're Changers. However many there were, they changed their appearance and assumed the personas of Bystanders and—"

"And Punks?" Slade interrupted.

"Yes, and Punks," Ryker said. "We had our guard down. We blame ourselves for this. We lost a lot of people."

"Guard up or down, how could we see that?" Stringer asked. "Of course they change and we don't notice. I blame the Changers, those bastards."

"We agree," Dion said. "We trusted them. Why wouldn't we after all this time?"

Slade pushed his chair back and stood. "We run a tight ship at the Perimeter."

Ryker looked across the table at Slade. "Yes, you do. But we have reason to believe the Changers have been coming and going for at least the last year, if not longer."

"What's your reasoning?" Slade asked.

"Because the Changers blended in. They didn't just come in on the night of the Lottery and get over five hundred people to trust them enough to get so close that they were able to absorb them."

Slade sat down. "How can people not see that happening?"

"In many cases," Ryker said, "we didn't see it either."

"We? Punks?" Slade asked.

"Yep. We believe there are Changers within our ranks, not just the Bystanders."

Curtis was standing against the wall to Dion's left. He raised his hand. "So, Ryk, how do we plan to counter that? I mean, if a Changer is passing himself off as a Punk, how would we know?"

Ryker motioned to Winter, sitting on Dion's left. "Winter, you're heading this up."

"Acid testing," she said.

"You gotta be kidding me," a Punk on the wall protested.

Dion stood. "Anyone has a problem with this, see me and Ryker after the meeting."

"Gonna fuck up our tats, man," another Punk said.

"We're doing what has to be done," Winter said. "We all have tats. If you're clean, consider it a badge of honor."

"How are you going to know who to acid-test?" Curtis asked.

"We acid-test everyone, no exceptions," Winter said. "We've already started in Tremayne. For Punks, we start tonight. Right here."

CHAPTER 18

Going Home

THE SUN PREPARED TO PEEK its brow above the eastern horizon as Drew and Sydney led the small group of escapees past the city limits sign. "What the heck? See that, Syd? There's a barricade up there."

"Yeah, I see it. Looks like Punks."

Two armored vehicles sat in the middle of the road, blocking both the inbound and outbound lanes, facing toward Drew and Sydney. The vehicle doors were fully opened, with a guard behind each door. Four guards stood behind the vehicles, watching the activity. Two Punks with semiautomatic rifles approached the group. Four additional armed Punks hurried around to the back of the group.

"Hi," Drew said. "What's happening?"

Krystal, obviously in charge, pointed her rifle at Drew. "Stop. What's your business here?"

Drew frowned. "We live here."

Krystal looked around Drew and Sydney at the others in the group. "All of you?"

"Yes," Sydney said. "All of us. You know us, Krys. What's going on?"

Krystal motioned to her partner. "Follow this man, please."

Drew and Krystal locked eyes. "Come on, Krys."

"I'm following orders, Drew. It's for everyone's protection."

Drew shrugged and stepped behind the other Punk. The group followed.

"Single-file, please," Krystal said.

The second-in-command Punk stopped at a steel cage, about four feet square and seven feet tall. There was a guard on each side of the cage door. A third guard was stationed inside a separate, enclosed side housing attached to one side of the cage.

"What's this all about, anyway?" Sydney asked.

"Acid testing, ma'am," the guard said. "Step into the cage, please."

Drew dropped the gimpy man from his shoulder and stepped between Sydney and the guard. "Hang on a sec. What's acid testing?"

Two guards moved swiftly from behind one of the armored vehicles and pointed their rifles at Drew. "Step back. Now."

The second-in-command forced Drew backward with the butt of his gun. Drew raised his hands and turned to look at Krystal. "What are you guys doing, Krys? What's acid testing?"

Krystal waved the two guards back to their posts. "Hold up, Bucky." She turned to Drew. "Look, Drew. Because of what happened at the Lottery—"

"You mean a whole ton of us getting kidnapped by Changers?"

Krystal glanced at Bucky. "I don't know anything about that. But haven't you heard? Last count, over five hundred people are missing from Tremayne. We believe Changers are responsible."

"Holy cow," Sydney said.

"Wow. No, we didn't know." He looked beyond the cage and the armored vehicles toward Tremayne. "So what's this operation about? What's acid testing."

"Okay. The Punks, I mean *we*, have found a way to distinguish a Changer from a non-Changer. It's only mildly uncomfortable, but it has to be done. We've locked down the Perimeter and every route into and out of Tremayne."

"How's it work?" Sydney asked.

Krystal turned to face the group of people waiting in line. "We put a minute drop of acid on your forearm. If your skin shows a specific reaction to the acid, we'll know you're a Changer. If not, we cross-reference your DNA and you're on your way."

"But you know us, Krys," Drew said.

Krystal walked over to Drew. "You're right, I know you." She kept one eye on the guards and lowered her voice. "Look, I've gotta prove myself here. I have to follow the no-exceptions order." She nodded to Sydney. "Might as well go first, Syd."

Sydney threw up her hands and stepped into the cage. She winced when the metallic latch on the cage door clicked into place.

"Place your hands in here, please," the guard said.

"It's okay, babe," Drew said.

Sydney slipped her hands through a custom-made slot. The steel bar squeaked as the guard rotated it over Sydney's wrists and locked it into place. A female Punk stepped up to the cage. She lifted a lid from a shiny black box sitting on a rigid table next to the cage. She removed the lid from a container of acid and withdrew a syringeful of the yellowish liquid. A gun barrel slid out through the side housing into the cage.

Bucky stepped forward as Drew lunged at the side housing. "Back." He shoved Drew to the ground and trained his gun on him.

"Easy, Drew," Krystal said.

The female Punk with the syringe placed the pointed instrument on Sydney's forearm. A tiny drop of acid oozed from the tip onto her skin. The Punk watched as Sydney clenched her fists and writhed in pain. As she dropped to her knees, her wrists secured in place, the female Punk calmly sprayed a mixture of water and baking soda onto Sydney's forearm.

"She's clean," the Punk said. "Now head over to that truck and wash it off with soap and lots of water."

A guard removed the cotter pin and swung the squeaky bar upward, releasing Sydney's wrists. He opened the gate.

Sydney rushed to Drew and helped him up. "Bastards," she said as she looked up at Krystal.

"Blame the Changers," Krystal said. "Who's next in line?"

Drew stood and looked into the tired but wide-eyed line of people. "Let's get the gimpy guy up here. He's probably worse off than the rest of us. Then the boy."

"Where is he?" Sydney asked.

"I don't know. I left him in line right there…in front of that… kid?"

"Heavens, I didn't know we had another teenager with us," Sydney said. She stepped over to the boy. She noticed his dirty, baggy clothes and her heart went out to him. "Hi. What's your name?"

The young man's huge eyes teared up as he looked at Sydney. His rosy cheeks were streaked with dirt from the overnight trek. "Sam," the boy said.

"Okay," Sydney said as she put her arm around his shoulders. "Where's your mom and dad?"

"On the train."

"Goodness." Sydney hugged him.

"Do I have to go in the cage?" Sam asked.

Sydney looked up at Krystal. "Of course you don't, honey."

"I'm sorry, guys," Krystal said. "It won't take long."

"Really, Krys?"

"I'm sorry, Syd. I know he's just a kid." Krystal motioned to Bucky. "Go easy, Buck."

Bucky guided the boy toward the cage.

The boy squirmed. "No. I don't want acid testing." He began to cry. "No, no, no, no, no."

"Come on, Krys," Drew pleaded.

Krystal watched as Bucky nudged the boy to the cage. Sam stopped struggling long enough to look at Krystal over Bucky's shoulder. He pointed at Krystal and frowned. "No acid test!"

Krystal blinked.

Bucky forced the boy into the cage.

Sydney rushed past Drew's guard to the cage. "Let me get in with him."

"I don't recommend it," Krystal said.

Sydney rushed into the cage and slammed the metal door behind her. She placed her hands on the Sam's shoulders. "I'll be right here with you, hon. Don't worry. Just think happy thoughts."

"Suit yourself," Bucky said. "Get his hands into the slot."

"Come on, buddy," Sydney said. But the boy wasn't cooperating. He slapped at the air, catching a wad of Sydney's hair between his fingers. Sydney managed to grab Sam around the waist and hold him in a bear hug. "Someone help me."

Bucky and the other guard reached into the cage, wrangled Sam's hands through the wrist slot and shackled his arms through the door. "Strong little shit," Bucky said as he motioned to the female Punk with the syringe.

The Punk stepped up to the cage and expertly administered the drop of acid to Sam's arm.

Sydney held Sam around the waist and watched the drop of acid turn a bluish-green. She saw the spot rise and harden into a scaly crust. She felt the boy twist and contort as Sam's waist ballooned. Sydney's interlocked fingers slipped away and she fell against the back of the cage as Sam's legs stretched to fill his pants.

A woman in line screamed.

"No shot from here," the Punk in the side-housing shouted.

Krystal rushed to the cage door. "Sydney, stay back."

The metal bar holding the Changer's wrists rattled.

"Keep his hands locked down," Bucky said.

"I got it, I got it," Krystal said as she pointed her 9mm at the Changer's head. "Get down, Syd."

Krystal squeezed the trigger. The Changer's head whipped back, then forward, and clinked against the cage door.

Sydney sat curled up with her hands covering her hair. Blood sprayed onto her arms when the bullet exited the back of his head. She heard the bones in the Changer's forearms, still bound in the wrist clamp, snap from the weight of his body when he went down. Liquid poured from the hole in his head and trickled down to the grate in the floor of the cage.

Bucky rushed to the cage and freed the Changer's wrists from the steel bar. Two additional guards stepped into the cage and removed the body. They carried it to an armored dump truck parked on the shoulder of the road.

Drew stepped past Bucky and met Sydney at the cage door. He smoothed her hair from her face. "Are you all right, babe?"

Sydney looked over his shoulder at Krystal. "I'm fine now. This is bullshit, Krys."

"Look, Syd. I'm a Punk, through and through. The Punks are in charge. We provide protection for all the Bystanders, including you. It's for your own good."

"Uh-huh," Sydney said. "And I got locked in a cage with a Change—"

"You were advised not to be in the cage with the boy."

"Fine," Drew said. "Just finish up so we can get these people home. But I gotta tell you, you haven't heard the last of this. I'm going to follow up with the police, the city council, the mayor, whoever I have to. Someone has to have approved this. You guys can't just be running around doing what you want like this."

"If you can think of a better system, tell whoever you want. I intend to carry out my orders." Krystal turned around to face the weary convoy of people. "Next."

DREW AND SYDNEY SAT ON the side of the road. The Punks' system of acid testing proceeded without further incident. When the last man stepped out of the cage, Drew helped Sydney to her feet and brushed off the seat of his pants. "Let's get these people into town. I'm sure they all know their way."

"Except the boy," Sydney said. "How old is he, twelve?"

"Yeah. I suppose we should give him a ride. Let's just get to my truck."

BY THE TIME DREW AND Sydney reached the downtown area, the group had thinned down to the two of them and the twelve-year-old boy. Drew pulled his keys from his pocket and turned to the youth. "You don't mind if we take you to your house, do you?"

"I guess not," the boy said. "I'm hoping my mom's home. She didn't get on the bus with us, and I never saw her on the train."

Sydney's eyes softened. She put her arm around the boy's shoulders. "I'm sure she's waiting for you," she said.

The trio rode in silence, except for an occasional "turn here" from the boy. When they pulled over in a relatively affluent neighborhood, he got out of the truck, leaving the door open. He turned to face Sydney on the passenger side of the vehicle. "Thanks for gettin' us all home."

"Aw, you're welcome, honey," Sydney said.

Drew waited until they saw the boy step into his house before pulling away from the curb. He looked across the seat at Sydney. "How tired are you?"

"Not so tired that I don't want to pay a visit to city hall," Sydney said.

"I was thinking the same thing." Drew smiled. "We look like shit, you know."

Sydney looked at the dried Changer blood on her arms. "I guess you're right. Let's get cleaned up and grab something to eat first. As tired as I am, I don't feel like sleeping. This whole ordeal—first the fiasco at the unveiling, then getting kidnapped by Changers, acid testing—"

"You actually touched a real Changer. That's weird, too. I don't know how they do it, but at least you weren't killed, or eaten, or whatever it is they do to people." Drew pulled into their garage and tapped the remote control to close the door behind his truck.

CHAPTER 19

Fool Me Twice

WELL, I GOT MY SECOND wind," Drew said as they headed back downtown.

"Me, too," Sydney said. "I guess there are two things we want to find out. First of all, I'd like to know why the police haven't figured anything out about what's going on."

"Changers moved into town and took people," Drew said. "As cold as it sounds, those are the facts."

"Okay, but why? That's my thing. Who holds the Punks accountable? The mayor? City hall? The police?"

Drew found a parking spot on the street in front of city hall. "Well, if it's city hall, we're not going to find out today."

Sydney looked out the window at the CLOSED sign on the set of double glass doors. "Nice. Now what?"

"I say screw the police," Drew said. "Let's go right to Mayor Kutch's house. He always says everyone's welcome."

"I'm down. Let's go."

It was a short ride to Kutch's house. He lived in one of the older homes, a few streets away from City Park. Pale green with white trim, the house was a large five-bedroom, two-story wood-frame structure on a double-sized lot. The porch stretched all the way across the front on both sides of the door, which was situated dead center, then wrapped around about half the length of the house on the right side. There was a detached garage to the back, with both front and alley access. Two dormer windows from the attic loft looked out over the front yard.

The front yard was small, but like the house, it was impeccably neat. A concrete walkway split the near-perfect lawn exactly in two and welcomed visitors straight to the front porch steps. There were rose bushes in a planter below the porch rails with begonias scattered in between. No fence enclosed the front of the house, just the sides and back.

Drew parked parallel to the curb, two houses down from Mayor Kutch's. "Well, his car's here," Drew said, motioning to a late-model Tesla in the driveway. The couple approached the house from the side, walking up the porch steps to the kitchen door. Drew knocked. A flash of lightning appeared in the distance over the mountains. There was no answer. The wind chimes hanging at the edge of the porch briefly swung horizontally, pushed by a gust of wind. Drew knocked again. Still no sign of life from inside the house.

"No one's home," Sydney said.

"Try another door, babe. I'll wait here in case he answers."

Sydney's steps echoed on the raised wood plank porch as she hurried around to the front. She pushed a button to the right of the door. Drew heard bells sound inside the house. Sydney used the knocker on the door and waited. She walked back to Drew on the side porch. "No answer."

"Wait here a sec," Drew said. "I'll be right back." He hopped down the steps and strode back toward the garage. Stopping at the fence, he grabbed the top of the wooden gate and stood on his tiptoes to survey the backyard. He reached over the gate and unlatched it from the back side. Looking over his shoulder, he motioned Sydney to follow him.

The two entered the backyard through the open gate and walked to the far side of the house. Drew held his arm out and stopped. "Did you hear that?"

"Yeah. Sounded like someone crying, only distant."

Drew crept up to a window and shielded his eyes with his hands. "It's hard to tell." He moved his head from side to side. "There's curtains here, but there's a little crack where I can kind of see something. I can't tell, but it looks like someone is sitting in a chair in this room."

"Let me see," Sydney said. She traded places with Drew. "Well...it splits a little further down here." She moved down the window, keeping her hands next to her face. "Oh no." Her voice began to quiver. "Oh no, Drew." She pulled away from the window and stumbled backward.

"What is it?" Drew asked as he stopped her fall. "Syd?" He bent down and looked through the bottom slit of the curtain. His eyes widened. "Holy shit, babe! That's the old man and that lady we saw forced into that van! They're tied to those chairs!"

"Yes." Sydney's voice was a raspy whisper. A wave of goose bumps washed over her. "There's that crying sound again."

Drew moved back from the window. "I think that sound is coming from down here. There's a basement." He and Sydney dropped to crawling positions and peered in through the basement window.

Sydney's heart leapt into her throat. She gasped. "Oh my God, it's that guy!"

Drew was wide-eyed. "What. The. Fuck."

TRAVELER TOWERED OVER THE MAN in the basement. He grabbed a wooden broomstick from the corner and tapped it on the concrete floor. "You'd best get on over there under the stairs."

The hair on the forty-five-year-old man's head was thinning on top and longish on the sides. He wore a holey green T-shirt, too small, with the faded image of a cartoon action hero on the front. He had on white brief underwear, no pants. "My knees are killing me, man. At least let me stand up."

A mutant, chained to the wall, watched intently from beneath the staircase. Its huge black eyes appeared to swivel as they reflected the light from the single lightbulb swaying from an electrical cord on the basement ceiling.

"C'mon!" *WHAP WHAP!* Traveler smacked the floor with his broomstick.

The mutant under the staircase growled.

The man shook on all fours as he squinted at the creature. "I…I…can't." His eyes watered and he began to dry-heave.

Traveler gripped the broomstick with both hands and whacked the man squarely on his lower back. "Move."

"Ow!" The man took two small crawling steps toward the mutant.

"There, that's more like it." Traveler poked the man with the pointed end of the wooden stick. "Now move on over there under the stairs."

The chains that secured the beast to the wall clinked against the floor as it pulled itself toward the man.

The man shielded his eyes from the lightbulb as he looked up at Traveler. "What's going on here, anyway? Where am I? Who are you?" He lifted his hands from the cold floor and held them out to Traveler.

Traveler backed away from the man. "Get over there under the stairs!" He poked the man with the broomstick again. The man grabbed the stick with one hand and pulled. Using both hands, Traveler yanked the stick from the man, then rapped him on the head with it. "Git, man!"

"Ouch! What the hell! What the hell…"

The mutant drew the chains taut as it moved out of the shadow of the staircase. Back on all fours, the man turned and saw it clearly for the first time. The man's face went white. His cheeks flushed pink while he retched again. "Wh…wh…" He tried to push himself away from the stairs.

Traveler's boot on the man's butt stopped his movement. He shoved the man toward the creature. Adjusting his grip, he aimed the stick at the man's upper leg and stabbed. "Hurts, don't it?" Traveler poked his broomstick again, raising a large red welt on the man's thigh. "Now, git, man!"

The man fell forward, scraping his cold, dirty hands against the floor. He lifted his head, now inches from the mutant. Its skin was smooth and white, as if from years of sunlight deprivation. It was bald, save for a few wisps of black hair on its head, now matted from sweat. Boils in various stages of coming and going— some healed, some popped open with mild infections—littered the pale body. The thin skin below the mutant's eyes hung wrinkled and heavy, exposing the red inside linings of its eye sockets. Its pointed teeth were green as if decayed, behind bluish, worm-like lips. The man stared at the beast's eyebrows. Pores where the hairs must have been were enlarged and filled with greasy globs of body oil. The mutant's fingers appeared withered, but strong. The fingernails were long where they weren't splintered or broken off. The pale skin hung on the creature's bones, its legs and feet like useless sticks protruding from beneath its grotesque abdomen. The legs moved randomly whenever its muscular arms pulled it across the gritty floor of the basement.

"Help!" The man's voice broke the brief silence.

Traveler moved forward and smashed the man square in the mouth with the broomstick. "Shut up, man!" A tooth flew out, struck Traveler's boot and bounced across the concrete floor toward the mutant.

"Helph…phleeze…" His words slurred from the blood in his mouth and the loss of teeth.

Traveler chuckled. "Well, you shoulda got closer when I told you, man. Git!" He poked the man's thigh again with the broomstick. Then he poked the man's thigh again. And again. And he laughed.

"Phsleeze heeelph phee—"

"Git, man!" Traveler poked the man's thigh in the same place. Blood drained from the new welt. "Git! Git! Git!" Traveler laughed.

The man rolled toward the stairs.

Traveler poked again. The wet, slurpy splat that accompanied each poke seemed to amuse Traveler as the victim struggled to stay away from the stairs.

"Git, man."

splat slurp

"Git."

splat slurp

"Git!"

splat slurp

"Git, git, git."

The man sprawled forward, his forehead, nose and chin scraping the cold concrete at base of the staircase. The mutant moved quickly, grabbing the man's neck behind his head.

Traveler stopped mid-poke and stepped back to watch. He removed his grimy Stetson and wiped his forehead on his coat sleeve. He dropped the broomstick, drew his duster upward, gathered it in front of him and tied the straps around his waist.

The man screamed as the mutant tore at the skin on his back. When the creature rolled him over, the man pushed his hands against the beast's slimy chest. The victim's screams turned to watery gasps as the mutant hunched over and tore a chunk of flesh from the man's throat.

DREW SCRAMBLED TO HIS FEET. "I'm getting in there." He sprinted through the gate and bounded up the porch stairs to the kitchen door.

Sydney was hyperventilating. She stared at the stomach-churning site in the basement, unable to move.

Drew pounded his fist on the kitchen door. "Hey! Hey! Open up!" The door rattled on its hinges as he pounded.

Sydney watched the man as he looked up toward the kitchen. He untied the sash from his waist, let the tails of his duster drop to the floor, removed his coat and hat and walked toward the short staircase leading to ground level.

Tears filled Sydney's eyes. Her pants were wet at the knees from the moist ground. She tried to push herself away from the window. Through blurred vision, she watched the man walk up the staircase and open the door to the house.

"Mayor Kutch?" she whispered. She felt her heart pound in her throat as she ran through the gate. "Drew! We have to go. Now!"

Drew was confused, but he knew the look on Sydney's face.

Without breaking stride, she grabbed Drew's hand and swept him off the porch, down the driveway, and into the street. She pulled Drew past the neighbor's house, jumped into his truck and slammed the door.

Drew hopped into the driver's seat, turned and grabbed her face with both hands. He searched her eyes. "What, babe? What is it?"

Sydney burst into tears.

CHAPTER 20

Door To Door

WINTER PULLED THE PARKING BRAKE on the Humvee and sat back in the seat. She grabbed her tablet from the center console and scrolled to the bottom of the screen. "Hallelujah, last house in the city. Looks like all the other teams have completed testing in every other sector. We're the last group at the final address. Three full days of testing, all we have to show for it is a city full of Bystanders with little round burn spots on their forearms."

"Agreed," Curtis said. "But at least we're done."

Winter clicked her seat belt off and grabbed her 9mm pistol. "Two residents here, according to the records. Let's get it done. Beer time after this, guys."

The older neighborhood consisted of mostly retired residents and vintage rental houses. Mature trees lining the street creaked in the wind.

"What the hell is that?" Krystal motioned to the house next door to the Humvee. A plastic baby doll hung from the eaves on a homemade noose, spinning in the breeze.

"Who knows?" Curtis said. "Some of the Bystanders are weird. This whole neighborhood is weird."

The three Punks crossed the street and approached the nondescript stucco house. They walked through the open gate on a four-foot-high chain-link fence protecting the front yard. Winter knocked on the door. No answer. She knocked again. "There's some rustling around in there. Let's try the back."

"There's an alley," Krystal said. "They should have a gate."

The alley was neatly lined with wooden and chain-link fences of various ages, some with gates big enough for cars. Other gates were walk-through only, but every yard with a rear fence had a gate in the alley. They found the chain-link gate to the house open. The trio strode through the gate and latched it behind them.

"Looks like the lawn's about two weeks overdue for a mowing," Curtis said. They stopped at the rear door on the small patio. Curtis knocked. No answer.

The sky flashed. Lightning.

"Door's locked." Krystal pressed her ear to the door. "I know someone's in there."

Winter pulled a five-inch fixed-blade knife from her boot. She leaned against the door for leverage and placed the tool against the doorjamb. The jamb popped and the door swung inward, slamming into a small plastic garbage can. Winter lost her balance and fell into the kitchen, catching herself between a chair and a slim wooden table. Her hand crashed down on a plate lying on the table. The plate flipped into the air and landed in one piece on the wooden floor. The Punks froze while the plate spun to a stop.

Curtis closed the door behind them.

"Piece o' cake." Winter looked around the tiny kitchen. "What the hell is that smell?"

Krystal suppressed her gag reflex. "Holy shit, breathe through your mouth."

"Yeah," Curtis said. "It's enough to make your eyes water."

The lights in the house were off. The neighbor's sodium vapor fixture cast an orange glow through the two kitchen windows. The trio peered through the doorway from the kitchen into the main living area of the house. Heavy drapes covered the front windows of the little residence, rendering the streetlights useless.

The floor creaked underfoot as the three searched the kitchen. Winter opened the refrigerator. "Well, the power's on. Whatever that smell is, it's not coming from the fridge."

The room flashed blue and white. The light from the refrigerator was extinguished when the neighborhood lost commercial power. Thunder followed. Then rain.

Krystal clicked her flashlight on and eyed the ceiling. "Storm's gonna be big."

"Nothing looks really out of place here," Curtis said. "Let's check out the rest of the house."

Winter led Curtis and Krystal into the darkened hallway. "That smell is stronger in here."

Thunder crashed again. The three moved along the creaking hallway floor toward the back of the house. The first step in, Winter's boot hit the slimy spot in the floor. Her feet went out from under her. She fell forward and kicked Curtis's shin behind her as she plunged down, clawing wildly into the darkness in front of her. Her flashlight flew out of her hand, hit the wall at the end of the hall, flipped off and bounced into a room on the right.

Winter landed on top of a heap of something soft but firm lying in the middle of the floor. "What the fuck?"

Curtis fell behind Winter. His head slapped something wet, hard and hairy lying on the floor in the pool of whatever Winter had slipped on.

Krystal stepped back and pointed her flashlight at the floor. "Oh, God." Her free hand flew to her mouth as she threw up, spraying vomit outward between her fingers. A mutilated body lay face-up under her two partners—only there was no face, just a round, concave bloody mess.

Curtis scrambled to his feet and grabbed the back of Winter's leather jacket between the shoulders. "Up we go."

The three stepped back into the kitchen. "What the hell did I slip on?" Winter asked.

"I think it was blood," Krystal said. She clenched her teeth together, suppressing a gag. "We gotta get out of here."

"No," Curtis said. "We have to find out what's going on here. Or what *went* on here."

"Who was that on the floor?" Winter asked. "Could either of you tell?"

"Couldn't tell. His face was gone," Curtis said.

Krystal shined her flashlight on Curtis. "You look like shit, man."

Curtis swiped a hand down his face, forehead to chin, and wiped it on his pants. "Blood, sweat, brain matter. Nice."

Winter glanced at the darkened doorway of the hall. "There's that sound again. Let's go."

"I'm not going back in there," Krystal said.

"Fine by me. Gimme your flashlight."

Winter and Curtis stepped over the body and moved toward the back of the house. She stopped at the doorway to the master bedroom and held her hand up. "It's coming from in here." The rustling turned to slapping, slurping and scraping. Winter set her flashlight on the floor and pulled out her 9mm pistol. "Shoot your light in there."

Standing behind Winter, Curtis held his flashlight waist-high and pointed it into the bedroom. He panned the beam left to right, stopping when the light shone on another body. A woman, partially dismembered. The slapping-slurping-scraping stopped when the creature straddling the body looked up. Its huge eyes reflected the flashlight.

Winter raised her pistol. "What…the…fuck?"

The white skin of the creature stood in stark contrast to the blanket of dark that cloaked the room. Its pointed teeth were caked with skin, fatty tissue and blood of the victim on the floor. The metallic fingernails of the creature stayed partially embedded in the victim's chest. Keeping its eyes on Winter and Curtis, the creature rose.

"That thing must be seven feet tall," Curtis whispered.

"I can't even tell if it's human."

"It's not," Curtis said.

"Then it's another fucking mutant…part human…"

The creature lunged. Winter fired three shots—forehead, mouth, neck. The hulking figure fell headfirst at her feet. It twitched. She put a bullet into the back of its head. A thick, opaque fluid spurted out through the hole onto Winter's boots.

The two Punks stood motionless as the liquid oozed down the side of Winter's boots and soaked into the grungy carpet. "You okay?" Curtis asked.

"Yeah. Test the DNA on these bodies and get some pictures of this mess. Dion's gonna want to see this."

CHAPTER 21

New Alliances

D REW CRUISED HIS LATE-MODEL PICKUP past the Tremayne city limit sign toward the Perimeter. "Even if the Punks don't let us team up with them, we're going to get to the bottom of this."

Sydney stared out the passenger window. Streaks of low clouds, leftover from the recent autumn storm, scratched the gray sky like scars. She thought about her childhood and the quaint neighborhood where she and Drew had grown up. She remembered how her mom had always fixed the neighborhood kids hot chocolate on days like today, and how Drew's dad had bought them all Popsicles from the ice cream truck in the summer. Drew's dad. He was a fixture, a constant, someone the kids counted on to fix bikes, wagons, dolls. He always had a warm smile and an open door for all the kids. Seemed so long ago. Now he was gone.

The overcast sky above the clouds gave Sydney an empty sense of loneliness. She pulled her sweater up around her neck and hugged her shoulders.

"Babe, you okay?" Drew asked.

His voice was soothing. Sydney turned to Drew. "Yeah, babe?"

"You were somewhere else."

"I'm sorry. I'm here with you, always."

Drew smiled and reached out his hand to Sydney. She clasped his hand between hers. "Can't live without you."

"You'll never have to."

Sydney smiled at him, but not inside. Inside she cried. She cried for Tremayne. She cried for Drew. Mostly, she cried for herself.

DREW SLOWED TO A STOP when he reached the main gate at the Punks' Establishment about a mile from the Perimeter. A black-hooded Punk stepped out of the guardhouse to meet Drew on the driver's side of the truck. The guard's AR-15 hung from a strap on his shoulder. The legs of his gray military fatigues were scrunched up above his boots, revealing a six-inch straight-blade knife at each ankle. He spoke through a red bandanna tied around his head inside the hood. "Greetings, sir. Your business here?"

"Hi," Drew said. "Yeah, you guys never used to have this guardhouse manned."

The guard adjusted the strap on his firearm. "What's your business here, sir?"

Two other guards, engaged in casual conversation, stopped talking and looked up when they heard the question a second time.

"Well, I'm Drew Bushong. This is Sydney. We're here to meet with your boss."

"My boss? And who would that be?"

Drew looked at Sydney. The guard peered into the cab of the truck. "Honestly, we're not sure," Sydney said. "We're friends of Curtis Dyer."

"One moment, sir." The guard spoke into a shoulder mic. "Jimbo, do you copy?"

The response from the two-way radio was prompt. "*Go ahead, Ace.*"

"Yeah, a Drew Bushong just pulled up here with some girl. Says he's here to 'meet with my boss.' Course, he doesn't know who my boss is."

"*Copy that. Did he say why?*"

"Negative. But he says he knows Curtis."

"*Stand by.*"

One of the other guards strolled nonchalantly to the rear of Drew's tuck and looked in the bed. He walked slowly around the passenger side toward the front of the vehicle, eying the truck. He stopped at Sydney's window. "Nice truck."

"Thanks," Sydney said.

"So is your husband a mechanic?"

"He's my boyfriend. And he's kind of a mechanic by trade."

The guard smiled under his bandanna. "Yeah? How's that?"

"He does computer programming and robotics. Contracts at home for a firm out of Los Angeles."

"Interesting. Did he do the mods on this truck? I mean, that engine sounds pretty powerful, obviously not stock. And this beauty's obviously modified for heavy off-road use."

"Yeah," Sydney said. "He did the work himself, with a little help from his friends."

"I'm impressed."

The two-way radio speaker crackled. "*Ace, do you copy?*"

"Go ahead."

"*Curtis cleared him. Tell him to wait. We'll send an escort.*"

"10-4." Ace motioned to a row of parking spots to Drew's right. "Okay, sir. Pull on over there and wait for the escort."

DREW FOLLOWED THE ARMORED VEHICLE slowly through the interior gate of Checkpoint One and took a parking spot at the end of a row of other vehicles. "Wow. I've never seen so many Punks in one place."

"I never knew it was like this," Sydney said. "It's like we just entered a different world."

Drew was wide-eyed. "So these are the Punks."

"We've been pretty sheltered in Tremayne, babe," Sydney said.

"And protected. Look at the armored vehicles," Drew said. Four armed Punks in military fatigues and hoodies stood guard at the door in front of a long, low building. Another eight guarded the entrance to a huge, round-roofed concrete and metal structure.

Drew scanned the compound and estimated fifty or so additional guards were on general patrol near the Perimeter Wall and roaming the grounds. "I never realized they were so organized."

"I think we've really taken the Punks for granted," Sydney said. "Everyone has, all the regular people."

Drew parked and turned off the ignition. He looked in his rearview mirror. An armored vehicle, the second of the two escorts, sat idling behind his truck.

Sydney noticed four Punks exit the Depot through the double doors at the front entrance. Two of the Punks were guards. One of the other two was tall, with thick, short-cropped bleached hair, dyed bright red on vertically pointed tips. He wore jeans, boots and a red long-sleeved thermal shirt under a black leather vest. The other one was Curtis.

"Here comes Curtis," Sydney said.

The two guards approached Drew's truck and stopped about six feet from the driver's door. The first guard turned to Curtis. "Sir?"

"I know them. They're clear," Curtis said. "You guys can take off."

"So these are friends of yours?" Dion asked.

"Yeah. Hey, guys. You can get out," Curtis said.

Sydney slipped out the passenger door and met the three guys on the driver's side of the truck. "Hi."

"Hi, Syd," Curtis said. "Drew, Sydney, this is Dion."

The gray sky released a mild drizzle. Sydney pulled up the hood on her wool sweater at the same time Drew zipped up his windbreaker. She shivered at the cold breeze that swept through the compound.

Dion rubbed his hands together. "Hey, let's go inside, where it's warm and dry." He led the group across the yard and around the side of the Depot. They walked down a long corridor and stopped at an unmarked door guarded by two Punks. The guards moved aside without comment. Dion opened the door and stepped back. "After you."

THE FOUR STEPPED INTO A large office that contained a desk, a leather sofa, two side chairs with a table between them, and a six-seat conference table. Behind a door on one wall was a guest restroom. Another interior door led down a short hallway to Dion's living quarters. Dion, Curtis and the two visitors seated themselves around the conference table.

"So," Curtis began. "What brings you guys here that we couldn't have talked to me about back in Tremayne?"

"Well, first, Curtis," Drew said. "I have to apologize, but we didn't come here to see you."

"Right," Sydney said. "We just used our relationship with you to get through the guards at the checkpoint."

"I'm really sorry," Drew said. "But we don't know your level or status here."

"Curtis is solid," Dion said. "We trust him. He's highly respected within the organization and holds a good rank."

Drew turned to Curtis. "Then maybe we could have talked to you in Tremayne. But we didn't know."

"Curtis also knows how to use discretion," Dion said. "He's loyal. Not likely you would have gotten much from him."

Sydney threw the hood back off her head. "Okay, so we dropped his name with the guard to get us get in here," she said.

"Fine." Dion shot a look at Curtis. "So you're in. What's your business?"

Drew looked from Curtis to Dion. "Are you the boss?"

"He's number one," Curtis said. "You're actually lucky to be meeting with him."

"Well, we thank you for that. So, the disappearances in Tremayne—we've heard, and we believe it, that the Changers are responsible." Drew waited a moment for an acknowledgment, or a confirmation.

Dion wasn't biting. "Go on."

"Okay," Drew said. "For the sake of this conversation, I'm going to assume we're right. The Changers are the only ones we know of that, one, are organized enough to pull off something like what happened at the Lottery, and two, have the incentive."

"Right," Sydney agreed. "They need to absorb human life to stay alive."

"Who doesn't know this?" Dion said. "We prevent them from just flat-out having their way with you people."

"But you didn't, not this time," Drew said. "You, I mean the Punks, are supposed to be protecting us, the regular people."

"Kind of a bold statement," Dion said. "We're human, too. We do what we can. And we lost people as well."

Drew shifted in his seat. "I know you are. And I don't mean to sound accusatory, or negative. Trust me, we appreciate what you do."

Curtis placed his hand on the table and looked at Dion. "They're not like that, really."

"Yes," Sydney said. "We've lost so many friends and loved ones. Especially the other night. The police, city hall, the mayor, no one is making any progress in either finding out what the problem is or putting a stop to it. It just seems to be getting worse."

"Which brings us to why we're here," Drew said. "We want to help."

"And how do you propose to help us?" Dion asked.

Drew looked at Sydney. "For starters, we can be your eyes in Tremayne. We have a lot of contacts, and both our families are very well connected to the community."

Dion sighed. "Did you know we killed a full-sized humanlike mutant in Tremayne the other day?"

Drew and Sydney looked at Curtis.

"No," Drew said.

"I was there," Curtis said. "So was Krystal."

"We didn't know," Sydney said.

"Actually, Winter killed it. Winter's one of Dion's inner circle." Curtis pushed back slightly in his chair. "Krystal and I were with Winter when she killed it."

Dion leaned forward. "Look, that shows you stuff goes on in Tremayne that you guys don't know about. We have members living in Tremayne. Why would we need you? You're just two additional people who aren't connected to either the Punks or the Changers. How can you help?"

"Okay, we don't see everything," Drew said. "But you could consider us another resource, another set of eyes. We go places the Punks don't go. We hang in different circles. We provide information to you."

"Okay, we're happy to receive any information you provide."

"Okay, but the deal is, we trade information with you," Sydney said. "We tell you what we find out, and you tell us what you know."

"There's no doubt in my mind we know more than you do," Dion said. "You'd have to have some pretty valuable information. What do you have?"

Sydney looked at Drew. "Well, nothing specific, yet."

Dion stood. "Well, it was nice meeting you two. I'm sure you're very nice people, and well intentioned."

"Drew's a computer and robotics specialist," Sydney blurted out.

"I heard. As soon as we knew his name." Dion pointed at Drew. "We ran the info through our system. We know his father disappeared, as yet unsolved. We know the name of the company he works for in Los Angeles, including his salary and Social Security number. If you can get information that deep and fast, maybe we can talk." He opened the door. A cold mist blew into the room from the exterior corridor.

"Wait," Sydney protested. "Drew, tell him."

Curtis pushed his chair back from the table and stood up. "I'm sorry, guys."

"Curtis, call an escort for your friends," Dion said.

"Drew?" Sydney pleaded.

"Mayor Kutch is a Changer," Drew said.

Dion stopped, his back to the room.

"Dion?" Curtis said.

Dion closed the door and turned to face Drew. He remained standing and folded his arms. "Okay, tell me about it."

CHAPTER 22

Tunnels

TWO PUNKS IN MILITARY FATIGUES stood guard at the walk-through gate at Checkpoint One. The mud caked on the soles of their boots made it feel like they were standing on two-by-fours. The constant moisture rolling off their rain-soaked parkas contributed to an already-sour demeanor. Dion and Ryker, each carrying an insulated bag, exited a side door of the Depot and approached the two guards.

"You guys look like you could use a break," Dion said.

"Just suffering for the cause," one of the Punks said. He lowered his weapon and swiped the bandanna from his face. "Nice to see you guys, though. It's been a long shift."

Ryker smiled. "Well, we brought sustenance." He and Dion handed the bags over to the two guards. "It's been pretty quiet tonight. Stay on post, but kick back a little and take a break."

The hot steak sandwiches on French rolls with deep-fried potato wedges and huge slices of cheesecake were the perfect relief for the weary Punks.

"Wash it down with this," Dion said. "Only one each." He handed each of the guards a twelve-ounce bottle of beer. "Just enough to take the edge off. There's a thermos of black coffee in that bag for later."

"You guys are awesome. Thanks, man."

"We appreciate the work you put in," Ryker said. "Big rewards later, you know that."

"Before you get started," Dion said, "open up. We're gonna pay a little visit to the crew outside."

As the two exited, light from the interior of the compound spilled across the wet ground outside the Perimeter and crawled up the rear of a BearCat parked just outside the door.

"Lock it behind us," Ryker said.

The heavy metal door slammed shut behind the pair. Light from the third-quarter moon highlighted the edges of the armored vehicles. The rain slowed to an irritating mist. Gusts of wind whipped the Punks' dusters up to their knees, causing the harassing moisture to soak their jeans down to their boots.

"Shitty weather," Dion said.

"Yeah," Ryker agreed. "We got hot meals on the way. Everyone's working overtime, including the kitchen."

A low-volume, high-pitched chirping turned their attention to the front row of vehicles. Light bars atop three vehicles clicked on, flooding the expansive murk. Dion and Ryker ducked behind the nearest BearCat. The door at the walk-through gate burst open. One of the interior guards stood in the doorway, silhouetted against the light from the inside. He motioned to Dion and Ryker. "Get inside, quick."

"Let's go, man," Dion said.

"Go ahead," Ryker said. "I'm gonna wait a few and see what's happening."

"All right. Don't hang out too long. You're not wearing anything."

Ryker smiled. "You know me and Kevlar don't get along. I won't be long." When he heard the door slam behind him, he crept between the rear bumpers of the vehicles and the Perimeter Wall to the furthest BearCat, last in line. He stopped moving when he heard the familiar *pop-pop-pop* of AR-15s. He slipped up to the passenger side of the vehicle and pounded his palm on the door. The Punk riding shotgun glanced at Ryker through the window and hopped between the seats into the rear of the vehicle. The door lock clicked and Ryker jumped inside.

"What's happening?" he asked the driver.

The driver never took his eyes off the wide swath of muddy scenery illuminated by the light bars. Peaks and edges of the soggy terrain reflected the white light from the four-wheel-drive machines. The incessant drizzle and gusts of wind made the surface appear to move like whitecaps on the ocean.

"Mutants. Shitloads of 'em. But none like we've ever seen before." He pointed to a small stand of rocks to the right, about fifty yards away. "There's another one."

"Holy shit, that's butt-ugly," Ryker said. The intermittent windshield wipers swiped across the glass in front of him, giving him as clear a view as the wet atmosphere allowed. "And damn fast."

The driver spoke into his two-way. "Six, Eighteen here. Do you copy? Another bogey at three o'clock."

The creature appeared to be naked, its pale, slimy skin the color of bleached pea soup. Ryker estimated its height at about seven feet. It ran upright, like a human—but its awkward movements were robotic and stilted. Through the thick windows of the Bear-Cat, Ryker heard a metallic *chink* with each step attained by the mechanical monstrosity.

"Six, do you copy?" the driver repeated into his mic.

Pop-pop. The momentum of the pale behemoth carried it forward as it tumbled downward onto the slick, gloppy ground and slid toward the vehicle. A whitish liquid spewed from its face where the bullets hit their target. Ryker could see the eyes, still open, but lifeless and black.

"I gotta check this thing out." He opened the door and hopped out, his boots sinking two inches into the swampy earth.

"I don't advise it," the driver said as Ryker closed the BearCat's door. "Two of you go with him," the driver barked. Two Punks piled out the back door, semiautomatic rifles in hand.

Ryker knelt, one knee in the mud, and grabbed the freak's shoulder, rolling it over, face-up. He grimaced at the sight of the creature's face. It looked familiar, yet distorted, abnormally muscular. The skin of the beast was smooth all over, except in places where there appeared to be scratches or minor gouges into the surface. There was no facial hair, no eyebrows or eyelashes. Its lips were slightly parted.

Ryker pulled a straight-edged knife from his boot, stuck it sideways in the mouth, and leveraged the jaw open. The teeth were not white, but some kind of shiny metal. He noticed the toenails and fingernails appeared to be the same metallic construction.

"Get back to the truck!" one of the Punks shouted.

Ryker looked up to see both Punks waving their arms at him, like they were swatting flies. Then he stood and turned and glanced toward the darkness beyond the light. Six mutants were running in his direction. Their anamorphic gait appeared exaggerated from the swirling mist in the air.

"Oh, shit." *Pop-pop. Pop-pop.* He slipped on his first frantic step toward the vehicle as he saw another Punk exit the rear of the BearCat, also waving his arms. "Get back inside the Perimeter!"

Ryker recovered his footing and ran twenty yards away from the row of vehicles to avoid the Punks with guns and the flying bullets. He pivoted as best he could through the mud and muck and ran to the Wall before heading toward the walk-through gate. The corner of his eye caught two more mutants running behind him from the darkness along the Wall's edge. The *pop-pop-pop* of the ARs sounded in the distance. Behind him, he heard the mechanical *chink-chink, chink-chink* of the two mutants behind him gaining ground. His feet were heavy from the mud caked on the soles of his boots and his jeans, now soaked through to the skin and wet to the top of his thighs. *Holy shit, somebody shoot these guys!* The *chink-chink, chink-chink* grew louder. Ryker's heart pounded as sweat mixed with the drizzle pouring down his face.

Ryker saw the door to the walk-through gate open as light from the inside broke the darkness. The *chink-chink* slammed his eardrums as he felt the tug on his duster. His upper torso stopped abruptly and his feet slid wildly forward as his head smacked the mud. The metallic chinking stopped and he listened to the slopping and slurping of the mutants moving above his head. He looked up the see two sets of nasty metallic teeth exposed behind parted lips. He felt a strong tugging on his ankles.

"They've got your coat!" a voice shouted. "Slip out of your coat!"

The tugging at his feet persisted as the creatures pulled his duster. Ryker felt himself slipping downward, dizziness scrambling his brain. His head throbbed as his coat was ripped from his outstretched arms and the sensation of falling feetfirst took over.

The fall was short. Ryker's boots landed on a concrete floor and his knees buckled. A bolt of lightning-like pain shot up his spine when his butt hit the floor. He heard the sound of a steel trapdoor slam above his head. Nausea washed over him, and he threw up on the concrete between his legs. As he passed into unconsciousness, he heard another voice in front of him.

"Good job, Will."

Dion radioed the Punk in charge on the front line outside the Perimeter. "Zane, do you copy?"

"*Go ahead.*"

"What's the status out there? We lost track of Ryk."

"*He was in Unit Eighteen. Stand by.*"

Dion looked at Pops. "I heard a lot of activity out there."

Pops sat on one of the workbenches inside the Hangar. "Heard it, too." He spat into a glass jar. "Definitely something going on."

Geezer stroked his goatee. "Guards opened the door a few minutes ago. The low-level alarm was goin' off."

Dion looked at a clock over the workbench. "I got back in about twenty minutes ago."

"*Dion, do you copy?*"

Dion whipped the microphone to his mouth. "Go ahead."

"*Eighteen says Ryker exited the Unit about fifteen minutes ago. They had a dozen or so mutants coming down on 'em. One of the troops from Eighteen said he saw the walk-through open up. That's the last they saw of him.*"

"He's not inside," Dion said. "Get a team out of Row Two and start a search."

"No can do, Dion. Mutants are coming at us nonstop right now. We're picking 'em off, but any let up and they'd be all over us. Anyone in the open has to be on the offensive. Can you send someone from the inside? We'll protect 'em."

Jimbo was monitoring from the office. "I'm on it."

"Good job, Jim," Dion said. "Copy that, Zane?"

"I got it. Back to business out here. We gotcha covered. Let us know what you find."

"Man, you were almost the main course at a mutant feast," a boy said.

Ryker's head throbbed. "Ow." He looked around at the small dimly lit room and the concrete landing he was sitting on. "Where am I?"

"You're still outside the Perimeter. But you're safe."

Ryker noticed the concrete shelf he was sitting on didn't fill the space inside the little room. A ladder directly in front of him ran down the wall, past the floor and into a tunnel.

"We might as well take him inside," a voice under the landing said.

"I agree. Looks like he's been through the wringer. A close shave with those mutants will do that."

Ryker looked at the concrete between his legs. "That's my puke, isn't it?"

"Yeah. You can clean it up later."

Ryker looked at the boy and raised an eyebrow. The boy smiled. "Just kidding, okay? Follow us."

"Wait," Ryker said. "Who are you guys, anyway?"

"Oh, I'm Will and that's Joey."

"Okay, and I'm Ryker. Nice to meet you. Who's the voice in the tunnel down there?"

"Uh, that's Mr. Tunnel. You get to meet him now."

Will and Joey scrambled down the ladder on the wall and landed on the tunnel floor, where a third boy was waiting. Ryker followed much more slowly. A sharp pain jabbed his lower spine with each rung. When he reached the tunnel floor, he saw the other boy.

"Hi, I'm Ryker. You must be Mr. Tunnel."

"Mr. Tunnel?" He shot a look at Will. "That figures," the boy said. "I'm Adam."

"Let's go, guys," Will said.

RYKER HADN'T BEEN IN THE tunnel in years. He was confident Pops and Geezer had adequately maintained it. The walls of the tunnel were smooth concrete like the floor and ceiling. Lighting fixtures protruded from the ceiling every twenty feet or so. He remembered if he walked closer to either wall, he could progress without ducking under the fixtures. The tunnel allowed enough room for four to walk abreast. The group walked in silence for about a hundred yards. Will turned left into an alcove and hurried up a short flight of concrete steps. He grabbed a handle next to an electronic box. A lock clicked open, and he pushed the trapdoor upward with the assistance of hydraulic arms on each side.

DION GLANCED OVER GEEZER'S SHOULDER when he heard the loud click from the vehicle inspection pit in Bay Three inside the Hangar. "What the heck?"

Geezer tapped his pipe into his hands and dumped the remnants into a trash can as he turned toward the inspection pit. He saw Will pop his head over the edge of the pit at floor level. "Hep, that's Will," he chortled. "Prolly got Joey and Adam with him."

Dion followed Geezer across the Hangar to the pit. "Are you kidding me?" He pointed at the three boys and looked at Pops, who was still sitting on the workbench.

Pops smiled. "There's a story behind that," he said.

"There better be," Ryker said as he ascended the short ladder inside the pit.

Dion turned, wide-eyed. His jaw dropped.

"Haven't seen that much emotion outta you in a year," Geezer said.

"All right," Dion said. "First things first." He pointed at Pops as he pressed an intercom button on the wall. "Then you and me are gonna talk."

"I figured," Pops said.

"Jim, do you copy?"

"*Go, Dion.*"

"Cancel the search detail on Ryk. We got him here in the Hangar."

"*Got it. Guess I'll get the info later.*"

"Yes, you will. And notify Zane, Ryk's safe inside." Dion turned around and leaned against a well preserved jet-black 1972 Buick Riviera. With his fists pushed up under his folded arms, his muscular physique looked more intimidating than usual. He eyed Pops. "Well?"

Geezer nervously cleaned his already-clean spectacles. "Aw, he's puffed up, Pops."

"I'd like to know what's going on, too," Ryker said.

"First," Pops said, "you two cool your jets. I was gonna tell you all about this."

"When?" Dion asked.

"Okay," Pops said. "You know how fucked up things have been around here lately. I've been real close to talking to you about this for a while. Just, the timing hasn't been right. You all have been busy."

"Wait," Ryker said. "I got a question before we get too deep into this."

Dion's eyes remained fixed on Pops. "So ask your question, Ryk, before I get started."

Pops was unfazed by Dion's demeanor. He swung his feet back and forth under the workbench he was sitting on and lit a fresh cigar. The three boys sat down cross-legged on the Hangar floor and leaned back on their hands, facing Dion. Geezer kept cleaning his specs.

Ryker stood in front of Will, Joey and Adam. "My question is, who are these guys?"

"Wait," Will said. "We told you—"

"Hey!" Dion cut him off. "Who are they, Pops? They're obviously not Punks. From the looks of those boots and what little leather they have on, they look like wannabees, posers."

Pops pointed at each boy, one at a time. "That's Will. That's Joey. That's Adam."

"C'mon, Pops," Dion said. "Who are they?"

Geezer snickered and stopped cleaning his glasses. He looked at the boys. "I call 'em the Three Amigos."

"All right," Pops said. "That's who they are. Now that all the introductions are done, I'm gonna give these guys a little history lesson."

"Fine. Go for it," Dion said.

Pops hopped off the workbench and strolled over to the inspection pit. "You know, boys," he said, "back when the Changers built that monstrosity out there, they conscripted the Bystanders. Forced 'em to build a wall to contain themselves. Ain't that the shit?"

"Sounds like it sucked," Will agreed.

"It did," Geezer said. "Before they built that sucker, the Changers came and went as they pleased. If they needed to absorb humans to extend their lives, they'd just send a party of armed vehicles into Tremayne. They'd load the Bystanders up in boxcars and freight 'em outta town."

"Right," Pops said. "So the Bystanders got fed up fast and they started to scatter. Who wants to live in the City when it's literally a feeding ground for Changers?"

"I get it," Will said. "So the Changers built the Wall to keep the people from scattering."

Geezer leaned one hand on the nearest workbench. "Exactly." His eyes narrowed and he pointed a bony finger at Will. "But the bitch is, they made a bargain with the Bystanders that if they helped build the Wall, the Changers wouldn't take 'em away. That's how they built it so fast. Almost every resident of Tremayne worked to build the Wall, for self-preservation."

"Uh-huh," Pops agreed. "This caused a shortage of people for the Changers to take, since most people were working on the Wall. That's where the Punks stepped in. They made a deal with the Changers to provide people to absorb. They figured out they could use prisoners, death row inmates and lifers, to placate the Changers."

"And the Tunnels?" Adam prodded.

Pops wouldn't be rushed. "That was about fifty years ago," he continued. Pops flicked his cigar ash into a large ash can by the pit. Geezer grabbed a clean rag from a cupboard over the workbench and walked over to the Riviera.

"Back then," Pops continued, "the Punks weren't as organized as we are today. They scrambled around doing their best to protect the Bystanders while this Wall was going up. Had their leaders, you know. Punks would steal weapons from the Changers just to protect the poor sap Bystanders. Slow, but sure, the Punks got more disciplined and orderly. Developed the ranking system we still use today. The Punks made friends with some of the Bystanders that worked at the manufacturing plants so they could start making their own weapons. They eventually forced this treaty we're under now, because the Punks became a force to be reckoned with."

Joey looked at Will. "Nice. The history of the Treaty." He looked at Pops. "Ironic that the barrier the Changers had intended to keep the people in is now used to keep the Changers out."

Geezer was doing his best to polish the Riviera. "Tell 'em 'bout the Tunnels now." He bumped Dion's thigh, stopped, and looked up at him over the rim of his glasses.

Dion stood up and uncrossed his arms. "Yes, tell them."

Pops scraped the cold ash from his cigar butt into the ash can. "The Punks came up with a great idea. They volunteered to help build the Wall. The strategy behind that was, if they got involved, they could customize the Wall right under the Changers' noses. So they built these escape hatches in the Wall, in various places around the Perimeter, and connected them with tunnels. They had a feeling this might come in handy someday. There was three guys got credit for the idea, and they led the tunnel-building effort. Risked a lot to do that. Took balls. Those three guys rose in rank within our organization. Ended up leading the Punks for many years."

Will tried in vain to brush the dried mud from his jeans. "Kind of a cool story."

"It is cool," Pops continued. "They further proved their worth through various guerrilla operations. Once huge sections of the Wall were finished, they ran stealth trips in and out of the Perimeter through these tunnels and gathered information on what the Changers were up to."

"Who were these guys?" Joey asked.

Pops stroked a handlebar on his mustache. "Well, the leader of these guys was my daddy."

Geezer stopped polishing the Buick. He stood up and pointed the rag at the Three Amigos. "Yep, early Punks was cool." He smiled. "And ballsy, like you guys."

CHAPTER 23

The War Room

TECHNICIANS WITH HIGH-SECURITY CLEARANCE OCCUPIED the 101 computer stations in the Changers War Room in the Underground. The stations in the round room occupied four levels of progressively larger semicircles from the center, out to the exterior walls. Curved monitors on the upper wall displayed a 360-degree view of Changers Global Sectors.

Levi met with his inner circle around a huge conference table in a large alcove adjacent to the War Room. Sound-deadening glass enclosed the alcove, ensuring top-security information stayed within the confines of the conference room.

"Our Chybrid numbers are looking good, Leader," Thomas said. "We're nearing capacity in the Chybrid holding rooms."

"Just what I like to hear." Levi glanced around the table. "As my top commander, Garrison will require all weapons in place. The timing of the strike is essential." He locked at Scotty. "Van Buren, I commend you on your new numbers. The Changers are multiplying beyond my expectations. I trust the operation inside the Perimeter will be perfectly coordinated with the outside forces."

"Thank you, sir," Scotty said. "We're ready now. We'll be ready when the order is given."

"Excellent," Levi said.

"Are we talking strategy, Leader?" Ivan Duncan asked. "I know the goal, and of course, I know my orders. But I feel like we should all know what part each faction is—"

"Leave your feelings out of it, Duncan," Levi said. "No one here cares about your feelings. If everyone follows orders, this operation will go smoothly."

Marvellus raised his hand.

"Macey," Levi said.

"Well, sir, I'm thinking Ivan may have a point. Example, if I know how Ivan will react under certain conditions, that knowledge will increase the effectiveness of my own actions."

Scotty frowned. "Makes no sense, Macey. The left hand doesn't need to know what the right hand is doing. The left hand merely requires knowledge of what it will do under a given set of circumstances."

"I tend to agree with Van Buren," Fred said. "You have orders to react according to a specific set of actions. You don't need knowledge of where the action originated. In other words, action happens, you react."

Silver agreed. "Pretty simple concept if you ask me." She looked across the table at Krystal. "What do you say, Peterson?"

"I can agree with the rule with respect to Macey and Duncan," Krystal said. "But it shouldn't be a hard and fast rule for all commanders."

"Explain yourself, Peterson," Levi said.

"I think I should know how each team member will react to specific actions—"

"Why?" Levi interrupted. "You have your orders."

Silver smirked and raised an eyebrow. Krystal looked directly at Silver. "Because I'm on the inside. I can direct activity within the enemy ranks—something not all of us can do."

"I can," Johnny said.

Krystal shook her head. "You're inside, Logan, but you fucking absorbed the only Punk that trusted you. You have no power on the inside."

"Climb down off your high horse, Peterson," Silver said. "You have an incomplete assignment on your record. You're walking on thin ice with each passing day."

Krystal looked across the table at Silver and mouthed, *fuck off.*

Levi scanned his inner circle. "Doc, we haven't heard from you. What's your opinion about this?"

The doctor removed his glasses and tossed them onto the table, watching them slide until they hit the multidirectional mic in the center. He leaned his chair back and put his hands behind his head, interlocking his fingers. He took a deep breath and slowly exhaled. "Well…" Felix closed his eyes.

Ivan stared at the black-rimmed spectacles touching the mic at the center of the table. Marvellus twirled his pen like a miniature baton, occasionally dropping it and swiping it back off the tabletop as if someone else was trying to steal it from him. Krystal glared at Johnny as she sipped water from the wineglass in front of her, while Scotty poured himself more from a pitcher. Silver busied herself jotting notes down in a tablet. Fred nudged Thomas, who was reading his tablet, and motioned to Felix.

Levi leaned forward, resting his elbows on the table. "Doctor!"

Felix's eyes fluttered opened. He scratched what hair he had left on the back of his head. "Leader?" he said.

Levi raised his eyebrows. "Your opinion?"

"Well," he said gazing at his glasses on the table, "I agree with Peterson."

"Makes sense to me," Thomas said.

"Yeah, now I agree, too," Marvellous said.

Levi raised his hand. "All right. What matters is that *I* agree. We will do whatever is necessary. Before and during the operation, all information is fed to Peterson. Let's not lose sight of the goal—total annihilation of the Punks."

CHAPTER 24

Acid Testing

JOHNNY LOGAN SMILED AS HE sailed his nondescript twenty-year-old Cadillac sedan down Main Street in Tremayne at five miles per hour over the speed limit. *Green lights all the way. I'm one lucky son of a bitch.* He turned right, toward the garment district. Five blocks in, he slowed his pace. Laundromats, boarded-up buildings, pawn shops, and liquor stores with bars on the windows lined both sides of the street. Scattered scraps of trash dotted the road and gutters on both sides. Remnants of rain on the asphalt held down any attempt by intermittent gusts of cold air to loose the debris from its resting places. Low clouds had earlier gloomed over what would have been a blue-sky day, so it mattered little that the sun had set. It was that time of day when you'd best turn on the headlights, but not so dark that they made any difference. Johnny rolled the driver's-side window down and zipped up his jacket. He turned the car's heater up to high as he leaned forward, scanning the sidewalks on both sides of the street. *Where are you, sucker? Come to Johnny.*

Two women in leggings and heels, bundled in fuzzy coats, strolled down the sidewalk on Johnny's side of the vehicle. He slowed to a crawl. "Hey, ladies. Either of you looking for a date?" The women ignored his advance and continued walking. "Hey ladies." The woman on the outside glanced over her shoulder and shot Johnny a dirty look. "Aw, c'mon, lady. I'm just looking for a good time. One of you? Either of you?"

The two stopped and turned to face the Cadillac. "What the hell do you think we are?" the one on the outside said. "Buzz off, creep."

"Whatever, man," Johnny said. He pressed the accelerator and steered the Cadillac into the next alley on the left. Taller brick buildings made the passageway seem narrower than it really was. It didn't help that dumpsters lined both sides of the alley. He continued at the pace of a tortoise and crossed the next street into a second alley. Half a block down, he spotted a man digging around in one of the dumpsters. *Okay, Johnny boy, maybe this is your lucky alley.*

Johnny pulled to the right, rolled up the driver's window and hugged the wall with the car, blocking the rear entrance to a tattoo establishment. Inside the Cadillac, the windows fogged up, hiding the momentary blur in the driver's seat. Johnny checked his new look in the rearview mirror before opening the door. He left the motor running and approached the man at the dumpster. "Hey, guy. What are you looking for?"

The man pushed himself backwards and jumped down off the huge garbage bin. He stood still, sizing up the good-looking professional man in the gray suit.

"Nothing," he said, swallowing hard. "Okay, just food. I'm kinda hungry."

Johnny smiled. "Oh, well, I can help. I mean, I help hungry people like yourself." The man at the dumpster smiled. "If you'd like to come with me," Johnny said, "I was about to have dinner myself. What say we both go sit down for a nice hot meal?"

The man dusted his grimy hands off and wiped them on his loose-fitting, equally grimy pants. "Okay, yeah, sure," he said, picking up a blanket roll and a small canvas backpack. He followed Johnny back to the Cadillac and squeezed in through the passenger door. "Where do you think we'll eat?" the man asked.

"Oh, I know a little place just outside town," Johnny smiled. "Good burgers, soup, hot coffee."

"I love a good burger," the man said.

Johnny drove past the city limits sign and increased his speed.

"You know," the man said, gazing across the seat at Johnny, "I don't usually dig around the dumpsters looking for food. I have a good job and my own place and all."

Johnny stared straight ahead. "Oh, I didn't think anything. I just like helping folks in need, you know?"

The man turned his attention to the road, gazing wide-eyed out the windshield as he clutched his backpack atop his blanket roll on his lap. "Well, I'm not *needy*, really. It's just, well, something *different* tonight…kinda…you know?"

Johnny remained silent. About a mile outside Tremayne, he slowed the vehicle before making a left turn onto a dirt road.

"Say, I don't know of any places to eat out this way," the man said.

Johnny loosened his necktie and smiled. "Oh, it's a well-kept secret. But the food's great." The further from the main road the two men traveled, the taller the wild weeds and various bushes on the roadside became. Eventually, the growth was taller than the car, forming a wall of foliage on both sides of the dirt road.

The man grabbed the dashboard in front of him as the vehicle bounced up and down, jostling the precious cargo in his lap. "You know, I'm not really feeling hungry like I was. I think I'd just like to go on back to town. Think maybe we could just turn around?"

Johnny ignored the question and yanked the steering wheel to the left, through the wall of weeds. The man's head banged against the passenger-side window. He grabbed his head with one hand, holding onto his belongings with the other.

"Ow!"

The Cadillac came to a rest in the wet weeds, perpendicular to the dirt road. Johnny pushed the driver's door open, forcing it past the heavy brush. He ran around to the passenger side and yanked the door open. The man, still clinging to his backpack, looked up at Johnny.

"Wh…what?"

"Out of the car, guy. This won't take long." He grabbed a fistful of the man's grubby shirt and wrenched him from the warm comfort of the velour seat.

The man lost his grip on the backpack and landed on his back in the wet weeds. He held his hands to his face and screamed. "What? What!"

Johnny straddled the man's waist and swiped his hands away. He wrapped his fingers around the man's throat and squeezed, leaning forward, pushing the man deeper into the brush. Mild malnutrition and a vagrant's lifestyle contributed to his inability to fight back. He was an easy target. The man's futile thrashing subsided quickly as his eyes glossed over in a cadaverous stare.

Johnny never took his eyes off the man as he stood upright. He paused for a moment to regain his Punk appearance, then stepped over to the still-open passenger-side door, tossed the backpack and blanket roll into the tall weeds, and took off his leather jacket. He threw the jacket on the seat and removed his fingerless leather gloves. Reaching down to his boot, Johnny removed a hunting knife from its sheath and used it to slice through the dead man's shirt. He split the material from the chest and cut down to the cuff on the shirtsleeve. He held the victim's hand up and away from the body. With surgical precision, he carved neatly around the man's elbow, then continued with a lateral incision up the inside of the forearm, all the way to the wrist. Like an experienced hunter, he stripped the skin from the dead man's arm and shook it out like a wet blanket.

Johnny rolled up his right-hand shirtsleeve and used fresh zip ties to secure the corpse's skin to his forearm before putting his leather gloves back on. He closed the passenger door of the Cadillac, jogged around the car and jumped into the driver's seat. The tires spun as he backed out of the brush and slung the front end of the car onto the muddy road.

"HEY, WHAT'S HAPPENING, MAN?" ACE said through his red bandanna.

Johnny smiled. "I'm here for the acid test."

"Awesome, dude. There's nothing to it. Had mine earlier today."

"I'm not worried," Johnny said. "Who all's there?"

"Well, we're almost done with this sector, so it's mostly higher-ups at the Depot right now. I guess they're doing reverse order of seniority—rank-wise, not age-wise."

"Sounds good to me, man," Johnny said.

Ace motioned to the Punk in the guard house. The boom gate swung upward, allowing Johnny's Cadillac to pass through the checkpoint. "Later, dude," Ace said. Johnny tipped his chin up in acknowledgment.

JIMBO SAT INSIDE THE OUTER office, staring at a monitor when Johnny stepped past the guards and entered the Depot. "Hey, man," Johnny said. "I'm here for the acid test."

Jimbo remained seated as he looked up from the display. "Oh, hey." He thumbed over his shoulder to the conference room door on the back wall. "Go on through that door. Everyone's in there."

Johnny didn't enter the conference room unnoticed. An involuntary pinprick jabbed Ryker's forearm when Johnny stepped in. Ryker's tendency to prioritize events in life put his fight with Johnny in his top ten. Since the Melody incident at Checkpoint One, the mere presence of Johnny caused that damned pinprick pain in his forearm.

Johnny surveyed the Punks present—Dion, Winter, Curtis, Lace, Stringer, Wade, Raymond, Griffin, Pops, Geezer, Krystal and others—before allowing the door to close behind him. He smiled his cheesy, full-toothed grin.

"Hey, guys," he said. He sauntered slowly toward one wall, strutting like a peacock, impressing no one.

Raymond stood by the door, scanning an electronic tablet. "Logan, right?" Raymond's question was rhetorical, but Johnny replied anyway.

"You know it."

"Good timing," Raymond said. "There's only two in front of you. Hang loose, I'll call you up."

Geezer stood at the front of the room on an elevated stage, the acid-testing paraphernalia on a table to his right. Pops assisted the procedure, standing on the opposite end of the table, with a spray bottle of water mixed with baking soda, and stacks of neatly folded cloths. A first-aid kit rested open behind the stacks of folded cloths. There was a tripod with a camera in the center of the table. A monitor on the wall, above and behind the table, displayed the image from the camera. Everyone in the room had a view of the monitor.

Lace stood in front of the table with her forearm outstretched. The image of Lace's forearm was visible on the monitor. Johnny watched as Geezer administered the drop of acid. He noticed a digital timer on the wall begin to count down—seven seconds, five seconds…two seconds… Lace's eyes watered. Her knuckles whitened as her clenched fist tightened…one second.

"Clean," Geezer proclaimed. "Good job, girl. Now go to the first-aid station and give it a good cleaning with soap and lots of water. Then Pops will do yer DNA swab."

A smattering of *attagirls* and *way to go*s mixed with loud single claps and fists in the air as Lace smiled and bowed. She stepped off the stage as another Punk handed her a bottle. He smiled. "Beer time."

"You're up, Griff," Raymond said from the back of the room.

Griffin stepped onto the stage. He took off his denim jacket and tossed it to the beer Punk at the end of the stage. "Keep one cold for me." Griffin looked at Geezer straight on. "See that snake?" he asked, referring to his tattoo. "Those are the most badass snake eyes you'll ever see. Miss his eyes."

Geezer cackled. "No sweat, man." Geezer dropped the acid precisely in the center of the O in *MOM* on Griffin's upper forearm.

"Ow, holy fucking shit!"

Geezer cackled again. "Hang in there."

For a full six seconds, Griffin stood like a statue, his eyes locked on Geezer, his fist clenched, his left hand squeezed around his right wrist. When the timer hit one second and Geezer declared him clean, Griffin raised his fists in victory, turned around to the room full of Punks and smiled. He knew he wasn't a Changer.

He just reveled in the accomplishment of standing still for seven seconds with a drop of acid on his arm. The spray and the beer welcomed him as he stepped off the stage and fist-bumped Lace on his way to the first-aid station.

"Logan," Raymond said.

Johnny smiled at Geezer when he strutted up onto the stage. "Yeah, uh, hey, nice that *we Punks* are real affirmative action types." He looked around the room, nodding like a rooster. "I mean, look at all the broads in charge. Yeah, I like that."

Geezer glared at Johnny above the rims of his spectacles. "Ain't affirmative action, numbnuts. We put 'em in charge 'cause they deserve it. Ain't because they're female."

Johnny stopped smiling and looked down at Geezer. "Whatever, old dude. Just do the test, man."

Krystal moved forward for a better view of the monitor. Ryker's hand moved to the back of his waistband. Winter unsnapped the strap over her holstered handgun and rested her thumb on the grip.

Johnny left his fingerless gloves on and unbuttoned the cuff of his long-sleeved shirt. He neatly rolled the cuff up his arm, exposing the dead man's skin. Geezer had a look on his face like he'd just eaten a turd. His brow furrowed. "What the fuck is that smell?" He leaned back as he stared at Johnny's forearm. At the side of the stage, Pops frowned. A low buzz of chatter developed among the roomful of Punks. Johnny faced the crowd, preening and nodding his head. He threw his arms out to his sides and puffed his chest, challenging the crowd.

"What? So what?" He turned back to Geezer. "Just hit me with the acid, man. I'm clean."

Geezer applied the drop of acid to Johnny's forearm and stepped back. The drop perched momentarily, then spread flat. Seven seconds later, Geezer called out. "Clear." Johnny turned to the crowd and held his hands out, nodding his pompous nod.

Krystal's jaw dropped. Ryker raised an eyebrow. Winter remained still, unfazed, her thumb still resting on her pistol grip.

"Just go git yer DNA swab and wash up," Geezer said.

Johnny laughed as he stepped off the stage and eyed Pops. "Swab nothing." He pulled out his butterfly knife and flipped it open. "Stick this in your test tube." He scraped several hairs and minute layers of skin off the cadaver membrane covering his arm.

Pops shook his head as he gathered Johnny's DNA sample into a glass tube.

"You're up next, Krys," Raymond announced.

KRYSTAL HAD BEEN STANDING NEAR the back of the room trying to look as small as possible. She hadn't anticipated being at Checkpoint One when the Punks began acid testing their own. Still, she knew her time would come.

A wave of nasty butterflies swept over her. Sweat burst from every pore on her body. The blood fled her face as she turned pale. Nausea washed over her as the shaking began.

"You okay, babe?" she heard Curtis say. His voice was distant, muted by the throbbing in her ears. The room was spinning when she heard Winter's voice.

"Get on up there, big girl."

Winter moved to the stage, beating Curtis by a step. "Let's help her up," he said, looking at Winter.

Krystal's knees felt like jelly as Curtis supported her under the arms. She looked into his eyes. Through her tears, she saw that his eyes were soft and sympathetic.

"I love you, babe," she said. Her voice quivered as she stepped up to the table in front of Geezer.

"Don't be scared, hon. It's not that bad," Geezer said.

Winter stood on the stage next to Krystal, in front of the table between Pops and Geezer. Curtis stood on the other side of Krystal and rolled up the shirtsleeve on her right arm. She became compliant, having accepted her fate. Her thoughts drifted to the time when she had been a crippled homeless girl. She remembered the severe auto accident. She saw her reflection in the mirror—burns over thirty percent of her body, most of her face badly scarred. She remembered her twelfth birthday party, when she had run away from the foster home. She saw Scotty Van

Buren's face. He had found her living on the street when she was seventeen, and she remembered how handsome he'd looked. She was the perfect Changer candidate—no place to go, no family, no contacts of any kind.

The room continued to spin—round, and round, and round—when Krystal felt the drop hit the skin on her forearm. She guessed someone must have stuffed cotton in her ears, because the roar from the room full of Punks sounded so distant. She heard the shot from Winter's 9mm and Curtis shouting "*No!*" as everything went black before she hit the floor.

SPARKS FLEW FROM THE OVERHEAD monitor. The wall behind it was visible through the hole in the spiderweb of broken glass. The 9mm bullet had gone clean through the monitor when Curtis had struck Winter's arm, deflecting her gun from its intended target.

Winter frowned, gun in hand, and stared at Curtis. "What the hell, Curtis?" She pointed at Krystal, crumpled on the floor, unconscious. "That's a fucking Changer. It's a fucking Changer that should be dead. What the hell is going on with you?"

"I love her!" Curtis blurted.

Dion stepped onto the stage and stood next to Winter. "Looks like you've got a problem, Curtis."

CHAPTER 25

Skull Caps

Thomas Dennis sat in front of Fred Garrison's desk in Fred's office. "Last night's dry run sent five hundred Chybrids to Checkpoint One outside the Perimeter," Fred said. "The Punks succeeded in destroying the Chybrids with a bullet to the head. Some units had three shots, some two."

"What about shots to the body?"

"Body shots inflict minimal damage. You already know the control center of the Chybrid is in the brain. Muscle enhancement and high-strength robotics throughout the torso provide adequate protection for the unit. The Achilles' heel is in the head."

"The Punks have been killing Changers with head shots for years," Thomas said. "Seems like a weak spot in the Chybrid design someone should have spotted before now."

"Agreed. However you look at it, the Punks terminated all five hundred Chybrids with head shots."

"I understand how Levi would see that as a problem," Thomas said. "Does he know?"

"Silver is addressing it with him now."

"So what are we going to do? Good news for us is bad news for Levi and the organization."

Fred leaned forward. "Actually, Felix has found a solution."

Thomas frowned. "What the heck? I thought he was on our side."

"He is. Look, Felix hasn't failed us in the past. He wants us to meet him in Holding Room Five." Fred glanced at the clock on his desk.

"When?"

"In about ten minutes. He's got Ivan and Marvellus doing busywork right now, so there shouldn't be any questions."

DOCTOR YAZ GREETED THE TWO with a pair of sterile surgical masks. "Put these on," Felix said. "Follow me." He led Fred and Thomas through a side door to a small laboratory. Felix secured the lock on the door and walked over to a work area at the back of the room. He put on a pair of disposable latex gloves and reached into an oven-sized box. He pulled out a large, hollow life-size synthetic head and handed it to Fred.

"Okay," Fred said. "I'm intrigued."

Felix inhaled deeply and closed his eyes. "This," he said.

Thomas looked at Fred, then back at the doctor. "Yes, Felix. This?"

Felix exhaled slowly. "This…is the solution I will present to Levi. The solution to the problem of Chybrids dying by a bullet to the head."

"What's the solution?" Fred asked.

"I have successfully woven together titanium and a combination of synthetic aromatic polyamide polymer." Felix paused and flitted his fingers in the air. "And…well…some other secret ingredients. We simply attach these hulls to the exterior of the Chybrid skull. With a specially enhanced contraction process, these caps will shrink to envelope the Chybrid skull and form a super-strength shell around the head."

"So the Chybrids will all have a similar look," Thomas said. "White heads, no hair, nearly flush facial features. And this hinged jaw facilitates destruction of the victim."

"And makes the Chybrid skull bulletproof?" Fred asked.

Felix closed his eyes and held up his index finger. "Ah…"

Fred and Thomas turned the skullcap over to view the underside. "Looks like a helluva helmet to me," Thomas said.

"For the average armor-piercing bullet," Felix said.

"Most of the Punks are using AR-15s and 9mm handguns," Fred said. "Are you saying these skullcaps are impervious to those weapons?"

"Yes, I am. It's what Levi has ordered, and what he expects. Far be it from us to disappoint our leader."

"Nice," Thomas said. He glanced at the door, then turned back to face Felix. "So what happens when the Chybrids are all equipped with these new caps?"

"As you have heard Levi say," Felix said, "the Changers' goal is total annihilation of the Punks. They are what stands in the way of setting up breeding districts with the Bystanders. With the Punks gone, the Changers can breed humans for food to their hearts' content. No Punks equals no impediment to the food supply."

Fred grew impatient with the Doctor's pontification. "We get all that. Have you figured out a fix for that? I mean, with the Chybrids running around with protection of this significance, how do we counter that?"

"Exactly what I'm thinking," Thomas said. "Have you built anything into these skullcaps to give the Punks a defense against them, or are they now sitting ducks?"

Felix shook his head. "Of course, boys. There is a substance." Felix motioned to Fred and Thomas. "Right this way."

The two followed Felix back out the door of the small laboratory and into Chybrid Holding Room Five. He led them between the center row of suspended bodies to another door at the back of the room. A sign on the door read BALLISTICS. Felix held the door open for Fred and Thomas.

A lab technician greeted the trio as they entered the room. "Good evening, Doctor Yaz."

"Ah." Felix nodded. "I'll not be needing you here at the present. You may complete the rest of your shift elsewhere."

"Yes, Doctor."

Felix smiled at Fred and Thomas. "Putty in my hands, you know. I do appreciate how compliant my technicians are."

Fred knew better than to let Felix ramble on. "Awesome, Felix. You were about to show us a substance that can be used to defeat the new skullcaps on the Chybrids."

"Of course I was." Felix nodded. "Let me demonstrate." He proceeded to a raised floor at the side of the large room. He stepped onto the raised floor and stood behind an AR-15 clamped to a firing bench. "This AR-15 is currently loaded with the most commonly used cartridge for this weapon. At the other end of this table, in that enclosure, is a new Chybrid skullcap. The bullet from this weapon will move through that barrel, enter the enclosure and strike the skullcap. Observe."

Felix fired the weapon. When the bullet hit the skullcap at the far end of the room, it ricocheted off the cap, bounced off the interior of the bulletproof enclosure and landed in a holding tank full of water below the cap. "Now, go look at the Chybrid skullcap."

Fred and Thomas examined the cap through the clear enclosure. "Okay, good," Fred said. "Not even a mark. Now what?"

Felix closed his eyes and smiled. "That, my friends, is the demonstration our leader will see. I guarantee he will be pleased." He opened his eyes.

Thomas walked back to Felix, who remained at the business end of the firing table. He gripped Felix's shoulders. "How do we counter this? With these new skullcaps in place, the Punks don't stand a chance against the Chybrids."

Felix reached into a pocket on his lab coat. "This cartridge contains a bullet made from the very ingredients I used to manufacture the Chybrid skullcap." He held the cartridge between his thumb and index finger. "However, there is one difference."

Fred was intrigued. "And the diff—"

"And the difference is," Felix interrupted, "although the ingredients are the same, I have altered the quantities of specific materials in the bullet. When you combine my alterations with the density and bulk of the bullet, the thin shell of the Chybrid skullcap is at risk. Watch this demonstration."

Felix loaded the modified cartridge into the AR-15. He stood to the rear of the pneumatic firing mechanism and pressed a remote control switch.

Fred heard a loud crack at the enclosure containing the skull-cap. He peered inside. The synthetic bullet had penetrated the cap. "I'm still seeing the synthetic bullet, Felix. It's lodged in the skullcap, but the cap is intact other than that."

Felix ejected the spent cartridge case. "Now stand back and watch this." He loaded a second synthetic cartridge into the AR-15 and pressed the switch.

The sound inside the chamber housing the Chybrid skullcap was like glass shattering. The skullcap was gone, its pieces in the water tank below. Fred smiled. "Now I'm impressed."

"I only have two questions, Felix," Thomas said. "First of all, how do you explain the use of all this material to make these synthetic bullets?"

"So simple, my friend. We collect the excess waste expelled through the manufacturing of the Chybrid skullcaps."

"Okay," Thomas said. "Then you throw in your mixture of custom ingredients to make the bullets stronger, right?"

"Precisely." Felix held up an index finger.

"And question two—how are you manufacturing the thousands of synthetic bullets the Punks will require to strike down the Chybrids? Looks like they'll need two head shots per Chybrid, once these new caps are in place."

Felix closed his eyes, smiled, and slowly shook his head back and forth.

Fred walked to Thomas and Felix at the other end of the firing table. He looked at Felix.

Thomas sighed. "Wait him out?"

"Remember"—Felix opened his eyes—"I am in control of the Changers' munitions manufacturing. I am transporting scrap material from the Chybrid skullcaps to our munitions plant. Upon arrival, the technicians take the scrap material and combine it with additional ingredients which we have produced in our laboratory. I have devoted ten percent of the facility to making the synthetic bullets."

"How will you get away with that?" Thomas asked. "Without questions from the technicians?"

Felix rubbed his palms together. "Putty in my hands."

"There's a third question," Fred said. "How do we get the synthetic skull-buster bullets into the hands of the Punks?"

CHAPTER 26

Tough Decisions

RYKER AND WINTER SAT ON opposite ends of a black leather couch in Dion's private quarters at Checkpoint One. Dion stepped from behind a wet bar and strode across the room. He handed a beer to his two friends on the couch before settling in his favorite chair.

"We've got an issue."

Ryker took a long triple-chug of beer from his bottle. "We got two, Dion—number one is Krystal, the other is Curtis."

"Agreed," Winter said.

Dion put his feet up on the heavy glass coffee table in front of him. "Look, I didn't ask you here because you're top commanders. You two are close friends. Shit, we grew up together in the same neighborhood. You two know me best and you don't feed me shit. I need input."

"You okay, man?" Ryker asked.

"Yeah, you really look beat," Winter said.

"I am. And you're right about having two problems, Ryk."

"Okay, let's break it down," Winter said. "The easiest solution to problem number one is one bullet."

"It's not that simp—"

"Sure it is," Winter said. "I had my nine right there, bam."

Ryker stood and walked over to Dion's pool table. "Yeah, you did—till Curtis."

"Exactly." Winter hoisted a leg onto the couch and turned sideways toward Ryker. She rested her beer-free arm on the sofa back. "And what if he hadn't done that?" She looked at Dion. "Problem one solved."

Dion took a swig of his beer and lit a cigarette. "But without problem one, problem two wouldn't exist."

Ryker sorted the balls on the table and guided them into the rack. "You're making your own point."

"Something else to consider," Winter said, "what Curtis did exposed a weakness in him."

"Yeah," Ryker said. "May sound corny, but it seems like he really loves that girl."

Winter stood, removed her vest and hung it over the back of the couch. "Loves, or *loved*? I wonder if he still does after all that."

"So now what?" Ryker asked.

Dion blew a smoke ring. "That's the question of the hour, my friend. I gotta think about things."

Ryker stabbed his cue stick into the carpet and rested his elbow on the tip. "You know we're here for you, man."

"He's right," Winter said. "Want to make a decision now?"

"Yeah," Dion said. "Get a hold of Jimbo, Curtis and Lace. Have them back here in half an hour. I'll run things past all of you then."

"You got it," Ryker said.

Winter grabbed a cue from the wall. "Play ya."

"Let's do it." He looked at Dion. "Three-way, bro?"

Dion put his empty bottle on the side table next to his chair and stood up. "Nah. You guys go ahead. I'm gonna take a walk first."

Geezer stood atop his and Pops' latest project in the Hangar. The engine on the tank-sized armored vehicle sat idling while Pops eyed technical data coming and going on a monitor at the main workbench. When Dion walked in through a side door,

Geezer whipped his specs off his face and yanked a rag from his back pocket. He squinted in Dion's direction as he slowly rubbed one of the lenses.

"Hep," he said. "I'm feelin' a consternation, Pops."

Pops stood and backed away from the monitor. He looked up at Geezer. "What's up, Geeze?"

Geezer paused his lens-buffing and motioned with his rag to Dion.

Pops turned and watched Dion as he walked toward the vehicle. His gait was slow, his head turned down.

"Hey," Pops said. "What's up, man?"

Dion stopped, thumbs hooked in his jeans pockets, and looked up at Pops. "I gotta talk to you."

"Welp," Geezer clucked, "I got some shit to do in the office." He hopped down off the top of the vehicle and climbed down a three-step ladder. "Be in the office if ya need me." He shuffled off to the far end of the Hangar.

Dion remained in place. Pops walked to the vehicle and leaned against the front end. He pulled his tobacco pouch from a pocket in his coveralls. "It's about the acid test, ain't it?"

"Yeah."

Pops stuffed a wad of tobacco between his cheek and gums. "Let's hear it."

"You know," Dion began. Then he stopped.

"Had feelings for that girl, didn't you?"

Dion looked his dad in the eye. "Not *feelings*, but yeah, I liked her."

"That's what I meant, son. I liked her, too. Me and Geeze had a real soft spot for her."

"Does it make me an asshole that I wish Curtis hadn't intervened?"

"You wish that now?" Pops asked.

"Yeah, I do."

"I gotta ask—why? Is it because you wouldn't have this dilemma on your hands and your life would be easier right now?"

"It's more than that." Dion scooped up a shop stool and set

it next to the armored vehicle. He straddled it, resting his arms across the back, facing Pops. "You know, I was that close to issuing Krystal quarters here at the compound. I trusted her."

Pops spat into a jar. "So you want her dead because your ego's hurt, because you made a bad judgment?"

"In my heart, I don't feel that. Right this very moment, I feel like it would have been best for the Punks."

"Then that's your answer. Didn't you approve acid testing for all of us?"

Dion lit a cigarette. "Yes."

"That alone proves you put the organization first. You knew you had to pull out the weeds, if there were any. But you're torn about what to do with her now."

"Right," Dion said. "Now it would be like an execution, not a split-second solution, like it should have been. I don't know what to do with her now."

"It's your decision, son. Maybe something you talk over with your top crew."

Dion pressed his hands hard onto his forehead and ran his fingers through his hair. "Yeah, I got a meeting with them at my place in a few minutes." He rested his forehead on the back of the stool and stared at the seat between his legs.

"So what else?" Pops asked.

"Curtis. I don't know what to do with him, either."

Pops stood and walked to the workbench. He placed the spit jar on top of a bench vise and threw his tobacco wad into a barrel. "What're you thinking?"

Dion looked up. "I trusted him—certainly more than I trusted Krystal."

Pops turned around to face Dion. "As much as you trust Ryk? Or Winter? Jimbo?"

"I'd put him up there, but not with those three."

Pops crossed his arms. "I gotcha. So where's he fall now?"

"I'd rank Lace where he used to be. He's dropped now, what can I say?"

Pops walked over and gripped his son's shoulder. "Nobody ever told you being in charge was easy." Their eyes met. "You're the leader of all the Punks, including me. I'd say you just made your decision."

JIMBO RECLINED SIDEWAYS ON DION'S leather sofa, watching Ryker and Winter finish their game of eight ball. "So I'm figuring Dion's gonna talk to us about Krystal's acid test."

"Eight ball in the corner," Ryker said. "You'd be figuring right." The cue ball cracked into the eight ball. Ryker stood up and smiled at Winter. "Nothing but net."

"Lucky shot," Winter said. She tossed her stick onto the table. "Winner cleans up."

"Hey," Ryker objected. "When did that rule start?"

"Just now." Winter strolled over to the wet bar and sat on one of the four barstools. "Tired of losing to you."

"Guys," Jimbo said. "Krystal's acid test?"

"What about it?" Winter asked. She leaned back, elbows on the bar.

Jimbo interlocked his fingers behind his head. "I know it's a big deal. You had her dead to rights, Win. I was wondering if Dion's gonna want you to finish it off."

Ryker hung the ball rack on the wall and walked over to the sofa. He swiped Jimbo's legs off the couch to make room to sit. "Guess that's what we're going to find out. Either he comes back in here to get some final input from us, or he's already decided."

"I sensed a little hesitation when we talked earlier," Winter said. "Something in his eyes. Did you notice, Ryk?"

"Hard to say. He's usually pretty poker-faced when it comes to big decisions."

Jimbo sat up and lit a cigarette. "I got a question. Why's he including Curtis and Lace in this meeting?"

Winter tossed a cork coaster at Jimbo. "Ha. That should be obvious, bonehead," Winter said.

"He really fucked up, Jim," Ryker said.

"C'mon, man," Jimbo said. "How could we know she was a fuckin' spy? Changers change. None of us saw that coming."

"That's a separate issue. Stopping the execution is what put Curtis in deep shit. Hell, he jumped in headfirst."

Winter tossed another coaster at Jimbo. "He stuck his heart out there in front of all of us."

Jimbo stood and frisbied the coaster back at Winter. She kept her elbows on the bar, leaning back slightly to avoid the flying disk. "Literally," she said. "He put his feelings before the Punks."

"Good point," Jimbo said. "So why's Lace coming?"

Ryker stood and walked to the bar. "Dion's got his reasons." He grabbed another bottle from the fridge. "Beer, anyone?"

"Me," Jimbo said, holding up a hand.

Ryker tossed a cold one across the room to Jimbo. The door opened as the bottle smacked Jimbo's palm. Lace walked into Dion's living room, followed by Curtis.

"Hey, guys," Lace said, looking around the room.

"Hey," Ryker said. "You guys want a beer while I'm back here?"

Lace smiled. "You know it."

"Sure," Curtis said. "Got any whiskey?"

Winter walked over to the couch and put her vest back on. "I think you'd best be sober for what's coming, my friend."

Curtis took a seat at the bar. "You're probably right."

Winter turned to face Curtis. "It'd be an order if you didn't think I'm right."

Dion opened the door and stepped into the room. He stood tall, looking refreshed and alert. He looked around the room, mentally taking attendance. "Ryk, Winter, Jim, over here." He strode across the room to his desk in the corner.

Lace hopped onto a barstool next to Curtis. Ryker, Winter and Jimbo stood behind Dion's desk while he leaned on the front, facing the bar. He folded his arms across his chest.

"Does anyone *not* know why we're here?" Dion looked between Curtis and Lace.

THE ROOM FELL SILENT. EVERY eye was on Curtis as he shifted on his barstool.

Curtis looked Dion in the eye. He saw the distance across the room, and felt the chasm that now existed between Dion and him. *I'm getting kicked out.* He felt the muscles in his neck tighten as he became conscious of the weight of his body on the barstool. *This is my* family. He fought shaking. *God, I'm sorry.* He held his eyes steady on Dion.

Dion broke the silence. "Curtis?"

Curtis swallowed. "Okay, I get that I fucked up, big-time." He knew his voice was unsteady. "I owe everyone an apology." He gulped down the lump in his throat. "I can't even say I don't know why, or what happened."

"Where's your head right now, Curtis?" Dion asked.

"Do you mean, do I still love Krystal?"

Winter crossed her arms. "Get serious, Dyer. This isn't about you. This is all bigger than you."

"It's bigger than any one of us," Ryker said, leaning against the wall.

Dion uncrossed his arms and gripped the edge of the desk. "I speak for all of us, Curtis—all Punks. We don't care about the love affair between you and Krystal. Number one, first and foremost with us, is the Punks. We have a history and a common bond that ties us together. This is a bond that's older than any of us here, including Pops and Geezer. Punks died for that bond. I thought you knew this."

"I do," Curtis said.

"We're like a fabric—a shield of chain mail. Each of us is a link in the shield. If that link has a weak spot, it has to be fixed."

"Or removed," Jimbo said.

CURTIS FELT HIS EYES MOISTEN as his stomach churned. *Please don't remove me. I'll prove myself.* "I understand. What does that mean for me?"

Winter glared at Curtis. "He still doesn't get that it's not about him."

"Curtis," Ryker said, "if you think about Dion's first question, you'll know how to answer. You shouldn't be the one asking questions." His eyes softened. "You should answer the big question that's right under your nose."

Jimbo grew impatient. "C'mon, pick a side, dude."

Dion raised an eyebrow. "Curtis?"

Curtis's eyes darted back and forth between the Punks in front of him. He saw the determination in Winter, the agitation in Jimbo. He took slim comfort in Ryker's demeanor. Dion remained stone-faced. *I can't read your eyes, Dion.* He knew whatever he said next would be the basis of his future, if there was a future, with the Punks. He took a deep breath and exhaled slowly. "I'm with you, with us, the Punks, first and forever."

"Do you understand the weight of your actions?" Ryker asked.

"Yes. I get that it's not because of my relationship with Krystal. I didn't know she was a Changer, none of us did. I know my feelings for her caused me to act the way I did. And because of that, I put the lives of all of us in jeopardy. I put myself, my feelings, and an outsider—worse yet, a Changer—before the best interests and safety of the organization. That includes everyone in this room, and all Punks. I'm apologizing to all of you, and to all the Punks. I'll do whatever I have to do to make up for that."

"Okay," Dion said. "I'm going to ask everyone here a question." He walked to the pool table, turned and faced the room. "Krystal Peterson: dead or alive?" He looked at Ryker. "Ryk?"

Ryker looked at Curtis. "Dead."

"Winter?"

"Dead."

"Dead," Jimbo said, before Dion had a chance to ask.

Dion looked at Lace. "Lace?"

Lace raised her brow. "Oh, I didn't know I was getting a vote. I'm a third-level commander."

Dion eyed Lace. "As of tonight, Lace, you're officially second level. I had Geezer poll all second-levels. Your vote counts here."

"In that case, I say dead. She's a Changer."

Dion turned to Curtis. "Curtis, as of now, you're no longer second level. Lace no longer reports to you. You are fourth level.

All your third-level lieutenants have already been informed that they now report to Lace. Lace will determine which of your former lieutenants you will report to."

Curtis felt every muscle in his body weaken. His head was spinning. "Yes, sir."

"However," Dion said, "given the circumstances, I'm giving you a vote tonight."

Curtis sat up straight. "Okay, guys. This is hard for me. I just want to reiterate, for me, it's Punks first, above all. But I just have to ask you to think about one thing. Krystal was a regular person before she became a Changer. I fell in love with that person." He looked at Dion. "I know you hate bullshitters, so I'm saying it straight. I vote to let her live. Kick her out, beat her up, whatever you want. But I vote to let her live."

"That figures," Jimbo said.

"I respect your honesty," Dion said. He turned to face the others. "So the vote isn't unanimous. That means she lives." He looked at Ryker. "Ryk, you three hit the conference room with the level two commanders and determine Krystal's final outcome. Bottom line is, she's out of the Punks Organization and she's outside the Perimeter. I don't want to see or hear of her in any city, anywhere."

Without a word, Ryker, Winter and Jimbo turned and exited the room.

"Lace," Dion said. "Move into Curtis's quarters." He turned to Curtis. "Curtis, move your stuff out. Lace will tell you where your bunk is and who you report to. Keep in mind, you will be reporting to someone who used to be subordinate to you. The burden is on you to make the relationship work."

"Yes, sir," Curtis said.

Dion turned to Lace. "If you have any special orders for Curtis, have at it. See you in the conference room in ten minutes."

CHAPTER 27

Branded

SEARING PAIN ON THE SIDE of Krystal's head awoke her from a black sleep. She moved her fingers tentatively through sticky, crusty hair to touch the wound. The skin on her scalp stung as she felt the raw, open slit. *What the shit*, she thought. The pain of stiff muscles hit her before she realized she was lying in a fetal position on a hard steel floor. Her neck felt like someone had replaced her muscles with a two-by-four. Stretching her legs proved useless. Her boots hit the steel bars on the other side of the cage, preventing full extension.

She remained on the cage floor and surveyed her surroundings. *Some kind of manufacturing place. No, wait, it's a repair shop.* She winced and grabbed the back of her neck as she looked around. *Oh, shit*, she thought as she spotted the boat-tail Buick Riviera. *I'm in the Hangar.* She pushed herself up on all fours before grabbing one of the vertical bars and pulling herself upright. *Damn. How long have I been here?*

Krystal leaned against the cage and gazed at the door leading to the conference room—the room where she'd failed the acid test. *The acid test.* She checked her forearm. The bluish-green lump resembled a huge wart. *Ow, shit.* Picking at it was futile. It was stuck. Tiny tentacles spread out from the growth in every direction. *Looks like I'll be wearing long sleeves in Tremayne from now on.*

"Guess she's come to now."

A sharp pain shot from her neck to the top of her head as Krystal whipped her head around. The room spun to catch up with her eyes. She squeezed them shut to shake off the nausea.

"Geezer."

"Yep. Wish I could ask how you're feeling, but I gotta say, I don't much care anymore."

"Geeze," Krystal said. "You know me."

Pops was standing next to Geezer by the main workbench. "Thought we did, kid. Surprised the shit out of everyone, seeing you fail that acid test."

"You're lucky you're alive," Geezer said. "Winter popped off a shot that shoulda kilt ya."

Krystal touched her blood-encrusted hair again. "Then how—"

Pops picked up a mason jar off the workbench and spat into it. "Curtis saved you."

Krystal slid down the bars and sat, knees up. She held her head in her hands and stared at the drain hole in the center of the steel floor. The clatter of raised voices in the conference room were gibberish to her ears. She listened to the rain tapping relentlessly on the metal roof of the Hangar.

"So what's going to happen to me?" she asked, not looking up.

Pops put the mason jar back on the workbench and spat his wad into a trash barrel. "That's what they're in there deciding right now."

"Why are you guys out here, then?"

Geezer pulled himself up backwards and sat on the workbench. "We didn't want to be part of the deciders."

"You know we always had a soft spot for you, girl," Pops said. "Now we know you're a Changer. It's messed up they're in there making a decision about your life. We didn't want to be a part."

"Yeah," Geezer said. "They needed someone to keep an eye on you, so me and Pops volunteered."

Krystal looked up at Pops. "So they're playing God."

Pops slammed a wrench into the toolbox and turned to face

Krystal. "Helluva thing for you to say, Krys. You're a Changer. How many lives have you taken just to stay alive?"

"I—"

"Then what do you expect?" Pops picked up a shop rag and began wiping down some hand tools. "To live?"

"I don't know. I guess not." Krystal hung her head.

The door connecting the conference room to the Hangar burst open. Krystal scrambled to her feet. She turned to face the door, each hand gripping a bar on the cage. She watched Dion, Ryker, Winter, Jimbo and Lace walk toward the cage. Behind them, the door opened again. Her eyes widened. *Curtis!*

The five Punks stopped in front of the cage and eyed Krystal. Dion motioned to Geezer and handed him a slip of paper.

Geezer read the paper, shook his head, then stuffed the paper, unfolded, into the back pocket of his coveralls.

Krystal kept her eyes on Curtis as he moved toward the group. Curtis avoided her gaze, positioning himself at the end of the line, next to Lace, but a step behind. He didn't want to see the disheveled clothes, the bloody hair, the look in her eyes. Mostly, he didn't want to see the mark. He knew he couldn't stand to have his heart shattered twice tonight.

"I'm going to make this quick, Krystal," Dion said. "This was not a unanimous decision. All votes were in favor of your termination, except one."

Krystal looked at each member of the Punk delegation standing in front of her. All eyes were on her, except Curtis's.

"As a result of the vote," Dion continued, "we are sparing your life. However, the decision to let you live comes with specific consequences." He motioned to Lace.

Krystal watched as Curtis and Lace walked across the Hangar to retrieve a large rolling table from behind a wall of cabinets. Krystal noticed the heavy adjustable struts supporting the stainless-steel table, and the eight-inch-diameter solid rubber wheels. She eyed the flexible steel straps atop the smooth surface. *That thing would hold Frankenstein*, she thought. *What the hell does it have to do with me?*

She looked at Dion. "So you're strapping me to that?"

"You're damaged goods, Peterson," Dion said. "Your choice is to get strapped to the table, or meet Winter's bullet. I guarantee she won't miss this time."

Pops unlocked the cage door behind Krystal and stepped back. Krystal turned around to face him. *They're letting me live*, she thought. *This isn't the time to wimp out.* She stepped out of the cage and walked over to the table. She hopped up and lay down, spread-eagle. Curtis and Lace fixed the straps to her ankles, thighs, waist, upper chest, biceps and wrists. *What the shit?*

Lace moved around to the end of the table and gripped Krystal's head with both hands. Krystal strained as Curtis used the remaining strap to secure her head to the table. *Dammit. He won't even look me in the eye. I could have completed my assignment and absorbed you.* She wished in vain that he could read her mind, hear her thoughts at this very moment. *But I didn't trade your life for mine because I love you, Curtis. If you'd just look into my eyes, you'd know.* She heard the familiar sound of Geezer's portable tool cart wheeling across the floor. The cart stopped by Krystal's head. She saw Geezer take a syringe from the cart and she strained against the strap.

"What are you doing?" Krystal managed to move her head slightly back and forth.

"Winter," Dion said, "give her some incentive to hold still." Krystal stopped moving when she felt Winter's 9mm against her temple. She stared at the Hangar's ceiling as tears pooled in her eyes. *Fuck me.*

She felt Geezer's gloved hands adjusting her head. "Now, hold still, or bad shit's gonna happen, girl."

Krystal tried to focus her peripheral vision on the syringe as it moved toward her. She felt a cold line on her face that began between her eyebrows and traced its way above her right eyebrow, around the outside of her right eye, and ended mid-nose near her right nostril. Then, the burning began. Krystal trembled as she felt the barrel of Winter's gun press harder into her temple. *Seven seconds, right? It's been seven seconds! What the hell?* Krystal heard her skin sizzle as Geezer backed away from the steel table. She felt relief from the pressure of the gun barrel as Winter retreated. She closed her eyes, resigning herself to the pain—accepting it, overpowering it.

After what she determined was fifteen seconds, at minimum, the sensation of drowning began when Lace poured a two-gallon bucket of cold water on her face. The streaming gush flowed through her nose and down her throat. The overflow drenched her leather jacket, T-shirt and bra.

Then, Krystal changed—old man, middle-aged fat woman, the cutest little girl you've ever seen. The steel straps scraped her extremities as her body pulsed and undulated through multiple changes. Krystal's eyes shot wide open at the last change—a seventeen-year-old girl with thin, greasy hair and burn scars. *Please don't look at me now, Curtis. Of all times, not now.* His words flashed through her mind. *"You're the most beautiful thing my eyes have ever seen."*

Curtis and Lace quickly released the straps that bound Krystal to the Frankenstein table. She felt Jimbo and Winter squeeze her shoulders and drag her to the floor. She fought to gain her footing as the Punks hurried her to the main exit of the Hangar.

The icy rain stung Krystal's face when Winter and Jimbo handed her off to two Punks in military fatigues. She felt moisture seeping into her boots as the Punks rushed her to the walkthrough gate at the Perimeter Wall. A guard at the Wall opened one of the doors, and another guard shoved Krystal outside. She slid through the mud and stopped, now on all fours. The light from inside the Perimeter was extinguished when she heard the door slam shut.

Krystal stared down at the mud, her thin hair passing the rain off her head as soon as it hit. She lifted a muddy hand to her face and felt the new wartlike growth. She traced the growth with her index finger. *It's a C,* she thought. *They* branded *me with a C.*

CHAPTER 28

Chybrid Project

LEVI AND SILVER RODE THE high-security elevator to Level One of the Underground. Two armed Changer guards greeted them at attention in the corridor. The couple strode past the guards toward the Underground Terminal. Levi's wingtip shoes clicked on the polished floor of the wide pedestrian thoroughfare, in near-perfect sync with Silver's high heels.

"I'm looking forward to the demonstration tonight," Silver said. Without breaking stride, she reached up and brushed a speck of lint from the shoulder of Levi's blue uniform coat. "You look splendid, by the way."

"Of course," Levi said. "As do you. Inasmuch as we represent perfection, I expect nothing less from our subordinates."

"I issued the order this morning to the top military brass. I have no doubt you'll be impressed."

"And the troops?" Levi asked.

"Four thousand will be on display for inspection tonight. And the first phase of our Chybrid project is complete and in the Terminal as well."

Levi smiled. "Chybrids."

Silver flashed her hand across a palm reader as two guards at the Terminal entrance stepped aside. Two heavy doors protecting the Terminal split slowly in the center. An infrared security beam scanned the couple as they stepped across the threshold. Levi involuntarily pushed his chest out at the sound of eight thousand heels clicking together.

"I trust you're impressed," Silver observed.

"Yes, but not how you think. I am impressed that the troops are at the ready. I am impressed at the sharpness and formality of this display. I am also pleased with the strength I know is housed in this Terminal. Above all, I am impressed with myself, and the power I command in this army of Changers."

Tight, immaculate rows of Changer infantry soldiers, grouped by company, brigade and battalion, stood at attention before Levi in the expansive, brightly lit terminal. Their pure white formfitting uniforms were polished and pressed.

Levi smiled broadly as he stepped behind a raised lectern, front and center, facing the troops. He picked up a small microphone from the lectern and hooked it around one ear.

"As you were." His voice was clear and crisp, echoing off the pristine walls, ceiling and floor. "I am proud of what I see before me. You were chosen to be here tonight because of your dedication to the organization, and your willingness to make the ultimate sacrifice for our cause. Your demonstrated abilities, both on and off the battlefield, will ensure that Changers worldwide will not only survive, but will prevail. You are the elite, the Number One military division. You are winners. And winners win."

Silver initiated the applause. The response from the troops was immediate and deafening—cheers, shouts and hurrahs filled the Terminal. Levi held the lectern like a steering wheel, as he surveyed the throng. He allowed the thunderous ovation to continue for two minutes before raising his hand. The cheering ceased as suddenly as it had begun.

"Some time ago," Levi continued, "when the humans rose up against the Changers, leadership was unprepared. A treaty was established. The Treaty tied the hands of the Changers and caused us to become reliant upon a renegade organization, the Punks, to provide the sustenance we require to extend our lives.

The best the former leaders obtained from the Treaty was a wall. To their credit, they intended the Wall to act as containment for the humans. But today, that Wall works against us, keeping us out, preventing us access to the nourishment we need to survive.

"You are under new leadership now. Your new team of leaders has the insight and vision to see that the Two-Hundred-Year Treaty spells eventual death for the Changers. Your leaders recognize the slow but steady depletion of natural resources—human resources, as determined exclusively by the Punks.

"The humans do not consider the lives of their fellow men expendable, as we do. As Changers, we know we have evolved beyond the finite lifespan afforded to humans. Our evolution provides us the opportunity to live forever. That we have this ability puts us a notch above the regular humans. In other words, their lives are of less value than ours. As such, your leadership has determined we will no longer live under the confines of a treaty that allows lesser humans to dictate the terms of our existence.

"Which brings us to tonight," Levi continued. "You are on the cusp of a new era, beginning here with you. Our new weapon, Project IX, will facilitate the annihilation of those who stand in our way.

"Throughout the past several decades, the Changers have assembled a world-class team of scientists, biologists, chemists, engineers and technicians. Our team is unmatched in quality, research, knowledge and innovation. Tonight, you are privileged to witness an amazing demonstration of our newest, most deadly weapon—the Chybrid." He looked down at Silver. "Where is Dennis?"

Silver glanced at her tablet. "He and Garrison are here—back of the Terminal, behind the troops."

Levi faced the Changers Division. "Thomas Dennis, our chief engineer, is here tonight. He will provide a demonstration of Project IX." He raised his chin, looking to the back of the Terminal. "Dennis?"

From behind the troops, Thomas raised his hand and strode between the center row of infantry toward the lectern.

"Ladies and gentlemen," Levi announced, "Thomas Dennis."

Thomas quickly mounted the three steps to the lectern. He hooked a microphone over his ear. "Good evening, troops. I'd like to thank you all for being here. The show of force is impressive." Thomas held the lectern in the same manner as Levi had moments before. His grip was tight, unlike the relaxed posture of the Changers' leader. "I'd like to introduce to you our two top scientists. These two have been instrumental in the development of the Chybrid project from its inception. I would be remiss in not giving them the credit they are due. These are the gentlemen who will conduct the demonstration of the power of the Chybrids. Without further delay, ladies and gentlemen, I present to you Ivan Duncan and Marvellus Macey."

Thomas swept his arm to his right as he backed away from the lectern. Ivan and Marvellus bounded up the steps to the center of the stage, in front of the lectern. They waved at the troops, then turned to gather microphones for the presentation.

Thomas hastily made his way between the center of the troops and rejoined Fred at the back of the Terminal.

"Greetings," Ivan said from the rostrum. "Ladies and gentlemen, please direct your attention to the west wall of the Terminal. For your convenience, the monitors on the walls will provide a view of all activity pertaining to the demonstration." He glanced at a technician stationed to the side of the stage and nodded. "Lights, please."

The house lights in the Terminal were extinguished and a blue glow illuminated the perimeter of the room at the floor and ceiling. An array of spotlights lit a huge floor-level alcove at the west end of the Terminal. Filling the alcove was a large enclosure.

"Ladies and gentlemen," Ivan announced, "what you are looking at is a specially constructed rectangular cage comprised entirely of bulletproof glass. We call this enclosure the Quadrangle. The Quadrangle is divided in the center by an additional panel of the same glass. The six individuals on the north side of the Quadrangle are humans and Changers. Let me clarify this by stating that three of the six subjects are regular humans from Tremayne. The other three are Rogue Changers. Although the Rogues have determined they no longer wish to be Changers, they *are* Changers, nevertheless."

"For the purpose of this demonstration," Marvellus broke in, "we have attired all six subjects in the same clothing so that there is not a distinction between the Rogue Changers and the Bystanders. This is to show the ability the Chybrid has to distinguish between Bystanders and Changers."

"We have programmed the Chybrids," Ivan said, "to recognize a Changer from a greater distance than that which we, as regular Changers, are currently capable."

"For example," Marvellus said, "as Changers, we are able to recognize each other from a distance of one meter or less. The Chybrid has been programmed to recognize a Changer from a distance of ten meters. Testing of this ability has been documented as ninety-nine point nine percent accurate across one hundred percent of the units. The point one percent anomaly was not a failure in the unit itself to make the Changer-Bystander distinction. Rather, the distance-to-recognition value varied slightly."

"The Quadrangle is soundproof," Ivan said. "However, microphones inside the enclosure will allow us to hear the activity."

The six test subjects inside the Quadrangle mingled about— some attempting to find a weakness in the enclosure, others pounding on the glass walls.

Marvellus stood beside the Quadrangle. "This side of the enclosure contains six Chybrids. Momentarily, we will raise the panel dividing the two sides of the Quadrangle, giving the Chybrids access to the test subjects on the other side. Just prior to this, the storage unit you see on the wall in the Changer-Bystander side will open, releasing six fully loaded, safety-off AR-15 rifles."

Ivan turned to face the alcove. "Without further delay, I will now release the weapons." He pressed a button on his tablet and watched the storage door inside the Quadrangle open. The six subjects inside scrambled for the rifles. It quickly became clear that only two of the victims knew how to use the weapons. "And now, I will raise the center panel, releasing the Chybrids."

As one of the victims quickly briefed two of the others about how to point and pull the trigger on the AR-15s, the other knowledgeable victim fired his rifle at the rising panel of glass. The two remaining subjects backed into a corner of the Quadrangle and braced themselves for what was to come.

The bullets from the AR-15s smacked into the glass panel, creating tiny spiderweb patterns at each point of impact. When the panel cleared the ceiling, the Chybrids rushed in, their shiny black eyes scanning the victims. The two experienced gunmen connected quickly with four of the Chybrids, their bullets bouncing off the Chybrid foreheads and ricocheting around the Quadrangle. The other two with rifles—a man and a woman, both Bystanders—achieved haphazard body shots but were quickly overwhelmed by four of the robotic humanoids. The weight of the Chybrids forced the victims to the floor of the enclosure.

The woman's knees snapped as they bent backward, preventing flight. She held her hand up in a defensive posture. "Shoot these things!" she screamed as the creature grabbed her arm, stretching the skin and separating the limb from its socket at the shoulder. The Chybrid stepped on the artery that extended from her shoulder, still connected somewhere inside her severed arm. One creature's hand came down on the woman's head, shattering her skull like an eggshell. Brain matter squeezed out of the cracks, deforming the skin between skull and scalp.

The man was more fortunate. One upward slice from a Chybrid slit the man's abdomen from crotch to neck, spilling blood and intestines at his feet as shock took over.

Sounds from the AR-15s inside the glass prison echoed throughout the Terminal over ceiling speakers. The Chybrids continued their onslaught, unfazed by the continuing hail of bullets.

The third Bystander, a man in the corner, was attacked mercilessly by the other two Chybrids. His shrieks were hideously loud, but short-lived. Razor-sharp metal claws and teeth sliced through his skin like hot knives through butter. The Rogue Changers recoiled at the streams of blood from the severed arteries. The high-tech humanlike automatons' frantic activity ceased as their victims' hearts stopped beating.

The entire altercation lasted less than sixty seconds.

The Chybrids stood and once again scanned the remaining humans. The three Rogue Changers stood stunned as they realized they were not targets of the Chybrids.

The house lights in the Terminal came up as a sliding door moved across the alcove, hiding the bloody Quadrangle from view. The monitors around the room clicked off and Levi jaunted up to the lectern.

"Bravo," he said.

CHAPTER 29

Rumors of War

THE THREE AMIGOS ROUNDED A corner on skateboards in the concrete Tunnel under the Perimeter Wall. Their routine patrols had turned up nothing new for the past week. Even mutant sightings were down to nothing. The west quadrant of the Perimeter seemed like a good place to cruise, since they hadn't been there in a couple of weeks.

"Who brought food?" Will asked.

"Got it," Joey said.

Will and Adam skated side-by-side, with Joey bringing up the rear. "Well, get on up here," Will said.

Adam wore his gear bag like a backpack over his shoulders. Joey accelerated and grabbed one of the straps. "Trade me places." Adam braced himself as Joey pulled himself forward, riding up even with Will.

"Here you go," Joey said, flipping a Twinkie at Will.

Will watched the Twinkie sail through the air. He held his hand up but deliberately let the creme-filled sponge cake bounce off the wall and hit the floor.

From behind, Adam made a quick, unsuccessful attempt to avoid the cellophane-covered snack. He hit it dead center with his front wheels. Joey looked behind just in time to hear the package pop and see a glob of the white filling splat against the Tunnel wall.

"What the heck?" Joey said.

Adam lost control of his board. He sailed off the front, kicking the skateboard backwards as he dove hands-first to the concrete floor.

Will looked back in time to see Adam's antics and jumped off his skateboard, doing a quick run before falling on the floor laughing. "That was awesome!" he said.

Adam sat up smiling and shook his head. "What a perfect shot."

Joey looked at Will. "Why didn't you catch it?"

Will tried hard to suppress his laughter. "I thought you had Slim Jims. I thought it was some kind of oversized grub flying through the air at me."

Joey couldn't help smiling. "Did you see that splat on the wall? It was like a cannonball."

Adam retrieved his skateboard and the flat Twinkie. "Been pretty quiet lately," he remarked. "What do you make of that?"

Will flipped his board on end and stood up. "Changers are up to something," he said. "What they fail to realize is that for geniuses like us, keeping their heads down makes them stand out, you know what I mean?"

"I know what you mean," Joey agreed.

Adam chuckled. "Maybe they're tired of playing whack-a-mole."

"Give me one of those Twinkies," Will said.

The boys resumed their trek toward the west quadrant. Will stopped at Tunnel Exit number 17 and dropped his gear bag on the concrete floor. "Let's have a look-see up top."

Outside, at ground level, all the Tunnel exit lids were camouflaged in some way. Some had deliberately random-looking but organized arrays of tin cans and miscellaneous debris. Others had strategically overgrown weeds, mixed with abandoned sticks and stones of various sizes. The debris held fast to the lids to maintain the facade of neglect after they were opened and closed.

"Fiber scope?" Adam asked.

"You know it," Will replied as he scaled the short ladder to the concrete shelf below the lid.

Adam handed Will a custom-made handheld scope attached to a fiber-optic cable. A thirty-six-inch-long flexible braided-steel sheath protected the fiber-optic glass inside. Will removed a plug from the lid and threaded the cable up through the hole. He peered in through the attached scope and adjusted the thumb wheel to focus the lens.

After angling the cable first one way, then the other, he stopped. "Well, well. What have we here?"

"You need the infrared adapter?" Adam asked.

"No, I'm good. And from what I see, we've got a little investigating to do."

"What's happening?" Joey asked.

"Punks. They're in an old Chevy Blazer, top's off."

"Anyone we know?"

Will turned the cable slightly and adjusted his position. "No."

"Strange," Adam said. "It's a little nipply out there to be riding around with the top down. Plus, there's no train tracks out this way."

"Yeah," Joey agreed. "And no roads, either. A couple of dirt trails—"

"Shh." Will held his hand out. "They're headed away from the Perimeter, but angling this direction. Mostly east, though. They're pretty far out there now." He refocused the lens. "Brake lights. What the heck is out there?"

"There's a couple of Changer outposts out this way," Adam said. "We ran across them in the Manx once, remember?"

"I do now," Will said. "And, yep, they're all getting out of the Blazer now."

"What are they doing?"

"I don't know, playing ring around the rosie. Jeez, gimme a minute." Will focused the lens again. "Pretty much surrounding the outpost on foot. They sure have some bright flashlights. Dang, it's hard to tell, but it looks like the door to the outpost is open."

"We need to check it out," Joey said. "What are Punks doing at a Changer outpost?"

"Agreed," Will said. He pulled the cable back out of the hole and replaced the plug before scrambling back down the ladder. "Since we left our jackets at the Hangar, all we have are windbreakers in the gear bags. So buck up, wussies. It's wet and cold outside."

"Got it," Adam said. "Ready, Joe?"

Joey flipped off the two tunnel lights on either side of the opening. "Let's do it."

THE THREE AMIGOS CLAMBERED UP the ladder and slipped out the tunnel exit to ground level. A cold gust of wind whipped the trio's faces as Adam secured the tunnel lid. "Holy shit, it's cold."

The boys stood facing the Changers outpost, their backs to the Wall. Will raised his biocular to get a closer look. "Okay," he said. "Four of these dudes are standing at the door. The other two are off to the sides." His narration of the activity was slow and deliberate. "There's definitely someone inside that they're talking to. The guy inside is like waving his arms. Doesn't look like he's friendly. At least to the Punks."

"Let's sneak on over," Adam said. "It's freezing just standing here."

Will lowered his biocular. "I'm going to assume these guys came from the west. So we'll head east, same direction they were headed."

"Good point," Adam agreed. "If we can get a little ways past the outpost and they head back west, they won't run into us."

"Or over us," Joey said.

The Three Amigos set out over the muddy terrain, gear bags slung over their shoulders. The cold wind was constant, keeping their windbreakers stuck to their bodies like contact paper. The tall grass and low bushes provided partial cover as they kept an eye on the lights at the outpost.

About half a mile out, Will held up his hand. "Hang on a sec." The boys stopped and squatted. Will pulled the biocular from his bag and peered through the lens at new activity around the outpost. "Looks like they're packing up. Get your eyes out, guys."

Joey and Adam retrieved bioculars from their bags and joined Will.

"You sure they're leaving?" Adam asked. "Seems like they're doing a lot of walking back and forth between the Blazer and the building."

"I never said they were leaving," Will said, eyes fixed on the outpost. "I said it looks like they're packing up."

"Oh, they're packing all right," Joey said. "Unpacking."

"You're right about that, Joe," Will said. "What the heck, they're setting up tents."

"Wonder why they don't just stay inside?" Adam said.

"Burn barrel," Joey commented. "That's a Punk thing."

Will lowered his biocular and looked at Joey. "It's a keep-warm thing."

"Yeah," Adam said. "And staying outside in tents in this weather is a dumb thing."

"Have to agree," Will said. "It looks like those guys are kind of stationing in a semicircle, facing the building. We gotta get closer and see if we can hear anything."

"Let's try to stay low," Joey said.

The boys scurried through the foliage in a wide circle. They stopped when they reached the far east side of the small structure. Will held his hand up again. "We're about a hundred yards out," he whispered.

"This is a good spot," Joey agreed. "We can see the back of the place and still keep an eye on them."

Adam stretched out on his belly and pulled his biocular out of his gear bag. "There's two windows on the back, guys."

"I see them," Joey said.

Will watched the activity in front of the little building. "Those guys are drinking. Looks like they're kind of winding down, though."

"Think we can get closer?" Adam asked. "Since they don't have the back covered, we might be able to see inside. I'm super bugged about who's in there."

"I think it's safe right now," Will said. "The wind's blowing toward us, so they're less likely to hear any popping Twinkie bags."

The Three Amigos stayed clear of the light cast from the burn barrel as they snaked around to the backside of the outpost. The boys quickly found a shallow ditch and scrambled down into it. Tall grass at the top of the embankment provided near-perfect protection for the surveillance point.

Will made himself comfortable near the east corner of the property, affording him a view of the side and front of the compound. Joey took up the opposite side on the west.

From the center of the small trench, Adam scanned his biocular into one of the windows on the rear wall. *Dang, curtains.* He panned his lens to the other window. *Nice. Curtain's open.* He set the infrared control on the device. *Dark, dark, dark. What the heck?* He tapped his cell, sending a group text to Will and Joey: *Going to look in the windows.*

Will replied: *Gotcha covered. Cell on vibrate.* Adam read Joey's reply: *Got it.*

Adam opted to leave his gear in the ditch. He tucked his scope away, zipped the bag and peered into the darkness behind the outpost. His eyes adjusted slowly as he clambered up the small embankment through the tall grass. The windows on the back of the tiny cabin stared at him like lonely eyes—weary from the cold, the solitude and neglect. The wind had all but subsided as he scurried, hunched over, to the wall between the two lifeless windows. He squatted with his back to the wall and glanced at Will, then Joey—two thumbs up. He stood and turned slowly, hugging the wall as if he were on a narrow ledge. Silence enveloped the compound, save for the occasional click or pop from the dying fire inside the burn barrel out front.

Adam's ears ached from the cold. His muscles tightened as he slid his head sideways, cupping his hands around his face. His nose touched the cold, gritty glass, clearing the dirt in a single streak across the pane. *Dammit, can't see*, he thought, using one hand to clear a small round spot. He cupped his hands again and pressed his face to the window. *What?* He pressed the window harder, as if trying to pass through the glass. *It's gray...wait, it's something leaning against the window.* Adam exhaled everything he had in his lungs as the hair on his arms stood on end. *A face!* He pulled himself away from the window, falling backward onto a patch of slick mush. He scrambled in reverse, slipping and sloshing in the muck.

Adam suppressed a scream as he felt a hand on his shoulder. "Shh, shh, shh." It was Will. Adam turned to see his friend kneeling beside him, a finger to his lips. "You stuck your face right in that person's face," Will whispered. "Whoever it is."

Adam tried to catch his breath. "Holyfuckingshithell! That was nasty."

"Okay, get a grip, dude. Whoever's in there hasn't moved. They're still at the window. If they haven't alerted the Punks out front by now, they probably won't."

Adam took a deep breath and glanced at Joey, still at his post in the ditch. "Okay, I'm good," he whispered. "Let's go."

The two boys stood and moved carefully over the wet ground, back to the window. The person inside remained still, watching the friends as they approached.

Will noticed the person inside furiously cranking a little handle on the windowsill. The window opened sideways, about three inches. He peered inside at the face. For the first time, he recognized the person was female. "Hi," he whispered.

"Who are you?" she asked.

Will looked intently at her scarred face, the greasy hair on her head. He didn't know why, but he felt sorry for her. "I'm Will. This is Adam."

"What are you doing here?"

"Just out looking around," Will said, glancing at Adam.

"Don't you know you could get killed?" she said. "Or worse yet, captured."

"By who?" Adam asked.

The female shot a glance over her shoulder at the front door of the outpost. She turned back to the open window and pressed a cheek against the glass. "Look, you two. You gotta come clean. I will if you will."

Will and Adam looked at each other. Will shrugged. "All right, fine. We're from the Punks' compound. We stay at the Perimeter, Checkpoint One."

"Sure. I've never seen you there."

"Why would you?" Adam asked. "Who are you?"

She backed slightly into the room, trying to hide her face.

"C'mon," Will said. "We told you the truth. Who are you?"

"You know those guys out front are Changers, right?"

Adam's eyes widened. "Oh shit."

"Yeah, shit is right," she said. "You get within three feet of a Changer and they can tell by looking into your eyes you're not one of them." She glanced back and forth between Will and Adam. "You're not wearing any eye covering."

"So what's the deal," Will said. "Are you a Changer, too?"

"Look, you look like nice kids," she said. "The Changers are evil. You don't know what they'll do to you if they catch you here."

Adam leaned toward Will and whispered into his ear. "Let's just tell her what we do." He shrugged. "What do we have to lose?"

Will crinkled his face and looked at Adam. "You mean like our lives?"

"You guys should get out of here."

"All right," Will said, squinting into the dark space behind the window. "We're going out on a limb here. I don't want this to be a wasted effort."

"Make it fast," the female said.

"We work for the Punks." Will shifted his feet on the soggy ground. "Not on any official basis. It's like, they tell us we're not Punks, but they know we're on their side. We hate the Changers. All we know is, the Changers seem to be planning something. None of us knows what. We've just all been on high alert since the unveiling."

"So, do you know anything about that?" Adam asked.

"Oh my God, you guys. You have no idea."

"You're right," Will said. "So tell us."

The female disappeared from the boys' sight and shuffled around in the darkness. When she returned to the window, she had her face and head covered in a ragged sheet. "Okay, you two.

I'm probably a dead woman walking, so it doesn't much matter what I say to you, or anyone else."

"Can we help—" Will asked.

"I'm beyond help," she cut him off. "But you can help yourselves, and all the Punks. Bystanders, too. The Changers are going to attack the Punks. Their plan is to destroy them, every last one. They have weapons that you guys can't stand against."

"Like what?" Adam asked.

"You know those mutants you guys have been dealing with?"

"Yes," Will said.

"The Punks pick those suckers off with a bullet to the head," Adam said. "Bam, gone."

"No. The Changers have developed the mutants into super fighters. They call them Chybrids. From what I've heard, a single bullet to the head won't kill them. They're also super fast. You can't stop them."

Will was frustrated. "So what do you have to offer?"

"All I know is, the Changers are going to attack, full-force, at Perimeter One. They're bringing thousands of the Chybrids in front of their own army. I'm warning you so you can tell the Punks. Do whatever you can to be ready."

"When are they going to attack?"

"I don't know. I'd say any day."

"Why are you telling us this? Are you a Punk?"

"Or a Changer?" Adam asked.

"Look, I can tell you if I had a chance, I'd be a Punk." A tear rolled down her cheek. "Actually, I had a chance, and I blew it. In my life, I've seen some bad times. When I was at my lowest, someone dangled a new, beautiful life in front of me. I jumped at it, not knowing there was a price to pay." She looked up at the two friends. "Nothing's ever free, guys."

"Sounds tough," Will said, shaking his head.

"You know," she said, "I jumped too soon. After I committed to that new life, I met some other people. These people didn't judge me, even though I can really be a shit, you know? And I fell in love." She paused. "I'm telling you now, that low point in my life wasn't rock bottom for me, even though at the time it seemed like it was. I'm at the bottom now, guys. I'm in a pit. If I ever have a chance to make up for what I've done..." Her voice trailed off.

"What are you gonna do now?" Will asked.

"You mean if the Changers don't kill me?" She shifted her position, pulling the dirty sheet tighter around her shoulders. "I have a plan, if I can pull it off."

"Wait," Adam said. "You're going to go up against the Changers by yourself?"

"Not all the Changers are bad," she said.

Will looked at Adam. "That'd be a joke with the Punks. We hate the Changers."

"Yeah," Adam agreed. "What are you even talking about?"

"You guys know someone named Fred Garrison?" she asked.

"Never heard of him," Will said.

"Never mind, then," she said.

The boys' cells vibrated. Adam checked his and looked at Will. "Joey's calling us back."

Will looked at the woman. "We gotta go. If there's ever anything we can do to help you."

The woman sighed. "Do you know a Punk named Curtis Dyer?" she asked.

"Yeah, we know him."

"How's he doing?"

"He's going to be okay."

The tattered sheet ripped slightly as the woman tightened her grip. "Good," she said. "I swear, if the Changers don't kill me...I don't know. If this night ever comes up, you know, in conversation—I'm on the Punks' side."

"We gotta get outta here, Will," Adam urged.

The boys swung around to leave. Adam scurried toward the ditch. Will stopped and turned to the window. "We won't forget you." As the window slowly cranked closed, he ducked down and headed for the ditch. The woman in the window watched him disappear into the shadows as she backed into a darkness of her own.

CHAPTER 30

Nowhere To Go

Fred and Thomas sat at the bar in the Changers Lounge on Level Seven of the Underground.

Though dimly lit, the lounge exuded luxury and class. The floor was covered with dark blue sound-deadening carpet. Indirect lighting under the bar top and around the baseboards contributed to the laid-back atmosphere. Booths of varying capacity lined the walls and provided privacy for couples and groups alike.

Fred's ears twitched at the muted laughter emanating from a booth behind him as he stared at his reflection in the shiny black bar top.

"What'll it be, fellas?" the bartender asked.

Fred started. "Two martinis."

The bartender sniggered. His overbite caused an exaggerated sucking sound with each breath. "Shaken, not stirred?"

Fred's eyes narrowed. He gazed at the bartender, unsmiling. "I didn't give any special instructions. Just bring us two martinis."

The man's face went blank as quickly as he had smiled. "No problem."

"You know that guy?" Thomas asked.

Fred watched the man fix the drinks at the other end of the bar. "I haven't seen him in here before. I'm pretty sure he's new."

"I've seen a lot of new faces here lately," Thomas said. "I guess Scotty's membership drive is paying off."

"He's the guy to do it." Fred grabbed a toothpick from a dispenser on the bar top. He eyed the bartender, who was now on the phone. "However, it makes the Changers' need for human consumption more urgent."

"Yeah. I feel for the Punks right now. The prisons have been running low for years. The death penalty actually means death, not like it used to be."

"Kind of a moot point, though," Thomas said. "The Punks are taking lifers to the platforms now. Death row is pretty much defunct. You know, a guy gets a life sentence, he can pretty much figure it's the death penalty anyway. The Punks are delivering those people within a year or two of sentencing."

Fred looked at the two martinis sitting at the end of the bar while Mr. Overbite continued talking on the phone. "I'm gonna go get our drinks." He stepped off the barstool and strolled to the end of the bar. "I'm taking these," he said to the bartender.

The guy looked up from the phone. "Hey, payment, man." He held out a cell phone–sized scanner. Fred swiped his hand across the screen, picked up the martinis and motioned to Thomas.

Thomas followed Fred to a booth in the corner of the lounge. "Good idea," Thomas said. "I'm not too fond of Big Teeth over there."

"We gotta be able to talk," Fred agreed. "I'm pretty sure our quarters are monitored. I don't think anyone suspects anything. I just know how Levi is."

Thomas chuckled. "Yeah. The guy would monitor his own mother if she was around."

"Right. So, Felix did well. I knew he would."

"I agree," Thomas said. "But you had a valid question. How do we get the skull-buster bullets to the Punks?"

"I've been thinking about it. We have to work with someone that's free to come and go in both environments—Changers and Punks."

Thomas scoffed. "That doesn't give us many options. We have

quite a few members doing that now. The real problem is whether anyone with dual access would be on our side."

"Agreed. The only other choice for us is to go full Rogue and make the break ourselves."

Thomas slid an olive off its plastic spear, crunched it twice in his mouth and swallowed. "We'd have Silver up our ass so fast, we'd hardly know what hit us."

"Think about it, though," Fred said. He sipped his martini. "Us getting out is one thing. The the question of getting the skull-busters out, too? Even if we were able to pull that off, how do we convince the Punks we're friendly?"

"That's easy. We just don't tell them we're Changers. You know, we're just good citizens trying to help."

"You know about the acid testing, right? The Punks are acid-testing everyone coming and going. You either show your burn mark, be in their database as *clean*, or get tested."

Thomas waved his hand. "Those marks don't last long on Bystanders. Their skin isn't artificially manipulated like Changers' skin. Normal human skin heals pretty fast. Second-degree burn at most."

Fred shook his head. "You mean, like, show them our forearms and tell them we were tested but we're healed? Won't work. They perform an on-the-spot DNA test, cross referenced to the National DNA database. Becoming Changers skewed the original DNA pattern. Consequently, we'd no longer be in the database."

"I didn't think about that." Thomas shook his head. "You know what's ironic about it? The Punks were against DNA registration at birth. The protests were brutal." He pushed his glass to the center of the table. "Now they're using the very thing they were against to their advantage."

Fred drained his glass. "Yep. The Punks are smart. They're taking no chances these days. They shoot first and ask questions later—if they even ask." He made a gun shape with his hand and pressed his forefinger against his temple. "Pop, bullet to the head."

Thomas raised an eyebrow. "So all of our plants inside are gone?"

"From what I hear, there's a few still outside the Perimeter that haven't been tested. Interestingly, Logan passed the test—*at the Punks' headquarters.*"

Thomas sat forward. "What the hell? How'd he do it?"

"I'm not sure. Last I heard, Scotty was going to check with him."

"Speaking of, how'd *he* make it? He's still coming and going, right?"

Fred nodded. "He is. But he's in tight with the mayor in Tremayne; lives with him, right? No one went up against the mayor, and the mayor prohibited Van Buren's testing."

"I'm surprised we haven't had a meeting about this. What have you heard from Peterson?"

"That's the most intriguing thing. She called me the night Logan passed his test. She told me she failed."

"At the Punks' headquarters?"

"Yes, at their headquarters. She sounded bad, Thomas. Said she'd call me in three days at eight p.m. That's why we're here and not in our quarters."

Thomas looked down at Fred's cell. The screen lit up. "Looks like she's true to her word. And right on time."

Fred swiped his cell off the table, nearly dropping it in his lap. "Peterson!"

"*Fred. I need help.*" Krystal's voice was shaky. "*I don't know what to do.*"

"Okay." Fred looked across the table at Thomas. "What's happening?"

"*Oh, God, Fred. I don't know who I can trust. I don't—*"

"Okay, first take a deep breath. I've been trying to get a hold of you. I left several messages."

"*I know. I got your messages.*"

"What happened since we last talked?"

Krystal sniffed hard. She didn't try to hide the fact that she had been crying. "*Since I got kicked out of the Perimeter and totally banished by the Punks—*" She stopped. Every muscle in her body tightened. "*Oh, Fred, I'm so screwed.*" She sucked in a breath. "*Levi wants to see me.*"

"Did you actually hear that from Levi?" Fred asked.

Krystal's staccato breathing overpowered her voice. *"There's some Changers outside the Perimeter...at the platforms. They're changed like Punks. Infiltrators. They play both sides. I don't know how they found me."*

Thomas motioned to Fred. He mouthed, "What's happening?"

Fred glanced across the room at the bartender. He noticed the guy was busy wiping a one-by-one-foot corner of the bar top with his damp towel. "Is ol' Overbite staring at us?" he asked Thomas.

"Looks like it," Thomas said.

Fred held up two fingers. The bartender smiled and nodded.

Thomas sat sideways in the booth, back to the wall, feet on the bench seat, facing the bar. "I don't trust him."

"Sorry, Krystal," Fred said. "Hang on just a sec."

"I've got nowhere to go, Fred."

The bartender stepped from behind the bar with two more martinis and walked to the booth. "On the house, fellas." He set the two drinks on the table, collected the empties, and returned to the bar.

"Okay, Krystal, I'm going to put you on speaker. I'm with Thomas. We're in a corner booth in the seventh-level lounge. It's safe here."

"Oh, man. I don't even know if it's safe to talk to you." Krystal sniffed again. *"I just thought—"*

"It's safe." Fred tapped the cell and turned the volume down. "Go ahead, Krys."

"You never call me Krys."

"You have to trust me," Fred said. "Where are you?"

"I'm at one of the abandoned outposts on the east side. This place is a dump. There's running water, cold only. And no power."

"Okay," Fred said. "So how'd you get a message from Levi?"

"These fucking Punks, or Changers. About six or seven of them found me. One of them had a cell. I don't know, they somehow got this message to Silver. When they found me, they called her."

Fred shook his head. "And you talked to Silver?"

"Yeah. She told me Levi knows everything. Fred, the Punks branded me."

"Branded?" Fred looked at Thomas.

"How, Krystal?" Thomas asked.

"*Acid.*" She sucked in another hard breath. "*The same acid they test everyone with. It doesn't come off of Changers skin.*"

"Krystal," Fred said. "We can have Felix look at it."

"*How?*" she practically shouted. "*I can't even really trust you guys. Now you're bringing in a third fucking Changer?*"

"Why'd you call me if you don't trust me?"

"*I always thought you were fair. You're Levi's right-hand man. If anyone has sway with him, it's you. I figured maybe, just maybe, you'd go to bat for me.*"

"Okay, hang on, Krys," Fred said. "How are you branded? It's a small round spot on your arm, right?"

Krystal fought a chuckle. "*It's all over my face. They put the acid on my face, around my forehead, my cheek, my eye. It's in the shape of a C. It's hideous. I can't hide that.*"

Thomas looked up at Fred. "True. It's permanent on Changers' skin. You can't even hide it with a charge."

"Okay," Fred said. "Let's accept that for now. What did Silver say?"

"*You guys know about my* assignment, *right?*"

"Yeah, absorb a high-ranking Punk. Send a message."

"*Right,*" Krystal said. "*And my consequence for not completing the assignment?*"

"Holy shit," Thomas said. "Please tell me it's death."

Krystal didn't hide her sobs. She managed to squeeze out one word. "*No.*"

"Okay, Krys, you have to try your best to hold it together. So Silver's the one that told you to report to Levi?"

"Krystal," Thomas said. "Why show up at all? Being on the run is better than facing Levi."

Rustling noises emanated from the cell's speaker on the table. They heard Krystal's heavy breathing and creaking boards under her boots. "*They're camped outside, guys,*" she said. "*They're waiting for me.*"

Fred glanced up at Thomas and noticed the bartender was at

the adjacent booth, slowly wiping down the table. "Hey, buddy. Are you eavesdropping?"

The bartender caught Fred's gaze. He stopped wiping the table and made a feeble attempt to appear disinterested. "Who, me? No."

"Then finish up and beat it," Fred said, jerking his head toward the bar.

The big-toothed bartender stood up and walked toward the bar. He picked up his cell from the bar top and tapped the face.

Thomas nodded toward the bar. "Mr. Teeth is back on the phone."

Fred shrugged. "Okay, Krys. When's your meeting with Levi?"

"*Thursday night.*"

"Fine. I'll make sure I'm at that meeting."

"*Thursday's Arena night, Fred,*" Krystal said. "*I have to meet with Levi first.*"

"That gives us a few days to put a plan together."

"*I gotta go, Fred.*"

"Krys?"

The call ended.

"Finish up, partner," Thomas said. "I have a hunch about something. I'll be right back." He slid out of the booth and strode across the room to the bar.

The bartender hung up his cell as Thomas approached. He tipped his chin at Thomas. "'Sup, man?"

Thomas leaned across the bar and looked deep into the bartender's eyes. "You need to mind your own business, Logan."

CHAPTER 31

Punks on Defense

Pops walked over to the main workbench in the Hangar and pressed the intercom button. "Jim, do you copy?"

"*Go ahead,*" Jimbo answered from the control panel in the Depot.

"Hey. Dion around?"

"*Him and Ryk's outside in the compound somewhere.*"

"All righty. I got the Three Amigos here, just come up from the Tunnels. They got some news you guys are gonna want to hear."

"*I'll call 'em in. Gimme five.*"

"You got it. Just come to the Hangar as soon as you can. It's urgent."

"*10-4.*"

Pops strolled to the fridge and grabbed three canned sodas from the door. He tossed them, one at a time, to the boys. "Good job, you three. Dion's on his way."

Geezer polished his lenses and smiled at the boys. "Y'all's got some balls," he clucked. "That's some dangerous shit, talking up close and personal with Changers like that."

"You know," Will said, "we hate the Changers. If we have to make nice to get information, we'll do it."

"That's more than makin' nice," Pops said. "You guys risked your lives."

"It is what it is," Joey said. "What good is anyone's life if you're just sitting around waiting for the Changers to eat you?"

"It's still ballsy," Geezer said. "You risk your lives for the rest of us—Punks *and* Bystanders."

"Punks risk their lives every day for the Bystanders," Adam said.

Joey took three hard swigs from his soda. "It's what we do." He belched. "It's our thing."

The three boys laughed at Joey's burp. "And we have the best burps, too," Will said.

"Hep," Geezer said as he nodded at one of the side doors.

A cold breeze swept through the Hangar as Dion and Ryker walked in. "Pops," Dion said. "What's the priority level?"

"Top," Pops said.

"All right, have Jimbo bring Winter in from Platform One. And get Lace in here, too. She's in Tremayne." He looked at the Three Amigos sitting on high stools by Bay Three's inspection pit. "So you guys have some information?"

"Yes," Will said.

Adam smiled. "Guess we're causing a commotion around here."

Ryker eyed Adam sideways. "Don't get cocky. We're on alert because Pops said Level One. We don't know what you told him, but his word is gold."

"He's not *getting* cocky," Joey said. "He's always been."

The intercom crackled. "*Pops, do you copy?*"

"Go ahead, Jim."

"*The girls are already on their way in. ETA from Winter: three minutes. Lace: about two.*"

"10-4. Call someone to cover the Depot and get in here."

"On my way."

Dion lit a cigarette. "So give me the gist, Will." He clinked his Zippo shut and tossed it to Ryker.

Will shifted on his stool. "Well, bottom line is, the Changers are going to move against us, I mean you guys, the Punks."

Dion raised an eyebrow. "What do you mean, *move against?*"

"They want to get rid of the Punks, once and for all. I guess they've been building up for years. Now they're ready to attack."

Ryker lit a cigarette and stuffed Dion's Zippo into his pocket. "How reliable is this information? Where'd you hear this?"

Will leaned forward and glanced at his two friends. He brushed his hair back off his forehead. "We talked to someone out on the east side. It was at one of those Changers outposts."

"Who was it?" Ryker asked.

"Don't know. She didn't actually say she was a Changer. But Changers were guarding her. There was six of 'em out in front of the outpost."

"Wait, she?" Dion said.

"Yeah," Will said. "We couldn't tell until we got up to the outpost. When she opened the window to talk to us, we knew it was a she—a woman."

Ryker's eyes widened. "Let me get this straight. You guys went to a Changers outpost on the east side, walked up to the outpost—that just happened to have six Changers guarding it—and talked to someone inside?"

Will shrugged. He looked at his friends. "Yeah."

"Holy shit, that's ballsy!" Ryker said.

Geezer cackled. "What I said."

Dion leaned against the custom Riviera, still parked in the Hangar. "So who was this person you talked to? Did she say?"

"Never gave her name," Adam said.

"What did she look like?" Dion asked.

"It was dark," Adam said. "There were no lights, inside or out. We didn't get a good look at her. But I can say she was not good-looking."

"And she's the one that told you they were Changers out front?" Dion asked.

The side door to the Hangar opened. Jimbo walked in with Lace.

"Yes," Will said. "We asked her if she was a Changer, but she didn't tell us either way."

"Oh," Adam said. "Funny thing about those Changers guarding the place. We thought they were Punks until she told us they were Changers."

Dion looked at Lace. "This explains some of the missing personnel in Tremayne."

"Agreed," Lace said. "How many are we talking?"

"These guys said there were six Changers," Ryker said. "They looked like Punks, guarding some woman at an outpost on the east side."

"Interesting," Lace said. "The Changers all but abandoned the outposts on the east side a while ago."

"Okay," Dion said. "Jim, you fill Winter in when she gets here." He looked at Will. "Let's get down to business. Pops said this is a Level One priority. What did this woman tell you about the Changers attacking us?"

Will took a deep breath. "She said the Changers are going to attack the Punks. Their goal is to completely get rid of the Punks so they can have the Bystanders any way they want them, anytime."

Ryker propped himself on a dirt bike next to the Riviera. "How and when?"

"*When* is anytime. She didn't know. She just said the attack is going to be overwhelming, and soon. They're going to send thousands of those mutants, the man-style mutants. She called them Chybrids. The plan is to overwhelm us with Chybrids to weaken us, then close in with their own Changer Army to finish us, I mean the Punks, off."

"No big deal," Jimbo said. "They tried that. We popped 'em easy with a head shot. Bam, gone."

"No," Will said. "They've modified the Chybrids since then. That was a trial run. This chick said a bullet to the head won't kill them. These are like super Chybrids, I guess."

"Why should we believe anything this chick says?" Jimbo said. "Some nobody in the middle of nowhere?"

Will looked at Jimbo, expressionless. "She's on our side, man. She's on the Punks' side."

"How do you know?" Dion asked.

The Three Amigos exchanged glances. "She said some things that made me believe her," Will said.

"Spill it."

"Exactly what she said is if she had a chance, she'd be a Punk. Then she said she had a chance once and she blew it. She said if she could ever make up for it, she would. And she would be on our side. I mean the Punks' side."

"Is that it?" Dion asked.

"There was one other thing that convinced me," Will said. He looked around at the Punks in the Hangar. "She asked about Curtis. She asked how he was doing."

Dion and Ryker looked each other in the eye. In unison, they said, "Krystal."

"ARE YOU GUYS TALKING ABOUT Krystal Peterson?" Adam asked.

"Yep," Ryker said.

"What the heck?" Joey said.

"It's a long story, guys," Ryker said. "Someday we'll explain it."

"We've got work to do," Dion said as Winter entered the Hangar.

Winter stopped as the door closed behind her. She rested her right hand on the grip of an AR-15 that was slung over her shoulder. "What kind of work?"

Dion looked around the roomful of Punks. These were his friends, his brothers and sisters, his dad, his family. "This is it, guys. I'm going to put out a red alert to all Punks. We're going to begin in full defensive mode. You all know your parts. You all have loyal down-line commanders. I don't have to tell you, this isn't a drill."

"I say we take the fight to the Changers," Jimbo said.

"That will be next. But for now, everyone plan on assuming full-on defensive posture." He looked at Lace. "If you have anyone in any of your crews that are suspect, take them down. Have them escorted here immediately to report to Pops for acid testing. Anyone gives you more than a 'what for,' cap 'em. I'll take full responsibility for any errors. You have my trust."

"Sir," Lace said.

"Winter," Dion said, "when you hear from me, shut down the platforms and pull everyone in. Once we're out of the platforms, the Changers will know we know something. That's why you need to wait for my signal. I want to make sure we're secure before we alert them. You can leave now. I'll be in touch."

Dion nodded to Jimbo. "Send the alert now."

Jimbo left without a word.

"Lace, the Bystanders in Tremayne are going to have a sense something's up. You'll have to assign crews to handle traffic. We need to get people into their homes. I don't want a huge exodus from the City."

"I already have that covered," Lace said.

"How?"

"You remember those Bystanders you met with a while back, the ones that wanted to help so bad?"

"I remember them well. Drew Bushong and Sydney DiLuca. What about them?"

"Well, when you told me to look them up that day, I paid them a visit. We figured out a way they'd be able to help. Drew is a downright computer and electronics communications whiz. He's already tapped in to Tremayne's traffic signal system. He can control any and all lights, including train crossings."

"Awesome," Dion said. "I knew you were a good choice for second level."

"Oh, that's not all," Lace said. "Years ago, the telecommunications companies set up nationwide and global emergency-alert networks via fiber optics and cellular towers. These systems have access to all the emergency and first-responder organizations worldwide. Even though these are ultrasecure systems, Drew has hacked them. He has the ability to intercept, direct, and redirect at will."

"Sounds like you've got things under control at your level," Ryker said.

"Oh, but there's more," Lace said. "Drew has access to and controls all the security cameras in all the cities in this sector. That's about a hundred cities and towns."

"Are you done?" Ryker asked.

"There's one more thing," Lace said. "Any agency that has remote control capabilities for drone aircraft—he can intercept and control them, too."

"Holy shit," Will said.

"I have one question," Ryker said. "For my own curiosity, who's Curtis working under?"

"I got him assigned to Stringer," Lace said.

Ryker winced.

"He requested the assignment, sir."

Pops looked at Dion. "I'd like to thank these guys for getting us this information. I know we're gonna lose some people, but in my opinion, they probably saved a lot of lives."

Will lit up. "Hey, is there anything we can do to help us, I mean the Punks?" Joey and Adam sat up.

Dion eyed the Three Amigos on the stools. "You guys aren't going with any of us."

"Oh," Will said, slumping down in his seat.

Dion nodded to Ryker as he dismounted the dirt bike.

"Guys," Ryker said. The Three Amigos looked at Ryker as he approached them. He took off his trademark black bandanna and handed it to Will. "You need to keep that hair out of your face." Then he stepped back and addressed the friends. "For your first official assignment, we need some good Punks to report back to headquarters on Changers activity, using the Tunnel checkpoints."

CHAPTER 32

Demotions

O<small>N</small> T<small>HURSDAY</small> <small>MORNING</small>, S<small>COTTY</small> V<small>AN</small> Buren and Johnny Logan sat in the Executive Dining Room on the seventh level of the Underground.

Each table in the spacious, brightly lit room was suspended from the stainless-steel ceiling by a single rod. There were no legs on the tables to interfere with foot room. Regular maintenance gave the highly polished white floors a look of hospital sterility. The shiny electric-blue tabletops required no tablecloths. The scent of bacon, fresh-brewed coffee, cinnamon, and various spices filled the air. Though crowded, there was never a wait for a table. Levi ensured the dining establishment employed no waitresses—only waiters in tuxedos.

A waiter landed at Scotty's table. "The usual, sir?"

"Yes, I'll have the usual," Scotty replied. "But I think today calls for a celebration." He looked across the table at Johnny. "Champagne?"

Johnny leaned back in his chair and clasped his hands behind his head. "Champagne with steak and eggs sounds about right."

The waiter bowed. "As you wish."

"Hey." Johnny held up his hand and snapped his fingers at the waiter. "Bring us the whole bottle."

"I can't wait to see the look on Garrison's face when he finds out about his new position," Scotty said.

"It's gonna be rich," Johnny said, smiling his full-toothed smile. "And Dennis, too. You believe that little shit told me to mind my own business?"

Scotty looked at his cell. "I'd say they should have received word by now."

"Speak of the devil," Johnny said, tipping his chin up.

Scotty turned around in his chair and looked toward the entrance. Fred and Thomas strode across the room and approached Scotty. Fred nodded to the two seated at the table. "Van Buren, Logan."

"Join us?" Scotty offered, motioning to two empty chairs.

"Not today," Fred said. "We have a little business to discuss."

Johnny snickered. "You can talk in front of us."

Thomas eyed Johnny. "I think we both know that's not true."

"Don't be butt-hurt, my little friend," Johnny said. "Are you referring to your little hissy fit at the bar the other night?"

"You made every attempt to eavesdrop. And let's be clear—we're not friends."

"Now you're hurting my feelings." Johnny couldn't stop smiling. He looked at Scotty. "Think they know?"

Scotty remained cool. He held his hands out, palms up. "I don't know. I'm not sure it's our place to say anything."

"What are you guys talking about?" Thomas asked.

Johnny leaned back in his chair and hooked his thumbs in his pockets. "Have you guys met with Levi?"

"Cool it, John," Scotty said.

"All right," Fred said. "I'll bite. What's happening?"

"You guys are in deep shit," Johnny blurted.

Scotty shook his head slowly, eying Johnny across the table.

Fred motioned to Thomas. "Have a seat." He sat down in the remaining chair at the square table.

The waiter approached with fresh coffee cups for Fred and Thomas. A second waiter on his heels placed hot wheat toast with trays of butter and assorted jams in front of Fred and Thomas. "I'll return with your orange juices," the first waiter said after pouring the coffee.

"Thank you," Fred said, placing his napkin in his lap. He took a sip of his coffee and turned his attention to Scotty. "Okay, I'm all ears. What's the scoop?"

"Obviously, you two have *not* met with Levi."

Thomas buttered his toast, trying to ignore Johnny. "Not recently."

"Okay," Scotty said. "Then I have to say up front, you need to confirm what I say with Levi. You outrank me, Fred—at least you did before today."

Fred bristled. "What's that supposed to mean?"

"It's a fact. Logan and I have both been promoted. You two are bumped down."

"Why?" Thomas demanded.

Johnny could hardly contain his enthusiasm. "Collaboration, boys. Collaboration."

Fred wiped the corners of his mouth with his napkin. "Collaboration? With who?"

Scotty sipped his water. "Peterson."

"Peterson?" Thomas said. "How's that? She's inner circle."

"Not anymore," Scotty said.

"Oh, things are changing around here, big-time," Johnny said. "You guys are busted." He looked at Thomas. "Yeah, I was eavesdropping at the lounge the other night. You know you guys were scheming with Peterson."

"Wait." Fred held up a hand. "Assume we were talking to Peterson. So what? No one knows what we were talking about."

"I do," Johnny said. "She's in a heap of trouble. She told you she was. And you two were talking to her about helping her out. I recorded everything you said."

"It's true," Scotty said. "I've heard the recording."

"So Krystal is in trouble," Fred said. "She told us she got kicked out of the Punks because she was outed by their acid test. So what?"

"Not that I have to," Scotty said. "But for old times' sake, I'll explain the situation. You guys were plotting against our leader. We know Peterson told you she was kicked out of the Punks. We also know she advised you they branded her with acid. All of us know that when Changers are in a changed state, they can't erase the acid burns—"

"Actually," Fred interrupted, "I didn't know for sure until Krystal told me that on the call the other night."

Scotty waved his hand. "Regardless. You know what was said, and you know how you reacted. Both of you plotted to assist Peterson in going up against Levi."

"Hang on, Van Buren—"

"Don't," Scotty said. "You'll just make yourself look pitiful. Levi heard everything. The recording doesn't lie."

"You also know Peterson had an assignment from Levi that went unfinished," Johnny said. "And that's a big no-no."

Fred left his toast unfinished and threw his napkin on the table. "I'm missing the deal here, Van Buren. We haven't even met with Levi. This kind of restructuring isn't something that he'd deliver to us through two lackeys like you and Logan."

Scotty glanced around the dining room. He lowered his voice. "Look, Fred. You two are lucky to be alive. Levi is this close to branding you Rogue. If I were you—"

"I'm not asking for your advice." Fred looked across the table at Thomas. "Let's go. I want to hear this from Levi." He and Thomas stood and pushed their chairs in. Fred pointed a finger at Johnny. "I owe you one, *my friend*. You and I *will* have this out."

Johnny held up his hands in mock fear, his eyes wide.

Fred and Thomas headed to the exit. Scotty leaned back in his chair and turned his head. "Hey, Garrison. Check things out. You'll find you don't have the friends around here you used to have."

Fred turned to catch up with Thomas.

The waiter set up a huge tray next to Scotty's table. "Well, that went well," Johnny said. "Champagne's here just in time."

Scotty shook his head again. "I'm glad we're on the side we're on, John. But don't ever count those two out."

FRED AND THOMAS HURRIED THROUGH the corridor on level seven toward the elevator. Residents of the Underground crowded the wide pedestrian thoroughfare. "So what's our next move?" Thomas asked.

"If my instincts are correct, we don't have much time here in the Underground. Levi didn't meet with us because he's got his mind made up. He doesn't just demote. I'd say we're as good as dead."

"Or worse," Thomas said.

"I'd rather be out of here before we have to plan for that." Fred nodded to four men exiting the elevator as he and Thomas stepped in. He waved off two women attempting to enter behind them. "Sorry, ladies, official business," he said, pushing the button for level three.

"Let's say we leave the Underground," Thomas said. "Where do we go?"

"When was the last time you received sustenance?"

Thomas frowned. "Look, we're out, right? Whether Levi has pegged us as Rogues or not, let's come to terms with it now. We're Rogues."

"I got it. So what are you saying?"

"It's absorption. It's 'absorbed a human.' The question is, 'when was the last time you absorbed human life?' Let's just call it what it is. Fuck the Changers and their bullshit vernacular."

"I'm with you. This is a messed-up world we live in, Thomas. I'm so sick of it."

Thomas nodded. "So, to answer your question, I have about six months left."

"Okay, same here," Fred said. "So we have time, but not much. All the more reason I need to get to my quarters."

"The formula?" Thomas asked.

"Yep. I'm the only one with access to that. It's in my safe. Felix is the only other one who knows what's in that safe."

"I'm glad you told me. All this time, I thought only Felix had it."

"Oh, he has it. It's all in his head. That man has the mind of a supercomputer, outward appearances notwithstanding."

Thomas glanced at the light bar above the elevator doors. "Almost there, partner. What do you need me to bring?"

"If we haven't been locked out of the system, secure electronic copies of the Underground schematics. Get all the information on architecture, infrastructure, and backup systems."

"That's easy," Thomas said. "What else do you have?"

Fred's eyes narrowed as he smiled. "I have everything on personnel, including our spies—who's infiltrated the Punks and the Bystanders. I've also got the backgrounds on everyone—who their parents are, when they became Changers, their real names."

"Everyone?" Thomas asked. "Including Levi?"

"Including Levi."

"Well, here's to Rogues," Thomas said as the elevator came to a stop. The two stepped off and the doors quietly closed behind them. They were alone in the corridor.

Fred tapped the face of his cell. "Levi's schedule has him at a meeting in the War Room at twenty-one hundred. That's Krystal's meeting."

"Wow," Thomas said, "You still have access to his schedule?"

"I'm surprised, too. But it gives me more confidence we can get everything else we want."

Thomas's brow furrowed. "What about our chips?"

Fred looked Thomas in the eye. "Felix can disable them remotely. The problem is getting that message to him. We don't want to contact him or be seen with him. I don't want to take the chance we'd out him as a Rogue. Once we're gone, he'll be our only access to the Underground."

"Got it," Thomas said.

"All right, then. Meet me here at twenty-one-hundred hours."

CHAPTER 33

Banished

TWO ARMED GUARDS STOOD SENTRY outside the War Room in the Underground. Their bright white uniforms appeared freshly pressed. Indirect lighting in the corridor glinted off their matching patent-leather boots. Fred raised an eyebrow as he and Thomas approached the guards. "Helmets tonight, guys? This must be some special meeting."

The two guards spread their legs and straddled the opening. "No entry, sir," the lead guard said. "I have orders, only specific personnel allowed in the War Room at this time."

"Well, since you're the spokesperson here," Fred said, stepping up to the guard, "let me ask you, who gave you your orders?"

"My commanding officer, sir—General Hendricks."

"And you know who I am?" Fred asked.

"Yes, sir."

"Then you know I outrank General Hendricks. Now step aside."

"Sir." The two guards brought their feet together and stepped to either side of the sliding doors, facing each other. Fred swiped his hand across the palm reader and the doors swished open.

Technicians seated at the computer monitors around the room remained fixed on their tasks, seemingly oblivious to Fred and Thomas's entry. The two Changers strode swiftly through the circle of technicians and walked up the short rise to the adjoining conference room.

Levi and Silver were at the conference table, viewing stats on a tablet when Fred and Thomas entered. Silver stood next to Levi, palms on the table. Fred and Thomas stopped when the doors closed behind them.

"As of two minutes ago, darling, the Chybrid Surge is underway," Silver said.

"Most excellent, my dear," Levi said. "Most excellent!"

"This looks cozy," Fred said.

Silver stood up. "What are you two doing here?"

"Important meeting tonight, right?" Thomas asked.

Levi's eyes turned to slits. "How did you hear of this meeting, Garrison? I only sent the orders to specific personnel."

Fred tried to prevent his mouth from turning downward into a wry grin. He raised an eyebrow. "Word gets around, sir." He looked at Silver. "I'd say you've got a security leak. Might want to be looking into that."

Levi glared at the two. "You are the latest and greatest security leak, Garrison."

Silver swiped her tablet from the table and entered several quick keystrokes. "I gave Hendricks specific orders to keep these two out. He'll be hearing from me."

Levi found it increasingly difficult to contain his ire. "God knows what Peterson has told them."

Silver sat down in her chair to Levi's left. Her eyes darted between Fred and Thomas. "So do you two know what this meeting is about?"

The two Rogues took seats at the conference table. Fred was noncommittal. He knew crashing this meeting would push Levi to his limit. He looked at Levi, then back at Silver. "Something about a problem with a high-ranking official in the organization?"

Thomas folded his hands in front of himself on the table. He followed Fred's lead. "One of our inner circle?"

"That's about all we know," Fred agreed. He shrugged. "Grapevine stuff."

The conference room door swished open and Felix entered. He stopped midstride and put his hands out to his sides as if to steady himself. He looked around the table over the rim of his glasses, then down at his wristwatch. He tapped his watch with a forefinger while he surveyed the ceiling. *What are these two doing here at this meeting?*

"Have a seat, Doctor," Levi said. "Our guest of honor will be here momentarily."

"I just received word they're off the elevator now, sir," Silver said.

Two armed guards led a procession through the center of the round War Room. Krystal was sandwiched between two additional guards behind them, with guards five and six bringing up the rear. Technicians behind monitors at floor level paused to watch the minor spectacle.

Thomas suppressed a gasp when Krystal entered the conference room. Her clothes were muddy and torn. Scrapes, cuts, dirt and grease covered the once-beautiful tattoos on her arms. Her hair hung in stringy locks over half her face. *Her face*, he thought. Burn scars spread down the left side of her face, from forehead to chin, and extended down her neck. Her eyelashes were short, her eyebrows nonexistent. The guards stopped, released their grip on her and stationed themselves in a semicircle behind her.

Krystal stood tall and steady. She raised her head to look around the room, the greasy remnants of hair falling away from the acid branding. Dark circles under her eyes stood in stark contrast to her pink and tan scars. She faced Levi head-on, but her eyes darted between everyone at the table.

Silver's hand moved silently, slowly, unconsciously to her mouth.

Thomas stopped looking and stared at the multidirectional microphone in the center of the conference table.

Felix had not accepted Levi's invitation to sit. He stood behind Thomas, hands folded in front of him, watching Krystal.

Fred's gaze remained fixed on Krystal. His attempt to be strong for her was unnecessary.

Krystal addressed Levi. "So, here I am—*Leader*," she said.

Levi smiled broadly. "So you are. So you are. And looking quite dapper, I must say."

"Just get on with it. Am I dead?" Krystal asked.

Levi laughed. "Oh, don't you wish." Then the smile disappeared. "You're a disgrace, Peterson. You look like shit. You'll never again be one of the beautiful people." He looked around the table, motioning with his hand. "Like us. Just look around the room. We are beautiful. Change if you feel like it." He leaned forward. "I dare you. That scar is a disgrace. You're not even good enough for those dreadful Punks. You were rejected as a kid, as a teenager—a burned-up piece of garbage."

"I became a Changer," Krystal said. "But I was never really one of you—"

"That's right!" Levi pounded his fist on the table. "From day one, you've been defiant, a misfit, a blemish. You don't fit in with anyone, with any group. You've been rejected your entire miserable life because you're ugly, Peterson."

Krystal scoffed. "You have no clue, little man. The Punks never judged me for my looks. They don't judge anyone because of their outward appearance."

"Oh, but you were cute, hon. You were *beautiful* when you were a Punk. One has to wonder how they would receive you now."

"They didn't kick me out because of my *looks*. They kicked me out because I'm a fucking Changer! You'll never get that." She pointed at Silver. "And you. What do *you* look like without the change? You're homely, mousy, weak. Hell, you're weak now. You became a Changer because you didn't like your looks. And guess what? Had you been a Punk instead, you might not have had the ability to live forever, but you'd be accepted, looks or not." She surveyed the room. "All of you bastards. You trade other people's lives for your own vanity—just to be one of the beautiful people. Well, get this—deep down, *you're* the ugly ones."

Levi mock-clapped his hands. "Nice speech, Peterson. Are you quite through?"

"Yeah, I'm through. But remember this—from now on, I am

who I am, scars and all. And inside, where it counts, I'm beautiful." She pounded her chest with her fist. "I'm Krystal fucking Peterson. And I'm not putting up with any more shit from any of you!"

"Aren't you fierce, missy," Levi declared. "Get down off your pedestal. You're as sick as anyone else. You've taken lives just to remain pretty, just to advance your own pathetic existence."

"Whoa," Krystal scowled. "What we have here, ladies and gentlemen, is the world's biggest hypocrite." Krystal's eyes narrowed as she pointed at Levi. "I know who you are. I know what no one else has figured out, you son of a bitch."

Levi's smile disappeared.

"You're Levi Aldrich, leader of the Changers. You're also Mayor Tobias Kutch of Tremayne. And you're Traveler, the most vile, sadistic piece of shit to walk the earth!"

The roomful of Changers stood stunned. No one noticed the step backward Krystal had taken until she was standing behind guard number three, her arm around his neck. Krystal grabbed the guard's 9mm pistol and pressed it under his chin, holding his jaw shut. With her back flat against the stainless-steel sliding doors, she motioned to the other guards. "All you assholes get over there by your asshole leader."

Still gripping the guard's throat from behind, Krystal turned and pointed the gun at Levi. "No one's dying tonight but you. All three of you!"

Levi fixed his eyes on Krystal. "You don't have the—"

Krystal squeezed the trigger. The 9mm bullet slammed into Levi's forehead.

Silver screamed when the bullet ricocheted off his skull, down onto the table and passed through her left hand. "You bitch!"

Krystal's eyes widened. Fred's jaw dropped. Thomas ducked. Every guard hit the floor as Krystal shoved number three to the ground with a boot to his ass. Felix watched from the side of the room, standing in his white lab coat, hands folded in front of him.

Levi laughed again.

"Levi," Fred said, the incredulous look still on his face. "How—"

Levi looked at Fred. "Surely, Garrison, you have seen the new skullcaps Dr. Yaz has fashioned for our Chybrids?"

"Y…yes, but…"

"I have undergone a most unusual procedure, thanks to our dear doctor. He has retrofitted me with the same bulletproof skullcap below my skin." He laughed again. "There was some deformity from the operation. But that didn't matter, did it? I'm a Changer! I am Levi!" he shouted.

Fred turned to the doctor. "Felix?"

Felix looked at Fred. He closed his eyes and nodded.

The distraction left Krystal enough time to aim the 9mm and blow out the electronic panel next to the doors behind her. The doors slid open and Krystal darted through the War Room between the rows of shocked technicians. She repeated the 9mm treatment to the panel leading to the corridor and disappeared into the nearest elevator.

"After her, you imbeciles!" Levi shouted.

CHAPTER 34

Abandon the Platforms

RYKER GLANCED AT THE ZONE map on the wall in the Depot. "Looks like Lace has the crews in Tremayne moving nicely."

"Agreed," Dion said. "She's a little light in the southwest quad, but she's ahead of schedule right now."

Ryker ran his fingers through his hair. "Looks deliberate. Patrols in that quadrant have reported zero activity for the last week or so. I think she's bulking up where we think they're coming in."

"It's a good strategy," Dion agreed. "Hopefully, the Changers aren't using some kind of diversion by keeping that area quiet." He looked at Ryker. "You know what I mean?"

"Listen, man. Don't doubt yourself. You're making good moves."

"I know. I'm trying to cover every contingency."

"I got that," Ryker said. "Just don't beat yourself up over this. Lace can handle it. Besides, man, we're pretty mobile. We can move damn fast if necessary."

Dion sat down on one of the barstools in front of the broad control panel. He propped his feet up, crossed his legs and leaned back. He cupped his hands behind his head and surveyed the huge monitor. The tiny blinking lights representing the Punks' troop movements blurred as his eyes unfocused.

"You know, Ryk, it's shit what this world's become. Did you ever imagine we'd reach this point?"

Radio banter from troops in the field, emanating from an overhead speaker, faded to distant background noise. Ryker strolled across the room and sat next to his friend. He spun the barstool around and faced the door leading outside to the compound. "You mean, like leading the Punks into a war against the Changers?"

"Yeah, there's that. But think about what's out there. It's dark. It's cold and desolate. It all seems so hopeless. And when the sun comes up tomorrow, it's still going to be cold, desolate, and hopeless."

"Yeah. Except places like Tremayne. That's like a huge splash of color on a gray background."

"Sure it is, physically. The Bystanders are already like sheep. They go about their daily lives with pretty much not a care in the world."

"I know what you mean," Ryker said. "We've made it that way for them. For the most part, they live in relative peace and safety, courtesy of the Punks."

"Wasn't always that way. Remember the stories Pops used to tell us? Stories about how it was before the Wall, before the Perimeter."

"I remember," Ryker agreed. "The best stories were about how it was before the Changers arrived."

"It's hard to imagine a world without those evil bastards."

"I guess it was like Tremayne all over. Pops never saw that, though."

"Yeah, but he kept the memories alive. His granddad told him things that his granddad's grandfather told him. Just handed down through the years."

Ryker looked at Dion. "Was the world ever really all that?"

"I think it was," Dion said.

"You don't think they ever embellished?"

"Everyone embellishes to a degree." Dion closed his eyes. "But I think these guys had good hearts. They said it was good because they chose not to remember the bad stuff."

"And now, their descendants are stuck in a shithole, defending a way of life that we ourselves don't even lead."

Dion held his reclining position and looked over at Ryker. He smiled. "And I wouldn't trade this life for any other."

"It's not the shithole you're in that matters, my friend," Ryker said, smiling back. "It's who you're in it with."

The two bumped fists as Dion swung his legs down off the countertop.

"*Dion, do you copy?*" Zane's voice crackled over the ceiling speaker.

Dion pressed a button on the control panel. "Go ahead."

"*We're set,*" Zane replied.

"10-4. What's the mood out there?"

"*Everything's been pretty quiet. It's a little breezy, but that seems to be dying down. We're ready for whatever those mothers throw at us.*"

"That's what I like to hear. Orders stand, though. Stay in your vehicles, hold your positions. We want to make the Changers pay for this incursion."

"*Spirits have never been higher. The crews are flexing their muscles. They're ready.*"

Ryker clicked a row of rocker switches on a nearby console. "Eyes are up." A series of monitors displayed views of the exterior Perimeter via remote cameras mounted atop the Wall.

Dion glanced up at the zone map. "Check out Lace's formation at Tremayne."

"Badass," Ryker said. "She looks ready. No notification yet."

Dion lit a cigarette. "I'm antsy. You know we're gonna lose some when this all goes down."

"I'm calling Lace," Ryker said. "That formation hasn't moved for the last five minutes." He stepped up to the console. "Lace, do you copy?"

No return through the speaker added to Dion's agitation. "Try it again."

"Lace, do you copy?" Ryker said.

"*Go ahead, Ryk,*" Lace replied.

"How's it going out there?"

"*We're almost ready. Crew's set. Just waiting on Drew to get back to me.*"

Dion frowned and tipped his chin to Ryker.

Ryker shrugged. "Copy that, Lace. We gotta get Winter off the platforms, ASAP. We don't know if anyone's feeding info to the Changers."

The radio scratched. "*Stand by.*"

"*Dion, do you copy?*" Zane radioed.

Ryker replied. "Zane, go."

"*Oh, hey, Ryk. I gotta say, it's unusually quiet out here.*"

"10-4. Can you guys see anything?"

"*Not a thing. It's driving me crazy. Not even a rabbit. Just seems strange, that's all.*"

"Okay. Stay loose."

"*We're trying.*"

"*Ryk, do you copy?*" Lace said.

"Go ahead, Lace."

"*Radio's a little scratchy. Go to channel two.*"

"I got it," Dion said. "You stay on one with Zane." He hopped into a chair behind console two and radioed Lace. "Lace, do you copy?"

"*Gotcha, Dion. Drew's having a few issues. He's getting some kind of interference. Doesn't have full control yet. I'm gonna say we're good to go while he's troubleshooting. Let's bring Winter home.*"

"10-4. Stay on two. I'll get Winter on this channel so you can monitor."

"*10-4.*"

Dion picked up his cell and tapped the speed dial. Winter's answer was swift. "*Dion.*"

"Bring it home, Win," Dion said. "Use channel two. We got Zane's crew on one."

"*Got it. We started assembling about half an hour ago. There's been some activity on the other side.*"

Dion's stomach roiled. "Tell me about it on the radio. Just get your asses outta there, ASAP." He looked down at his cell.

CALL ENDED

"*Ryk, do you copy?*" Zane's voice was unsteady.

"Zane, go," Ryker replied.

"*Seems like something's out there on the rise. We can't get anything through the infrareds, though.*"

Ryker looked at Dion. "Don't get spooked out there, buddy," Ryker said. He stepped back to check the lights on the zone map before looking at the video from the Wall cameras. "I don't see anything on the cameras."

"*Dion, do you copy?*" Lace said.

"Go ahead."

"*Drew's picking up a jamming signal or something. Whatever it is, it's blocking his access to several remote systems.*"

Dion frowned. "Is this something new?"

The radio was silent.

"Copy, Lace?"

Silence.

Ryker swiveled his chair toward Dion and raised an eyebrow.

"*Losing you, Dion.*" Lace's transmission was weak, her voice distant. "*Radio's jammed.*"

"*Ryk,*" Zane radioed.

"Go, Zane," Ryker said.

"*Seems like it just got darker out here.*"

PLATFORM ONE WAS DESERTED, SAVE for two Punks standing on the ramp by the neutral zone.

"Where'd all the Changers go, Win?" Raymond asked.

"I don't know, but I feel like a sitting duck up here." Winter cinched the strap that secured her knife to her right boot. "Are all of our people out?"

"Yep. I double-checked," Raymond said. "Pops' count was perfect for the crew. We got six to a vehicle, one hundred and twenty trucks, mostly BearCats."

Winter glanced up the ramp to the top of Platform One. "Who the hell is that?" Instinctively, she slid the AR-15 off her shoulder and faced the platform.

Raymond swiveled and matched Winter's stance. "Can't be one of ours."

A Punk wearing jeans and a leather jacket trotted down the ramp. He waved at Winter and Raymond. "Yo," he called out.

Raymond squinted. "Shit, that's Wade. I swear I saw him get in one of the last 'Cats. He musta forgot something."

"Guys," Wade said. "Don't take off yet." He jerked a thumb over his shoulder. "There's a couple more of the crew on the other side of the platform."

Winter stepped up to Wade. "I ordered everyone into the Cats thirty minutes ago, including you. What gives?"

"Aw, man," Wade said. "Just some strays. They must not have heard the order. I was rounding them up. I chewed 'em out good, though. I think we should demote—"

Wade's head jerked backward as the bullet from Winter's rifle pierced his forehead and exited the rear of his skull. He stood, swaying momentarily before pitching forward and landing face-first at Raymond's feet. Raymond stared at Winter, eyes wide, mouth open. The ensuing silence was deafening.

"Hear that?" Winter asked.

"N...no," Raymond said.

"Exactly," Winter said. "Not a peep. Where's all the strays he was talking about?"

"I don't hear a sound, Win."

The color drained from Winter's face. "Get to the truck, now!" she shouted.

The couple turned and ran down the ramp, Raymond in the lead. As Raymond hit the dirt at the bottom of the ramp, his legs wobbled. "Wha—" The explosion behind him rocked the ground at his feet. He turned around to see a massive fireball engulf the platform as Winter flew headfirst off the side of the ramp. Smoke billowed from the back of her leather vest as she skidded, face-down, through the dirt. Raymond stood stunned, his head throbbing, his vision spinning.

"Come on, come on, come on!" Raymond heard a voice shouting. The words were muffled, distant. He rubbed his eyes and ran his hands over his head and down the back of his neck. The stinging sensation he felt at the base of his skull was like a dart through his skin. *Shrapnel*, he thought as he pulled his hands away and saw the blood on his palms.

"Come on!" The voice again. Raymond looked up and saw Jasper running toward Winter, still lying on the ground. Her face was in the dirt, the strap of her AR-15 twisted grotesquely around her arm.

"We gotta get outta here," Jasper yelled.

Raymond ran toward Winter, driven mostly by instinct and adrenaline. He bent down and seized Winter under one arm while Jasper grabbed the other. The two Punks carried her to a waiting BearCat, the toes of her boots leaving a double trough in the dirt behind them. An armed Punk was waiting beside an open door at the back of the vehicle. A hand reached from the inside, grabbing a wad of the burnt leather vest, and hoisted Winter into the back.

"Get in," Jasper said.

Raymond crawled in and flopped onto the floor of the vehicle. When the door slammed, he heard Jasper slap his palm twice on the outside. He stared at the spinning ceiling. His vision blurred as the ceiling faded to black.

CHAPTER 35

Lockup

Six armed Changer guards, dressed in bright white uniforms, ran past Fred and Thomas in the circular corridor on level ten of the Underground.

"Chasing Peterson," Thomas said. "Hope she gets out. That was about as gutsy a move as I've ever seen."

"I'll agree with that," Fred said. "But we have problems of our own. My guess is we've overstayed our welcome."

"Yes. I'll never forget the look on Levi's face."

"I couldn't wait to get out of the War Room," Fred said. "But now I'm second-guessing myself. Had we waited, we'd have a better idea what his next move is."

"Or, he could have had us taken into custody."

"He could have. But he didn't give any indication he had that inclination."

Thomas furrowed his brow. "Obviously, he doesn't trust us enough to tell us we were demoted. Why would he give any forewarning about arresting us?"

"Good point," Fred said. "But we still have to get out of here."

"I agree," Thomas said. "Up top, we don't have the Chybrids to worry about. But it won't take long for the Punks to eliminate us."

"However long that takes, I just have a feeling we'll stand a better chance out there than here in the Underground."

Thomas tipped his chin up. "We may not get to find out," he said as four Changer guards stepped off the elevator and blocked the corridor.

Fred and Thomas approached the guards and attempted to step between them. "Sorry, Garrison," the ranking guard said. "You two are coming with us."

"On whose orders?" Fred asked.

"Orders from Commander Van Buren, sir."

"We hold rank over you," Fred said. "I want to talk to Van Buren before I do anything."

"I'm going to ask you once to turn around and place your hands behind your backs," the guard said. His eyes were sympathetic, having served under Fred for years. "Let's not make this any harder than necessary."

The two Rogue Changers exchanged glances. "Do what he says," Fred said. "We have no choice at this point."

"You'll have a chance to speak to Commander Van Buren momentarily," the guard said. "He's waiting at the detention center."

CHAPTER 36

One of Their Own

LACE RODE SHOTGUN IN THE Lenco BearCat as she radioed the Punks set up on the south side of Tremayne. "Margot, do you copy?"

"*Yeah, go ahead, Lace.*" Margot's voice crackled over the two-way radio speaker.

"Confirm your position. I want the BEARs on the outer periphery, BearCats to the inside."

"*We're good, Lace. BEARs are blocking ingress and egress on the backside here. We're sittin' comfy and cozy, smack-dab in the center.*"

"Copy that. You got a 10-20 on Dyer?"

"*Haven't seen him, Lace. Stringer assigned him to reconnaissance at the VIP district in town.*"

"Copy that," Lace replied. "Keep me apprised of any activity back there. I think we got a handle front of the City."

"*How's everything on the inside?*" Margot asked.

"Dead quiet. All the Bystanders are holed up in their homes, except for a few stragglers."

"*10-4.*"

Lace hung up the two-way on the dash of the armored vehicle and looked at her driver. "Take a cruise over to the VIP district."

"You got it," the driver replied as he guided the BearCat

diagonally through a downtown intersection. He glanced at Lace and smiled. "I'm lovin' the red lights. Your Bystander, Drew, seems to have a handle on the traffic signals."

Lace surveyed the buildings on both sides of the street. The structures sat silent, their darkened windows staring back, like the lifeless eyes of rows of corpses. She gazed at the pale yellow wall behind Tremayne's downtown mall as the vehicle whizzed past. She read a large sign on the wall for the umpteenth time— MALL EMPLOYEES ONLY.

The driver slowed the BearCat to make a left turn. Lace's gaze drifted to a green garbage dumpster down an alley. A stray cat surveyed the dumpster, sizing up the jump from asphalt to lid. Yesterday was garbage pickup day. When Mayor Kutch had caught wind of the Punks' intention to shut down the City, he'd ordered the City's waste management to complete its work two days early.

Before the mangy feline made its leap, the two-way radio crackled. *"Lace, Nevada. Do you copy?"*

Lace grabbed the mic. "Go ahead, Nevada."

"Go to channel seven, Lace."

Lace switched to channel seven, available only to second Level Commanders. "Go, Nevada."

"Yeah, Lace. We got the east side locked down tight. But check out channel three banter. Sounds kinetic."

"Copy that, girl," Lace said. "Changers?"

"Negative. It's our people. Stringer's your level three, 10-4?"

"He's mine. Whadda you make of it?"

"Don't know," Nevada replied. *"Sounds like an altercation with Curtis. Just check it out when you get a chance."*

"10-4. I'm headed that way now. Thanks for the heads-up."

"You got it," Nevada said. "I'm headed back to channel one."

The driver downshifted and pressed the accelerator. "You got a 10-20 on Stringer?" he asked Lace.

Lace checked her cell. "Yeah, make a right at the next street, then an immediate left. Then slow it up. I don't want them to know I'm here yet."

"You got it."

Lace tuned the radio to channel three. She caught the tail end of a transmission from Curtis. "...*negative, String. That's a bad move.*"

"*Not your call, Dyer,*" Stringer said. "*Move your squad to the Main Square, mural sector. Turn your backs toward the VIP sector and stand by. That's an order, and it's the last time I'm gonna say it.*"

Lace's driver slowed the vehicle to a stop in an alley adjacent to Stringer's position. "That's a dead sector, Lace. That order doesn't make a whole lot of sense to me."

"It's a direct order from a superior," Lace said.

"Understood," the driver nodded.

"Turn it off," Lace said. "Let's get out and have a look-see. No helmets."

The two exited the BearCat and quietly pushed their doors closed, being careful not to alert anyone who might be nearby. Lace held up her hand for silence, then motioned to the driver to follow behind her. They crept silently up the alley, hugging the red brick wall of an old two-level hardware store. At the corner, where the building met the sidewalk, Lace stopped and knelt. She pulled a scope from her tool belt and placed it near the edge of the wall. The scope confirmed Stringer's location on the street. Her left ear bud popped to life.

"*I'm headed your way.*" It was Curtis.

"*Hold your position, Dyer,*" Stringer replied.

Lace looked back at the driver, who was kneeling behind her. "Go back and get the bolt cutters," she whispered. "I'm going inside this store through that door." She motioned to a gray door in the alley. The door was secured with a padlock and hasp. The driver held up a thumb and made his way back to the vehicle.

Lace peered through her scope as she heard a vehicle approaching Stringer's position. She saw Curtis's armored van pull up next to Stringer's Humvee, parked facing the wrong direction on the street. She watched Curtis exit the van and advance toward Stringer. Their conversation was animated, but muffled. She turned to see her driver hurrying up the alley with the bolt cutters.

She met him at the door and took the tool. The lock snapped off and clinked to the ground. Lace handed the cutters to the driver.

"Take my scope and keep an eye on those two. Tune to channel one. I'll contact you there if necessary." The driver nodded.

Lace crept through the gray steel door and closed it behind her. There were no security lights inside the hardware store. Lace noticed the faint scent of mildew, mixed with damp wood and the chemical smell of paint. The wooden floor creaked under her boots as she made her way around stacks of boxes and unpacked merchandise. The only light inside the store came from the sodium vapor lights on the street, cast through the huge display windows on the front of the building. She made her way forward, through the curtains blocking the Authorized Personnel Only doorway, to the main customer area.

She knelt down behind a small display of yard decorations, sandwiched between stacks of garden hose reels and shiny galvanized trash cans. *Perfect*, she thought, grabbing a new five-gallon plastic bucket. The white bucket sported the name and slogan of the store in bold blue lettering: *Tremayne Hardware—The Highest Quality for 300 Years and Counting*. She flipped the container upside down and used it for a seat. From her position, she had a full view of the street's activity.

Lace noticed Curtis motioning his arms earnestly, arguing whatever his point was to Stringer. She spied a handle on one of the storefront windows and reached down to crank it open. The voices on the street carried through the open window, loud and clear.

"Look, String," Curtis said. "Mine is the strongest, most experienced squad you have under your command. It makes no sense to pack us into an area where absolutely nothing is happening."

"You need to learn how to follow orders, Dyer," Stringer replied. "I could have you up on charges for insubordination today. You know Dion wants you to toe the line. Besides, you never know what's going to happen, and where. You could be sitting in a hot spot right now and not even know it."

"That's not all," Curtis said. "I didn't want to broadcast this all over the radio, but you've got some shady people you're relying on right now."

"Okay," Stringer said. "I'm all ears. State your case."

"All right," Curtis began. "I've heard you barking orders to Johnny Logan. What's his rank?"

"He's front line, two steps below you. So what?"

"So you're giving Logan info on Punk positions throughout the City. He has no business knowing that. He's got a senior officer to receive orders from. Why you? Why is a level three commander giving that kind of information to a frontline troop?"

He's got a point, String, Lace thought.

"That's your argument?" Stringer was defiant.

As Lace waited for Curtis's reply, she noticed two Punks walking up the alley across the street. The two turned the corner at the sidewalk and approached Stringer. She recognized one as Johnny Logan but couldn't place the other. *This ought to be interesting,* she thought.

Curtis looked behind Stringer. "Speaking of—" he said as the two-way radio transmitter on his shoulder sounded. "*Curtis, do you copy?*" a voice crackled from the speaker.

Johnny and the other Punk stepped up to Stringer.

Curtis turned his back on the trio to answer his radio. "Go ahead."

Johnny smiled at Stringer. "We got it laid out perfect, man. All Punk positions relayed to the Underground."

Stringer waved his hands, as if doing so would force the words back into Johnny's mouth.

Curtis jerked his head away from his shoulder mic—his eyes zeroed in on Johnny.

Lace's jaw dropped. Her hand instinctively flew to her waist, unsnapping the strap from her 9mm.

The driver waiting in the alley turned and hurried toward the steel door.

Lace stood, knocking over the display of shiny trash cans inside the store.

CURTIS GLANCED PAST JOHNNY AT the other Punk. The hair on his neck bristled. *Scotty Van Buren.*

"Wait!" Stringer's attempt to wave off Johnny and Scotty became more frantic.

Curtis raised his 9mm to Stringer's temple and squeezed the trigger. Stringer's body fell, seemingly in slow motion, as Curtis turned his pistol to Johnny. He squeezed the trigger again. The bullet hit the cinder-block wall of the building on the other side of the alley as Johnny and Scotty ducked back down the darkened corridor.

Lace burst out the front door of the hardware store from across the street, gun drawn, and ran toward Curtis. Her driver followed immediately behind, AR-15 in hand.

Curtis recognized Lace and the driver and immediately held both hands up. "Lace, Stringer's a Changer," he said. "So is Logan and Scotty Van Buren."

"Good job, Curtis. I saw and heard everything from across the street."

Curtis slumped his shoulders in relief. "I'll get this mess cleaned up."

"That's a negative. You're taking Stringer's crew. Whoever's your number one under you, they'll take yours."

"Wow, thanks, Lace."

"You earned it. You'll report to Margot now. I'll get the word out. Now you can *assign* someone to clean up this mess."

Curtis smiled. "10-4, Lace. I'm on it."

The driver surveyed the alley, panning his handheld spotlight from side to side. "They're gone, Lace," he shouted.

Lace turned to her two-way. "Dion, Lace. Do you copy, Dion?"

"Lace, Jimbo. Dion's tied up. What's happening?"

"We got a situation here, Jim," Lace replied. "Get the word out—Stringer's down. Confirmed Changer. I'm field-promoting Curtis to third-level."

"Holy shit. Copy that. I'll send a global."

"10-4. Also, put an APB out on Logan. He's a Changer, too. I couldn't take him out. He was too fast. And he's with Scotty Van

Buren, the mayor's Liaison. He's a Changer as well, dressed like one of us."

"*Good job, Lace,*" Jimbo said. "*By the way, why promote Curtis? Dion's gonna want to know.*"

"Curtis took Stringer down, no hesitation. No doubt that saved the operation here in town."

"*Sounds like a good move,*" Jimbo said. "*I'll let Dion know.*"

"Copy that, Jim. Bad thing is, from what Logan said, the Changers know our locations and setup now. I'm starting a contingency layout."

"*Copy that, Lace,*" Jimbo said. "*Let us know what you need.*"

"Will do."

CHAPTER 37

Overwhelmed

OUTSIDE CHECKPOINT ONE, ONE HUNDRED Lenco Bears parked side-by-side, facing the low rise of foothills to the north. Behind the Bears, three rows of BearCats full of Punk troops sat silent. Two hundred yards of thick, muddy terrain stretched between the rear of the vehicles and the Perimeter Wall.

The telltale vibration of multiple antennae atop Zane's BearCat accompanied the mild breezing blowing in from the west. Clouds moved in to block the last remnant of starlight. A single rain-drop sliced through the darkness and landed on the windshield of the center vehicle in the fourth row. It paused momentarily before sliding down the glass and disappearing into the dark space between the two windshield wipers.

Zane squinted through an infrared biocular from the driver's seat in his BearCat. *So fuckin' dark*, he thought. He adjusted the mouthpiece on his two-way. "See that, Griff?"

"*Come again, Zane?*" Griffin's voice hissed in the earpiece.

"Swear I caught something on the rise up there, ten o'clock."

"*I'm seeing it, too, Zane. Whatever it is, it's huge.*"

"Holy shit, it's expanding. Looks like it's stretched across the whole top of the hill. What the hell is it?"

"*Got me.*"

"All units, all units, red alert."

"*Thing's growing, Zane.*"

Sweat trickled down Zane's temples as the expanding blob came into focus. "All units, battle positions."

Floodlights on the front row of Lenco BEARs clicked on in sync, illuminating the base of the small hill. Roof hatches flew open in sync with side doors on the BEARs. Punks in BDUs piled out of the vehicles and took up positions behind the armored doors. Zane's heart pounded in his ears. He felt the blood rush from his face as he dropped the biocular between the seats. *Mutants.* He knew if he spoke the word aloud, his voice would shake.

"*Zane, do you copy? Zane, do you copy?*" Griffin's voice was frantic but firm.

Zane wiped his hand across his forehead after the sweat hit his eyes. He felt a hand on his shoulder—his partner, riding shotgun. "Fuckin' mutants, Zane. But badass. They're refined, upgraded." He gazed out the front window of the vehicle. "And fast."

"*Zane, do you copy?*" Griffin radioed. "*We need orders.*"

Zane realized the T-shirt under his jacket was soaking wet as he spoke into the mic. The words came as if by instinct. "All units, fire at will."

High-powered spotlights on top of the Wall sprang to life, their beams cutting through the pitch with razor-sharpness. The full extent of the onslaught was now crystal-clear in Zane's mind. His muscles tensed as sporadic pops from AR-15s began. Within seconds, the air filled with simultaneous gunfire from five hundred Punks on the front line.

"Griff, do you copy?" Zane said. "There's thousands of them."

"*At least two thousand,*" Griffin shouted. "*We need more firepower up here.*"

Nonstop noise from the barrage filled the air. "All second-line units, move up," Zane announced over the radio. Punks poured out of the second row of BearCats, taking up positions adjacent to the troops on the front line.

The swarm of Chybrids moved swiftly, unfazed by the onslaught of bullets. Their arrowhead-shaped formation struck the lead Punk vehicle, rocking the BEAR backwards. The driver pushed the brake pedal to the floor as the weight of the Chybrids forced the vehicle into the BearCat in the second row. Punk troops behind the doors fell to the ground. The relentless hoard of mutants stomped across the prone Punks and slammed into the third row.

"*Our guns are useless, Zane!*" Griffin shouted.

Zane scrambled between the seats and hoisted himself up through the roof hatch. He screamed into the mic. "All units, fire, fire, fire!"

The wall of sound from this vantage point vibrated his body to the bone. Punks from the first three rows of vehicles fired their weapons incessantly against the tireless Chybrids. The sound of clanking steel from the Chybrid claws and teeth mixed with the screech of tearing metal as the creatures ripped the opened vehicle doors from their hinges. Zane saw his brothers in arms racing backward to put space between themselves and the mutants.

He watched in horror from the fourth row of vehicles as the Chybrids continued their assault on his troops in the front. Tears of rage filled his eyes as the orange mist of blood drifted from between the armored trucks and filled the air. Punks ripped out from under vehicles became fodder for the humanoid creatures.

"Zane, do you copy? Zane, do you copy?" Griffin radioed. "I'm calling my crew in. Our rifles are doing nothing."

"10-4, Griff," Zane shouted. "All units, all units, scramble Snake Eyes. Repeat, scramble Snake Eyes."

FROM INSIDE THE DEPOT, DION fixed on the monitors. The rising smoke, the screams, the furious din of the ineffective firearms boiled his blood. He broke his gaze and turned to Ryker. "They're scrambling."

"Yeah," Ryker said. "I see that."

"Where's Will?" Dion demanded. "I need to talk to him, now."

"He's in the Hangar with Pops." Ryker pressed the intercom button. "Pops, you there?"

"*We're here, Ryk.*"

"Send Will to the Depot," Ryker said.

"*Gotcha. He's on his way.*"

THE THREE AMIGOS BURST INTO the Depot through the door leading to the outside compound. Dion wheeled around from the main console. "Will, I need some info fast."

"We're down for anything," Will said. "What do you need to know, and how can we help?"

"When you guys were at the abandoned outpost on the east side." Dion's voice quavered. "I need to know if there's anything Krystal said that you didn't tell us. Maybe something you forgot, or something that didn't seem important. I need something. Punks are dying out there."

Will looked up at the monitors. He saw Chybrids, thousands of them, on every screen. He saw the Punks' vehicles moving across the battlefield, scattering in different directions. He saw the bodies and body parts of fallen Punk troops. Armored vehicles plowed over Chybrids as they bounced away over the uneven terrain.

"Will," Ryker said, snapping the new young Punk from his trance.

The two-way radio crackled over the ceiling speakers. "*Dion, Lace. Do you copy?*"

Jimbo answered the radio. "Stand by, Lace."

"*Copy that, Jim. We're catching the action on channel one. Sounds like Zane's got his hands full. We're ready to move on your orders.*"

"10-4, Lace. All units, stand by."

Lace, Nevada and Margot all replied in the affirmative.

"What about Winter?" Will asked.

Dion held up a hand. "Awesome that you're on top of the activity. I need an answer to my question. I need to know everything Krystal said to you, no matter how insignificant it might seem."

Will's eyes darted between Dion and Ryker. "Okay, remember she said a single bullet to the head won't kill them. These are like super Chybrids."

"I remember," Dion said. "Knowing that, our plan was to use

an overwhelming response, like five to ten bullets instead of our usual one."

"Obviously, that didn't work," Ryker said. "Think, Will. Did she say anything else?"

"Yeah," Dion agreed. "Even if she said anything that didn't sound related to the Chybrids."

Will stared at the floor, slowly shaking his head. "Wait," he said, looking up. "Adam, she asked us if we knew someone. Not Curtis, but someone else."

"Yeah," Adam said. "Fred something."

Will snapped his fingers. "Garrison! Fred Garrison."

"Doesn't ring a bell," Ryker said.

"For me either," Jimbo agreed.

"What did she say about this guy?" Dion asked.

"Nothing," Will said. "When we said we didn't know him, she just kinda dropped the subject."

Dion looked at Ryker. "What do you think?"

Ryker shook his head. "Not much to go on."

"There was one other thing," Adam said. He looked at Will. "Remember, she said not all the Changers are bad. Right after that, she asked if we knew that guy."

"True," Will said. "Maybe he's a Changer that's not bad."

"I've never met a Changer I didn't hate," Jimbo said.

"Me either," Ryker agreed.

Dion folded his arms across his chest. "I agree. But what if it means something? I mean, putting two and two together, it makes sense that this Fred character is one of the 'not bad' Changers."

"If there is such a thing," Jimbo said.

"Let's assume two and two is four," Ryker said. "Where do we find this guy?"

"The Changers' Underground City?" Dion asked. "And if so—"

"How do we get to him?" Ryker finished Dion's thought.

Dion looked at Will. Will looked at the other two Amigos and smiled.

"Wait a minute," Dion said. "You're not thinking—"

Ryker couldn't help but smile, too. "If anyone can do it, it's these guys."

"I'm not approving that." Dion shook his head. "You guys aren't going to the Changers' Underground."

Will puffed up. "You can't stop us. But you can at least have our backs."

"Yep." Joey nodded. "We'll get in."

"Watch us," Adam said.

"DION, WINTER. DO YOU COPY?"

Jimbo was at the two-way. "Go, Winter."

"We're surrounded by mutants."

"Copy that, Win. Stay in your vehicles. Our weapons won't stop them. Did you catch Zane's banter at Checkpoint One?"

"Heard it all."

"Then you know the mutants will tear through the vehicles eventually. I'm hoping shelter in the trucks will buy some time for us to get help your way."

"10-4, Jim."

CHAPTER 38

Underground Interlopers

THE THREE AMIGOS ROARED EASTWARD on Interstate 10 through the Southern California desert. Against Dion's better judgment, Ryker had procured a fully battle-equipped armored Humvee for the boys. It wasn't so much that none of the three was old enough to drive, or that they were not battle-hardened. Dion felt it was a sure mission of death. Even if they somehow made it into the Underground, there was the issue of finding Fred Garrison and then getting back out safely.

The trio remained unfazed. Confidence in their own abilities and resourcefulness far outweighed any danger that might lie ahead. Having discovered the Changers' entrance to the Underground on one of many previous expeditions, they knew where they were going. The Humvee didn't facilitate this latest expedition, it merely enhanced it.

The Humvee sported 'Punk Security' decals on all sides, preventing questions or unnecessary traffic stops by local fat-bellied sheriffs or rednecks along the way.

High clouds provided cover for the moon and stars. The strong winds gave hint that the forecast rain storm was inevitable. However, nothing dampened the Three Amigos' disposition. This was their chance to make their impression, to solidify their standing in the Punks' organization.

"We're making good time, guys." Will glanced down at the speedometer. "Holy cow, we're doing over a hundred. This sucker is one smooth ride."

Adam was anxious. "I can't wait till we get there."

"Yeah," Joey agreed. "I can't wait to see what that place looks like inside."

"We're really winging it here," Will said. "You know they're gonna have some kind of security."

"Not outside," Joey said. "We've seen those mothers hop down into that hole with no one else around."

"Sure," Will agreed. "What we haven't seen is if they have any kind of keyless entry device while they're doing it. I mean, jumping down into that tunnel, or whatever it is, is one thing. But we don't know if it opens based on some security clearance, or if it's just open."

"Yeah." Adam laughed. "After all this time, we missed the 'Open to the Public' sign."

Radio banter from Checkpoint One dampened the boys' chatter. "It's hard to forget what's happening back home," Will said.

Joey gazed out the windshield. "Turnoff's coming up."

Will slowed the Humvee and took an old freeway off-ramp to access Highway 95, north. He sped through what was previously a small desert town known as Blythe. Stop signs meant nothing. Old traffic signals were useless since there was no commercial power provided to the little community.

"Bummer about this town," Joey observed.

"Yeah," Will agreed. "The place finally went to shit several years ago. Got left outside the Perimeter when they built the Wall."

Adam shook his head. "One of many. Pops said they herded Bystanders from little towns like this inside the Perimeter. It was either move or die."

Ten minutes north of Blythe, Will braked to turn west onto a dirt road. "Infrared goggles, guys," he said as he flipped off the vehicle lights. The friends rode in silence for about two miles before Will stopped the vehicle near a small group of rocky foothills. "This is about as close as we get," he whispered. "No activity doesn't mean we haven't been seen. I say the quicker we get to cover, the better."

A cold breeze hit the boys when they exited the Humvee. They donned their windbreakers and lightweight utility belts.

"Okay, guys," Will said. "Might as well leave the goggles here, but make sure you have your sunglasses." He looked at his friends and held out his hand, palm down, between them. Joey placed his hand on Will's. Adam followed suit, placing his hand on Joey's.

"All right," Adam said. "This is the hugest mission we've ever done. We're winging it. Let's do what we do best!" The Three Amigos nodded in silence and broke the circle. Will turned and led the trio toward the foothills.

The friends walked in silence up a low rise of randomly strewn rocks. Will held up his hand as he approached a small smoke tree bush adjacent to a large mound of jagged boulders. A hinge secured the bush to a rock base. He tilted the bush to one side, revealing a triangular opening in the rocks, wide enough to accommodate a large adult. The base of the opening was about two feet off the ground, with one tip of the triangle pointed downward.

"Well, there you go," Adam said.

There was a small ledge on the rock, about three inches above the opening. The ledge ran parallel to the opening, providing a convenient grab handle. Will shined his flashlight into the opening, revealing a downward-sloped shaft. The slick triangular shaft ended about eight feet in and appeared to dump into a hole. Just beyond the hole at the end of the opening was a wall of rock.

"I'm going in," Will whispered. He grabbed the rock ledge above the opening, leaned back and placed one foot into the opening. He hopped up, swung his other foot in and assumed a sitting position, facing into the darkness. He squinted at the black that touched his boots and scooted down into the shaft on his back.

When he had wormed his way down to the back wall, Will

stopped and pulled out his flashlight. He let his legs dangle into the opening in the floor. There was enough room in the three-sided shaft to swing around and shine his light down past his boots. About six feet below was another floor. He pointed his flashlight back toward the opening.

"Guys," he whispered loudly.

"Yeah?" Adam shined his flashlight toward Will.

"I'm going down and take a look."

"Do it."

Will left his flashlight on and placed it on his belt, beam down. He scooted as far into the opening as he could and braced himself on the rock wall before hopping down into the hole.

Adam held his beam fast and watched Will's head disappear below the edge of the triangular shaft.

When Will dropped, the floor gave under his weight. It bounced slightly like a springboard. The little room was like a rock cylinder. He knew four adults would fit, even if not comfortably. He grabbed his flashlight and pointed the beam around the tiny space. He found a gray aluminum lever in the up position on the floor. He held his flashlight up and clicked it off and on.

"Okay, Joe," Adam whispered. "There's the signal. Follow me down."

"Gotcha."

Adam mimicked Will's moves and made his way through the shaft. When his feet hit the opening at the end, Will grabbed his boots. "Hold up, dude. I'll guide your feet."

Joey followed Adam and the trio stood silently, panning their flashlights around the tiny, cylindrical room. "So, here's a lever," Will said. "I say, down is *down*."

"Yep," Joey agreed. "Let's go."

Will pushed the lever down. "Okay, everybody put your shades on." The spring-loaded device returned to its former position after emitting a soft click.

Immediately, the cylinder began its descent. The rock wall remained in place as the floor dropped. The boys found themselves standing in a cylindrical room of polished metal. The rock wall that was visible from above was merely a facade to hide the metal walls of the cylinder. They watched the triangular opening above disappear from view in the darkness. A glass-like ceiling slid over the opening, enclosing the capsule and silencing the wind noise from the elevator's descent. Within seconds, the elevator rushed downward at a rate of speed that caught the trio off guard. A soft amber glow formed around the perimeter of the floor. Just enough light shone for the boys to become accustomed to the darkness and see each other's faces.

"Awesome," Joey commented.

"And scary," Adam said.

"Yeah," Will agreed. "What are we headed into?" He estimated about fifteen seconds had elapsed before the elevator slowed to a stop. A curved doorway clicked open and slid around the outside of the elevator, revealing a long, dimly lit corridor. The gritty granite-mix rock floor sloped gently downward, becoming more smooth and polished as it advanced. The boys stepped into the corridor. They heard the doors slide shut behind them, followed by a soft *whoosh* as the elevator began the ascent to its original position above.

"Now what?" Joey asked.

Adam walked a few steps into the corridor. "It's a one-way street, guys."

"All right, then," Will agreed. "Here we go."

The three friends walked silently down the corridor until they came to the tinted glass wall blocking the corridor. The wall had a seam in the center where a closed glass door rested against the control booth. "Now, what? Knock on the door?" whispered Joey.

"Well, there's a button next to that intercom on the wall," Will said.

Adam had his ear pressed against the glass door. "Shit, I hear voices."

Joey glanced up at a camera on the ceiling. "We're on TV."

"If that door opens, just be cool and walk in," Will said.

When the door slid open into the adjacent wall, the boys saw a well-dressed company of individuals forming an involuntary blockade of their path to the inside. Will and Joey hurried through the opening. The group of people split to make room for the two to pass.

When Adam entered, a man in his midtwenties put his hand on Adam's chest. Adam attempted to brush off the gesture and go around the man.

"Excuse me," the man said. "Don't I know you?"

Adam stopped. "Um, ahem," Adam cleared his throat. "Yes, I believe so. Were you at the, uh, the Tremayne convention, uh, thing, the other night?"

"Oh, the Tremayne episode?"

"Yes! That's it, the *episode*. The Tremayne episode."

The man smiled. "Of course. I think I saw you at the park that night. You were hanging out with some other teenyboppers. I assumed your assignment was in Tremayne. So what brings you to the Underground?"

Adam was on his game now. "Garrison. Personal invitation from Fred Garrison."

"Oh?" The man stopped smiling. "Apologies for the inquisition. I meant no offense."

"And these are my friends. They're here at Garrison's request as well."

The man, and several others in the group, eyed Will and Joey. "Oh, hello," he said. "Well, uh, carry on. I mean, I didn't know."

Adam smiled. "What was your name? I'll ask Garrison if he knows you."

"Wait, uh, he doesn't know me. I mean, he wouldn't know."

The group of people nervously separated, ever so slightly, from the man.

One of the young women in the group took a step toward Joey. "Why don't you tell us your name, little guy?"

"Excuse me?" Adam raised his voice. "I don't think anyone addressed you. We're headed to see Garrison now. If you think you're somebody, let's see if you even know where he is."

"What?" The woman was taken aback by Adam's tone. "What do you mean?"

Adam approached the woman. He tilted his chin up to meet

her eyes. "You seem a little suspicious to me. Let's see if you can tell us where Garrison's, uh—"

The man tried to be helpful. "His quarters?"

"Yes," Adam said. Through his sunglasses, he kept his eyes locked on the woman's. "Yes, Miss Know-It-All. Where are Garrison's quarters?"

"It's…it's…room 3300." She looked around at the crowd of people. "You all know I know this." She turned to Adam. "I'm sorry, really. It's room 3300."

"Yes, you're correct," Adam agreed. "It's room 3300. But everyone knows that. So let's see if you belong here. Can you even tell me how to get there from here?"

"Of course I know that." The group eyed their companion suspiciously. "You take any elevator to the third level. Then follow the signs. You know that. I mean *I* know that."

"What's your name?" Adam asked. "I'll give your regards to Garrison."

"No, please, that won't be necessary," the woman pleaded. "And my apologies for any doubt—"

Adam held up his hand. "Just don't let it happen again. Go on about your business and I won't mention a word of this to Garrison."

"Thank you, sir," the woman nodded.

"Yes," the young man agreed. "Thank you, sir."

Adam eyed the crowd. "I won't say anything if you don't." He walked briskly past Will and Joey. "Let's go."

The small crowd parted and watched Will and Joey follow Adam around the corner of the corridor. The trio stopped at a set of elevator doors.

"Ballsy move, dude," Will whispered.

"Look." Adam held out his hand.

"Dang," Joey said. "You're shaking bad."

Adam smiled. "Yeah. Hope I don't have to do that again real soon."

Will removed his sunglasses and pressed the elevator button on the wall. The only direction was *down*. He watched the numbers on the lighted panel above the elevator doors. The numbers decreased as the elevator rose to the first level. He wondered why it hadn't occurred to him that this was the logical direction for an elevator in an underground complex.

When the doors opened, the boys noticed a man in a white lab coat standing in a back corner of the elevator. The man was oblivious to the three friends when they stepped in. Staring at the floor, he was lost in thought. Will quickly selected level three and pressed the button.

The Three Amigos stood with their backs to the man in the white coat, as if not looking at him would prevent his seeing them.

"Oh, hello." The man looked up. Without turning around, the boys watched the man's face, reflected in the highly polished doors inside the elevator. "I don't believe I've seen you boys here. Are you new?"

Taking a lesson from their earlier encounter in the hallway, Will thought it best to meet the challenge head-on. He turned around to face the man. "Yes, we're new." He held out his hand. "I'm Will. These are my friends, Adam and Joey."

The man took Will's hand and stepped closer. He leaned down and stared into Will's eyes above his black-rimmed spectacles. "Oh!"

Will attempted to end the uncomfortable handshake, but the man persisted. "Like I said, I'm Will. And who are you?"

The man let go of Will's hand and reached past him, between Adam and Joey. He placed his hand on a palm reader next to the control panel, then pressed a red button. The elevator slowed to a stop, but the doors remained closed. He stepped back to his original position in the corner of the elevator and crossed his arms in front of him. He took a deep, abrupt breath and slowly emptied his lungs.

"I'm Doctor Felix Yaz. And you're not Changers."

Will shot a look over his shoulder at Adam and Joey. He noticed their sunglasses were still on. He turned back to face Felix. "I...we—"

Felix held up his hand. "Do you realize, fellows, this is an offense punishable by death?"

The boys remained speechless, their machismo drained. Will's eyes darted rapidly at every nook and cranny in the elevator—the ceiling, the floor, the walls. *There must be a way out.* His muscles tensed.

"There is no exit but the one behind you, young man," Felix said. "It's time for you to answer some questions."

Will knew he looked pale. He felt his skin turn clammy as he fought to keep his knees from shaking. He wasn't as successful with his speech. He blurted out the only two words floating around in his head. "F-F-Fred G-G-Garrison."

Felix raised an eyebrow. "Hmm…"

Will suspected he had hit a nerve with the doctor, but his speech continued to fail him. He opened his mouth, but his hyperventilating prevented words.

"What about him?" Felix asked.

"Wha…" Will managed.

"What about Fred Garrison?" Felix said. "You brought him up. So, what about him? How do you know him?"

Adam stepped forward. He swallowed hard. "Actually, sir, we've never met him. We were told he might be able to help us."

"Now who on earth would have told you that?"

Adam looked at Will—no help there. "You don't know us, and we don't know you. I'm afraid if I tell you where we got his name, we may get someone in trouble."

Felix uncrossed his arms and moved his hands to the pockets of his lab coat. "Let us get a few issues out in the open, my friends. May I call you my friends?"

Will and Adam looked at each other.

"Yes," Joey said. "Call us friends. We mean no harm."

"This is a good start," Felix said. "Let's play a little game. I mean, we have time, no?" Felix took two steps toward the boys. Imperceptibly, Adam and Will flinched. Joey kept his eyes on Felix and leaned against the slick elevator doors.

Will found his voice. "Sure, why not."

Felix nodded once, bending at the waist. "Splendid!" He crossed his left arm over his chest and rested his right elbow in his left hand. He stroked his chin while pacing back and forth across the back wall of the elevator. "Here are the rules, my friends. I'm going to give you one fact—one single fact—about myself. I would consider that I am exposing myself greatly here. Although given the fact that none of you are Changers, obviously I hold all the cards, so to speak." He stopped pacing and looked up at the boys.

The Three Amigos watched Felix's every move. The sudden cessation of his steps and change in his posture startled the three. They stared at the doctor while he stood motionless in front of them, staring back.

Felix raised his eyebrows. "Well?"

"Well, what?" Adam asked.

Felix slung his head backward, nose pointed at the ceiling, eyes closed. Making no attempt to hide his exasperation, he sighed. "The *rules*. Do you agree to the *rules*?"

Adam frowned. "What *rules*? That you're going to give us one fact—*one single fact*—about yourself? That's *a* rule. *One rule.* That's not *rules*. What else is there?"

Felix looked down at the boys. "Huh? One rule? Oh, yes! I'm going to give you one fact about myself, then you tell me everything about yourselves—why you're here, how you got into the Underground…" He waved his hand in a circular motion. "All that stuff there."

The trio shrugged. Knowing they had nothing to lose, Adam said, "Sure."

Felix repeated his exaggerated nod. "Good, good!" He clasped his hands behind his back and resumed his pacing. "Now, fact one: Fred Garrison is a close friend of mine." He spun on his heel and stopped, holding up an index finger. "Not like the three of you and I are friends. We—we four"—he motioned back and forth—"we're just casual friends. Mr. Garrison is a dear friend of mine. Now it's your turn."

Will's shoulders dropped. "All right." He knew the possibility remained they were as good as dead. Might as well put it all on the table. He eyed Adam and Joey. "We're with the Punks. Right now, back in Tremayne, at the Perimeter, we're under attack by Changers. They sent these things called Chybrids. They're creaming us; our bullets aren't stopping them. Recently, we talked to someone named Krystal Peterson. She warned us this was going to happen. When we talked to her, she mentioned Fred Garrison, but since we didn't know him, she didn't say anything about him." Will wiped a hand across his forehead. "So we came here looking for Fred Garrison." He glanced at his friends and shrugged. "That's about it."

"Well, well," Felix said. "I commend you for your honesty. And I can help. I would tell you it's going to be dangerous, but the fact you're here reveals to me that it wouldn't bother you knowing this. Nevertheless, I must tell you, Mr. Garrison is currently in lockup. That is to say, he's been arrested by the Changers' leadership. Coincidentally, you have interrupted my visit to Mr. Garrison. I was on my way when you stepped into this elevator."

Adam's eyes widened. "You mean we'll be able to talk to him?"

Felix took a deep breath. "Of course you will." He reached between the boys again and restarted the elevator. He canceled the level three destination on the keypad and smiled. "We're going to level nine."

Within seconds, the elevator glided to a smooth stop and the doors opened. Felix stepped out and stood in the corridor. He turned to face the Three Amigos. "Well? Come out. You're safe. You're with me."

The trio followed Doctor Yaz down the wide hallway. Will noticed this level was not nearly as well lit as level one. However, black spheres staring down like lifeless eyes reminded him their every move was still under scrutiny. He relied on the doctor's sketchy assurance—*"You're safe with me"*—to assuage his fears.

When they approached the level nine lockup, four guards confronted Felix. The guard in charge greeted the doctor, blocking his path. "Good evening, sir."

Felix stopped, hands in his lab coat pockets. "Okay, you'll move now."

"Apologies, sir," the guard said. "No entrance at this time. Orders from Commander Long."

Felix stepped up to the guard. He gazed into the guard's eyes. The man looked down, keeping his head facing forward. "You'll move now," Felix repeated.

"Sir." The guard stepped aside, allowing the four to pass.

Felix approached two security guards outside the door to level nine lockup. The two officers stepped in front of the door, blocking the doctor's entry.

Felix rolled his eyes. "Move aside."

"Sir, we have been ordered to restrict entry to all personnel."

Felix fluttered his eyes and sighed. "Yes, yes. Both of you come here."

The guards moved together, shoulders touching, and stared down at Felix. "Now look into my eyes," Felix said. The guards complied.

"I want you both to take a ten-minute break. Join your comrades down the corridor. Tell them it is also break time for them."

"Yes, sir."

As the guards moved past Felix and the boys, the doctor turned and held up an index finger. "Oh, guard?"

The lead guard stopped. "Sir?"

"Make it fifteen minutes," Felix said. "And when you return, just forget about all this."

"As you wish, sir."

"Putty in my hands," Felix said as he used a wall-mounted palm reader to let himself into the foyer of the cell block. The boys followed him in.

Will surveyed the area. There was an unmanned console with a control board and—he estimated—about twenty monitors on the wall. To the right was a narrow hallway leading to holding cells for the City's prisoners.

Felix walked to the first cell block and peered in through the small window in the door. He smiled and waved.

The boys watched from the foyer as Fred's face appeared in the window from inside the cell.

"Good-looking guy," Adam whispered to Joey.

"Of course he is," Joey said. "He's a Changer—he can look

however he wants. They all choose *handsome* or *pretty* because they're nerdy-looking in their normal state."

Adam suppressed a chuckle. "So are we, nerd!"

"Yeah, but we're accepted—at least by the Punks we are. And we don't have to take lives or be loyal to a scumbag organization like the Changers to feel accepted."

"Yeah, good points," Adam agreed. "You're still a nerd!"

Will watched Felix unlock the first two cell doors, releasing two prisoners.

"Fred, Thomas," Felix said matter-of-factly, "you'll have to leave the Underground."

Thomas looked past Felix at the Three Amigos. "Who are these characters?"

Felix turned slightly and motioned to the boys. "Will, Adam and Joey, meet Fred and Thomas. I can vouch for you all."

"We'll take your word for it," Fred said.

Felix inhaled deeply. "Now get along with each other. You will need to work closely together." He exhaled.

"I believe we will," Fred agreed.

"This is quite the impromptu team," Felix said to Fred. "Use the elevator on level one by the South Supply Room for your escape. I've made arrangements with the guard at the security checkpoint. There will be no resistance from her." He looked at Will. "These new friends of ours will escort you to safety once you are all on the surface."

"Is there even a plan after that?" Fred asked.

Thomas eyed one of the monitors above the control panel. "We gotta go. Security is returning."

Felix closed his eyes and waved off the threat. "Ignore the guards. Beyond that, getting to where you need to go is up to you once you get to the surface. Contact me only if necessary."

Fred shrugged. "Let's go, then."

The group exited the lockup. Six security personnel stood in a loose group, blocking the corridor. Fred led the friends through the small faction of guards. Two of them glanced up, disinterested, as the newly formed team of Rogue Changers and Punks passed by.

The team hurried down the corridor toward the nearest elevator. They rode up to level one, exited the elevator and ran five abreast through the wide passageway.

Fred held up his hand and slowed the group to a fast walk. When they rounded the corner, Will and the other Amigos stopped.

"Okay," Will said. "So what's that big black wall up there?"

"It's the security checkpoint Dr. Yaz referred to. The one where he said he had made arrangements with the guard."

"So how do we get past?"

Fred looked at Thomas. "Well, procedure calls for a voice or retina scan, both directions. Let's see what happens."

When the five reached the black wall, a door slid into the adjacent wall, exposing the hallway on the other side. Fred stepped through, followed by the others. The door closed behind them.

"Well, that was easy," Adam said.

The group hurried past the South Supply Room. When they reached the elevator at the South Entry Portal, Thomas moved to slide his hand into a palm reader to activate the elevator.

Fred grabbed Thomas's arm. "Wait. I'm sure our security codes and IDs are flagged. They'll be all over us. Felix specified this exit. Let's give it a shot without clearance."

Thomas shrugged. "Here's to Dr. Yaz." He pressed the UP arrow. A red light on the panel above the elevator doors flashed three times. Thomas's scalp bristled.

The elevator descended. Less than a minute later, the team ascended to the desert floor.

CHAPTER 39

Platforms Destroyed

WINTER STOOD BEHIND THE FRONT seats of her Lenco BearCat, her upper torso exposed through the roof hatch. Unfazed by the light drizzle, she surveyed the throng of Chybrids surrounding her team of one hundred and ten armored vehicles. She glanced to her left. Raymond had assumed the same position in his vehicle next to her.

"Whadda you make of this, Ray? We're going on two hours and those fuckers are just standing there staring at us."

"It's like they're waiting for us to make the first move or something."

"Or waiting for orders."

"That'd be more like it, I guess," Raymond said. "Damn Changers are all about technology."

Winter shifted her position and adjusted her utility belt. "Yep." Her eyes glazed. "Ever wonder what things would be like if the Punks never stood up to them? I mean, what if we were all like the Bystanders—relying on the Changers to dictate our every move?"

Raymond looked at Winter. "I dunno, man. Those people don't seem to have a care in the world."

"You mean the Bystanders? They're oblivious. They admire the Changers and all the technology. They spend their days staring at video screens—cells, tablets, laptops, holographic displays. They communicate with each other almost exclusively through electronics."

"True that," Raymond agreed.

Winter shook her head slowly. "They get off work—if you can call it that—only to go home and stare at another screen. Shit, they send text messages to family members in the same house."

"So, like, where's the family time?"

"Exactly what I'm saying. So we'd all be the same. Sitting around in our living rooms or bedrooms, zoning on some artificial being on a screen, waiting for the least lazy person in the house to bring us something to eat."

Raymond scoffed. "Or we'd just order food online and have some nameless AI deliver it to us."

"Kinda makes you appreciate hanging out with real people at Checkpoint One."

"You got that right."

The two-way radio crackled to life in Winter's headset. "*Winter, Jasper. Do you copy?*"

"Go, Jasper."

"*All seven main platforms are destroyed. We'd be doing some major construction on all of 'em, if we rebuild.*"

"Copy that, buddy."

"*What's your situation, Win? I got ten trucks to bring home.*"

"Have you heard the traffic from Checkpoint One?"

"*Heard it,*" Jasper replied. "*Some heavy shit.*"

"We're the same here. Surrounded by Chybrids. They haven't made a move on us yet."

"*Sounds like it sucks there, too,*" Jasper said. "*How do you want us to proceed?*"

"We're blocked in. I don't know what would happen if you guys came into this mess right now. I'm gonna send you guys to Tremayne. Hook up with Lace when you get there."

"*10-4. What's the situation in Tremayne?*"

"Lace is repositioning. Stringer's dead. Curtis is promoted to third-level."

"*Damn.*"

"Contact me when you get in. Just want to know you guys are safe."

"*10-4, Win.*"

AT CHECKPOINT ONE, DION AND Ryker assessed the situation outside the Wall on the monitors inside the Depot. Drizzle from the latest storm continued to choke visibility for the Punks as the battlefield turned to mush. Lenco BearCats continued their scramble, led in packs by the Lenco BEARs.

"Nice scramble," Dion noted.

Ryker stood in the middle of the room, arms folded across his chest. "Snake Eyes was the right call."

Jimbo sat in front of the communications console. He leaned his chair back, checking the monitors. "Those guys are badasses." He watched the vehicles, front and center of the massive Perimeter gate, moving over the rough terrain in two perfectly synchronized, unbroken circles. Chybrids trapped inside the circles continued their charge against the hard, steel vehicles, fighting to tear through to the soft targets inside. All roof hatches were closed. The mechanical creatures slammed against the vehicle doors and windows. Chybrids bounced off one vehicle, only to be run over by the next one in line, and the next.

The seemingly endless horde appeared to have reached its limit. All the Chybrids were in the expansive battle zone—the sprawling flatland between the Wall on one side and the rolling hills on the other. Chybrids outside the moving barrier of vehicles fared no better, unable to keep pace or hang on. The Snake Eyes strategy was working.

"Zane's got it under control now," Dion agreed. "Chybrids aren't keeping up."

Ryker shook his head. "Go, Zane."

"Yeah, we're not sitting ducks anymore." Dion looked away

from the monitors and ran his hand over his head. "Can't believe I didn't see this coming."

Ryker took his eyes off the monitors and turned to Dion. "But we did, man. We were warned. Krystal said our ARs wouldn't stop them."

"A single bullet to the head. She said a single bullet..." Dion's voice faded. "Those bodies out there..." His eyes moistened. "Those lives are on me."

"On us, man. We share it." Ryker pointed at the door leading to the Hangar. "Everyone in that room heard what Will and the other Amigos told us. We all heard Krystal's warning about these Chybrids."

Jimbo swiveled his head toward Dion and Ryker. "Hey, guys. They're breaking formation."

"Yep," Dion agreed. "Taking them away from the Perimeter."

The number one vehicle in each eye broke the circle, leading the other trucks in a centipede formation toward the hills. One line headed northeast, the other northwest. Each long line broke off to form two. The four sets of armored vehicles pulled to a stop, resting in two double-line V-shaped formations about a quarter of a mile from the Wall.

Dion lit a cigarette. "Chybrids are confused. Look at that."

"Yeah, they're just standing there," Ryker said.

Jimbo stood next to the communications console. "Zane, Jim. Do you copy?"

"*Go, Jim.*"

"What's the plan?"

"*Not sure, man. These things are tough. We had to do something. I figured the best bet was to break up and try to get these mothers away from the Wall. If we can lure them out, we can outrun 'em when we hit pavement.*"

"Copy that. We're watching the monitors. Chybrids are frozen right now. They're not coming after you guys."

The downed Chybrids stood slowly, facing whatever random direction they were when they hit the ground.

"They're just standing there," Ryker observed.

The three Punks homed in on the monitors. The Chybrids on the battlefield remained still as drizzle from the low clouds trickled down their shiny white forms. LEDs inside their eye sockets glowed different colors—blue, violet, red.

Dion's brow furrowed. "Check it out. The ones with red eyes are turning this way."

The blue LEDs blinked slowly as they changed to violet. The violet LEDs blinked faster and changed to red. As the LEDs changed to red, the Chybrids turned in place to face the Perimeter Wall.

"Holy shit," Jimbo said. "Are they coming this way?"

Ryker turned to Dion. "They can't breach this Wall."

Zane's voice crackled over the ceiling speaker. *"Jim, do you copy? What's happening?"*

"Stand by, Zane."

Dion bolted to the intercom on the control panel. "Pops, you there?"

"I'm here."

"Evacuate everyone from the compound into the Tunnels."

Dion looked at Ryker and Jimbo. "Those Chybrids are remote-controlled. Check it out. I'd bet my life those blinking LEDs indicate they're receiving some kind of reprogramming signal."

"You may be right, bro. They're turning now," Ryker said.

Jimbo's eyes widened. "And they're headed this way."

CHAPTER 40

Krystal and Felix

K RYSTAL DUCKED INTO THE SMALL supply room on level three in the Underground. She flipped the light switch down. In the corridor outside, she heard the familiar sound of boots on the polished floor. *Security.* She estimated there were at least six. They were running.

She slipped into a corner of the tiny room and squatted behind a rolling cart. She stared down at her feet. A sliver of light shone in from the hallway. She wiggled her toes, exposed through the top layer of her once-cool creepers. Her nostrils flared as she bristled at the puke-inducing scent—cleaning solution, damp towels, soiled from a day's worth of work in the community restrooms, and cherry-vanilla air freshener. She stifled a gag, then held her breath as the light dimmed.

One of the security guards had stopped to peer through the narrow vertical window in the door. *So what if they find me?* she thought. *Put me in the Arena. Torture me, motherfuckers. I'm better than you are. You can take my life, but you can't have the real me. Not ever again. I'm me, and that means I win—losers.*

The light shone again on her feet as she heard a muffled voice in the corridor. "All clear."

Krystal waited until she heard the footsteps fade around the corner. She pushed the cart away and stood up in the darkness. Moving silently to the door, she pushed the handle down slowly and opened the door, just a crack. No one coming. No sound. She opened the door just enough to slip through sideways and stepped out into the bright corridor. *Gotta get to Fred*, she thought. *I know they're tracking me.* With no other choice, she hurried down the corridor toward room 3300. *Can't believe I haven't run into anyone. Wonder if they're on some kind of lockdown.* She knew her walk was awkward. Her feet slipped randomly inside her shoes. Huge holes in the damaged tops had them feeling two sizes too big. She strained to keep them straight on her feet while half-running through the corridor. Her mind raced. *Next curve, next curve.*

When she reached room 3300, Krystal took a chance and tried the door handle. Locked. She knew attempting to use the palm reader on the wall would confirm her location. She looked both directions before knocking lightly on the door. *Come on, come on.* She glanced furtively back and forth, dancing on one foot, then the other. After ten seconds that seemed like sixty, the door cracked open.

Krystal gasped. "Doctor?"

Felix poked his head out through the narrow opening and looked past Krystal in both directions. Without a word, he stepped back in, yanking Krystal's arm. She almost left a shoe in the hallway as it caught on the door when she stumbled into Fred's quarters. Felix locked the door and turned around to face Krystal. He folded his arms and inhaled.

"Dr. Yaz, I—"

Felix held up a hand and exhaled. "I've been waiting for you."

Krystal sized up the doctor. *I can take him*, she thought. *He's only an inch or two taller than me, but he's fluffy. Hasn't been to the gym in forever.* "All right, Doc—"

"Lest you say something you'll regret," Felix said, his hand still in the air, "you'll let me speak first."

Krystal felt her face flush. "Where's Garrison?"

Felix fluttered his eyes. "That's out of order. I said *me* first."

Krystal shuffled forward, her ragged creepers within an inch of the doctor's polished wingtips. "What have you done with Fred?" She hadn't noticed the syringe in Felix's raised hand until the needle pierced her soiled cotton shirt and sank into her neck. She managed to curl her right hand into a fist. Felix stepped back when she took a swipe at his face. Krystal's vision blurred as she watched the floor rush up to meet her face.

Felix paused briefly to stare at the prone Punk on the floor. He studied the tattered shirt, baggy pants and the gray-black shoes. He noticed Krystal's left foot was turned to the side, her big toe protruding through the top of the shoe. Resisting the urge to tuck the toe back in, he sighed and walked across the room to Fred's desk.

Felix pressed a series of numbers on a keypad on top of the desk. A voice sounded over the adjacent speaker. "*Yes, Doctor?*"

"Room 3300. Bring a gurney. Prepare my private library."

"*Yes, Doctor.*"

Felix turned from the desk and looked down at Krystal. He shoved his hands into the pockets of his lab coat and sighed. He glanced at the indirect lighting around the baseboard of Fred's office. A mechanical pencil on a side table next to the door caught his eye. *The lead is sticking out. Why didn't they click it back in?* He gazed at the pencil, considering the length of the protruding lead. *One point five millimeters*, he estimated. Eventually, his eyes wandered back to Krystal. He stepped slowly forward and knelt down on one knee next to her feet. Gently turning her twisted foot into a more natural position, he tucked her toe into the shoe through the hole in the top. *You did the hard part, girl—you fixed the inside. Now leave the rest to us.*

He reached into an inside coat pocket and pulled out a small battery-powered device. After entering some numbers into the device's touchscreen, he pushed the power switch. He gently gathered a handful of Krystal's greasy hair and exposed her neck. He placed the pointed end of the device against her scarred skin and moved it around. *Ah, here it is.* He stopped moving and pressed hard into the muscle.

Holding Krystal's head to the floor with one hand, Felix

expertly tapped the activate button on the device. Krystal's body convulsed as the device emitted a humming sound. *Easy, girl. Just disabling your GPS.*

Felix started at the knock on Fred's door. "Dr. Yaz?"

He powered the device down and dropped it back into his pocket before walking to the door. When he swiped his palm across the reader, the lock clicked. Two orderlies stood at attention next to a rolling gurney. Felix held the door open and pointed at Krystal. "There's the patient. You know what to do."

The orderlies moved past Felix and lowered the gurney to floor level. They turned Krystal over and gently placed her on the thinly padded platform atop the gurney. Felix frowned and waved his hand when one of the orderlies threw a strap over Krystal's legs. "Not necessary."

The two attendants raised he gurney and wheeled it into the corridor.

"Oh, wait," Felix said. He stepped into the hallway and covered Krystal with the sheet that was tucked under one end of the gurney. He pulled the sheet over her face and patted her foot. "Okay." Felix looked up at the attendants. "My library."

Felix stood in the hallway, gazing at the gurney until it disappeared around the wide curve toward the elevator. He pushed the door open and surveyed Fred's quarters one more time. He tapped a code into the control panel on the inside and let go of the door. As the door drifted closed, he reached in and grabbed the mechanical pencil off the side table. He clicked the end of the pencil, tapped the lead down and set the pencil back on the table. The door eased shut, and Felix walked quietly to the elevator.

WHEN FELIX STEPPED OFF THE elevator, he stopped short. Four security personnel stood waiting to board. Felix nodded and attempted to pass.

"Pardon, sir," the lead guard said, blocking the doctor's path.

Felix was eye level with the guard. "Yes, ma'am," he said.

"We have orders to question all personnel regarding the disappearances of two Rogue Changers."

"Well," Felix said. "I'm personnel. What's your question?"

The woman puffed up. "What's your knowledge of the disappearances?"

"I have none." Felix sidestepped the guard and turned around to face her back. "Good evening, ma'am," he said, turning to leave.

The guard spun on her heel. "Sir! Stop!"

The second-in-command grabbed his superior's forearm. "I wouldn't mess with him, ma'am."

"Who does he think he is?" The woman fingered the strap on her sidearm.

"It's Dr. Felix Yaz. I thought you knew."

The lead guard didn't hide her irritation. "Just get on the elevator."

"Yes, ma'am."

MEDICAL ATTENDANTS HAD COMPLETED THE final critical checks on Krystal when Felix entered his private library.

There was no bed, but Krystal rested face-up, naked, suspended in a gravity-controlled pod, an IV in each arm. Hair-thin wires, seemingly connected to every pore on her body, fed out one end of the sealed transparent pod to a small computer bank.

Felix stood to the side of the operating table and tapped a keyboard on the control console. Lines of numbers scrolled quickly up the virtual screen as the doctor's eyes flitted back and forth across the display. As his fingers moved expertly over the keyboard, a three-dimensional image formed on a second monitor. The human image on monitor two appeared as a wired frame. The faster Dr. Yaz typed, the faster the rows of numbers scrolled up on monitor number one.

The doctor never looked at monitor two while he typed. White pixels formed within the framed image, from the center of the body, outward. The pixels flashed colors as they populated the outer extremities. Pixel upon pixel upon pixel painted the entire image like an artist's brush until the image was full.

Felix ceased typing and looked up at the prone figure in the pod.

The lead medical assistant stared at Felix. "The procedure has stopped at the neck, Doctor."

Dr. Yaz raised his eyes to the assistant. "Neither the brain nor the face will be touched. If you'll notice, I manipulated the operation around these areas, but continued up the back of the neck and forward to the hairline at the forehead. I know this patient. She wears the scars on her face as a badge of honor. As for the brain, this patient's mind—through life lessons and experience—has reached a pinnacle we could not hope to achieve through artificial means."

"So—"

Felix held up his hand. "So the body is rebuilt to perfection. The face and mind stay as is."

"As you say, Doctor. I'll set the chromosome micromanipulator and cell regenerator."

"I have already configured the settings. The procedure will be complete in two hours. You are both dismissed. Find some chores to do, clean up your rooms, or wash the dishes."

"Yes, Doctor."

CHAPTER 41

Tesla in Town

Five Punks followed Curtis on foot in a zigzag formation through a darkened alley in Tremayne's downtown business district. The alleys were narrower here than on the outskirts of the City. Newer, contemporary-styled businesses, malls and restaurants stretched the City's outer perimeter in recent years. Here in the oldest area of the City, a recent renovation project helped smooth out rough spots in the streets, providing old-school lampposts and some fresh paint but little else. Emergency lighting on the main streets kept the storefronts illuminated. The alleys remained dark, save for the few old buildings where some random paranoid owner had hot-wired a single bulb around the City's security system.

Curtis walked upright, AR in hand, his head as if on a swivel. The two Punks bringing up the rear of the formation wore helmets with rearview infrared scopes attached. Curtis and the lead Punk to his left stopped to check each one of the City's green dumpsters that lined the alleys. Refuse pickup had occurred the day before the Punks had declared the shutdown in Tremayne, so most were empty. Stray cats did not observe the shutdown. A gray tabby skulked along—tail in the air—down the middle of the alley with the six Punks, stopping at each dumpster to observe the activity.

The group navigated quickly across Main Street to the next set of buildings, breaking the darkness one man at a time. The location of the low-voltage sodium vapor streetlights cast multiple shadows as they crossed the street. With no dumpsters adjacent to the first two businesses off the street, the Punks walked in two lines of three each. They hugged the wall of the first building and stopped when Curtis raised his hand. Curtis knew there was a parking lot immediately after the second building. When he glanced across the alley, his eyes glazed at the sight of a tiny darkened alcove. There was a single back door leading to the business. Nasty butterflies roiled his gut as he recognized the little alcove. He remembered the night of the unveiling. *Krystal.*

He remembered the warmth of her hand—how tightly she gripped his. How she needed him that night. He felt her body against his once again—how frail and vulnerable she was that night. He closed his eyes and tasted the scent of her breath once again. "*How can you think about love at a time like this?*" Her distant, cutting words. *I still love you, Krys*, he thought. *Wherever you are. I still want you.*

The pressure against his shin startled Curtis from his dream state. He looked down. *Dammit. Fucking feline!* He swished his leg hard against the body of the flaccid creature, immediately regretting his boot hadn't made contact. Yanked back into the present, Curtis signaled his crew to squat.

As the Punks lowered their profiles, Curtis switched frequencies and spoke into the radio mic on his shoulder. "Drew, do you copy? Drew, do you copy?"

The reply in his ear bud was immediate. "*Go, Curtis.*"

"Track my position. I need a spotlight thirty yards due north."

"*Stand by.*"

Forty-five seconds passed before Curtis heard the faint whisper of a propeller overhead. The pitch was sucked into the funnel of light from the drone, instantly illuminating all corners of the darkened parking lot. On Curtis's signal, the Punks moved in, rifles drawn, and formed a human blockade of the area's exit.

A white late-model Tesla roadster sat quietly in one corner of the asphalt lot. The black-tinted windows prevented visibility from all sides.

The drone hovered as if frozen in time.

The Punks were poised, fingers resting on the triggers of their rifles.

High-powered headlights on the Tesla flashed to life, piercing even the drone's conical beam.

The Punks lowered their goggles.

With no further prelude, the AC induction motor zipped to life and propelled the car forward.

The Punks opened fire as they lunged sideways, splitting their formation in the middle. Bullets from the rifles bounced off the modified exterior of the Tesla. The stunning acceleration of the vehicle afforded its occupants the advantage they needed to exit the parking area and hit the alley in mere seconds.

"Hit the tires," Curtis barked.

The roadster reached the end of the alley, power-slid to the left, and was out of sight before the Punks fired another round.

"Drew, do you copy?"

"I'm already on it. Get back to your van. I'm syncing video to your monitor."

"Got it." Curtis motioned to his crew. "Let's go!"

CHAPTER 42

The Codfish Assist

DREW SAT AT A WIDE countertop—modified to form the basis of a control console—in front of five huge flat-panel monitors. He had converted the spare room over his garage into a high-tech video command center. He used the capabilities of the command center to receive video feeds from hundreds of sources simultaneously throughout Tremayne and the surrounding area.

Unknown to the Changers and city officials, Drew received infrared and optical feeds from both homemade and confiscated drones, and the City's surveillance cameras. Using intercepted transmissions from satellites, cell towers and various microwave links, his capacity to monitor every corner of interest held few limitations. He selected specific cameras within a sector or drone, and directed the feed into a chosen display. Since he set up his system with two-way control, Drew also sent false images to certain cameras where he wanted to keep the current activity hidden from prying eyes.

Controllers with joysticks operated the drones. He had integrated the controllers—previously on separate, handheld tablets, mirror-cast onto the monitors—to operate directly from his main console. This eliminated clutter and internal linking/beaming issues in the command center.

Sydney sat next to Drew, monitoring an area map on a digital whiteboard. She fed information to Drew and acted as an additional set of eyes and ears.

Drew and Sydney had chosen sides. Using this technology to help the Punks was their way of unleashing the rebel inside, while remaining innocuous to friends, neighbors, and most importantly, the Changers.

"Tesla's fast," Sydney said.

Drew's bare feet moved subtly on the floor, guiding the drone with specially modified controls under the counter. His eyes remained fixed on a screen in front of him. "No match for these drones."

"They're obviously headed south," Sydney said. "Out of town. We've got one on standby that's directly in their path. A little distraction wouldn't hurt."

Drew raised an eyebrow and glanced at the whiteboard. "Not a bad idea." He tapped a number of controls on a panel to his left. A corresponding monitor displayed a POV camera from the second drone.

"Let me take this one," Sydney said.

Drew smiled. "Have at it."

Sydney moved around behind Drew and sat to his left. The POV image from the second drone's camera spun 360 degrees, showing the desolate area outside the Perimeter over the Wall, and circled back to display Tremayne's southern outer limits.

"Hmm," Sydney said. "Punks have quite a blockade in the south. I wonder if that Tesla driver has thought about his exit?"

Drew tapped the two-way radio control. "Lace, Drew. Do you copy?"

Lace's voice sounded a few seconds later. "*Go ahead, Drew.*"

"Yeah, there's a white Tesla headed your way. We've got a drone tailing it, and another one coming in from your position. It's headed straight down South Habiliment Boulevard. There's no traffic, and it's blowing all the signals."

"*Dumb move on their part,*" Lace replied. "*We got that street blocked big-time. Not to mention Checkpoint Four at Habiliment—*"

gate's closed, and we got vehicles parked inside and out. They're not going anywhere."

"Lace, Curtis."

"Go, Curtis."

"That driver's mine."

"Copy that, buddy."

Sydney guided drone number two toward Tremayne's garment district. "Oh." She smiled. "I see it now, about a mile in front of me."

"Good, babe," Drew said. "Bring it down in front and let's see if we can get a look inside."

"Heading in now." Sydney's eyes remained fixed on the flat-screen in front of her while her fingers expertly guided the unmanned aircraft toward a point several blocks in front of the roadster. "I can't believe how fast that car—" Her eyes widened as she flinched and flipped the joystick toward her. The drone narrowly missed the windshield of the Tesla.

Drew located the roadster and changed the display on one of the flat-screens. He watched the roadster attempt a hard ninety-degree turn to avoid the number two drone that was no longer there. Luck was not with the driver as the Tesla skidded sideways at Habiliment Boulevard and 112th Street. The car hit the center median, taking out a left turn traffic signal pole. It flipped over once, its tires touching the pavement momentarily before the momentum caused the Tesla to roll onto its roof. A contemporary building on the southwest corner was the unexpected recipient of the vehicle as it jumped the curb and slid upside down through the plate glass window of a furniture store showroom.

"Oops," Sydney said, glancing at Drew.

"Curtis, Drew. Do you copy?"

"Caught the whole scene in my van. Drone strike was perfect. Good move on the Tesla."

Drew looked at Sydney and smiled. "10-4, Curtis. I'll keep the area on your monitor."

"Curtis, Lace. Do you copy?"

"On my way, Lace."

"Copy that, Curtis. I'm sending trucks that way. We'll contain all four sides, one block out. He's all yours. Let me know if you need an assist."

"10-4, Lace."

WHEN CURTIS'S SQUAD OF VEHICLES reached the scene, he parked his van on the opposite corner of the intersection from the showroom. One of the BearCats drove past the building and did an about-face. The other two armored vehicles parked out of sight on 112th Street, facing the showroom on either side of Habiliment Boulevard. A fifth vehicle, a Lenco BEAR with a remote-controlled robotic arm mounted on top, rolled silently up behind Curtis's van and stopped three car lengths behind him.

Five Punks exited each of the three BearCats, leaving the driver in each vehicle. The Punks moved toward the showroom in SWAT formation, hugging the walls of the buildings. Curtis stood behind the driver's door of his van, waiting for his crew to set up. He watched the Tesla intently for movement.

Curtis spoke into his shoulder mic. "Codfish, do you copy?"

A gruff, raspy voice responded. *"Go ahead, boss."*

"Get your hook up there and flip that sucker over."

"You got it, boss," the driver of the BEAR replied.

The Lenco BEAR moved quietly around Curtis's van and maneuvered, front first, toward the shattered storefront. The tires of the huge vehicle pressed hard against the curb before Codfish applied the parking brake. Hydraulic outriggers extended from each side of the BEAR and rested firmly against the pavement.

Curtis watched the driver's window descend. A wad of chewed, spent tobacco flew out and splatted against a city trash can on the sidewalk. A raspy laugh came from inside the cab of the BEAR.

"Copy, boss," Codfish said. "I'm going in."

Curtis heard the whine of the hydraulic arm as it lifted and extended toward the Tesla. The arm pivoted downward near the tip, which housed a rigid hardened-steel hook. The capsized roadster remained still until the hook made contact with the driver's window. Slowly, the arm retracted back toward the BEAR, its center joint bending perfectly to bring the smashed roadster upright.

Codfish pulled the outriggers back to their original positions under the armored vehicle and put the BEAR into reverse.

For the first time since the roadster rolled, Curtis saw movement inside. The driver furiously tried to pry the hook from the door of his car. Curtis heard Codfish laughing inside the BEAR's cab.

As the Tesla's passenger door flew open, Curtis radioed his crew. "All ground units, move in. Suspect exited the vehicle into the structure."

The roadster's other occupant continued to flail about in the driver's seat. "Codfish, move your guys in on the driver. Looks like he's stuck in his seat belt."

Five Punks inside the Lenco BEAR exited the rear of the truck. They ran forward, shields in front. Curtis heard raised voices and watched the crew yank the driver from the vehicle, slamming him onto the sidewalk facefirst. He closed the door on his van and walked quickly to the scene.

"Stand him up," Curtis barked.

Two Punks gripped the driver and raised him to eye level with Curtis. The driver's hands were secured behind his back with heavy zip ties. The three other Punks, standing two paces back, trained their rifles on the driver. From inside the cab, Codfish lit a cigar. A puff of smoke exited the driver's window.

Curtis knew in his heart the Tesla driver was Scotty Van Buren, dressed as a Punk. "So, Scotty. What's your story?"

"What's there to say?" Scotty shrugged. "I was trying to help you guys out. Thought I'd dress the part."

"Sounds like bullshit to me, boss," Codfish growled out the window of the BEAR.

Scotty sneered. "So, Curtis. Word on the street is you're reporting to Marco now."

Curtis stepped up to Scotty. Only the peach fuzz on their noses separated the two. "I report to *Margot*, asswipe."

"Marco, Margot. What's in a name?" Scotty said. "The guy's a dude, man."

"Margot's who and what she says she is." Curtis head-butted Scotty. "Did I make myself clear on that point?"

Scotty winced as a walnut-sized welt formed on his forehead. "Becoming a Changer would have been a good option for him—" He flinched and closed his eyes. "I mean *her*. We could have protected *her*."

"That's your problem, Van Buren. You and all the Changers. Margot and people like her don't need your protection. And they don't need to change to be like you. All you can change is the outside. You can't change people on the inside. You can't accept that."

Curtis shouted over his shoulder. "Hey, Cod. Toss me the paintball gun."

Scotty snickered. "What, you're gonna shoot me with that?"

Curtis caught the gun and walked back about twenty feet from Scotty. He slung his AR behind him, over his shoulder. "It's not paint, Scotty. It's acid."

The smile fell from Scotty's face. "What the hell? You know me, buddy. We're friends. I'm on your side."

"I think we both know you're a Changer," Curtis said. "We're just gonna do a little field test for confirmation."

Scotty looked anxiously from Punk to Punk. "Wait, you wouldn't do that. You'll spread that stuff all over these guys."

"It's a gel," Curtis said. "Don't worry about these guys. It won't splatter."

"Why are you doing this, buddy?" Scotty begged.

"We got first aid on the trucks. If you're not a Changer, we'll fix you up." Curtis raised the paintball gun and aimed it at Scotty's face.

The two Punks holding Scotty turned their faces away.

The other three Punks lowered goggles, then reaimed their rifles.

A series of smoke rings exited the driver's window of the BEAR.

This one's for you, Krys, Curtis thought, as he squeezed the trigger.

The gel-filled projectile made contact with Scotty's face—

squarely between the eyes. The gel stuck to his face and bubbled into a greenish-blue, scaly mass.

"Fuck you, Curtis," Scotty said.

Curtis walked up to Scotty and looked him in the eye. "No, fuck you, *Changer.*" He glanced at the Punk standing two paces behind Scotty. "Do it."

Curtis heard the shot as he walked away. He didn't flinch, and he didn't look back.

Drew sat back and dropped his hands to his side. "I can't believe what I just saw."

"*Curtis, Lace. Do you copy, Curtis?*"

"Go ahead, Lace."

"*My crew's reporting shots fired at your location.*"

"No big deal, Lace. Just another dead Changer."

"*Copy that.*"

Codfish stepped out of the Lenco BEAR. "Hey, boss."

Curtis tossed the paintball gun into the cab of his van and turned around. Codfish jerked a thumb over his shoulder. Four Punks were escorting Johnny Logan, hands secured behind his back.

"What the hell are you guys doing? Lemme go!" The big Punk was defiant when Curtis met him in the middle of the intersection.

"So, Johnny. What were you doing riding around in a Changer's car with a Changer?"

Johnny's eyes sprung open. "What? That guy? Wow, I thought he was one of us, man. Holy Moses, I can't believe he was a Changer."

Curtis wasn't buying Johnny's act. "We did a field acid test," Curtis said. "What say we do one on you?"

"Aw, man," Johnny said, shaking his head. "I had one already." He tipped his head up. "You were there. You saw me pass. Flying colors, remember?"

"Yeah," Curtis said. "I saw you pass. Problem is, you were with a Changer in a restricted part of the City. Your commanding officer reported you AWOL hours ago."

Johnny looked around at the other Punks. "Well...he kidnapped me, man. You saw how he tried to escape." He smiled. "That car's fast, man."

"Right," Curtis said. "That doesn't jibe with what you said five seconds ago. How 'bout we check with headquarters? See what they say?"

"Whatever, man. They all saw me pass the test. They're just gonna tell you to let me go."

"We'll see." Curtis turned away and walked toward his van. He switched frequencies on his two-way. "Jimbo, Curtis. Do you copy?"

"*Go ahead, Curtis.*"

"Hey, Jim. I got Johnny Logan here in Tremayne. We picked him up fleeing with a Changer. He was reported AWOL several hours ago."

"*Copy that. What's your plan?*"

"Acid test, then decide."

"*He passed an acid test, 10-4?*"

"He did, Jim. But he's got conflicting excuses about why he was traveling with a Changer. Something's up with him."

"*Stand by, Curtis.*"

Curtis leaned an elbow on the edge of his van door and surveyed the intersection. The Punks stood around in loose groups, rifles at the ready, but shooting the breeze. They appeared relaxed and loose. He thought about what had just happened. His mind drifted to the days leading up to the unveiling. He remembered how Scotty had single-handedly taken down that mutant, saving those three young boys. He thought about being with Krystal that evening. He was glad he'd deflected Winter's arm the night of the acid tests. *Wish I was with you, Krys.*

"*Curtis, Ryker.*"

Curtis instinctively snapped to attention. "Go, Ryk."

"*Take custody of Logan.*"

"10-4. Consider it done."

"*Curtis, Jimbo. How's everything else out there?*"

"Calm now, Jim. I thought you guys had an ear on us from headquarters."

"*Oh, buddy. We've got our hands full, and then some. Just keep up the good work.*"

"Thanks, Jim."

"*Let us know if you need anything.*"

"Will do."

CHAPTER 43

Come Together

FRED GAZED OUT THE WINDOW from the backseat of the Humvee as it sped northbound on Interstate 99 toward Tremayne. "The highway's deserted, Will."

Will had the cruise control set at one hundred miles per hour. "Yeah, we shut everything down. We got word the Changers are going to attack the Perimeter—probably Tremayne, too."

"We, meaning the Punks?" Thomas asked.

"Exactly what he means," Adam said.

"I assume you have plans for us," Fred said.

Will glanced in the rearview mirror at Fred. "It's not up to us. We're kinda low on the seniority list."

Thomas snorted. "So the Punks sent the low-seniority guys into the Changers' Underground to spring a couple of Rogue Changers from lockup? Doesn't sound to me like you guys are peon Punks."

"They didn't send us, we volunteered." Adam smiled. "We're working our way up."

"Well, we haven't gotten out as much as we should have, I guess," Fred said.

"True," Thomas agreed. "You guys could be lying to us all the way and we'd never know it."

"Yes," Will said. "But you two were as good as dead if you stayed with the Changers, right?"

"We could only hope for death," Fred said. "We had no choice but to trust you."

"Right again," Joey said.

Fred leaned forward and looked out the windshield. "It wasn't you guys that convinced us to go with you. You know that, right?"

Will's interest was piqued. "Then why'd you leave with us?"

"It was Dr. Felix Yaz, the man who brought you to us in lockup. The doctor has some kind of innate ability to read people. There's something special about him that didn't come from the Changers."

"So you wouldn't have come with us if that Doctor Felix hadn't made it okay?"

"Let me put it this way." Fred sat back. "You wouldn't have known where to find us if not for Felix."

Adam's eyes lit up. "Oh, wait. I found out from some stupid Changers in the hallway where your room was."

"Sure," Fred said. "But we weren't in my quarters, were we? We were in lockup."

"So what are you saying?" Will asked.

"Let me ask you this," Thomas said. "How did you hook up with Felix in the first place?"

Adam looked at Joey. "Well, we got on an elevator, and he was already there. We ended up telling him why we came to the Underground."

"Exactly," Thomas agreed. "Felix also has a knack for being in the right place at the right time. You ran into him even though you weren't looking for him. And then he brought you to us."

"Plus," Fred added, "he set up the security systems that enabled us to escape. Even if you found us in lockup and we all made it safely to an outlet, there would have been no way of exiting without being discovered. Felix arranged that."

Will remained lost in thought. "You know who you guys really have to thank for even having a chance of getting out of there? Krystal Peterson," he answered his own question.

Joey puffed up. "Course, it was us Three Amigos that discovered Krystal—"

"Teamwork," Will declared. "Somehow we all formed this unusual team, can you believe that? I mean, Punks and Changers? Really?"

Thomas smirked. "Well, guys, we don't feel all that safe heading toward the Punks' headquarters."

Will glanced in the rearview mirror. "Punks never rejected anyone. Not for their beliefs, their looks, social status, sexuality, nothing."

"Not what I hear," Thomas said. "Punks are against just about everything you mentioned."

"That's what the Changers want everyone to believe. We're the ones with all varieties of everything I just said. We just don't want to be controlled by anyone without a reason. We don't want the government all up in our business."

Fred sat forward again. "So where do we stand with *your* government, your leaders?"

Adam and Joey deferred to Will. "They know we came to try and spring you guys. And they're taking a chance on you two, hoping you can help."

"We can help," Fred said. "But we've got less than six months. We'll have to work fast. You guys are way behind, technology-wise."

THE SCREEN ON WILL'S CELL—RESTING in a customized console mount—lit up the interior. Dion's picture displayed on the screen.

"Whoa," Fred said. "He's scary-looking."

"He's our leader," Will said, tapping the screen. "Hey, Dion."

"*Will! Where are you guys?*" Dion's voice sounded on the Humvee's dash speaker.

"We're about twenty-five minutes south of you on 99."

"*Did you make it into the Changers' Underground?*"

"In and out." Will couldn't help smiling.

"*So is that Fred Garrison guy with you?*"

"You bet. And we got another guy, too. Thomas."

The group heard Dion's muffled voice as he covered the

mouthpiece on his end. "*I don't believe it. Those guys actually got in and out of the Underground, with two Changers, Garrison included.*"

"*Wow.*" The boys recognized Jimbo's voice. "*Those little shits did it.*"

"*Never had a doubt,*" Ryker said.

In the background, they recognized Geezer's cackle.

Dion came back. "*Okay, good job. So, twenty-five minutes. How fast are you moving?*"

"About a hundred."

"*All right. You should be coming up pretty quick on Winter's location. Her crew's blocked off from us—surrounded by Chybrids.*"

Fred glanced at Thomas. "Great," he whispered.

Thomas was grim.

Will glanced anxiously at Adam. "*What do you want us to do, Dion?*"

"*Stay the hell away from her position, for starters. Your only choice is to go into Tremayne through Checkpoint Four. I'll let Lace know you're coming. She's got that side of the City secured.*"

"Okay, got it."

"*We've got all personnel from the Checkpoint One compound evacuated into the Tunnels. We also have thousands of Chybrids just outside The Wall. Let me know when you start heading this way from Tremayne. We'll open up.*"

"Okay, Dion."

"*I'm hanging up now. Just be careful. You're dead if a Chybrid gets hold of you.*"

JOEY FLOPPED BACK IN HIS seat. "Well, that was a wakeup call."

"Who's Winter?" Fred asked.

"She's one of the higher-ups," Will said. "She's pretty badass."

"So she's got a 'crew'?" Fred asked. "What's that mean?"

Will gazed intently out the windshield. "Like a group of Punks. In armored vehicles. She's got over a hundred vehicles in her crew." He squinted and pulled himself forward. "I'd say... that'd be them over there."

Fred looked out the side window. About a quarter of a mile off the highway, in an expansive flat area, he saw a circle of vehicles. The vehicles formed a tight circle. He shielded his eyes. "Looks like every available light on those trucks is on."

Thomas leaned across Joey and looked out. "You can see the Chybrids. They're attacking."

"They'll tear through that armor eventually. They're not programmed to stop. Once they expose a weakness or a tear in the exterior, they'll concentrate on the weak spot till they rip through."

"What if the trucks start moving?" Adam asked.

Thomas took a deep breath and exhaled. "They should have moved a long time ago. See how several of the Chybrids have wedged themselves into the wheel wells? Look closer and you'll notice there's no space under the trucks. They're programmed for those specific vehicles. Most likely, they've disabled the drive trains, probably ripped the drive shafts off the trucks."

Adam frowned. "How do you know all that?"

"I hate to say it now, but I wrote the programs for the Chybrids. It's only a matter of time before everyone in those trucks is dead."

"What if, by chance—let's just say it could happen—what if one of those BearCats broke out of there? Say the drive train was still working?"

"It's a pretty specialized program," Thomas said. "The Chybrids will go after the mobile unit first. Then they'll work to disable that unit and go for the soft target, or targets, inside."

Will looked at Adam. "You thinking what I'm thinking?"

"Yep."

Will swished his hair back. "Gimme my bandanna." He slowed the Humvee and tied the bandanna onto his head, steering the vehicle with his left knee.

Adam smiled. "Here's your turnoff, partner!"

Fred grabbed the back of the seat in front of him. "What are you doing, Will?"

Will braked hard and turned the vehicle to the right. With all four wheels locked up, the Humvee skidded sideways down the highway as he whipped the wheel back to the left, maintaining a perfect power-slide into the off-ramp. Within seconds, Will guided the Humvee onto the adjacent frontage road.

Joey looked up at Fred. "We can't just pass by and allow those Punks to die. We have to do something."

Fred stared ahead at the lights from the vehicles in Winter's formation. "You're going to kill yourself and your friends, too, Will."

"You're not scared, are you?" Adam asked Fred.

Thomas grabbed Adam's shoulder from the backseat. "The Chybrids won't hurt us. They don't attack Changers."

Adam yanked his shoulder away. "Then hold on for the ride. We have to at least try."

Will pushed four auxiliary rocker switches on the dash, activating light bars on all sides atop the Humvee. "Look for an opening, guys."

"Looks like one coming up," Adam said.

Will slowed the vehicle. "I see it." A chain-link fence, bordering the frontage road on the right, was missing a section. Will anticipated the opening and timed his turn perfectly. "Everyone hang on!"

The Humvee hit a shallow rise, forcing the front end into the air. When it recovered, the truck pitched upwards—the rear wheels cleared the ditch as the vehicle became airborne. It landed squarely on all four tires, the engine revving freely as Will accelerated toward Winter's location.

Thomas stared intently out the windshield. "I'd say you got their attention."

One by one, the Chybrids ceased their attack on the stationary BearCats and stood upright. They turned to face the Three Amigos and their new friends.

As the Chybrids began their move toward the Humvee, Will accelerated again.

And the Chybrids accelerated.

"Will!" Thomas shouted. "Get out of here!"

Thomas, Joey and Fred dug their fingernails into the seat backs in front of them.

Adam gripped a grab handle on the ceiling.

Will swung the steering wheel hard left, sliding the Humvee sideways on the slick terrain. Multiple mud rooster tails filled the air, coating the first row of Chybrids with the brown muck. He pointed the vehicle northward, paralleling the frontage road before guiding the truck toward the highway.

"Get Dion on the cell!" He had to shout over the sound of the powerful high-revving engine noise from the Humvee.

Adam snatched the cell from its mount on the dash and speed-dialed Dion.

Fred and Thomas opened their side windows and watched the persistent Chybrids.

"You're not making any progress," Thomas said. "They're keeping up."

Joey tapped Thomas on the shoulder. "Are you scared now?"

"No." Thomas turned and slunk into his seat.

"He knows what he's doing, man," Joey said.

"Dion," Adam shouted into the cell before activating the dash speaker.

"*What's up, guys?*"

"Dion, it's Will. Call Winter. Tell her to get her crew out of those trucks and into the Tunnel."

"*Whoa, what are you talking about?*"

"Don't ask questions right now. Just do it! We got the Chybrids chasing us! She has time to get everybody out of there! Tell her now—I don't know how long they're going to follow us!"

"*Do it, Dion.*" It was Ryker in the background.

"*I got it, Dion,*" Jimbo said.

"Dion," Will said. "Tell Winter—there's a pile of old tractor tires due north of where she's parked, about three quarters of a mile away. Tell her to make a beeline for those tires. Just beyond that pile of tires is the Wall, about fifty more feet. There's a Tunnel entrance under a bed frame and an old flattened trash can. Tell her to look for a T-handle and twist it. The Tunnel lid will pop up and everyone can get in."

"*Got it.*"

"We're doing about thirty-two miles an hour in the dirt right now. We'll keep those suckers chasing us as long as we can, or until we hit the highway. Tell Winter she's got about fifteen minutes, max."

Dion stood in the Depot staring at his feet. "*What am I gonna do with you guys?*"

"We'll call you when we meet up with Lace," Will said as Adam ended the call.

Nevada rumbled up to Checkpoint Three in her Lenco Bear-Cat. "Stop right here." The sultry rasp of her voice suited her rugged frame. Natural dark shading under her eyes contrasted with her light skin, giving her otherwise-average face the appearance of makeup—which she never wore.

Two identical BearCats pulled to a stop, a single car-length behind her. Three others parked behind the two.

She stepped out of the vehicle and sauntered up to the middle truck in the back row of fifteen BearCats.

The Punk riding shotgun stepped out to meet her at the rear of his vehicle. The lanky redhead stood a head taller than Nevada. "What's up, boss?" he asked.

"'Bout to ask you the same, Red."

Red stretched and yawned. "Damned slow on this side, boss. Damned slow."

"Been monitoring the radio?" Nevada asked.

"Yep. Oh, yeah," Red said.

"The Three Amigos are bringing two Changers into Tremayne. Gonna hit Checkpoint Four. Going through Lace's crew."

"Yep, heard that." Red nodded. He patted the gun on his hip. "Got my nine ready."

Nevada waved her hand. "They're friendlies. Want you to escort 'em from Checkpoint Four to Checkpoint One."

"Oh, can do, boss. Can do." Red nodded again and stood staring at Nevada.

Nevada rolled her eyes. "So head over to Checkpoint Four. Timing's about right. You'll get there by the time the Amigos are pulling in."

"Oh." Red clapped his hands once. "I'm on it." He spun on one heel and trotted back to his truck.

Nevada stood in place until Red hopped into his truck. She spoke into her shoulder mic. "Lace, Nevada."

"*Go ahead, Nevada.*"

"Red's headed your way to escort the Amigos."

"*10-4. ETA?*"

"ETA fifteen minutes."

"*10-4, Nevada.*"

CHAPTER 44

Badge of Honor

FELIX GAZED THROUGH A GLASS window separating his private library from the recovery room where Krystal rested comfortably. His ever-busy mind drifted as he clasped and unclasped his hands behind his back. He closed his eyes and thought back to when Scotty Van Buren had brought Krystal to Levi.

Felix knew Krystal had never cared about living forever. She'd wanted her beautiful face back—the face before the accident, before the fire. She wanted to belong. Scotty and the Changers had offered her that, and more.

Krystal's assignment with the Changers allowed her to choose a target within the Punks' organization. She had chosen Curtis, because she knew that with her new, beautiful appearance, Curtis Dyer was dating above his class. Krystal knew her beauty caught his eye, but he had told her it was her heart that he truly loved.

Then Krystal had committed the deadliest of sins for a Changer—she had fallen in love with her mark. From the day he'd met her, Felix had known she hated absorbing innocent lives. After the acid test, the Punks had rejected her.

Krystal Peterson's hat trick: Rejected by the Bystanders. Rejected by the Punks. Rejected by the Changers.

For a brief moment, Felix's mind keyed on the current

dilemma: help the Punks defeat the Changers. He thought about the weapons the Punks possessed. *Hmph*, he snorted. *The AR-15. The most popular rifle in the country.* The Changers had managed to confiscate or destroy all weapons and raze every munitions facility in the country. But not the AR-15s. He was glad the rebels had managed to hide so many from the Changers. Felix decided he would one day find out how the rebels had done it—hidden millions of AR-15s. Without them, there could be no rebellion.

And then, the truce. He shook his head slowly. The truce with the rebels was a farce. The Changers had never intended to uphold their end of the bargain. He knew when the Changers had built the Wall, it had been intended to contain the Bystanders. The Changers had needed a breeding farm to survive.

Felix opened his eyes and started. "Aagh!" He grabbed his chest and took a deep breath. It was only his own reflection in the glass. He removed his glasses and refocused on Krystal's bed. She lay staring calmly at the ceiling. He tucked his glasses into the top pocket of his lab coat and walked to the door.

Krystal turned her head toward Felix when he entered. "Doctor," she greeted him.

Felix touched a remote control and raised the head of the bed. "How are you feeling, girl?"

"Surprisingly, I feel great," Krystal said.

"Splendid. I'd like you to get up now. I have some exciting things to tell you, and we haven't much time."

Krystal looked around the room. Indirect lighting from the baseboards and around the upper walls provided the room with a peaceful atmosphere. There were no pictures or wall decor of any kind.

Krystal was wearing panties and a formfitting tank top. She ran her hands over her body under the blanket. She touched her face. The scar from the acid remained.

Felix held out his hand. "Come."

Krystal threw the covers back and swung her legs to the side of the bed.

The doctor took her hand as she slid off the bed to the floor.

He guided her to a full-length mirror on the back of the closed door.

Krystal stood facing her reflection. She lifted her hands to her face, one to each cheek. She lifted the hair from both sides, running her fingers through the long, silky smoothness. *Wait...hair! I have hair!* She crossed her arms over her now-firm shoulders, felt her breasts, and smoothed her hands down to her waist and over her hips. Unable to take her eyes off the mirror, she noticed her legs were also toned, the skin smooth, free of ripples and blemishes. Keeping her eyes on the reflection, she turned around and smiled. *Nice ass*, she thought.

When she finally looked at Felix, he smiled back. "I take it you approve?"

"I don't know how or why you did this," Krystal said, "but thank you!" She threw her arms around the doctor's neck and squeezed.

Felix resisted the urge to hug her back and grabbed Krystal's wrists. "No thanks are necessary," he said. "You have a new mission, and we have work to do."

Krystal put her hands on Felix's chest and pushed herself away. "I should have known there'd be a price."

He placed his hands on her cheeks and locked his eyes on hers. "There is no price. What I have done to you is for *you*. It is my gift to you. Nothing more, and nothing less. There are no strings attached. If you choose to walk away now, you may do so. I will help you out of the Underground, and your life is yours to do with as you please." He dropped his hands and shoved them into the pockets of his lab coat.

Krystal stood staring at Felix. She opened her mouth to speak but had no words.

Felix walked over to the bed and switched off the vital signs monitor above the headboard. "Your clothes are in the closet."

A rare twinge of modesty forced Krystal to open the closet. She surveyed the attire inside: a thick long-sleeved T-shirt, leather cargo pants, cotton socks, high-top leather boots, a leather vest, and a full-length leather duster—all black.

She nodded her approval. "Okay. So what about this *new mission?*"

Felix kept his back toward Krystal and smiled. "Get dressed and we'll talk."

WHEN THEY STEPPED BACK INTO Felix's private library, a wall of shelves, filled with books, rose from the floor to hide the recovery room. Felix tapped his cell and the adjacent wall of books lowered into the floor, exposing another room.

"Follow me," Felix said.

Light from the newly exposed room cast its bright white glow into the library. "Another lab?" Krystal asked.

"Aside from myself, you are the only person ever to enter this room," Felix said.

Krystal strode into the lab, marveling at the ease with which she had adapted to her new body. She felt taller, firmer and stronger than she ever remembered feeling—even after effecting the Change upon herself. She brushed her duster back and stood with her hands on her hips.

"I'm going to be brief, because time is of the essence," Felix said. "You should feel more physically fit than ever before."

"I do."

"I have performed a procedure on you that has never been applied to anyone. You are the first. If I am ever found out, I will be eliminated."

"Holy shit, Felix," Krystal said. "I feel awesome. Why would anyone not allow this?"

Felix breathed deeply and closed his eyes. "Because." He exhaled. "I have reversed the Change."

Krystal's jaw dropped and her eyes widened. "I thought the Change was irreversible."

Felix held up a finger. "Everyone thinks that. The procedure is extensive and costly and requires specific processes in a specialized sequence. I am the only one alive who knows the procedure. This is why I cannot perform it upon myself. If I could, I would."

"But why do I feel *so* good?" Krystal asked. "I mean, I feel strength and endurance I've never felt."

"Everything about you is stronger—skin, hair, muscles. Even your hearing and eyesight are enhanced."

"I had a feeling you were a Rogue, but I never—"

"There is not time for blather. I will give you what I can, and then you must leave the Underground as soon as possible."

"Okay," Krystal said. "Let's hear it."

"You have chosen a side. Your choice to fight for the Punks means your life is in danger from the Changers. Since you were exposed as a Changer, your life is danger from the Punks. However, you will prove yourself to the Punks, and they will accept you."

"How—"

"You must trust me on this." Felix stepped across the tiny room to a small workbench and clicked on a holographic display. "The attire I have provided you, that which you are wearing, is made from the same synthetic material used to form the Chybrid skullcaps and their new bodies. The material is impervious to rounds fired from the Punks' AR-15 rifles. Nothing else has been tested—except when you fired that guard's 9mm pistol at Levi's head. Most likely, the 9mm will also not penetrate. But I have not extensively tested this bullet. You can see by this video demonstration that the Chybrids are unaffected by the AR-15's bullet."

"That's awesome," Krystal said. "But why do I need this type of protection if the Punks are going to recognize I'm on their side?"

"Two reasons. First, some Punks may still shoot their rifles at you, until they realize you are not a threat to them. Remember, they feel you betrayed them. And secondly, see this additional demonstration?" Felix pointed to the holographic display. "Notice the Chybrids' power does not allow them to harm each other. Their strength lies in their ability to damage conventional steel and various other metals—not to mention human flesh. However, errant blows from one Chybrid to another have no effect. This means the Chybrids cannot harm you when you are wearing these clothes."

"Okay, I'm with you. But what about the parts of me not covered by the clothing?"

"You are vulnerable. That's why I am providing you this helmet, these goggles, and these gloves."

Krystal picked up the helmet and turned it over in her hands. "You always knew I liked black."

"Yes," Felix said. "There are a few more items."

But wait, there's more, Krystal thought, smiling to herself.

Felix turned to the workbench. "Take this utility belt. I have equipped it with various items you will need and appreciate."

"Is that it?" Krystal asked.

Felix raised his finger in the air. "I am going to escort you to my private elevator that will take you to the surface. When you arrive at the top, walk fifty yards due south. You will find an armored vehicle with the keys in it. This vehicle has a rolling storage trailer attached. Both units are constructed of the same material that is impervious to Chybrid damage. The trailer is fully stocked with special bullets. These bullets fit the AR-15s. Two bullets will pierce the Chybrid shell."

"I'm ready," Krystal said. "But one question, Felix. Why me? Why Krystal Peterson, the reject of rejects?"

Felix crossed his arms and looked into Krystal's eyes again. "Because I know the real you, Krystal Peterson. You have lived through every kind of rejection a person can live. What makes you different is your heart. You found yourself. You accepted yourself as you are. You know that true worth comes from within. You know you do not require the presence or approval of another human being to be worthy. You found that you are worthy because you are *you*. A simple truth, but so easily missed."

"Felix?"

"Yes?"

"Thank you for not changing my face."

"Wear it as a badge of honor. Now we must go."

CHAPTER 45

Checkpoint One

WILL PULLED THE HUMVEE TO a stop behind Red's BearCat outside the Depot at Checkpoint One. "Jeez, this place is deserted."

Thomas surveyed the compound. He noticed moisture on the concrete sidewalks and adjoining pads—remnants of the earlier rainstorm. "It would be impressive if there was anyone manning the area. Looks like you guys would have quite an operation."

Adam looked back at Thomas. "If no one's here, it's on purpose. Dion knows what he's doing."

"I'm sure he does." Thomas smiled.

"Just so you guys know," Will said, "we gotta cuff you before going in. No one in there knows you like we do."

"Is that supposed to scare us?" Thomas asked.

"Rule is, see a Changer, bullet to the head," Joey said. "You can take your chances if you'd rather."

"He's not scared, guys," Fred said. "He's just a little nervous. So am I. Just cuff us if that's what you have to do."

"Sorry," Thomas said. "I'm really not trying to give you a hard time."

Red strode back to the Humvee and leaned in the driver's

window. He glanced back at Fred and Thomas. "We'll cuff these guys for you."

Joey looked at Thomas. "Told you so."

Red stood back as two of his men opened the rear doors. Fred and Thomas dutifully stepped out. Punks on each side of the vehicle trained their rifles on the two Rogue Changers as two other Punks turned them around and frisked them.

Fred eyed the door to the Depot as the exterior radio speaker spewed forth banter from the two-way inside. "Is that where we're going?" he asked the Punk as the handcuffs ratcheted closed.

"You'll go where you're told to go," the Punk said.

"Of course."

Red led the way, accompanied by Fred and Thomas, with a Punk on either side. The two Punks with rifles drawn followed the Rogues. The Three Amigos grabbed Fred and Thomas's utility bags from the Humvee.

"Another successful mission," Adam said.

Will stood for a moment at the driver's door of the Humvee, facing the Depot. "Thanks to that Dr. Felix, dude."

Joey agreed. "I swear I almost peed my pants in the elevator down there."

"Didn't we all," Adam said.

"I have a feeling there's more hard work ahead," Will said as the trio headed to the Depot.

Red greeted Ryker inside. "Hey, bro," Red said as the two bumped fists.

Ryker looked past Red at the Rogues. No one spoke as the Punks herded the two into the control room.

Fred scanned the electronics, the control panels and the array of flat-screen monitors on the wall. *Impressive,* he thought. *These people are much more advanced than I anticipated.*

Jimbo swiveled around in his chair at the communications console. "Put those guys over there in the corner."

"Thanks for the escort," Ryker said. "We'll take it from here."

"You got it, man," Red said. He motioned to his crew. "Let's go, guys."

The Three Amigos squeezed in as Red's crew exited.

Ryker smiled. "Hey, you Punks. Get your asses over here." One at a time, he bumped fists with the three. "Nice fit on that bandanna," he said to Will.

"Thanks. You, too."

Ryker turned to the Rogues. His smile gone, he eyed the two, head to toe. "So." He looked at Will. "Why don't you make the intros?"

"Okay, so this is Fred Garrison, and this is Thomas." He looked at Thomas. "I'm sorry, man. I forgot your last name."

"It's Dennis," Thomas said. "Thomas Dennis."

Dion stepped in from the Hangar.

"Thomas Dennis what?" Jimbo asked, mocking the Rogue.

"That's enough," Dion said. He looked at Will.

"They're okay, Dion," Will said.

Dion motioned to Ace. "Take off the cuffs."

Ace stepped behind the Rogues and removed their handcuffs.

"Will says you guys are okay." He held out his hand. "That's good enough for me, unless you two prove otherwise."

Fred and Thomas each shook Dion's hand. "As foreign as this may sound to you, we're actually on your side," Fred said.

"For now, I'm going to ask you two to observe," Dion said. "No doubt we'll exchange information, but for now, we really have our hands full."

Thomas watched the camera feed showing the Chybrids outside the Wall. He knew their programming didn't enable them to climb the slick exterior—but he also knew that ability could be activated with a few adjustments. His efforts, half-hearted as they were, had been enough to satisfy Levi and the Changers' leadership.

"*Jim, Winter.*" Her voice crackled from the ceiling speaker.

Jimbo spun in his chair. "Go, Win."

"*I'm gonna feed an optical scope up through the hatch and stream it to you, so you guys can get a visual of what's happening here.*"

"Sounds good, Win. How's our stream to you?"

"*Looking good. Sucks what's going on there, though.*"

"Copy that."

"*What's Zane gonna do? I see they keep moving around, staying just out of reach from those fuckers. That's gotta be monotonous.*"

"*She's right, Jim. Zane here.*"

"Go Zane," Jimbo replied.

"*Winter's right. It's not just monotonous, the guys are wearing out. Not to mention, we're all running on fumes. We'll be outta gas here real quick.*"

"Stand by, Zane." Jimbo spun back to the room. "Any suggestions?"

"How far are they from solid pavement?" Thomas asked.

Ryker tapped a keyboard under the area map. The wide area zoomed to Zane's position, showing a single light marker for each vehicle. He used a touch pad to draw a temporary circle around Zane's caravan.

"So here's Zane's crew," he said. He drew another circle around a second set of marker lights. "And here's Griff's. Looks like they're both about equal distance from the nearest road. That'd be roughly a mile and a half."

"And how fast can they travel?" Thomas asked.

Ryker stood up from the console. "Oh, hell. Maybe thirty over that terrain, if they're lucky."

Thomas looked at Fred. "I'm surprised they haven't been overtaken by now. From what I can see, the Chybrids are on the move again."

The Three Amigos stood on tables at the back of the room—their equalizer against being the three shortest guys in the Depot.

"Hey, Ryk," Will said. "Give us a couple more Humvees full of gas and we'll do another Chybrid roundup!"

Ryker glanced at Dion.

"Get Pops in here," Dion ordered Jimbo. He looked up at the Three Amigos atop the table. "You guys game?"

Adam puffed up and pointed two thumbs at himself. "You ever see better game faces than these?"

"No," Dion said. "But that was Will's driving that got Winter outta that situation down south. How are you other two, driving-wise?"

Joey smiled. "You think we didn't take turns and lay a few donuts in the dirt on our way to the Underground?"

"Good enough," Dion said as Pops walked in.

"What's up, Dion?" Pops asked.

"That Humvee the Amigos took to the Underground. You got any more souped up like it?"

"You bet," Pops said. "We done three more of 'em that way."

"We only need two right now."

Pops scratched his beard. "Well, we'll just need to swap tires, street for off-road. Take about five minutes to get 'em ready."

"Do it, then," Dion said. He turned to Jimbo. "Jim, get word to Zane and Griff. Have one of them make a pass and get these mothers away from the main gate. Take 'em out about half a mile and circle up the trucks. Make sure each caravan's near a Tunnel entrance. They got ten minutes. When the Chybrids hit the trucks, the Amigos will move in." He looked at Will, Adam and Joey. "You got that?"

"Got it," they said in unison.

"And keep your two-ways on in the trucks. We want you guys to hear everything that's going on."

CHAPTER 46

The Call

*W*OW, *THAT'S BADASS*, KRYSTAL THOUGHT as she walked up to the armored vehicle parked above the Underground City. She strolled around all four sides before trying the driver's door. It was unlocked. When she opened it, she noticed the vehicle was electric—no internal combustion engine here. Indirect lighting under the seats, around the roof edges and on the dash, glowed softly. The proximity sensor device lay on the console between the seats. She picked it up and stuffed it into her vest pocket.

She noticed a brand-new cell attached to the dash. She noticed the background picture—a huge 3-D K. *Felix thought of everything.* She thought back to what he had said to her. *"You know you do not require the presence or approval from another human being to be worthy."* Try as she might to fight the feeling, she knew she had to call Curtis. She picked up the cell and stared at the face. *"…you are worthy because you are you."* She remembered the night of her acid test, how Curtis had saved her life. *"A simple truth, but so easily missed."* Krystal took a deep breath and dialed Curtis's number.

"THIS IS CURTIS."

Her voice sounded worlds away. *"Curtis, it's Krys."*

Curtis felt his heart leap into his throat. "Babe?"

"*Yes, it's me.*"

"Oh, babe, I've missed you so much! Where are you? How—"

"*I'm outside the Changers' Underground. But don't talk, Curtis. I have to tell you some things, and I need you to just listen.*"

Curtis felt the distance. "Okay, babe. I'm listening."

"*I've been through a lot.*"

"Oh, I know, babe—"

"*Please. Please don't stop me. I have to tell you I've changed. Things have changed between us.*"

An overwhelming loneliness consumed Curtis. He felt detached, like he was falling away from everything that held his world together. His face flushed and he felt nauseous.

"*I've discovered how to stand on my own. I know who I am. And I know my life has purpose.*"

Curtis sat still in his van. His stomach tightened and the buildings outside his van began to swirl. Tears he never felt coming fell from his eyes. "I love you. I need you, Krys." His throat closed up as he choked on his own words. They sounded small and insignificant.

"*And I love you, too,*" she said. "*But I don't need you now, Curtis.*"

Curtis retched. He opened his mouth and gagged. He threw the door open and stepped from his van, falling to his knees in the street. The stench of a nearby dumpster, mixed with wet asphalt and his own vomit, filled his nose as he dropped his head to the pavement. He sobbed silently on all fours in the middle of an abandoned street, in the center of a clueless city, filled with people he had sworn to protect, who couldn't care less that he was there.

KRYSTAL ENDED THE CALL AND pressed the power button on the dash. She heard a faint hum as the vehicle came to life. She tapped the button to engage the drive train, pressed the accelerator, and headed toward the highway leading to Tremayne.

CHAPTER 47

Changers Declare Victory

L EVI STOOD AT THE HEAD of the table in the Changers' War Room. All seats at the huge conference table were filled. The highest-ranking generals and commanders were seated among top-level Changers.

Levi stood. "As you all know, we have apprehended traitors in our inner circle. But do not despair. We have dealt with them swiftly. I am trusting our top security personnel to contain them until they face the consequences of their actions."

He picked up a full champagne glass and held it up to the crowd. "But now, Changers, rejoice in our successes. I direct your attention to the monitors." The curved screens on the wall displayed a view of Checkpoint One from various cameras mounted to specific Chybrids. "Images of our victory over the Punks are streaming to us from outside the Perimeter. The battlefield is littered with the bodies of our enemy. Remember this, my most loyal commanders, the only good Punk is a dead Punk. From all indications, they are in the process of retreating from Checkpoint One."

Spontaneous applause erupted from the attendees. Silver stood, prompting the others to do the same.

Levi smiled. "Please, please. And thank you. I encourage you all to adjourn to the main ballroom. Celebrate tonight until your hearts are full. You all deserve much credit for this victory. And tonight, I intend to sleep well, as should you all."

CHAPTER 48

Rescue The Rescuers

Dion stood next to Ryker, watching the activity on one of the overhead monitors. The two Punks had their arms crossed, their bodies flexed and tight.

"Dammit, Dion," Ryker said. "We've lost so many Cats. Half of Zane's fleet is totaled."

"Not to mention, Punks gave their lives out there." Dion's face took on the color of his red-tipped hair. "I can hardly tell the bodies from the mud. The Chybrids are eating them up."

Ryker looked down. "Didn't mean to minimize that, bro."

"Where the hell are the Three Amigos?" Ace shouted from the back of the Depot.

"Jim, do you copy?" Zane's voice wavered. *"Where's the help, man?"* Writhing, slashing, clanking Chybrids blocked his view through the windshield and the side windows of the BearCat. He squeezed his eyes shut and turned his face away. *"Jiiimmm! Ooohhh, help! Jimbo!"*

Ryker forced his way past Jimbo to the communications console. "Easy, buddy. We got help on the way now. Just hang in there."

Pops and Geezer hurried into the Depot from the Hangar. "The Amigos headed out five minutes ago," Pops said. "But you know we had to send 'em west first. We can't use the main gate."

"Auxiliary gate 'tween this'n and Checkpoint Two, Dion," Geezer said. "Quickest way out."

"That's a five-minute haul to the auxiliary gate, then five minutes back," Pops said. "They should be passin' by outside right about now."

Ryker looked up at one of the flat-screens above his head. "Will, Ryker. Radio check."

"*Copy, Ryk. Loud and clear.*"

"Then you got an ear on Zane. He's in trouble, man."

"*Copy that, Ryk. But Griff's fleet is coming up first for us. We can clear those suckers away from Griff, then head to Zane.*"

"That's a negative, Will. Clear Zane's fleet first."

"*Copy, Ryk. We're coming up on Griff now. Zane's a mile away.*"

"Clear Zane first, buddy."

"*Adam, Will. We gotta split up. The Chybrids are chomping big-time on Griff. You and Joey get Griff freed up. I'll head to Zane.*"

"*Got it, Will.*"

Ryker threw up his hands and walked away from the radio. "Whatever, man! We gotta teach those guys some discipline."

Dion looked at Pops.

Pops nodded, ever so slightly.

"Sounds like a good plan, Ryk," Dion said.

ZANE PUSHED HIS BOOTS AGAINST the floorboard under the steering wheel. He glanced up when the windshield cracked. "*Help me! Oh, help me!*" he sobbed into the radio. The interior lights in his vehicle went out. He dropped the radio and put his hands over his ears. The scraping, tearing sound of his BearCat coming apart pierced his ears like fingernails on a blackboard. The relentless rhythmic shaking of the truck nauseated him.

He started at the series of loud bangs from beneath him as his tires split, the exhaling air squealing above the din. His nerves were gone. His bladder emptied into his pants. The warmth was somehow comforting. Unconsciously, he curled into a fetal position between the front seats and rocked himself in sync with the hideous beasts on the outside. "Hmm, hmm, hmm, hmm..." He tried to calm himself with his own rhythmic monotone hum, and the clanking, sickening rocking motion continued.

The crash of the windshield didn't faze Zane—his brain sank into a defensive mode as his humming blocked out the threat, and his self-made cradle comforted him. His partner, riding shotgun, dove over Zane into the back of the vehicle as the shiny metallic arm swiped at Zane's shoulder.

Zane never felt the tug when the jagged claw ripped his left tricep vertically down the middle. The second strike from the intruding metallic beast slit Zane's skull down the side, sliced his ear off and split his neck, severing the jugular. The orange-red liquid spewed out from his vein and spray-painted the white face of the relentless Chybrid. As the beast withdrew for the next strike, Zane's heart pumped another load of blood onto what was left of the broken windshield and sprinkled the dash with the ensuing splash.

WILL STARED IN HORROR AS his Humvee skipped over the uneven terrain toward the circle of armored vehicles that was Zane's fleet. He saw a Chybrid buried waist-deep in the windshield of a darkened BearCat. *No, no, no,* he thought as the Humvee neared the stationary trucks. He saw most of the roof-mounted light bars. Below the lights, the scene resembled a mass of maggots devouring an unrecognizable roadkill.

Oh, God, that's Zane's truck! Will smashed the accelerator to the floor, tracking head-on toward the truck with the grotesque metal maggot-creature embedded in the BearCat. He calculated his turn—too close. When Will spun the Humvee in a deliberate one-eighty, the rear end of his vehicle caught the jagged metal on the front of Zane's vehicle, puncturing his right rear tire.

The Chybrids stopped their motion momentarily—while their preprogrammed chips zeroed in on the movement of the Humvee. Will straightened his vehicle and floored the accelerator again, heading away from Zane's fleet.

The Chybrids rushed toward the new movement. The right rear of Will's Humvee tilted downward, slowing his progress as the remaining tires labored to pick up the slack. Will grabbed the two-way radio mic from the dash.

"*Guys, I'm in trouble here!*"

Joey was on top of the two-way. "*We got you covered, Will!*"

RYKER PUSHED JIMBO AWAY FROM the radio. "Will? Joey? Ryker. Fuck that. Me and Dion are heading your way!"

Dion pointed at Jimbo. "Get the second levels back here ASAP. Those fuckers aren't even heading to Tremayne." He looked at Pops. "You got another Humvee gassed up?"

"You bet." Pops threw a quick thumb over his shoulder. "Parked in the compound. Keys are in it."

Fred and Thomas stood at the back of the room, near the door to the compound. Ryker brushed past Fred and held the door for Dion.

Fred placed his hand on Dion's arm. "The Changers' plan was never to send the Chybrids to Tremayne."

Dion's eyes narrowed. "What are you talking about?"

"The Changers never intended to attack Tremayne. They aren't about to destroy all those people. They need those lives for absorption."

Ryker grabbed a handful of Dion's leather jacket and squeezed. "We gotta go, man."

"You and me are gonna have a long talk when I get back." Dion shoved his finger into Fred's chest. He yanked his shoulder from Ryker's fist and followed, trotting toward an idling Humvee outside.

Fred stopped the door from closing and stepped past the threshold. "You played into their hands," he shouted. "I'm on your side!"

RYKER WAS WAITING IN THE Humvee when Dion hopped into the driver's seat. They fastened five-point harnesses before rolling the side windows down. The cool breeze whipped through the cab as the vehicle picked up speed.

"Compound looks pitiful with no one out here," Ryker said, hanging his arm outside the window.

Dion stared ahead. "What a fucking mess, Ryk. I don't even feel like a leader any more. We look like pussies hanging out in the Depot while our tribe's out there dying."

"Punks need a leader. You're our leader, bro. I'll fight to the death for that." Ryker looked across the cab at Dion. "No way we could have, or should have, been out there."

"Sometimes I lose track of what we're even fighting for."

"It's an old story, isn't it?" Ryker said. "It's all about freedom. Punks are free, always have been. Socialist bullshit from the Changers, all up-in-your-shit ain't where freedom is."

"And protecting the Bystanders?"

"Some people are oblivious to what's happening to them. That's the Bystanders. They're only free because we hold the Changers back. Bystanders would die without us. They're just too blind to see that."

Dion tipped his chin up. "Geezer's got the auxiliary gate open." He turned the wheel to the right and hit the brakes.

Geezer smiled, mouth open when the Humvee made the turn through the tight opening without stopping. "Yee-haw!" He rotated his raised arm, lasso-style, in a continuous, full circle. "Go get 'em, guys!"

"Gotta love Geezer," Ryker said.

Dion remained grim. "We got five minutes, then about a mile past that to Will—depending on how fast he's going."

Ryker snatched the two-way mic from the dash mount. "*Will, Ryker.*"

"*Gotcha, Ryk!*"

"*We're on our way. ETA seven minutes. Can you hang on?*"

"*You kidding me?*" Will shouted. "*I got a Chybrid hanging on my rear bumper right now! I'm spinnin' three-sixties just to keep him from standing up!*"

"*Ryk, Joey here.*"

"*Go, Joe,*" Ryker replied.

"*I'm about four minutes from Will. Adam's slow-rolling Griff's Chybrids out to the highway.*"

"Ryk, Jimbo."

"*Go, Jim.*"

"What's left of Griff's crew is safe in the Tunnel."

Dion glanced at Ryker. "Tell him to get them out of the Tunnel and back to the compound. They need food and rest. According to Garrison, the only place we have to worry about these fuckers is out front of Checkpoint One."

"*Copy that, Jim. Get Griff's crew into the compound. Get a head count and get everyone fed. Compound's safe.*"

"*10-4, Ryk.*"

"Guys!" Will shouted into his mic. "*A whole shit ton of Chybrids are breathing down my back!*"

"I'm on it, Will," Joey radioed. "*I see your headlights. Hang on!*"

"That must be Joey up there," Dion said.

Ryker squinted through the windshield. "I see him, barely."

Dion pressed the accelerator. The engine revved as the Humvee flew over the dips.

"Tear it up, bro," Ryker said, gripping the handle above his head. "Actually looks like we're catching up."

"He's going slower than we are, but he's still hauling ass."

"*I'm almost there, Will,*" Joey shouted.

"*I see you, partner!*" Will shot back.

Dion and Ryker saw Will's Humvee in the distance. The vehicle traveled about fifty yards and turned in a 360-degree circle before running straight another fifty yards or so.

"I see what he's doing," Ryker said. "He can't outrun them. So he hauls ass in a straight line until they're right on top of him. Then he redirects by spinning around. See how they pause when he spins? That's buying him time."

"I see it," Dion said. "But they get closer with every sequence."

"If he could shake that one off his bumper, he'd have a better chance."

Dion glanced to his left. "What the heck is Joey doing?"

The two watched Joey's Humvee angling about a hundred yards toward the front of Will's vehicle.

"I don't know, but he's sure taking the long way," Ryker said.

"Let's head toward the middle of the pack and try to get their attention."

"Oh, shit. Check it out." Dion nodded to Joey's Humvee.

Joey's angle was perfectly timed. Will completed another 360, then continued slogging through the mud in a straight line.

"He's not slowing down," Ryker said.

"Dammit," Dion said. "Looks like he's gonna hit Will."

Joey's Humvee slammed into the Chybrid dangling off Will's rear bumper. The mechanical beast separated at the arms and rolled under Joey's Humvee. The exterior lights went out and his vehicle bounced wildly, thrown off-balance by the debris now caught underneath. The arms of the Chybrid remained fixed to Will's bumper.

Dion floored the accelerator again as Joey's Humvee came to a stop. *"Will, Ryker. Do you copy?"*

"Go, Ryk!"

"Stop your truck! Stop your truck! That Chybrid's off your bumper!"

"They're still behind me, Ryk!"

"All right, listen. Dion and me are gonna get their attention. They'll follow us if you stop. They go for the motion."

"Guys?" Joey radioed. *"I'm dead in the water over here. Hittin' that Chybrid somehow killed my truck."*

"Gotcha, Joey," Ryker said. *"Sit tight. Will, when you see the Chybrids coming after us, go pick up Joey. He's about seventy-five yards behind you."*

"10-4, Ryk. Hang on, Joe. I'm slow, but I'll be there as soon as I can."

"I'm not going anywhere in this truck," Joey said.

Dion zeroed in on the center of the hoard of Chybrids. When they stopped their forward motion toward Will's Humvee, he hit the brakes and whipped the steering wheel to the right, power-sliding toward the throng of white humanoids. At the exact apex of his 180-degree spin, he hit the gas. The Chybrids reprogrammed and turned toward Dion and Ryker. Dion accelerated—the Chybrids followed.

"Will?" Ryker said. *"Go pick up Joey."*

"*Got it. I'm limping your way, Joe.*"

Dion glanced in his rearview mirror. "They're right behind us, bro."

Will slogged across the soggy terrain toward Joey's dead Humvee. Hang on, Joe. Almost there. His truck continued to slide off-track, the right rear tire now completely gone.

INSIDE THE DEPOT, ACE STARED at a monitor above the control console. "Check it out, Jimbo. Part of that pack following Dion's truck is breakin' off."

Jimbo glanced up at the monitor. "Holy fuck!"

Thomas was watching the flat-screen. "Will has to stop. The back of the pack has keyed in on his movement."

CHAPTER 49

Bring In The Troops

L ACE THREADED A TWO-WAY RADIO headset through her tightly woven hair. "Nevada, Lace."

"*Go, Lace.*"

"You catching the traffic on one?"

"*That's a 10-4, Lace.*"

"Stand by, Nevada. Margot, you hear it, too?"

"*Affirmative.*"

Lace fastened her five-point harness and glanced at her driver. "Tie your hair back, Murph. Head to Checkpoint One, outside the Wall."

"Girls, grab two of your best and catch up to me. I'm moving. Checkpoint One, Exterior."

"*Gotcha, Lace.*"

"*10-4, girl.*"

"My units—two and three—fall in behind me. Level three commanders, stand by."

The acceleration of the BearCat pressed Lace's head against the seat. "Jimbo, Lace. Do you copy?"

"*Copy, Lace. I heard your order. Dion wants all units 10-19. Return to the compound.*"

"I copy, Jim. Put out an all-call to my units and get 'em rolling your way. A couple of us are taking a little detour on the way."

"*Straight to the compound. No detours, Lace.*"

"That's a negative, Jim. Dion and Ryker's in the field. We're assisting. Three sets of three Cats."

"*Lace, Jim. Orders from Dion. Return to the compound.*"

"You're breaking up, Jim."

Murphy grinned from the driver's seat and shook his head.

"*Nevada? Jimbo.*"

radio silence

"*Margot, do you copy?*"

silence

MURPHY GUIDED THE BEARCAT SWIFTLY through the empty downtown streets. He took the center turn lane straight down Main Street, allowing the two BearCats behind him to follow abreast. With its modified suspension—courtesy of Pops and Geezer—the large Cats maneuvered like slot cars. All three drivers negotiated the 270-degree highway on-ramp with ease and hit the gas.

Murphy smiled at the smooth acceleration. He glanced at Lace. "Turnoff's right up here."

Lace checked the tracking screen on the dash. "Nevada's team is about a mile back of us. Margot's two miles behind her. After the off-ramp, cross over the highway and park off-road, facing the checkpoint. We'll set up there."

Murphy eyed his boss. "Set up?"

Lace opened the window and rested her elbow on the door frame. "Yeah…I have an idea."

JIMBO SLAMMED HIS HAND ONTO the transmit button. "Will, Jimbo. Stop your truck! Stop your truck!"

DAMMIT, WILL THOUGHT. I'M ALMOST there. "Joey, can you see me?"

"*I see you, man. Stop. I'm getting out.*"

"No!" THOMAS SHOUTED.

WILL STOPPED.

Joey opened the driver's door on the Humvee and sprinted through the mud toward Will.

The Chybrids increased their speed.

Holy shit, Joe! What are you doing? Will thought.

LACE OPENED THE DOOR AND began to dismount as her vehicle slow-rolled off the side of the paved frontage road. "This is good."

She left the door open and sludged through the mucky terrain toward the distant clatter of Chybrids.

Murphy finished parking and caught up to Lace.

The two stood side-by-side. Headlights from the BearCat cast ripply shadows onto the uneven terrain in front of them. "You can see Dion's Humvee out there," Lace said.

"Yeah, what a mess to be in."

"I'd say they're a little over a quarter mile way. His lights are bouncing all over the place."

Murphy gazed into the darkness. "They're going damn slow. Sure we got time?"

"I say yes." Lace swallowed hard. "This is a walk in the park for us, Murph." She glanced over her shoulder. "Nevada's pulling in now." The two Punks turned and strode toward the purple-camouflaged BearCat as Nevada and her driver exited.

"Hey, girl," Lace said. "Your paint job's gonna be showing the pain after we're done with this mud fight."

Nevada raised an eyebrow. "What can I say? I'm a badass girly-girl."

"Always a girl first," Nevada said. "Well, pull that purple beast over there next to Murph and me. Get your other trucks set up behind mine, lined up the way we are. Stagger them so everybody has time to react and we're not running into each other."

"No worries, Lace. By the way, Margot's about two minutes out."

Lace looked at Murphy. "Make sure the rear winches are set up and ready to go on these two Cats. Timing's gonna be essential."

"You got it," Murphy said.

"I'm gonna hang out with the trucks here and wait for Margot."

DION WHIPPED THE STEERING WHEEL to the left when he saw the pothole. "Shit," he yelled. The Humvee dove into the small but deep crater and bounced back out onto level ground. The front tires slid sideways through the mud when he accelerated.

"Oh, that's messed up," Ryker said.

"I swear I heard something break," Dion agreed. "Look at this." He spun the steering wheel back and forth. "Takes me twice the distance on the wheel to turn this thing now."

The Humvee fishtailed left and right as Dion fought to maintain a straight line through patches of heavy mud.

Ryker leaned forward and glanced in the rearview mirror. "We're still maintaining a decent distance."

"Yeah, but she's slowing down. I'm fighting to keep the speed up without doing donuts here. Every time I give it gas, we're back into a slide."

MARGOT'S MINI CONVOY PULLED OFF the frontage road and rolled onto the dirt/mud surface. Lace stood in front of the high-powered headlights, hands on her hips.

Margot used her exterior intercom. "What's up, girl? Looks like you already got a plan in the works."

Lace held up a closed hand, signaling the truck to stop. Margot stepped out of the passenger side of the truck and the girls fist-bumped. "We're pumped," Margot said. "What's the scoop?"

"We're gonna show these mindless mechanical mutants an old-school trick."

"Oh, do tell."

"Ever see someone get clotheslined?" Lace smiled.

"Oh, yeah! Where do you want me?"

"You're on a retrieve-the-survivors mission. Nevada and me got the winch cables. When the Chybrids go down, you get in there and snatch up our bosses. Get your other two trucks headed out to the Amigos *now*. No time to stand here shootin' the breeze."

Margot threw up her hands. "Ooh, you always get to have all the fun!"

"Yeah, well. You get to be the hero and rescue our people. Now get moving."

Margot pounded a fist on Lace's shoulder. "All right then, girl. String 'em up!" She turned back to her vehicle and pulled herself into the shotgun seat.

Lace trotted to her BearCat. Murphy and Nevada's driver were making final adjustments to the winches attached to custom rear platforms. "'Bout set, guys?"

"All set, Lace," Murphy said.

"You got the custom breakaway joint Pops made?"

Murphy looked sideways at Lace. "Has a cat got an ass?"

Lace smiled. "Gotta ask, partner." She glanced at Nevada's driver. "Ready?"

Both drivers signaled thumbs-up.

Lace rotated her arms in a circular motion as she walked backwards to her vehicle, facing the other BearCats. "Let's do it!"

As if by a single switch, every light on all the trucks illuminated the landscape.

"Copy, Nevada? Lace. We're cuttin' it close, but I'm feelin' good!"

"*Right behind you, girl,*" Nevada replied.

Murphy frowned. "No way they're making it to pavement at that rate."

Lace gazed through the windshield at Dion's injured Humvee, slogging mightily through the mire. "Hey, Nevada. When I get stopped, back up to my truck. Then move away far enough to give that Humvee about three car lengths between us. He's slippin' and slidin' that buggy all over the place."

"*Gotcha, Lace.*"

RYKER WATCHED LACE AND NEVADA'S BearCats through the windshield. "Heading straight at us," he said.

Every muscle in Dion's body felt banjo-tight as he fought the steering wheel against the uneven surface. "God, just get here," he said.

"Those girls are hauling ass," Ryker said. "I can't believe how they handle this. I would've thought a lighter truck would be better."

"It's that special suspension Pops and Geezer rigged up."

"They look like they're gliding over pavement," Ryker said. "Wait…what th—"

Lace held her hand up. "This is good. Stop here."

Nevada's driver followed suit and pulled to a stop before whipping a U-turn. He lined his bumper up to Lace's and pulled away—exactly three car lengths. Nevada jumped out and ran to the back of her vehicle. She grabbed the winch cable as her driver unwound the reel from a remote control in the cab.

Murphy met Nevada and connected his cable to hers via Pops' custom breakaway joint. Their eyes met. Both held up a thumb and trotted back to their cabs.

"*Lace, Ryker. Do you copy?*" Ryker shouted. "*Why'd you stop? These guys are almost on top of us!*"

"Relax, Ryk." Lace tried to hide the waver in her speech. "We gotcha covered. Just keep that truck movin' as straight as you can. Get her between me and Nevada—then just keep going. Margot's on the other side to pick you guys up."

"So close, Lace," Murphy said.

Lace rubbed her head, scratching the itch from beads of sweat on her scalp. Two drops broke through and trickled down her temples. "We're gonna do it, Murph…we *have* to."

"Something's seriously fucked up on this suspension," Dion said. "For the life of me, I can't keep this thing moving in a straight line."

Ryker gripped the ceiling handle with one hand, and the dashboard with the other. His fingers dug into the dash, flushing the blood from his knuckles. "We got those suckers off the Amigos' asses, only to put them on ours."

"Well, Ryk," Dion said. "I gotta tell you something, in case we don't make it out of this. I've always loved you, man. I've always considered you my brother."

Ryker gazed across the cab at his friend. "I know you have."

WILL STOOD ON THE ROOF of his Humvee, his legs shaking. It took every bit of grit left in the pit of his stomach to watch his friend. "Run, Joey, run!" he shouted. His voice quavered and the tears fell. "Joey!"

Joey hyperventilated at the clanking and humming of the Chybrids. He concentrated hard. *One foot after the other. Breathe, breathe, breathe. I'm almost there, Will! I'm—al—most—there...*

Will jumped down off the Humvee and threw open the rear door. *Gotta be something here! Anything! Anything!* His eyes locked on a flare gun. He turned quickly to face Joey and the Chybrids. "No!" he screamed.

Two Chybrids behind Joey lunged simultaneously. The closest one stumbled as the second Chybrid landed on top of it. Joey felt a searing pain down the side of his right thigh. His stomach turned as he heard his jeans rip.

Will pointed the gun at the Chybrids. A huge fireball erupted from the barrel. The fiery projectile burst into a shower of sparks when it hit the Chybrid to Joey's left.

Joey kept moving, involuntarily limping from the wound in his leg.

A flare gun! Will thought.

"*Will! Will! Are you there?*" Adam radioed. "*Will!*"

Adam's voice over the radio was muffled and distant. Will turned to see a BearCat blazing past him. His world spun in sickening circles and his skin went cold when he saw Joey hit the ground. *Sparks*, he thought. *The sparks.* Tears pooled in his eyes, blurring the fireworks from the flare gun as he lost consciousness. His legs turned to rubber as the dark mush of the battlefield rushed upward to engulf his face.

ADAM BRAKED HARD WHEN THE huge Lenco BearCat slid sideways to a stop in front of his Humvee. Two Punks rushed out of the Cat and ran to Adam.

"Get out and come with us," one of them shouted. "Now!"

The Humvee's door opened from the outside and Adam felt hands unlatching his harness. The Punks pulled him out of the driver's seat like a rag doll and dragged him—half-running, when his feet were able to touch the ground—to the BearCat. They threw him into the back of their vehicle and piled in behind him. Before the rear door slammed, the BearCat was moving.

Adam felt the rush of acceleration, and an unbearable centrifugal force, as the vehicle circled back toward the group of Chybrids that had been chasing Joey.

MARGOT'S THIRD BEARCAT NEGOTIATED A wide arc around the throng of Chybrids closing in on Dion and Ryker. The driver maintained his distance to prevent attracting the beasts. "Three? Unit Two here. Got a couple of bodies down in the mud," he radioed.

"*Copy that, Two,*" the Unit Three driver replied. "*We got one Amigo on board. Those are the other two, laying in the mud. You need an assist?*"

"That's a negative. Chybrids are chasing that flare right now. We'll retrieve the two Amigos' bodies and meet you at the highway."

"*10-4, Two. We're outta here. Safe driving, man.*"

LACE RADIOED NEVADA. "YOU READY, Nevada?"

"*You know it, girl. Waiting for you.*"

"Wait for my mark."

DION PUSHED THE ACCELERATOR TO the floor. The crippled Humvee slid forward one last time over the muddy surface before the engine died. The small ridge of mud in front of the BearCats' cable pushed the front end of the Humvee into the air. Ryker reached for the dash as the rear wheels of the truck left the ground. The Humvee flew over the cable between the BearCats and landed in a heap before skidding to a stop.

"Now!" LACE SHOUTED INTO THE mic.

The two large trucks sprang to life in opposite directions. The cable reels on the winches whined furiously as the heavy cables unwound.

Muddy rooster tails followed the BearCats, racing parallel to the oncoming hoard of Chybrids.

"On my mark, Nevada."

Dion and Ryker turned in their seats, wide-eyed at the approaching mass of mechanical monsters.

"Now," Lace shouted.

The winches locked in place.

The Chybrids advanced.

The cables tightened, then stretched like a guitar string.

The hair on Dion's neck bristled at the shrinking space between the Humvee and the Chybrids.

In front of the Humvee, Margot's truck slid to a stop.

"Hey, guys!" she yelled. "Hop on in!"

The two Punks needed no further encouragement. They threw the doors open and sprinted to the open door on the back of Margot's BearCat.

The front row of Chybrids hit the taut cable and stopped. Each row of the creatures collided with the row in front. Lace and Nevada's trucks slid backwards toward each other as the weight of the Chybrids bore down on the cable.

The Chybrids began their descent, falling row upon row upon row.

"Hit it!" Lace cried.

The drivers accelerated, stretching the cable to its limit.

And the breakaway joint detached.

"Woo-hoo!" Murphy shouted as the huge truck lunged forward. "Good job, boss!"

Lace lifted a weak fist to her driver and looked out the passenger window. "Just get to the highway."

Murphy frowned. "What's up, man? That was an awesome rescue."

Lace shook her head. "Something about retrieving bodies from the battlefield bothers me, you know?"

THE CARAVAN OF NINE LENCO BearCats raced up the highway in formation toward Checkpoint One, led by Lace and her crew.

"Jimbo? Lace here."

"*Go, Lace.*"

"We're 10-19. Nevada and Margot are with me. Nine Cats, intact."

"*Copy that, Lace. How's everyone? Sounded like we took some casualties.*"

"Contact Margot, Jim. Her crew's got 'em aboard."

"*10-4. Everything okay with you, Lace?*"

"I don't know yet."

"HEY, JIMBO."

"*Go ahead, Dion. It's good to hear your voice!*"

"I'm with Margot. Ryk's with us. Margot's number two has Adam—he's safe. The other two Amigos are in Margot's Three."

"*Copy that, Dion.*"

"Will's conscious and alert. Joey has a nasty gash in his leg. He lost a lot of blood, but he'll recover."

"*Good to hear. Stitches?*"

"The crew stitched him up. Did an awesome job."

"*10-4, Dion.*"

"How's everything at the checkpoint?"

"*We lost over half our fleet, Dion. The Chybrids are outside the Wall. They're tearing at the main gate—*"

Dion listened to mild static over the radio speaker.

"Copy that, Jim."

Static

"Copy, Jimbo?"

"*Thomas Dennis said the Chybrids have been reprogrammed,*" Jimbo said. "*They're learning to climb the Wall.*"

Dion looked at Ryker.

"Let's just get home, bro," Ryker said. "If we're going down, might as well go down with the crew."

CHAPTER 50

Stranger on the Hill

WINTER TROTTED UP THE SHORT set of steel steps inside the inspection pit in Bay Three of the Hangar. "Let's go! Let's go! Let's go!" Punks in various stages of military dress emerged. One at a time, they received a fist-bump and a hefty slap on the ass from their boss as they hit the Hangar floor. "Everybody assemble in the compound. I'm right behind you!"

Raymond followed the last of the crew and stayed with Winter in the Hangar. He glanced at the flat-screen monitors over the main workbench. "What the hell is that god-awful noise?"

"Chybrids," Geezer said. "They's attackin' the Gate."

"Fuck me, it looks like a mass of tangled arms and legs." Raymond looked at Winter. "What are we doing about it?"

"I'm gonna meet with Dion and Ryker. We're gonna have to come up with a plan of action."

Raymond was mildly indignant. "Nice, Win. So what are we supposed to do in the meantime?"

"The crew is hungry and tired. Some of them need first aid. Get out to the compound and handle that. Get everyone fed and let them rest up."

"The compound? If those mothers break down that gate, we're all sitting ducks out there."

Winter stepped up to Raymond, locking her eyes on his. "This isn't a debate, Ray. I need you to handle the crew." She pointed at the door. "They need you right now."

Without a word, Raymond headed toward the exit. He stopped at the door and turned around. "You know, Win. We got some good people out there. Smart people. They might have some ideas how to defeat those bastards."

"You come up with something, let me know."

Pops walked into the Hangar from the Depot. "Hey, Win? Dion's pulling in with Ryker."

"On my way, Pops."

JIMBO PUSHED HIS CHAIR AWAY from the communications console and stood up to stretch. "You know something, Dennis? You really screwed us over with those Chybrids. We don't stand a chance against them."

Thomas leaned against the wide countertop under the area map. "I did what I had to do to survive, Jimbo."

Jimbo's face reddened as he stepped toward Thomas. "By setting up the Changers to slaughter us? That's all you guys are about. Kill Punks, absorb the Bystanders. You're disgusting, Dennis."

Fred casually stepped between the two. "Look, we're like you guys. We hate the Changers. We—"

"You're not like us. You don't know the first thing about us."

Fred crossed his arms. "We'll accept we don't know enough about you to say we're exactly like you. But you're helpless against the Changers. You need our help—"

Jimbo lunged forward, now inches from Fred's face. "Then fucking help us!" he screamed. "If you can help us, why are you just standing here watching our people die out there? At least we're fighting for something!"

WINTER STEPPED INTO THE DEPOT and let the door close quietly behind her. Her eyes narrowed. "Hey, Jim," she said softly. "Who are these pukes?"

Jimbo threw up his hands and turned away. "They're fucking Changers."

Winter drew her 9mm as Dion entered from the compound. "No!" he barked.

Ryker strode in and stopped behind Dion. "Whoa!" He held up both hands. "Steady, Win."

Winter stood motionless, both hands on her pistol—aimed at Fred's temple. "What's going on, Dion? These two are Changers."

"I know, Win. Stand down."

Winter trained her pistol on Dion. Her eyes took on a look of desperation. "What…the…fuck is going on? Ryk, help me out here."

Dion swallowed and felt beads of sweat break out on his scalp. His body braced for the shot.

Ryker stepped between Dion and the 9mm. He looked Winter in the eye. "Trust me, Win. It's okay."

Winter dropped her arms, but retained the grip on her gun. "I'm listening."

Ryker reached down and clasped his hand slowly around Winter's wrist. "Put this away. This is really Dion. And yes, these two are really Changers. They're on our side."

Winter didn't move when the tears of fury pooled. She gazed deep into Ryker's eyes. She searched his face. "Ryk?"

"I'll explain it all to you, sis. We're all on edge, for every reason in the world." Ryker's heart went out to her. He knew he was the only one who could talk her down. "Trust me right now."

Winter refused to wipe her tears as she holstered her pistol.

Dion turned to Fred and Thomas. "You two wait in my quarters."

Ace jumped down from the tabletop at the back of the room. "I'll take 'em, Dion."

Dion motioned to Jimbo. "You go, too. You and Ace wait with them till I get there."

Raymond poked his head in through the door from the compound. "Hey, Dion. The Three Amigos are here."

"Okay, Ray. Have Margot's crew get Joey to the infirmary. Let Will and Adam in here."

"You got it."

GRIMNESS HUNG OVER THE COMPOUND like a shroud. Punks moved with purpose in all directions, but their energy was somehow subdued. Exchanges between superiors and subordinates were low-key. Harsh reminders of the untimely deaths of their comrades weighed on the Punks. No one was unaffected. BearCats that had entered the battlefield with four team members on board returned with eight—the result of damage inflicted upon the fleet. Some vehicles limped in with only the driver left. Other Punks died with their trucks outside the Perimeter. The Chybrids had not only ravaged and destroyed the bodies of trucks and human beings—they had stolen the energy, the pride and spirit that was the Punks.

Lace stood with Nevada next to a concrete bench in the center of the compound. "I've never in my life seen the Punks so down."

Nevada shook her head slowly. "Me either. The edge is definitely off right now."

"You know, we lost so many people. But this mood is only partly about that. If that was all, we'd make it through."

"What are you saying?" Nevada asked.

"It's that noise outside the main gate, outside the Wall. We don't have anything that can stop them. It's that hopeless feeling that the lives lost were in vain, because we're next in line."

"Yeah…"

Lace scanned the compound. "Look at our people. There's no hope out there. It's like we're destined to take a number, then wait our turn to die."

Margot walked up behind the two and pounded her fists on her friends' shoulders. "How are you guys doing?"

"Just talking about how everyone else is doing," Lace said.

Margot stepped over the bench and sat down between Lace and Nevada. "Obviously not good. Most of 'em look like zombies. It's like the Changers took the lives of our people and sucked the life out of the ones they didn't kill."

"Exactly what it is," Lace said. "Question is, what's next? What are we gonna do?"

"I just talked to Raymond," Margot said. "He said Dion and Ryker are meetin' with the others to try an' figure that out. Me, I'm at a loss."

"Well, Dion wants everyone back here. You guys call your crews in?"

"Mine are back," Nevada said. "I left a small contingent in Tremayne for regular security patrol."

"Good," Lace said. "Margot?"

"My crew's back. Except Curtis. I can't get a hold of 'im."

Lace looked down at Margot. "What's that mean?"

"He's not answering his radio, or his cell. I tapped his next in line and made sure everyone else was comin' in."

"What about his GPS?"

"I checked that," Margot said. "His tracker is disabled."

"Well, you gotta get a hold of him," Nevada said. "We need Curtis."

"I got Racer on it. I told 'im to keep tryin' till he makes contact."

"CURTIS? CURTIS, DO YOU COPY? Come back, buddy. You out there?"

Curtis looked at the red light on the two-way radio on the dash in his van. He knew the voice—Margot's driver, Racer. He reached out and clicked the power off on the radio. He picked up his cell and glanced at the face. *Seven missed calls.* He powered it down as he drove his van through downtown Tremayne toward the city limits.

He glanced in the rearview mirror. "Tie your hair back, pal. I intend to haul ass."

The passenger in the backseat remained silent.

Curtis smiled. "Loosen up, Logan. We have plenty of time to get to know each other."

The 270-degree highway on-ramp was empty. There were no headlights on the highway in either direction. He headed south toward the Underground City and set the cruise control to one hundred miles per hour.

THERE WAS ONE EMPTY BARSTOOL in the conference room in Dion's quarters. Pops, Geezer, Fred, Thomas and Jimbo sat on barstools, facing Dion, Ryker and Winter.

"Where's Curtis?" Dion asked.

Winter shrugged. "Margot's been trying to contact him for the last hour."

"We need that boy," Dion said. "Ryk, does he even know he's up for promotion?"

"No one's heard from him since yesterday."

Dion looked down and ran his hand over his head. "Well, we can't wait." He paced around the room momentarily before settling on a pattern between the pool table and his leather couch. "Fred, what's your best idea?"

Fred reclined comfortably with his elbows on the bar behind him. "Reprogram the Chybrids."

"How do we do that? We can't even get close to them."

"That's a good idea," Thomas said. "But it would take some time—"

"We don't have time," Ryker interrupted.

Thomas stared at Ryker, waiting for Ryker to finish. "If I may?"

"Sorry," Ryker said. "Go ahead."

"Reprogramming means we will first have to obtain the proper frequency to transmit a signal to the proper circuit within the Chybrids to send the reprogramming command. But there are issues we must overcome before we can even begin that process."

"Like what?" Dion asked.

"First, we will have to jam the signals the Changers are sending—the signal they are sending for their own reprogramming purposes. Even that presents challenges."

"Why?" Ryker asked. "If you know the frequency they're using to transmit, just jam it. Can't be that hard."

Fred sat forward. "The problem is, the transmit frequency isn't static. It's different each time. The way it's set up, when a new command—or program—is sent, it also sets the future frequency to receive the subsequent program."

Dion stopped pacing. "So jamming is the only way. Can't we jam a wide band of frequencies, make sure we hit anything?"

Thomas looked at Fred. He took a deep breath. "There's a bigger problem than all that."

Jimbo hopped off his barstool. "Spit it out! What's the problem?"

Thomas braced himself. "The Chybrids are AI."

"Hep! Artificial intelligence!" Geezer elbowed Pops. "What we was sayin'. We knew it!"

"Then we have to stop them physically," Winter said. "It's gotta be muscle on might. Fight to the finish."

"I agree," Jimbo said.

Dion's cell buzzed. *Lace.*

"Hey, Lace. What's up?"

Lace was uncharacteristically frantic. "I'm organizing the fleet. The monitors are showing the Chybrids are almost through the main gate."

The commotion and voices in the background unnerved Dion. Adrenaline flooded his body. "What's happening out there?"

"Tons of the crew are crowding into the Tunnel through the Hangar. I can't stop them. We're losing control out here."

"All right. If everyone goes into the Tunnel, we're going to lose the entire fleet. We can't leave all those Cats sitting in the compound."

"Dion, what's going on?" Ryker asked.

Jimbo stood next to Ryker. "Do we need to get out there?"

Dion stuck a finger in his ear and strained to hear Lace on the other end. "Lace!" he practically shouted into the cell. "Those guys are creating their own coffin out of the Tunnel. The hatch inside the Hangar is nothing compared to the main gate. Those Chybrids will tear that door off without even thinking twice!"

"No one's listening, Dion...oof!" Lace took an anonymous shoulder punch in the back. "Get off me!" she shouted.

The look of desperation on Dion's face alerted Winter. "I'm going out there."

"Lace, is there anyone left who can, or will, drive those Cats?"

Geezer jumped off his barstool, followed by Pops. "We'll drive." The two old-timers fist-bumped.

"Count us in," Fred eyed Thomas.

Thomas nodded.

"Lace, get as many as you can who'll drive. We're on our way!"

Dion surveyed his quarters. Everyone was standing, looking to him for direction. He felt an unfamiliar weight on his shoulders. He had never felt this way before. No decision he had ever made as the leader of the Punks was more critical. From somewhere deep inside, he summoned a calmness. An inner strength he had never felt, consumed him.

"Everyone follow me."

Dion exited his quarters and strode boldly down the gray concrete hallway leading to the compound. Ryker and Winter followed him, taking their strength from his. Jimbo and the two Rogue Changers fell in behind—Pops and Geezer brought up the rear.

Lace, Nevada and Margot stood firmly at the center of the compound, surrounded by a ragtag group of about a hundred lower-ranking Punks. The entrance to the Hangar was not visible behind the throng of people trying desperately to crowd in. Noise from the mass of bodies scrambling in all directions was unsettling.

Dion stepped onto a concrete bench and raised his hand. He turned in a circle to view the gutsy remnant of the Punks. "Everyone listen up!" he shouted. "I'm going to get into the driver's seat in that BearCat right there." He pointed behind the crowd. "Ryker's getting in the second one, Winter in the third. I want each of you to find a vehicle and get in the driver's seat. Fall in behind us, in order of rank—don't crowd each other. Remain as calm as you can and follow us. Now, let's do it!"

Dion jumped down off the bench. The crowd dutifully parted, creating a concrete pathway with two walls of leather, denim and camo fatigues. Dion fist-bumped every extended hand as he strode swiftly through to the waiting vehicle.

Ryker and Winter followed. Ryker caught Lace's eye. "Let's do this, Punk!"

The remaining Punks each climbed into a vehicle and followed one after the other. Dion circled the compound toward the exit, then turned back toward Checkpoint One's main gate. The Hangar door was still crowded with bodies squeezing in as he roared past the entrance. When he reached the main gate, the clatter from the Chybrids outside drowned out the sound of his engine. He maneuvered the BearCat as close to the entrance as he could. He deliberately guided the vehicle against the gate, shearing off the exterior right-hand rearview mirror. Sparks flew from the right side of the truck as he scraped metal on metal against the gate. As he neared the hardened-steel-and-concrete pillar that formed the gate's frame, he gassed the BearCat, crunching the front end against the pillar.

Ryker recognized the strategy and followed Dion's path identically, crushing his front bumper against Dion's rear. He exited the BearCat and met Dion on foot as Winter slammed her truck into Ryker's. Jimbo, Lace, Nevada and Margot followed, creating a barricade. As the BearCats wedged into line, blocking the entrance to Checkpoint One, Dion directed traffic with the ensuing trucks. When the reinforced obstruction was three vehicles deep, Dion held his hand in the air.

Dion trotted up to the thirty-first truck in line. He hoisted himself onto the exterior step and grabbed the rearview mirror as the driver rolled the window down. He looked at the scared skinny blond kid in the driver's seat. "What's your name?"

"Nico," the driver replied.

"All right, Nico. You're in charge of this truck and about seventy trucks behind you." Dion unclipped the two-way from his shoulder and belt and handed them to Nico. "When you use this radio, everyone will know the communication is coming from me, no matter whose voice comes over. You get this fleet down to Tremayne and set up a blockade of the City. Let me know when you get there and you're all set."

Nico took the radio set. "Yes, sir!" He smiled. "Thanks, Dion. I mean, thank you, sir!"

Dion smiled and pushed back off the truck. "Call me."

"Oh, I will," Nico said as he pulled away.

Dion trotted back to the remaining drivers. "We bought ourselves some time. Let's get back to the Depot and see what these things are up to."

Dion, Ryker and Winter jogged side-by-side to the Depot in front of the others.

"Sun's about to come up," Winter said. "Maybe we can get a good look at the damage then."

"Sun up doesn't change anything," Ryker said. "God, listen to that. They're climbing the Wall."

The hideous noise against the Wall permeated the compound.

Dion stopped at the Depot entrance and issued instructions to everyone except his inner circle and the Rogues. "Secure everything that's important. Prepare to evacuate, but don't make a move until you hear from me."

Ryker opened the Depot door and stopped short. "What the heck, guys?"

The Three Amigos spun around on their barstools to face the door.

"Hey, Ryk," Will greeted.

Dion stepped in behind Ryker. "What are you guys doing here?"

"What, you think we'd abandon you guys?" Adam said. "You need us."

Dion noticed Joey was holding a crutch, his leg heavily bandaged. "How's your leg?"

"The doc says I'm going to live. No one's ever heard of the Two Amigos."

Inside the Depot, the ceiling speakers monitoring the outside activity set everyone on edge.

Winter stared at the flat-screens above the communications console. "Oh my God! They're almost to the top!"

The cameras showed the Chybrids stacked one upon the other. They climbed on top of each other, incrementally extending their reach—every metallic body forming a step for the next series of Chybrids.

"They're learning," Thomas observed. "We don't have much time here."

Geezer keyed in on video of the camera at the main gate. "They're breachin' the gate!" He pointed at the monitor. "They're breachin' the gate!"

"Holy hell, Dion," Pops said. "We've gotta get out."

Joey's eyes widened. He pointed at a monitor, his mouth open. He attempted several times, but no words came.

"They found a Tunnel entrance!" Jimbo screamed.

"Oh dear God," Fred said. "You people better go!"

"And leave our people to be fodder for those beasts you and your friend created?" Dion said. "I'll die first. I'll die with them."

"Wait, guys," Will said. "They're stopping. The Chybrids are stopping! They're unpiling! They're retreating!"

Every eye in the Depot was fixed on the monitor above Will.

"They're not even going for the gate anymore," Pops said.

Thomas stepped closer to the monitor. "They're literally falling off the Wall. They're disassembling the staircase they just built."

Adam pointed to another monitor. "Look at that." The screen displayed a wide-angle view of the battlefield outside the checkpoint. "Are they retreating?"

"There's activity on the hill out there," Ryker said. "I can't quite see what's going on. But they're being drawn to movement up there."

Dion moved next to Ryker and pressed a button on the communications console. "Drew? Drew, you out there?"

"*I copy you, Dion. This is Sydney. Hang on, I'll get Drew.*"

Dion remained fixated on the monitor above his head. "What the heck?"

"*Dion? Drew here.*"

Dion jumped at the console. "Drew! Get a drone out to the hill in front of Checkpoint One. The Chybrids are retreating because of some activity out here. We don't know what it is."

"*Got one airborne now. I'll stream you the video.*"

Jimbo turned one of the Wall cameras off and switched to the stream from Drew. The pixelated image flickered sporadically before syncing in clearly. "Got it," Jimbo said.

"Full speed ahead," Drew radioed.

Every person in the Depot fixed on the screen as if they were one set of eyes. No one blinked. They seemed to breathe in sync. The drone's camera zoomed past the Tremayne city limits sign and continued toward Checkpoint One.

Nico set that up nice, Dion thought as the drone passed over rows of BearCats lined up just outside the City.

As the compound came into view, the Punks crowded together. Video of the Wall flashed across the monitor as the drone sped toward the hill. Dion placed a hand on Ryker's shoulder, never taking his eyes from the monitor.

The drone passed over the wreckage of Lenco BearCats and what was left of the bodies of fallen Punks. The battlefield was strewn with destruction, the stench of death, and a mass migration of Chybrids moving away from the checkpoint.

The drone slowed as it approached the hill.

The group crowded closer to the monitor—everyone was touching someone.

A figure at the top of the hill was shooting the Chybrids.

"What the heck?" Ryker said. "Whoever that is, they're killing those suckers with a rifle."

"Drew?" Dion radioed. "Get in on that person on top of the hill. I gotta see who or what that is."

The drone zoomed down onto the battlefield directly in front of the figure on the hill.

The Chybrids continued to move up the hill, and continued to fall lifeless into the dirt.

The figure moved slowly, deliberately, confidently. There was a rifle in each hand. The figure stopped to reload each rifle in record time, without looking up at the oncoming throng of humanoids. Each rifle cracked twice, so quickly it was hard not to hear them as one shot.

And the Chybrids fell.

"Who the fuck…?" Jimbo said.

The drone's camera zoomed in on the figure silhouetted against the skyline, partially glowing from the imminent sunrise. A long black duster swayed in the breeze, exposing black pants and black boots.

The face of the figure came into view as Drew focused the drone's camera.

"I know her!" Will exclaimed.

Fred and Thomas exchanged glances.

Winter could not have fallen harder into the chair behind her if she had tried. "That bitch."

CHAPTER 51

Epilogue

L EVI AWOKE TO A SHRILL chirping sound. He opened his eyes and stared at the ceiling in his quarters, the sound not yet registered in his consciousness. His peripheral vision caught the red light flashing over his door. His mind drifted to the night before—Chybrids slaughtering Punks. He closed his eyes and smiled. His hands smoothed over his silk nightclothes under the covers as he attempted to return to the peaceful sleep state he had felt just moments before. But the chirping persisted.

His eyes shot open and he sat upright. He tapped a touch pad on his nightstand, illuminating the room. Glancing at the digital clock on the far wall, the time incensed him. *This better be an emergency.* He threw back the covers and moved swiftly toward the door to his private elevator. His change completed as the door swished closed behind him.

As usual, two armed guards awaited Levi when the elevator door opened on level ten. Their attempt to escort him to the War Room was in vain—his furious gait put him three steps ahead of them.

Technicians filled every seat at the computer terminals. Levi strode swiftly through the center of the round room and entered the adjacent alcove. Silver, Marvellous and Ivan stood at the head of the familiar table, their eyes fixed on a curved monitor on the wall. Six of Levi's generals occupied seats on one side of the table, facing the screen.

Levi's eyes were drawn to the monitor. His ire arose as the image on the screen registered in his mind—the figure on the hill outside Checkpoint One. Chybrids dropping to the ground. The face of the figure was in focus, crystal-clear.

"Sir—" Silver said.

"Shut up!" Levi surveyed the room. He turned to his top general. "There's only one person capable of pulling this off."

"Yes, sir."

Levi picked up Silver's electronic tablet from the table and threw it at the monitor. Sparks flew and the screen flashed to black. "Find him!"